Other titles by this author

The Bequia Mysteries

Dead Reckoning

Deadeye

Deadlight

Davidia's Seed

Michael W Smart

Cover Illustration Copyright © 2015 by Michael Smart
Cover design by: Denise Kim Wy
http://www.coveratelier.com)
Editing by: Amanda Hough, Progressivedits
http://www.progressivedits.com
Author photograph by: Camilla Sjodin
(www.sjodinphotography.com)

Published by Michael W Smart at CreateSpace

ACKNOWLEDGMENTS

I want to acknowledge and thank my editor Amanda Hough, whose diligence, insights, and love of my characters contributed immensely to completing this novel, including her invaluable assistance in choosing its title. And to my cover designer Denise Kim Wy, who expressed initial trepidation when I approached her with this project, having never designed for science fiction before. She hit it out of the park on the first pitch. Thanks Denise, you are a wonderful talent. My thanks also to numerous authorities in the scientific community, whose research papers and journal articles on cosmology, astrophysics, astrogeology, astrobiology, and particularly the study of Chiroptera species, informed the concepts presented in this novel. Finally, to all of you who took the leap to purchase and read this novel, thank you, and enjoy.

Ezekiel

The enormous ship shuddered. It rolled onto its side like a charging beast felled by a hunter's bullet. Ezekiel tumbled weightlessly within the pitch-black compartment. The dim artificial lighting winked out, replaced by bright explosive flashes and flickering firelight. Ezekiel slammed against a bulkhead, arresting his uncontrolled inertia in the confines of the small compartment.

The battle had been lost. Each brief flash of light illuminated the chaos around him. Energy relays and conduits exploded. Fires burned out of control. Beams buckled. The bulkheads and decks they supported crumbled. The acrid odor of burning equipment, machinery, and flesh, reached him through the ventilators.

And the whiff of toxic fumes. If the poisonous gasses didn't kill him first, the failing life support system would, merely prolonging the inevitable. Unless the compartment decompressed first. He'd sealed it upon entering, but how much longer before it imploded? The ship doomed, as explosive decompression consumed it section by section. It'd reach him soon.

The end of life closed in on Ezekiel, clouding his consciousness, clouding his mind as he sought direction, as he waited for instructions directing the actions required of him. Instructions, which never arrived.

Ezekiel pushed himself off the bulkhead, in the direction of the scout pod he'd been servicing. His actions directed by an overriding instinct, focused solely on reaching and entering the pod.

A sudden rush of flying debris drew Ezekiel's attention as he floated through the scout's open hatch. The fires in the compartment snuffed out as though smothered by a giant hand. A maw-like opening in the far bulkhead grew wide, exposing the compartment to empty space beyond. Not empty. Through the breach, Ezekiel observed a vast field of fast moving debris, the mangled remnants of a once mighty fleet.

The compartment's atmosphere vented into space, sucking the air from his lungs. A light-headedness descended upon him. And a lightness in his body, apart from the absence of gravity.

Ezekiel secured the pod's hatch as the doomed mother ship collapsed around the scout. He activated the scout's systems, pressurizing the tiny, cramped interior. Life support and flight controls powered on. He'd been trained and conditioned to pilot the pod, scouting beyond the range of the mother ship's sensors.

Before he'd been able to release the dock clamps, the final explosive demise of the mother ship jettisoned the small single person scout violently into space, one more piece of debris, hurtling amidst the fragments of the mother ship.

Inertia flung Ezekiel out of the pilot seat, pinning him against the ceiling. The sound of metal impacting metal resonated through the cockpit. Alarms flashed their dull illumination on the control panel. Ezekiel's inner ear perceived a tumbling motion.

He reached out. Grasped the back of the pilot seat. He maneuvered his weightless body into the seat and secured the restraints around his torso and hips. Disjointed, unfamiliar thoughts rushed through his mind as he donned the control headcap. He activated the scout's maneuvering jets and stabilized the pod's tumbling motion. He scanned the panel, and the silent, pulsing, beckoning alarms. Borinian instruments emitted no sounds. And none of their vessels possessed transparent surfaces permitting visual sighting beyond the hull.

He observed the energy spikes on the instruments, depicting the explosive end of the mother ship. The only sounds in the scout the thud of debris impacting the hull. Ezekiel also observed the flying flotsam displayed on the instruments. The debris spread out in all directions, travelling at speeds to keep them in perpetual motion through space, until halted by some other force.

Another instrument indicated damage to the propulsion system. Only the maneuvering thrusters functioning. Life support also functioning, but the pod was leaking atmosphere, probably punctured by a piece of debris. The pod's power cells were draining and unable to recharge. Soon there'd be insufficient power to sustain life support, sealing his fate, if the space borne debris didn't destroy the pod first. His escape in the scout a temporary reprieve.

Such a fate held no meaning for Ezekiel. He'd been bred to serve, and die. His every thought, every action, directed and controlled by omnipresent minds superimposed on his own. His mind linked irrevocably to his masters.

Until now. The sudden silence in his mind overwhelmed him. As frightening as the gagged chunks of metal hurtling around him. And the thoughts rushing through his mind were not of the masters, but more like the visions possessing his mind during sleep. The masters absent. The headcap he wore silent. Now all departed, along with the mother ship.

For the first time in his life, Ezekiel experienced the sensation of being utterly alone. It disoriented and frightened him. Threatened to consume him as he sought to comprehend the strange unfamiliar impulses compelling him to act. Who had directed him into the scout? Provided the instructions to escape the doomed mother ship? What actions was he required to perform next? The headcap remained ominously silent.

Absent instructions, Ezekiel was lost. He waited for death in the silence surrounding him, accompanied by the strange new voice in his mind.

Seraphina

Seraphina observed the scattered remnants of two space fleets depicted on her instruments, and through the viewports of her cockpit. A scavenger's dream. But she needed to determine which items to retrieve. The debris moved swiftly, spreading outward into space.

Seraphina activated her ship's thrusters, maneuvering from behind the small orange and red hued moon where she'd hidden while the battle raged. She'd waited for the last surviving stragglers to limp away, their damaged ships venting plasma and other gases in their wake. She studied the instruments indicating the stellar wind's strength and direction, and deployed the ship's collectors, spread like sails on either side of the craft. She engaged the drive which converted the star's streaming particles into thrust.

Her attention returned to the instruments as she closed on the debris. Seraphina tweaked their calibrations, searching the debris field for the particular nuggets she hoped to find. In order of preference, fuel cells, power cells and generators, weapons, engine and navigational parts, food and water processors. And finally, anything of value she might be able to sell or trade.

The flying flotsam represented her livelihood. The ship her home. She lived a solitary existence, without the encumbrance of friends or familial attachments. Or her past, and the harsh, brutal lessons, which had taught her how to survive. She'd learned to trust her instincts. To rely on no one but herself.

Seraphina selected and locked her targets. She deployed the metal mesh scoop and grappler as deft hands maneuvered the ship into the field, comfortable in her complete familiarity of her ship, its handling, its capabilities. A familiarity bred of countless hours in space together.

She focused on the targets, but did not ignore the other sensors. She'd learned from past mistakes to be situationally and spatially aware. Alert to the hidden, unexpected danger. She preferred being the stalker, rather than the stalked.

The cockpit viewports provided a one hundred and eighty degree field of view. She visually inspected the debris, now floating around her ship as though motionless as she matched their speed. She grappled the first haul into the cargo hold in the belly of her ship.

Seraphina worked the field, noting the passage of time, and the mass accumulating in the hold, careful to not exceed her ship's weight limit when it entered atmosphere. As she moved in on the last selected target, an alarm chirped on the console. A small energy spike. An object ahead emitting power.

A cold shiver tingled her spine. Instinct kicked in. She prepared to fight.

Seraphina locked a targeting sensor on the object. Other sensors remained on wide field and long range scans. She secured the grappler. Expert hands on the controls, Seraphina shortened sail, trimming them amidships as she maneuvered the ship to present the smallest possible target profile. She coupled the targeting sensor to the particle beam cannons mounted on the aft dorsal and ventral bulwarks. She prepared to fire.

Target locked. Cannons charged and ready. Seraphina's index finger hovered over the trigger. The sensors depicted a small vessel, shaped like a pea pod. Powered, but weakening, its energy signature waning. And it hadn't maneuvered to attack, or escape. It merely floated along like all the other pieces of debris.

Seraphina engaged maneuvering thrusters to close on the object, maintaining her attack posture. In visual range, she observed the object clearly. A clicker long range scout. Intact. A line of mist, no thicker than a thread, vented from a pinhole breach in its hull.

The find of a lifetime. More than she'd hoped for or imagined on this hunt. No one had ever captured an intact scout before. The stories she'd heard claimed the scouts were booby-trapped. Set to self-destruct if captured, destroying itself and its captors. Spacer factions simply destroyed the scouts from a distance.

Caution dictated she not discount the booby-trap story. But such scouts were deployed ahead of a fleet, Seraphina reasoned, performing reconnaissance and presumably under control. This one had been aboard the mother ship. Jettisoned into space by the mother ship's destruction. No one remained to control it, or destroy it. Unless a clicker happened to be aboard. And happened to still be alive.

The scout presented a conundrum. Clicker hulls were resistant to penetrating scans, and no spacer faction had yet developed a means to scan the interior of clicker ships. And to Seraphina's knowledge, no one had ever seen a clicker up close. A few claimed they had. A claim Seraphina placed little faith in. Clickers left few survivors, and removed their own dead and injured. When they attacked they'd arrive in overwhelming numbers, immense swarms turning the sky black, the air filled by a clicking noise, the source of the name used to describe them. And they'd strip a settlement, town, or city, bare of human inhabitants, like lotus swarms stripping grain fields on Antrobus.

Seraphina continued to observe the little bee shaped ship. Her finger never far from the trigger. The ship displayed no signs of active control. And its energy signature continued to dim, falling below the level capable of maintaining life support aboard.

Seraphina decided to chance it. The prize too valuable to simply abandon. She maneuvered her ship into position. She deployed the grappler and secured the scout, ensuring the grappler neutralized any residual electrostatic charges built up on the scout's hull. She drifted away to the bitter end of the grappler's cable, the distance between her ship and the scout eight one hundredths of a league, a little more than half a mile. Hopefully sufficient to escape an explosion if she reacted swiftly enough.

She towed the scout clear of the debris field, extended and trimmed her ship's sails, and waited. Her fingers poised to detach the grappler cable, close the cargo hatch, and apply maximum thrust. Her stare glued to the sensor console and its energy readings. The slightest spike in the little ship's energy output, she'd immediately cut it loose and flee.

Zanthinvolar Abydynus

General Zanth exited the communication center. The death throes of the mother ship, the fleet, and all aboard the doomed ships echoed in his mind. Over twenty thousand souls. Not to mention the quiri. Did quiri have souls? He wondered.

Zanth grasped a moving rail outside his office, hanging head down from his taloned toes. He transferred to another rail at an intersection in the tunnel network within the mountain peak housing Borinorhnus's military headquarters. The tunnels wide and spacious, accommodating the shining railways resembling moving walkways or escalators. The rail system ferried personnel to and from the various sections and offices within the complex. The office chambers accessed through portals in the smooth tunnel walls. Carved busts of memorialized military leaders, and depictions of historic battles, decorated the tunnel walls. And at each intersection, elaborately carved arches overhead. The tunnels bathed in dim ultraviolet light.

Zanth rode the rail to a terraced exit in the cliff face. As the rail neared the end of the hallway tunnel, he checked the fit of his headcap. The elastic metal used in the headcap's construction ensured a snug fit, preventing air from entering beneath it, holding the headcap in place during flight. Strands of Zanth's long flaxen hair hung below the headcap's nape, flowing over a tuft of bright amber fur circling his neck. The headcap's lower hem fitted tight below the prominent ridge of his wide cheekbones, and a U shaped hole cut on either side exposed his high pointed ears. The front covered his sloping forehead, the smooth gleaming metal shaped into an elegant point just at the bridge of his flat, wide nose. The cap's top smooth and flat, except for a small ridge running along its center from front to back.

More than an accessory, the headcap a sophisticated electronic device linking Zanth's mind to his command center, and providing control interface. The cap also shielded thoughts he wished to keep private. Finally, a badge of office, the embossed crest on the headcap's front indicating his military affiliation and rank.

At the terrace Zanth released the rail, diving head first from the cliff. He spread his arms and stretched out his fingers, unfolding thin wings on either side of his body. The wings a continuous layer of skin, attached to a spinal ridge running down his back to a stubbed vestigial tail. The skin covered his arms out to his palm and single, clawed prehensile thumb. The other four fingers of each hand long and flexible, his wings formed by the membranous skin connecting them.

Air rushed past him. Swept over him. Ruffled the furry hair around his neck and down his back. Thin, buoyant air, lifting him after four beats of his outstretched wings. He rose, and soared, joining a dark swarm of flyers filling the twilight sky above the city. Tiny tactile hairs embedded in his wings sensed variations in the air, autonomously adjusting the shape and angle of his wings as he flew toward the capital citadel.

In the distance on his right, a dark horizon delineated the boundary between twilight and perpetual night. To his left another horizon, brighter, the sun scorched side of the world.

As he glided amid the swarm toward the city center, foreboding images lay heavy in Zanth's mind. He did not relish the meeting he'd been summoned to. The unpleasant news he had to deliver. Yet another defeat. Yet another fleet lost.

His headcap electronically shielded his tortured thoughts from reaching every other mind in the city. Eventually to spread to every mind around the world. Each sharing thoughts, images, memories. His headcap provided a secondary level of privacy beyond the mental control he'd learned and exercised during a long military career.

Zanth navigated the capital city's jagged peaks. Returning echoes of sonic waves he emitted reached his large sensitive ears, painting detailed images in his mind of the peaked landscape. Rocky spires towered thousands of echospans into the pale pink sky. The barren landscape unchanged over the millennia, shaped by the early volcanic upheavals of the planet. Many of the steep slopes swirly smooth, like the sides of a softie ice cream. Others, like black stalagmites, pierced the sky, the tips of the tallest peaks covered in chalky blankets of snow.

Other images filled Zanth's mind. The exact location, direction, and velocity of each individual in the swarm surrounding him, heading in myriad directions around the city. High above in the thin atmosphere, transports plied their routes to and from other regions of the continent, other far flung cities around the world.

His wide nostrils gathered the city's scents borne on the prevailing wind from the dark east. When storms brought a westerly wind, the scent of livestock farms, food processing plants, waste disposal, and other industrial odors filled the air.

At short distances, visual acuity in the mid electromagnetic spectrum blurred. But vision in the ultraviolet spectrum distinguished shapes and patterns. His other senses rendered the indistinct shapes in crisp detail upon his mind. The citadel's tall irregularly shaped peak approached, rising above the others around it. The citadel's cave like openings, adorned by decoratively carved protruding terraces, lined the peak at multiple levels from its base to just below its highest point. Zanth flexed his fingers, beating his wings, and soared for the highest terrace.

The rail transported Zanth through ornate tunneled hallways to the council chamber. A uniformed sentry opened the portal for him to enter. Zanth stepped into a large open cavern. Its walls converged overhead, indicating its location at the top of the peak. Narrow shafts bored to the outside allowed faint natural light to seep in, augmenting the ultraviolet illumination, and circulating fresh air. An aide attending an office console informed Zanth the governors were assembled, awaiting his arrival.

Zanth strode across a wide rock ledge jutting from the wall, stretching across the deep cavern like a bridge, almost to the opposite wall. Reaching the stairway, Zanth clasped the handrail on both sides. His talons grasped the carved rounded steps. He stepped around and below the ledge to the assembled Council of Governors, each in their assigned place, hanging head down in the roosting position. He assumed his place among them, relaxed his muscles, enabling his hanging body weight to tighten the grip of his talons around the roost.

Zanth removed his headcap, held it against his chest. His closed fingers folded his wings close against his body. The council chamber clear, the aide having set the privacy field and departed, the minds he had feebly sensed upon his arrival now flooded full force into his. The thoughts of the assembled governors merged into his.

Each governor recognizable by the unique quality of their thoughts, by their individual pattern of oral sounds, by their unique facial features and ultraviolet markings, by their distinctive scent. Each wore the red and gold trimmed uniform of government. Their chest coats bore the distinctive emblem and sash of their office. The headcaps, held against their chests, the crests of their office.

All of the governors were elders, wise and cunning in their own right. The council a kratocracy, whose members had acquired their status through social maneuvering and political cunning. Even through physical force, like Law and Security Governor Zepharinlenar, whose ruthlessness Zanth did not underestimate.

"General Supreme Zanthinvolar Abydynus," each individual mind greeted him formally, using his matronymic, Volar, and his birth colony, Abydy.

"This is not favorable news," said their thoughts, as Zanth relayed the images of the destroyed fleet. The audible clicks, chirps, and loud scheeping of the assembled governors indicated the depth of their displeasure and dismay.

The Loudest, the head of the council, Governor Supreme Khorabinjolen Khucharnus. Khorab born of Jolen, of the Khuchar colony, an elder from a long line of 'Keepers', Borinorhnus's traditional leaders.

Borinorhran history told of the first 'Privys and Seers', individuals of unusually strong mental powers, able to shield their thoughts and probe deep into another's mind, to the extent of controlling and directing another's thoughts. How one such ancient leader had possessed both abilities, a Privyseer, and had united the Keepers, gathering their scattered and disparate colonies into the first collective. The first Keeper Supreme.

Successive Keeper Supremes possessed these mental abilities to a greater or lesser degree. A few not at all, surrounding themselves with privys and seers of lesser ancestral lineage. Governor Supreme Khorabinjolen one of these, possessing the lineage but not the mental abilities. But possessing the strength, cunning, and social connections to rise to the top.

A staunch traditionalist and self-proclaimed guardian of Borinian culture, Khorab loathed change as much as failure. Close spaced, fierce onyx eyes stared from a long narrow face, their burning intensity equal to his agitated oral clicking, and the ferocity of his thoughts.

"It is the third mother ship destroyed. Such losses are unacceptable. We must maintain and increase our quiri herds," using the colloquial contraction for the Borathquiri, literally, ground walkers. "We need to replenish our stocks, and we have not yet found a means to speed up the breeding process."

"Not to forget the loss of our own people," thought Laskarinadya, Governor of Space and Technology, a short rotund Borinian, his round pudgy face covered by close cropped brown facial hair.

"Indeed," concurred Sorkahringorol, Governor of Health and Habitats. "Our own population growth is in decline. The downward trend over the past five decades is increasing. And we reproduce even more slowly than the quiri.

The losses we are encountering in space will soon be unsustainable."

"Decreased fertility appears to be an underlying factor," from Science Governor Tovarinkara, his lean face aged, but the evenly spaced eyes shrewd, intelligent, and perceptive. "We have yet however to determine a cause."

"The population question is a separate issue," snapped Governor Supreme Khorabinjolen in their minds. "The loses in space are a military issue, and the immediate issue of this meeting. What do you intend to prevent more losses general?"

"As to who may be controlling these wild quiri?" inquired the portly Space and Technology Governor.

"We have not been able to discern that governor," Zanth responded. "Nor do we have any indication quiri in the wild are being directed."

"You must search harder," demanded Governor Supreme Khorabinjolen. "It is preposterous to consider these mindless quiri are capable of destroying our mother ships and entire fleets without direction."

"It must be a priority," insisted Laskarinadya, his frustration betrayed by loud elongated clicks.

Zanth shielded his true thoughts and doubts concerning any such control of off-world quiri. None of his intelligence reports, including close reconnaissance by their own quiri scouts and checkers, revealed any indication of such control. The council's conventionally held belief quiri lacked intelligence and self-control, an unproven conception, perhaps a conceit. One Zanth no longer subscribed to.

"The quiri are not the only resource we are consuming at unsustainable levels," the errant thought from

Antrozinpanar, Governor of Industry and Farming, prompting Zanth to probe deeper into the minds sharing his.

"Increasing individualization and fragmentation in the collective is a growing concern," Zanth heard in the thoughts of Information and Culture Governor Mokharinsephin, as the governor pondered whether the problem might not be connected to the wild quiri question. "Perhaps these dissident factions are responsible for both."

"The immediate issue is the military situation," repeated Governor Supreme Khorabinjolen, his sudden strident clicks and chirps reminding the other governors to control their own thoughts. "Governor Zepharinlenar's security colony is handling the dissident situation."

"Indeed," Zepharinlenar's response registered in each mind. Zanth glanced at the Law and Security Governor without turning his head. Zepharinlenar younger than the other governors, his small, slate black eyes, sunk within deep wells formed by prominent protruding cheekbones, and a heavy brow ridge. The eyes always suspicious, always malicious. Zanth maintained a mental struggle to shield his intense dislike and distrust of the governor.

"General?" prompted Governor Supreme Khorabinjolen.

Zanth refocused his thoughts on the issue at hand. Chiefly on the meeting he'd arranged following conclusion of the council meeting, and the plan he intended to set in motion.

"We approve of your plan," the assembled minds assured him.

"I will proceed," Zanth responded.

"You have the information you require from Zepharinlenar?" inquired Khorabinjolen.

"We met earlier," Zanth responded, mentally burying the lingering distaste of the earlier meeting. "The governor's staff provided intelligence reports on the dissident groups. It is not much, but provides a starting point from which I may trace a connection to these off-world quiri."

Dismissed by the council, Zanth returned to the terraced entrance. Sonic echoes depicted his waiting transport before he'd observed it visually. He released the rail and leapt the intervening distance. The free articulating thumbs of both hands grasped the transport's receiving ring. Zanth swung inside, heard the soft hiss of the hatch closing behind him. The military pilot operating the transport applied power and the vehicle rose through the sky, merging into a transit lane high above the city's peaks.

Zanth settled onto a seat. In reality a flat shelf protruding around the perimeter of the vehicle's interior hull. Seats not a feature in Borinian vehicles. And the sitting posture uncomfortable, unnatural. While his skeletal anatomy permitted sitting, even for long periods, it entailed tucking the stubbed vestigial tail and attached wing skin between his legs, sitting on it. And closing his fingers to wrap the silky smooth wings against his body. Normally he'd hang by his talons in the natural roosting position, but he needed to change garments for his next meeting. His destination lay beyond the city, in a broad valley between a peaked mountain range on the edge of darkside.

In the privacy of the passenger compartment Zanth removed the poly-carbon breastplate, and his chest coat. He loosened the collar and unfastened the waist belt of the one-piece uniform garment, pulling it down around his legs, stepping out of its leggings. He stepped into the leggings of a nondescript grey suit, the material heavy and insulated, tugging it up around his legs and thighs. The rear section fitted just below his short protruding tailbone. He tightened the belt around his waist, lifted the garment's upper shirt to his chest and dropped the collar loop over his head, fitting it beneath the ring of fur encircling his neck. He cinched the collar tight. Next, he donned a heavily insulated chest jacket to fend off the cold temperature at his destination. He tucked the jacket's crutch flap between his legs, looped the straps over his hips, and fastened them to the jacket's hem on either side. And last boots, open at the toes to permit extrusion of his talons.

Zanth tucked a short-barreled projectile weapon into a concealed holster on the jacket's right side. The weapon an old design, capable of being fired from a standing or roosting position, but useless in flight. Crude but effective. And easily concealed. He'd loaded the weapon with alternating sonic explosives and penetrating projectile rounds. In another concealed holster on the jacket's left side, he carried a shokra charge lance.

"Approaching your destination general." The thought from his pilot penetrated a corner of Zanth's mind. Much of his mind he'd walled off during the flight, relegating the aide's continuously streaming thoughts and mental images to background chatter, while he'd ruminated and pondered the implications of his plan, and the individual he'd chosen to implement it.

And the death toll such a plan was certain to entail.

Scout

No explosion. The sensors indicated no energy output from the scout. Seraphina retracted the cable. Pulled the scout closer. The pod small enough to fit into the cargo hold. But its mass put her ship over the limit. She'd have to jettison other portions of her haul. An intact clicker scout worth whatever she had to throw back into space.

The scout also required her to reconsider her next move. Rethink her intended destination. And decide how to turn the little ship into profit. If word of her prize escaped prematurely, it'd attract all manner of scavengers and pirates, like carrion to a corpse.

She secured the scout in the hold, secured the grappler, closed the hatch, and pressurized the hold. She transferred sensor readouts and basic controls to the hold before exiting the cockpit and heading below.

Seraphina's eyes widened in wonder. A smile parted her lips, spread across her creamy chocolate face, lifting her cheekbones. She approached the inert cylinder. Her impression of its bee-like resemblance reinforced up close. Its thin wing-like sails folded neatly into a recess running along its smooth, trisected body. The front section, like a bee's head, contained the control cockpit. The thorax-like center section the scout's sensor arrays. The aft, tail-like section, the propulsion system.

No ports anywhere. The rounded head closed. Seraphina reached out, gingerly touched the smooth surface. Pulled her hand back as though receiving an electric shock. A nervous reaction. She reached out again, maintained the contact, and caressed the smooth curved sides. Her smile grew wider.

Her apprehension of booby traps long abated, Seraphina marveled open mouthed at the sleek functional beauty of the craft. Unexpected. Unlike other clicker ships she'd previously encountered. All hideous, amorphous things, resembling an asteroid with spiked peaks erupting on its surface.

A series of smooth indentations, low on the hull between the head and mid section caught her attention. Steps. She fitted one booted foot into the lowermost indentation, her other booted foot in the next one up. She climbed to the dorsal surface of the hull, discovering a small square entrance hatch sealed flush against the head section. She observed no method of opening it.

Seraphina prodded, probed, and explored around the head section of the craft until the hatch sprung its locking clamps, opening a mere crack. She pried it fully open. A strange unidentifiable odor assaulted her nostrils. Remnants of the scout's internal atmosphere she reasoned.

She lowered her head through the open hatch. And recoiled with sufficient force to propel herself from the scout, her grasp torn from the hatch coaming. She fell onto the hold's deck, sprawling flat on her back.

Recovering, Seraphina gazed around her. Dazed. Confused. Unable to focus on the heaps of junk lying in scattered piles around the hold. Unable to believe the thing she'd seen in the cockpit. Or imagined. She hadn't expected to discover much in the little scout, expecting it to be empty. Certainly not a body. And not the kind she'd seen. Or thought she'd seen. Hallucination she decided, recalling the strong odor. Probably a strange residual gas in the alien ship. But no chemical, bio-hazard, or environmental alarms had sounded in the hold.

She sat on the deck, allowing the scout time to air. Still no alarms. Her thoughts preoccupied and disturbed by the imagined sight.

Estimating she'd allowed sufficient time, Seraphina rose from the deck and approached the scout again. Using the footholds she hoisted herself to the hatch. Cautiously, she peered inside.

No hallucination. Not her imagination. A man sat strapped in the pilot seat. A Human man.

She shimmied forward, head and torso hanging upside down through the hatch. Seraphina reached out, touched the skin of his face. Warm. She reached farther, placed her open palm on his chest. A hard smooth surface hid the rise and fall of his respiration. She held her hand close beneath his nostrils. A shallow, barely perceptible exhalation of air tickled her skin. Alive.

Seraphina gazed around the tiny cockpit, barely registering the unfamiliar instruments, the alien design. Her thoughts preoccupied by her shocking discovery, the astounding implications not yet registering. Her immediate task, she decided, removing the man from the cramped cockpit.

Seraphina was confident she possessed the upper body strength to lift him. But the confined cockpit provided insufficient room to maneuver. The space behind the pilot seat, providing access to the sensor section, capable of accommodating another person. But the hatch only large enough for one body at a time.

Seraphina squirmed backward out of the hatch, her plan formulated. She headed to a far bulkhead of the hold, retrieving the harness she needed. She worked fast. Uncertain how much longer the man might survive. And not wanting to linger any longer than necessary in this section of space. The sensors indicated no other ships in her vicinity, but she doubted it'd remain clear much longer.

The harness Seraphina carried reminded her of one other item. She might not need it, but she had learned never to throw caution or instinct overboard. From a bulkhead locker she retrieved a weapons belt. She fitted it around her waist, snapping closed quick-release fasteners on the belt, and the straps around her thighs. Cross draw holsters on both hips contained hand pistols, and a kukri shaped blade next to the pistol on her right hip.

Seraphina activated the hold's cargo hoist, positioning it above the scout. She returned to the hatch and climbed in behind the pilot seat. She discovered the seat swiveled. She turned it to face her. The man's features registered for the first time. A strong masculine face. Pleasant proportions. His jaw and chin concealed beneath crudely trimmed facial hair, uneven and stubbly in spots. Strands of long straw-colored hair flowed from beneath a peculiar metallic cap on his head. A pungent odor surrounded him.

She rechecked his respiration. Still shallow. Still alive. She rigged the harness around his torso, snug under his arms, forgoing the leg loops and straps between his legs, which she'd be unable to secure.

Seraphina climbed onto the back of the scout, straddling it aft of the hatch. She activated the hoist, the control in her right hand, her left guiding the hoist chain hooked to the harness. The hard covering of the man's strange garment prevented the straps from biting into his flesh.

The soft clinking of chain running over the hoist's sprockets accompanied the slow rise of the man from the scout. First his head, covered by the strange cap, followed by shoulders, torso, waist, legs; like an infant's birth. Seraphina guided the chain as the man rose, arms limp at his sides. She halted the hoist when his booted feet cleared the scout's hatch.

Seraphina slid from the scout. She directed the hoist to a clear area of the hold. Suspended above the deck, the man turned slowly at the end of the chain. Seraphina lowered him to the deck. She removed his headcap, and strapped a breather connected to an air cylinder onto his face.

The material covering his body not a garment, she noted. More like a shell. She tapped it with her knuckles. Rigid, like hardened leather around the arms, legs, chest and back. Flexible at the joints. A ringed collar around the neck, and an attachment, similar to the collar of her environmental suit. But the design alien and unfamiliar. No obvious openings or seams. Seraphina unable to discern how to open or remove it.

Agarinzelar Trionalnus

Zanth plunged head first from the transport. He flexed the fingers of both hands, spreading his wings. His mouth opened at the shock of frigid air hitting the thin membranous skin, emitting a long shriek with the ultrasonic waves spreading out in all directions.

The sky dark, speckled by twinkling pinpoints of light high above, and a lingering hint of twilight before the opaque blackness covering the far side of the world. Returning echoes provided detailed images of the colony sandwiched in the valley below, on the edge of perpetual night.

Scents reached him, borne on the cold breeze blowing westward. Industrial fumes released by processing plants. The raw odor of ores mined from the darkside. The individual scents of the miners. Other strange, unfamiliar odors, emanating from the inhospitable darkside.

A dangerous place, this close to darkside. Not only the proximity of wild carnivorous creatures inhabiting the area, sometimes preying on the unwary miner. But the miners themselves, who seemed to assimilate the predatory aggressiveness of darkside carnivores as though by osmosis. A hardy group, the miners. Able to withstand the harsh conditions, exhibiting none of the cold weather torpor typical of the average Borinian. Their quiri herds even more so. Aggressive. Ornery. Nasty. Requiring strong mental and brutal physical control. Must be something in the air Zanth mused.

No fancy carved terraces or transport rails in the mining town. The location a primitive outback on the edge of civilization. Zanth flew into a dark opening in the cliff face, merging with a stream headed deeper into the wide tunnel. On his left, a swarm headed in the opposite direction. The tunnels, like their occupants, crude and rough hewn, unlike the art festooned tunnels, smooth walls, and decorative arches in the cities.

Countless minds connected to Zanth's, their thoughts revealing occupation, destination, personal histories, and memories. For his part, Zanth revealed only superficial thoughts and images. Unconnected bits and pieces of memory. An assumed identity he projected to the minds populating the colony.

Echoes of more openings ahead. Smaller tunnels branching in all directions. Streams of miners broke from the main swarm, rushing into various tunnels on beating wings.

The main tunnel emptied into an immense cave. The space crowded and cramped despite its size. Zanth landed on a ledge just inside the entrance. His sharp talons, protruding through toeless boots, dug into and clutched the granite wall. Zanth surveyed the room.

Dark. His ultraviolet vision rendered the crude furnishings and machinery dispensing food and drink, and the individual patterns of the raucous miners. A dozen, two dozen, more, grouped around each dispenser. The sound of dispensing tubes being suckled and gnawed filled the public eatery. Accompanied by a cacophonous chorus of excitable chirps, screeches, and clicks.

The minds Zanth had dimly perceived on his flight through the tunnels burst full force upon him. Wave upon wave of ultrasound bounced off him, sizing up the newcomer. Not an individual the miners readily recognized, but new miners rotated in and out continuously. The more adroit might image his weapons, just as Zanth's pulses, tuned at a specific frequency, located crude weapons they carried.

A mind at the edge of his thoughts beckoned. Zanth responded, emitting a long low frequency pulse. The returning echo provided the information he required. He released his grip on the wall, fell headfirst a short distance before outstretched wings swept him upward, toward a lone occupant roosted beneath a ledge in a corner.

"General Zanthinvolar Abydynus. It is an honor to meet again," the solitary figure greeted him formally.

"The honor is mutual Agarinzelar Trionalnus," Zanth responded, his senses roaming over his companion, registering his non-descript scent, a different one whenever they met, and the thick brown fur circling his neck, covering his head and back. And facial hair, like many of the miners occupying the eatery. Their heavily furred bodies another defense against the cold.

The facial hair on Zanth's companion also obscured atypical Borinian features. The ridges of his cheekbones and brow not as prominent, but flatter, smoother. The broad forehead not as sharply sloped. The eyes larger; dark pools exuding a quiet intelligence, intense and penetrating.

Zanth probed his companion's mind. The cover identity accessible on the surface. Blank below. Agar a strong privy, adept at compartmentalizing and blocking his thoughts. A natural, even before the rigorous military mental training. And one of the few among millions possessing a fission personality, capable of living a solitary life, harboring solitary thoughts, apart from any colony and the collective. Agar a powerful seer too. An ideal candidate for covert intelligence gathering.

Zanth's innermost thoughts similarly blocked. But Zanth and Agar shared a mutual respect born of their long association, rooted in battle, cemented in loyalty, allowing them to share their thoughts freely, without reservation.

"Have you eaten general? May I request something for you?"

"Not sure I could stomach it. The stench is unappealing."

A string of short clicks signaled Agar's amusement.

"You are correct. The holders here serve the usual fare. Quiri, and a few creatures hunted on darkside. Vegetation and fruit is imported, and there is a variety of local produce, but most have a vile taste. All unappetizing. They are not particular regarding preparation. You get used to it I suppose. On the other hand the spirits are exhilaratingly potent," Agar offered, accompanied by another series of amused clicks and cheeps.

"I will pass," Zanth thought. "I also do not wish to put you in jeopardy by remaining here longer than necessary."

"Though I am pleased by your presence I wonder at your wish to meet here?"

"You are familiar in this colony, and also familiar with it. And the assignment I have for you will probably have its beginning here."

"Command me general," Agar's response unhesitant and unequivocal.

Zanth's thoughts flowed freely into Agar's mind. "The council is concerned by our continuing losses in space. In truth my perception is of a matter much more disturbing they do not wish to share. Therefore they shift the burden to me. And the blame. My head in the block when they fail."

"You anticipate failure general?"

"Not to your mission. But the problem may extend beyond any successes we may achieve. The council believes the quiri spacers are directed by dissident factions. And these factions must be receiving support from networks on Borinorhnus yet to be identified and purged."

Agar bared pointed teeth in a snarl-like expression. The hiss of air escaping his open mouth, and string or low clicks, expressed his contempt.

"The Council underestimates the quiri and their spacer kin to their detriment. The quiri are more intelligent than is commonly believed."

"We are in agreement Agar. I do not underestimate their capacity for innovation and aggressiveness. Nor do I discount the possibility of an as yet unidentified enemy."

"What is your command general?"

"I am providing you the commissioned rank of Captain Commander. I've assigned you an attack cruiser and crew. They are at your disposal, as are the full resources of the intelligence colony. You are to search out this dissident network, identify its members, trace its activities off world, and determine what, if any, connection they might have to the spacer quiri. And the true nature of our enemy."

"I understand why you suggest I initiate the operation here. Mining colonies are ideal hiding places for dissidents. And the mining operation often exposes archeological artifacts attractive to a particular type of dissident."

"Exactly Agar." Zanth hesitated, uncertain whether to release the thought stirring in the depths of his mind. Decided their relationship permitted it.

"What are your thoughts on this dissident theory regarding an evolutionary kinship between Borinian and quiri?"

"It is of no consequence to me general. I am a soldier. Not a scientist. Why do you ask?"

"The question appears increasingly prevalent in the collective. And I believe it is the matter occupying the council. The reason they wish such strong action. And I fear the aftermath which may befall us may be of our own making."

"The dissidents when I find them?"

"The consensus of the council is to halt the spread of this infection."

"Understood general."

Awakening

Ezekiel's mind drifted in a dark timeless void. Consciousness awakened. A vague sense of being. Higher and higher, through successive layers of consciousness, surfacing from the darkness like a drowning man bursting above the water gasping for air. Sensations returned. A pounding inside his head. Disoriented. Consumed by sudden panic. Every cell in his body revved for survival. A strange apparatus attached to his face. His hands ripped it away.

His eyes fluttered open to reveal an impossible sight.

Ezekiel recoiled in panic. His mind gripped by an overwhelming instinct to flee. His conditioned passivity in the presence of the masters replaced by a different imperative. New. Unfamiliar. A dormant instinct awakening. The sight before him not a master. A vision perhaps, like when he slept. Perhaps he'd died. Memories of the recent battle surfaced in his throbbing head. The ancient myth passed down through countless generations must be true. A new life after death. A place where the newly dead are reunited with those who'd gone before. A place without masters.

The figure gazing down at him fenori, female. But unlike any fenori he'd ever seen. Her face smooth, her skin dark, like quiri bred on the sun-scorched plains of his homeworld. Her hair also dark, colored a bluish hue. Long and shiny, falling below her shoulders. The front cropped short, covering her forehead, hanging just above large liquid brown eyes.

Her garments familiar as the type worn by quiri in the wild. But as strange to him as his garments were to her. The bottom all of one piece, tightly enclosing her legs, circling her flared hips and small waist. The upper piece black, shiny, covering the round mounds of her chest, her shoulders, and her arms down to her elbows.

Seraphina amused by the man's reaction. His shock similar to her own when she'd first discovered him. And just as troubled. She was undecided on how to proceed. What to do regarding him. She had no plan for such a bizarre circumstance.

"What is your affiliation?" she asked. "How do you come to be in a clicker scout ship?"

A blank stare the man's only response. His grey eyes uncomprehending, bewildered.

"What are you called? What is your affiliation?" She tried again in another of the many dialects spoken by the space faring factions.

Still no response. His eyes swiveled back and forth in fleeting glances around the hold. His gaze rested on the scout, his expression perplexed and terrified. He noticed the headcap she'd removed from his head. He grabbed desperately for it, plucked it from the deck and placed it on his head.

Ezekiel aware the woman had spoken. As his people did among themselves. Using vocalizations instead of thought images as the masters did. But her words incomprehensible, devoid of meaning. Unintelligible to his ears.

He noticed the scout, wondered why it'd been transported with him in death. Maybe to carry his body into the afterlife. The headcap he'd grabbed from the deck and placed on his head silent. Empty. No thoughts reached his mind. Not his masters. Not the woman's. Though he hadn't expected it from her, not if she were similar to fenori of his kind.

I am perished, he concluded. And this is the afterlife.

The woman continued to stare down at him. Her initial surprise turned to incomprehension, and bewildered uncertainty.

"We must leave this place," Seraphina said, turning from him and heading toward a control console on one side of the hold, conscious of the weapons hanging at her sides. She did not consider the strange man a danger. Probably a clicker captive. But the weight of the weapons on her hips comforted her.

She'd remained in the area longer than expected. The clickers had arrived to hunt on the only habitable world in the system. The factions controlling the system had ambushed them and destroyed the fleet. But more might be on the way. And she expected scavengers like herself to arrive soon.

Seraphina headed toward her cockpit. The man responded to her exasperated beckoning and prodding, timidly following her from the hold.

Darkside

Agar entered the cave, which bore no tunnels beyond the short passage inside the entrance. Instead a hole opened onto the cave floor. Not natural. Artificial. A deliberately dug square shaft. Deep and old. Ultraviolet hues in the rock face attested to the shaft's antiquity. Agar had been led to the cave by bits and pieces of errant thoughts gathered in the crowded eatery.

He noticed talon tracks in the walls of the shaft. Hundreds of them, indicating numerous trips up and down, by many individuals.

Agar's mind reached out, probing the depths. Unable to detect another presence. But the shaft deep, perhaps obscuring the thoughts of anyone below. Agar closed his mind, preventing his thoughts from revealing his presence.

He wore combat gear. A stiff leather chest coat over a plain brown suit. The combat chest coat incorporated a dull matte black poly-carbon breast shield, low-slung side holsters, and ammunition and equipment pockets. The bottom of each holster secured by straps around his thighs. He retrieved a small capsule from a pouch on the left front of the coat, raised it above his head, and crushed it between thumb and palm. A gaseous mist enveloped him, erasing his scent.

Weapons ready in holsters on each side of his waist, and along his thighs, Agar commenced the long descent. He used the toe tracks already gouged into the wall, avoiding any displacement of stone from his own talons gripping the shaft. He descended into the dark abyss.

Agar halted at the bottom of the shaft. His acute senses alert for any movement, any sound, any scent. Talons protruding through open toed combat boots gripped the wall as he lowered himself headfirst to the opening.

An empty cavern. Long and wide. Black as darkside. His ultraviolet vision scanned its features. Without sonic echoes, Agar was unable to determine the cave's details or dimensions, but emitting ultrasonic waves posed a risk. Still no one in sight. But he noted a number of tunnel openings on the far side.

Agar dropped to the ground, his boots dispersing a fine mist of dust where he landed. Other boot prints embedded in the powdery dust covered the cave floor, heading to and from one of the tunnels. Agar followed them.

The tunnel sloped downward, deeper into the mountain. The first whiff of a scent reached him. He paused. Heightened senses on alert. More scents, accompanied by sounds, scraping, scratching, shoveling. Loud vocal clicks and cheeps echoed through the enclosed space.

Agar reached the chamber where the sounds and smells originated. From concealment, he peered around the edge. A small cave, bathed in dim diffused ultraviolet light. Supplemented by light emitted from mechanical tools and instruments. A half dozen individuals, busy excavating a section of the cave, and recording the activity on data recorders.

Agar paid particular attention to the recorders. A device rarely used in the collective, where each individual's mind is connected to the thoughts, images, and memories of each other. Where knowledge is stored and preserved in the minds of Librarians, the collective's historians, accessible to all. The recorder used primarily by the military to transmit information securely, and during off-world and deep space missions, given the uncertainty of a ship or its crew returning home.

Agar examined his options. The stocks of his weapons silently telescoped outward. Their thin metallic butts rested beneath each armpit. He carried a long barrel rifle and a short-range pistol. Both snug in quick release holsters.

He opted for the shokra charge lances, effective in controlling unruly quiri, and in close quarters. He reached down and drew them from their holsters on each thigh, one in each hand. As he gripped them between palm and thumb, he activated the triggers in each handle. The lances silently charged. Their collapsible sections telescoped to their full length.

Agar leapt into the cavern, startling the occupants into momentary immobility. Sufficient for Agar to move in close among them. His arms swung left and right as his body twirled in a graceful choreographed combat ballet, fingers tightly curled to keep his wings closed against his body. The outstretched lances contacted their targets, discharging incapacitating energy in a blue ultraviolet glow. His targets fell to the ground unconscious amid loud panicked shrieks.

The workers farthest from him regained their mobility and leapt to attack. But Agar already crouched on bent knees, twirling and spinning, his aim unerring, catching one attacker in midair, another moving in on him from his left side, dispatching the final two with forward sword-like thrusts.

Agar surveyed the scene, straightening to his full height. The six workers occupying the cavern lay in unconscious heaps around him.

He moved to examine the activity he'd interrupted when an errant thought touched his mind. He turned. Two figures stood in one of the tunnel entrances. The figure on the left raised a projectile weapon. The other poised to attack.

Agar dropped the lances as his right hand fell to his side, palm flat against his pistol's handle. His thumb curled around the grip, yanking the pistol forward from its spring-released holster, raising it bear on the target, the butt jammed into his armpit. He fired, all in one fluid motion lasting a mere fraction of a second.

The charged projectile tore a hole in his target's chest, hurling him backward. The weapon fell from the astonished assailant's grip, unfired.

The second figure already hurtling through the air at Agar, feet forward, sharp wicked talons outstretched and reaching. Agar spun away, firing as he turned. The blast jolted his attacker to a stop in midair. His lifeless body crashed to the ground in an eruption of dust.

Agar returned his weapon to its holster, pressing it against the inside latch which closed the spring loaded front opening snug around the pistol. The stocks of both holstered weapons retracted, the butts receding from beneath his armpits.

Agar spent the next hour examining the caverns and tunnels. The caves similar, exhibiting signs of old and new excavation. He studied skeletal remains unearthed from the sediment. Quiri and Borinian among them. Old. Ancient. Long since buried. The excavated bits and pieces of artifacts and tools designed for quiri hands. Not Borinian. Agar documented his findings on his own recorder, and retrieved the recorders used by the workers.

Retracing his path up the shaft Agar paused at intervals, placing small marble sized charges from a low pocket of his combat coat into the claw holes and crevices in the wall. He exited the shaft and strode to the mouth of the cave. He leapt head first from the cliff face, simultaneously triggering the charges. The detonations reached his acute hearing as he spread his arms and fingers. The stretched membrane between his fingers bit into the thin frigid air, lifting him upward as the shaft collapsed into the cavern below, burying everyone and everything beneath it.

Junk

Space is silent. Yet permeated by sound. Receptors arrayed around the hull of Seraphina's ship collected signals across a wide electromagnetic spectrum. The converted cosmic chorus filled the cockpit at low volume. The background hiss of galactic space, the static crackle of the nearby star, the rhythmic popping of the solar wind, the low hum of the portal the ship had exited.

The man occupied the seat next to her in the cockpit, the main sensor console before him. The console's screens depicted processed images across the visual wavelengths. The man sat in silence, incomprehensible, casting furtive glances at her as she piloted the ship. His gaze studied the controls and instruments, as though understanding their function and the data they displayed.

The ship sailed across the dark void at tremendous velocity. The solar wind impacting its sails processed into harmonic sound by the sensors. The portal no longer visible to the naked eye against the star's blinding brilliance. The portal's presence depicted only as radiated energy in the X-ray band.

The strange portals were seeded across the galaxy. Each orbited close to a star, from which many believed the portals drew their energy. The origin of the portals forgotten in antiquity, including how or why they functioned. The technology had survived the ages, along with the ships transiting through them, plying the vastness of space. Spaceship mechanical components and ship construction well understood on many space faring worlds. But like the portals, the science behind the working parts understood as little more than magic. The knowledge lost to time.

Seraphina wondered what the man knew of such things. Had he learned of the portals from the clickers? The clickers possessed sophisticated ships and technology. Much of their technology believed to be based on sound. And they too used the portals. Many believed the clickers had built the portals. But much regarding the clickers remained unknown. Mostly conjecture and speculation. Stories told to frighten children into obedience. Stories Seraphina discounted as too outlandish and farfetched. Her only certainty, they preyed on Humans, and were an enemy to avoid, or kill on sight.

Seraphina's destination Ecibor, the fifth world circling the star. At the ship's current distance a mere energy blip on the navigation console. A luminous dot to the naked eye, like a star in the night sky. The system itself at the intersection of four known functioning portals, making Ecibor a center of commerce offering an eclectic variety of trade goods. Under strict control by the Guild, an ad-hoc collection of merchants who set trade standards, laws, and maintained the peace with hired enforcers.

Seraphina considered Ecibor the safest destination given the nature of her cargo. Though she intended to exercise her customary caution. She'd also have time prior to orbit to sort her salvaged haul, setting aside items she'd keep for her own use and upgrades to her ship.

Her glance fell on the man. She'd have to communicate her intentions to him. She kept an assortment of male garments on board for trade. Something among them might fit him. And she needed to clean him up. Eliminate his peculiar odor for one, she reminded herself, wrinkling her nose.

For his part, Ezekiel continued to study the instruments around the cockpit. Their design alien to him, like the fenori. But he'd gleaned a pilot's intuitive understanding of their purpose. His mind, free of interference and control, processed the sights and sounds around him. An entirely new perception of space, including the incredible vision beyond the ship, seen through its transparent ports. A feature absent and inconceivable on the masters' ships.

He'd noted their passage through the portal, and scanned the instruments for a familiar pattern. But the area of space the ship had exited into as alien as everything he'd encountered since awakening. He glanced at the fenori who'd risen from the pilot seat, speaking to him.

"Come. Come," Seraphina repeated, to no avail. Her words provoked only a blank stare. But her gestures by now familiar, beckoning him to follow.

She led him through a short passageway. Other areas of the ship hidden behind closed portals embedded in the ship's circular bulkheads. A flight of metal steps led down. Ezekiel recognized his surroundings, recalling the route from the hold to the cockpit. Now retracing their earlier steps, they emerged at the bottom of a companionway into the ship's cargo hold. The scout sat like a shiny insect surrounded by piles of debris.

The fenori moved among the piles, sorting the debris.

"Power cell," Seraphina said, pointing to an object Ezekiel didn't recognize. She set it aside.

"Conduit," she continued. "Useful for the ship," indicating a new pile she'd created. "Also useful for trade. In demand, some of it scarce. Expensive. They'll fetch a good trade," indicating another new pile.

Shrugging her shoulders, Seraphina ceased speaking, continuing to work in silence. The items she placed in the different piles unfamiliar to Ezekiel. Until an area she'd cleared revealed a cylindrical object at the bottom of the pile. Ezekiel pounced on it, his sudden movement startling Seraphina.

"Shokra," he exclaimed, the single word eliciting raised eyebrows and a wide-eyed stare from Seraphina.

"You speak?" she said, the incredulity expressed in her clear brown eyes also present in her voice. "You speak," she repeated in a softer voice.

"Shokra," Ezekiel repeated, pointing to the object as she had done while sorting.

Her turn to stare at him blank-faced. The word meant nothing to Seraphina. It's meaning less significant than hearing it spoken, the first sound the man had uttered since awakening. She also noted the narrowed eyebrows and dark dread expressed in his grey eyes as he spoke, still pointing at the strange object he held in his hand.

Ezekiel noticed Seraphina's uncomprehending stare. He held the lance away from his side, pointed at the deck. His thumb activated the trigger.

Seraphina observed the object in the man's hand extending outward, tripling its length as hidden sections telescoped out.

Ezekiel touched the tip to a piece of debris on the deck. A blue-white sparkle of energy erupted at the point of contact. The burst flowed into and across the deck, dissipating quickly, but not before leaving a mild tingling sensation on the soles of their feet.

Seraphina's arms instinctively fell and crossed her body as the weapon discharged into the deck, and a tingling current swept across her toes and feet, even through her thick-soled boots. Her right hand gripped the handle of the pistol, her left the carved hilt of the blade. She had no doubt the object the man held was a weapon.

But she hadn't drawn hers. Her hands poised to pluck them from their holsters as she gazed into the man's eyes, attempting to discern his intent. No belligerence or aggression present in them. Instead a benign smile parted his lips and curled the corners of his mouth. But she couldn't be certain. The man undoubtedly belonged to a faction she'd never encountered before. Captured by, or working for the clickers. Too many strange occurrences for her to be certain of anything.

She observed his thumb pressing down on an area of the handle. The extended sections drew inward on themselves, collapsing into the short, innocuous cylinder it'd been before activation.

Ezekiel observed Seraphina's stunned apprehension and reaction to the lance's discharge. Her hands still rested on the implements at her sides, no doubt weapons, though of a type alien to him. He meant her no harm, and did not wish to be harmed by her. He deactivated and closed the shokra. But didn't hand it over.

A thought surfaced, to wonder why weapons were required in the afterlife. Other thoughts surfaced on the heels of the first, positing contrary conclusions given all he'd witnessed since awakening. This ship, the space beyond it, the debris from the destroyed fleet lying at his feet, the portal. Why were portals necessary in the afterlife? Or was existence in the afterlife constructed in the same manner as the life he'd departed? Not according to the ancient tale.

Most perplexing of all, the random thoughts arising of their own volition. A product of his own mind. At least he considered them as such. He had no way to be certain. No reference point beyond the many minds and thoughts comingled in his brain since his birth.

Seraphina continued working in the hold. Ezekiel joined her, extracting parts from the rubble, offering them to Seraphina for inspection.

"Plasma conduit.....junk.....fuel core.....piece of sensor processor.....more junk," Seraphina said for each item Ezekiel handed her, resuming her commentary after hearing him speak. Aware he hadn't handed over the weapon, instead tucking it into a concealed pouch she hadn't noticed before on the thigh of his garment.

Before long he imitated her, "Command relay.....echo sounder....pulse meter," he said in response to her perplexed expression at the alien objects he handed her. His words as unfamiliar as the objects, spoken in a language she had never heard before. But he'd point to the useful ship parts pile, astonishing her by his swift inductive learning.

Her jaw fell open when he uttered "junk," tossing a piece of burnt machinery onto the scrap pile.

In the passing days of the long voyage, they worked together in the hold. Their efforts complemented each other as though they'd been accustomed to working together for a long time. Each expanded their vocabulary of the other's language as the days wore on. During the ship's night, Ezekiel slept on the hard deck next to the scout, occasionally using the disposal chute to relieve himself, flushing the contents into space as he'd seen Seraphina do with the junk.

The last item stowed, Seraphina surveyed the hold. The items she'd designated for trade arranged in containers and sealed shut. The scrap loaded into the disposal chute. The final chore had been to move the scout into a corner of the hold, where a stack of empty containers, cargo pallets, and a lubricant stained canvas tarp, hid it from view. Seraphina explained the activity to Ezekiel as they concealed the scout. Or attempted to explain. His expression blank, but seeming to comprehend the nature of the activity, as he adjusted the containers and the tarp to ensure proper concealment of the alien craft.

Seraphina paused at the auxiliary control console, checked the displays, and their progress. A bit to go before the course change to intersect the planet's trajectory. And given the vast distances in space, nothing in even close proximity to their position. No other ships, no errant objects, natural or otherwise. Just an empty void.

Time to address the man's odor, she decided. It had grown into an obnoxious presence in the confined cargo hold as the sweat of their daily labor accumulated. He had not changed since she'd found him. She had no idea if, or how, he'd relieved himself since regaining consciousness. And she still had not observed a means of getting in or out of the strange garment he wore.

Ezekiel followed her up the metal companionway from the hold. The time spent working below oddly exhilarating. His mind unobstructed, wholly occupied by the activity, and learning the fenori's words. The work strenuous at times, requiring his undivided concentration. And allowing him time to grow comfortable with the pattern of thoughts in his head, accepting and recognizing them as his own. And although he did not fully comprehend the purpose of concealing the scout, he instinctively accepted it, and followed the fenori's lead.

Heading through the now familiar passage toward the cockpit the fenori halted, turning to one of the closed portals along the passage. She activated a mechanism on the portal and it swung inward, emitting a soft hiss. Interior lighting flickered on, revealing a small compartment decorated in white and beige. Soft, cushioned padding on two chairs and a footstool matched the décor of the curved bulkhead. A large mirror fixed above two oval shaped shiny metal sinks occupied one bulkhead. A built-in locker of flush fitted drawers occupied the other. And at the far end, another, smaller compartment behind a transparent enclosure.

Seraphina turned to the man. Her hands pantomimed a rubbing motion across her body, then his.

"You need to wash," she said in accompaniment to her gestures. "Do you understand? Of course you don't understand," she said to herself. "From the way you smell does your kind even wash at all?" Aware she'd been smiling in a rare moment of amusement. "I don't even know how in hella's flame to get that thing off. If it even comes off."

Seraphina again turned to gestures, attempting to penetrate the man's uncomprehending stare.

Ezekiel marveled at his surroundings. Unable to believe his eyes. The thought of being in the afterlife resurfaced. He'd never seen, even imagined, a place like the one he stood in. His attention drawn to the fenori before him, her gestures, attempting to convey her thoughts to him. Her words meaningless.

Seraphina threw her arms up in exasperation. She flung open the shower enclosure and repeated the gestures. Her raised outstretched arms triggered a thought in Ezekiel's brain.

"Washing. You want me to wash." But the thought incongruous. The chamber bore no resemblance to a cleaning pen. Not large enough for one thing. Not empty for another. And he observed no ultraviolet emitters embedded in the walls.

Seraphina gestured in a renewed rush of enthusiasm at his words, sighing when the brief flicker of understanding in his eyes turned to confused bewilderment.

She needed a different approach.

Though she no longer considered the man a danger, Seraphina habitually wore her weapons belt. Its weight an unconscious part of her attire, and comforting. She unsnapped the straps, set the belt aside, but within easy reach. She untied the fastenings of her coat, shed it, and set it aside. She removed her blouse, tugging the material over her head, leaving her naked from the waist up.

Ezekiel observed Seraphina removing her garments. Uncertain of its significance. Strangely moved by the smooth texture of her brown flesh, the enticing supple mounds of her chest, a lighter shade of brown, and creamy smooth. Dark red nubs at their center.

Seraphina studied his reactions as he observed her. She held his eyes in her stare, alert to the slightest shift in their expression, or change in his demeanor. She unhooked the waistband of her pants, unfastened the lacing at the front.

Peeled the material clasping her legs until the garment fell to the floor, covering her boots. She stood naked before him, suddenly aware of her predicament. With the pants bunched at her ankles, she'd be unable to move.

Seraphina continued to study the man's eyes. Unconcerned by her naked exposure. Long accustomed to it. Inured to it. To men ogling her naked body, and grappling and pawing at her flesh like beasts. Used for their entertainment. She'd survived it. Had learned from it.

Exposing herself to danger another matter. But she'd borne and survived danger too. Conscious of the weapons within reach, she studied the man surveying her nakedness. Apprehension. Maybe confusion. But non-threatening.

Ezekiel's conflicting thoughts confused him. The fenori's actions at first indicated she wanted him to wash. Not certain how she'd perform it in the small compartment which did not resemble a cleaning pen.

Followed by her removing her garments, a prelude to mating. But equally unreasonable in Ezekiel's' mind. Mating and breeding controlled by the masters, who selected the breeding partners and controlled the process. Nori and fenori crowded into breeding pens, the grunts and cries and screams of copulation on an industrial scale filling the air. Commanded and directed. A process of sexual impregnation and nothing more.

Convinced the man posed no danger, Seraphina reached into the shower and twisted a control. A jet of mist hissed from nozzles recessed around the top of the enclosure. She mimed the follow me gesture, aware he understood that much. She indicated the shower, before again throwing up her arms in resignation. Bending to reach for the pants around her ankles, she missed the broad smile spreading across Ezekiel's face.

A low tearing sound drew Seraphina's attention as she tugged her pants into place. The man's right hand squeezed inside the circular collar around his neck. The sound produced by an invisible seam opening down both sides of the strange garment he wore, from under the armpits to above his ankles, opening the garment into front and back halves, releasing trapped air and a stench which threatened to overpower her nostrils. He grasped a sleeve in one hand, bent his elbow, and pulled his arm out downward. He repeated the maneuver on the other side.

Both arms free, Ezekiel grabbed the ring collar and pulled it over his head, freeing his body of the suit, except for his feet. He dropped the rigid suit to the metal deck, bending at the waist to extricate his feet from the attached boots. Ezekiel stood before her clad only in a sweat-stained tunic, the skirt reaching to his knees. He untied a fastening around his waist, releasing the bottom half of the material wrapped between his legs, covering his genitals and bottom. The flared sides of the garment formed the lower skirt. He tugged the soft, flimsy one-piece garment over his head, forgoing the tied fastenings at the sides. He untied straps around his upper thighs, dropping a pair of leggings to the deck at his bare feet.

Seraphina stared open mouthed at the naked figure before her. Noted its strong male features, the wide muscled chest and shoulders, the firm striated abdomen, the limp organ between his legs embedded in a bushy mound of straw colored hair. The pale whiteness of his skin, the dark, reddish, blotchy scars across his lower sides and shoulders, and a mark like a brand, burned into the flesh of his upper right arm.

Aware of a catch in her breathing. And a strange sensation infusing her, warm and liquid. A mysterious desire, like an unquenchable thirst.

Ezekiel stepped into the enclosure, smiled, and raised his arms.

Lightside

Agar dove from the peak. The operation completed. Information from the darkside miner's cave, pieced to other intelligence provided by General Zanth, had led him to the location. He'd recovered additional information on the dissidents and destroyed the site, as he had the first site on darkside.

He noted the twin suns high in the sky, like a mating pair. Always together. Always in the same place. The smaller sun a dim red companion to its larger mate, which blazed bright and brilliant in the twilight sky. The eve of another interval, 'Ketu', the dimming, or rebirth, when the smaller sun eclipsed its larger companion, dimming the larger star's light and creating a dark ring in its center. Followed eight days later by the interval 'Rahu', death, when they reversed roles, and the large sun covered its smaller mate, blocking it out altogether, as if consuming it.

Borinorhrans believed the eclipses represented a symbolic cycle of death and rebirth. Celebrated with rituals and festivals performed during the events. Agar subscribed to no such notions. Content in the predictable reliability of the eclipses, from which their civilization derived their measurement of time.

Agar opened his arms and spread his fingers, extending his wings. A rising current of air lifted him as a fleeting echo alerted his brain.

Imminent danger. The exact location unclear. The echo arrived from above and to his right. No time to ponder the situation. Or the inexplicable lack of sonic pulses impacting his body, which might have alerted him to another's presence. Instinct commanded his reflexes. Agar flexed the fingers of both hands, adjusting the trailing edge of each wing, rolling onto his side. He continued through the snap roll onto his back, closed his fingers, folded his arms, and dove as the charge crackled and singed the air he'd occupied a moment before.

He pinpointed the shot's source. Returning sonic echoes depicted a cave opening west of the one he'd exited. And a solitary figure, rendered in crisp detail, taking careful aim with a high-energy particle rifle. Agar's mind touched his assailant's. A dissident. A sentry who'd been posted along a different entrance to the cave complex.

He hadn't eliminated everyone after all.

Agar continued the dive, increasing the range. Contemplated whether to continue on his way or engage the shooter. He'd completed the mission. He'd retrieved the information he needed. One survivor of no consequence.

The decision forced upon him when the dissident launched from the peak and dove toward Agar. The attacker held the advantage, his dive allowing him to intercept and fire on Agar from above and behind.

Agar spread his wings and soared upward as another blast split the air beside him. But the attacker unable to fire again as he too spread his wings, arresting his dive, and maneuvered for a firing position. Firing in flight required different dynamics and tactics given the weapon's orientation, pointed to the side along the outstretched arm, the butt jammed firm under the armpit. The attacker needed a flight path allowing the weapon to bear on target. Not the other way around. Movement of his arm also moved his wing, altering his flight configuration.

Agar rolled out of his soaring loop on an interception flight path, feet forward, intending to strike with extended talons.

Perceiving the changed dynamic the dissident drew his legs tight against his body, reared his head and upper torso, braking in mid flight. His weapon off target and useless.

He extended a leg as Agar swept toward him, talons poised to rip Agar from neck to groin. Agar flexed his fingers a moment before contact, adjusting his wing spread, colliding into the dissident and blocking his opponent's thrusting feet. They fell together, entangled from the mid air collision. Agar spread his fingers, opening his wings to their full span, and looped over backward to fall into a dive. As he did, one taloned foot ripped the rifle from his opponent's grasp, sending it twirling through the air into the mist-shrouded gorge below.

The dissident recovered from their collision and dove after Agar. But Agar had already changed direction, dipping his left arm, maneuvering into position for the pass he'd anticipated.

The returning echoes near instantaneous. The tiny moments ticked down in Agar's mind. Agar timed his turn. He raised his right arm. The upswept wing abruptly changed his direction and spun him in midair. The spin kick found its target. The blow landed on his opponent's back, just below his neck. A tear appeared in the thin membrane stretched across his shoulders. Anguished thoughts and terrified clicks reached Agar as the dissident fell away. But not done yet.

Agar's mind remained connected to his opponent as the dissident fought to configure his wings, ignoring the pain in his back. He arrested his fall and caught a rising current, finding sufficient lift to maneuver toward the cliff face. The dissident landed heavily, but intact, his talons in a tight grip holding him to the vertical rock face.

The dissident's returning echoes pinpointed Agar's position, swooping in from above. As Agar closed the dissident leapt up the cliff face, talons gripping, powerful legs pushing, wings folded against his body, leaving his arms free to reach and pull. His clawed thumbs grasped at every crevice, every crag. He scaled the rock at a rapid pace.

Agar perceived the danger, halting his gliding flight before it placed him too far below the climbing dissident. He grudgingly admired the move.

As Agar braked, the dissident leapt from above, spread his wings, talons extended and poised to strike. He dove straight at Agar, rushing at him with ferocious velocity, and ferocious intent. Agar heard his thoughts, focused on a single outcome. A willingness to sacrifice himself to ensure his opponent died too.

The instant before contact Agar flexed his fingers, rolling onto his back. A face-to-face encounter. His attacker struck first. Deadly talons missed Agar's mid section by mere inches as Agar spread his fingers and arched out of reach. His legs reached out as he swept over and upward, his opponent passing beneath him. Solid contact. Agar's talons ripped into the dissident's shoulders, tearing away flesh, muscle, and sinew.

Agar rolled facedown. Observed his opponent's final fall. Anguished thoughts of defeat and failure and a lifetime of memories filled Agar's mind. The vocal death shrieks swept away on the wind. One wing flung upward and back as the dissident fell. The other hung limp, useless, no longer supported by the shattered shoulder.

Agar observed the impact on a lower ledge of the cliff. The dissident's body shattered and lifeless as it bounced, and continued its final plunge beneath the cloudy miasma into the gorge.

Agar flew on. A curious anomaly to any observer. A solitary individual beating wing for the far side of twilight. Toward the sun scorched peaks of the world's sunlit hemisphere. Far from the city's teeming swarms.

Agar's senses on high alert. He sifted returning echoes for any other presence in his vicinity. His vision scoured the mountain range ahead. Decidedly alone.

He sensed the change in air density as he flew farther into daylight. The atmospheric pressure lower. The air thinner. Heat building across his body. The sunlit side of the world characterized by vast stretches of open space between mountain ranges. Some areas desert like. Others covered by vast lakes and oceans of water circulating heat around the planet and governing its weather patterns. The water fresh in certain areas. Brackish in others. Deadly acidic in others. Immense processing plants stood on their shores, supplying fresh water, minerals, food, energy, to far-flung cities across the continent.

Abundant water also flowed beneath the surface. Accessed by the larger cities through wells drilled deep into the ground. And frozen water on the dark side. Mined and processed and piped into cities on the borders of darkside.

The daylight side also dotted by large quiri farms, the environment more suitable to their rearing than the twilight or dark zones.

Echoes reached Agar's ears, informing him of his approaching destination, a range of sharp, steep peaks, sloping more gently toward the desolate desert floor. Sustained flight more strenuous as he crossed a wide valley. Soon he caught the heated updrafts flowing up the peak's side as he neared his destination.

Agar entered the dark cave. The air hot, musty, and dank. Heavier and cooler the deeper he penetrated. He reached the large open cavern deep within the mountain. One of many solitary roosts he used around the world. A safe, isolated haven.

His talons closed around deep, familiar grooves in the overhead wall. He removed his combat coat, the one-piece tunic, and leggings, hanging them in place among other garments surrounding his roost. Naked, he relaxed, hanging head down, arms folded and fingers closed. Wrapped in the cocoon of his wings, fatigued by the deadly encounter, and long flight, he succumbed to a deep restful sleep.

Ecibor

Seraphina set her ship down in a vast open field of the port. Unaccustomed to the amount of available parking space, but not surprised. At one time the port had been a bustling center of commerce. Arriving ships had to wait in orbit for a berthing spot to open up on the surface.

Over a span of decades commerce had dwindled. Not for lack of trade goods, but fewer traders. Various accounts attributed it to portals gone dead in other regions of space. Others to clicker raids in nearby sectors, dwindling populations, or fear of travelling into space unless heavily armed and in protective convoys against the clickers and other raiders.

The population on Ecibor dwindling also. Seraphina had noticed more abandoned areas of the city on her approach. Probably insufficient commerce to support the population, which in better times had swelled around the port.

The man, Ezekiel she had learned, paid close attention as she shut down and secured the ship. He wore the clothing she'd provided him following his shower, more like many showers. A mismatched assortment of male clothing she'd pulled from among her trade goods. Tan trousers, black laced boots, and an oversized tan shirt fitting him more like an outer coat.

The memory of the bath evoked a smile. Her smiles less rare than they used to be. He'd stepped into the shower, raised his arms, and waited. She hadn't understood initially. Until it occurred to her he expected her to bathe him. Any other man she'd have planted a steel-toed boot between his legs. But the innocent expectant smile on his face, his harmless strangeness, had overcome her instinctive impulse. Besides, she'd been unable to abide his odor a moment longer.

The experience had been perplexing. Had stirred emotions she didn't recognize. She'd used the ultraviolet bath constructed from salvaged components on him first. He'd seemed to understand its function, turning in the enclosure as the rays swept over him. She'd used the mister next, producing a confused consternation as the hot vapor enveloped him. Finally, her favorite, a method not much in use anymore, but one she preferred, and the most amusing part of the entire process. When the jets of water had hit the man's naked body he'd yelped, skipped, and fought like a distraught dog, attempting to flee the strange phenomenon. She'd held him squirming against her in the shower, water cascading over them both, soaking her pants and boots. He'd eventually relaxed, allowing her to lather and rinse him.

She'd washed his long gold-brown hair, on the verge of matting, separating it with her fingers, when the absurdity of the situation smacked her in the face like a screen door. She'd been bathing a naked man, half naked herself, who she'd salvaged from wreckage in space, whose name she didn't know. Which produced a further absurdity. She'd pointed at herself under the running water, slowly, painstakingly pronouncing her name. Pointing at him in turn. Repeated several times before a gleam of understanding sparked in his strangely compelling grey eyes. He'd blurted out a word. Ezekiel.

Ezekiel barely able to contain his astonishment, his enthusiasm, his raw delight at the port. Experiencing a quiri world for the first time on his own, without command or direction from the masters. A prelude to the hunt. The notion of afterlife long abandoned. At least the one following death. He'd survived the battle. Had been found by the fenori who called herself Seraphina, who had transported him to a different afterlife. Amazed by his increasing acceptance of the thoughts in his mind as being his own. Of his surfacing individuality. Of a freedom he had never before experienced.

Stepping into the bright sunlight outside the ship reminded him of Nivalinorhnus, the other inhabited world of the masters' domain. Former masters he reminded himself. The light hurt his eyes, long accustomed to the darkness the masters preferred. Ezekiel squinted in the harsh glare, his fascination undiminished by his discomfort, instead heightened by the new experiences.

He drew his hand along the hull of Seraphina's ship. She called it Dauphin. The hull color a bluish black, like her hair. His pilot's eye appreciative of its sleek lines and functional design. An appreciation he'd never been allowed to experience before. At rest, the ship's broad blade-like wings folded back against its sides, resembling the grass hopping insect native to Nivalinorhnus.

He followed Seraphina as she strode across an open field toward a warren of low buildings. The sights and sounds around him produced further amazement. Boisterous laughter, and music, unlike any he'd ever heard. Quiri everywhere. But not quiri. Not like him, domesticated and controlled. They existed in the wild. Their behavior uncontrolled and independent. Now he'd live among them in the wild. Among his own kind.

Seraphina maintained a wary eye on Ezekiel lest he stray. But he remained at her side, like a loyal puppy. His head swiveled side to side, observing everything around him in wide-eyed wonder. She questioned her worry. And why she should care. Still undecided regarding him. She'd considered simply leaving him behind after conducting her business. His welfare not her concern. She'd already done enough by saving him. But the idea didn't sit well. Unable to understand why.

Her first task to secure a port agent. A person to hold her trade goods, and transport and hold the items she acquired. Representing the Guild, the port agents also recorded all transactions and ensured the Guild received their percentage. The person she sought was an agent she'd used on other trips to Ecibor. A person she trusted. Observing the empty stalls and shops as she navigated the maze of lanes within the bazaar, she hoped he'd still be in business.

Seraphina approached his building in a far corner of the compound, close to the main thoroughfare heading into the city. Relieved to see the agent remained in business. The entrance open, she strode in, accompanied by Ezekiel. A short hallway opened into a cavernous interior. The walls and two center aisles lined by shelves bearing a multitudinous assortment of parts, appliances, machinery, items of every shape color and sort. Confounding to the naked eye, but Gebediah possessed an uncanny ability to precisely locate any item you cared to request.

Seraphina found the agent in a cramped little office close to the entrance.

"Princess," he greeted her in surprise, lifting his gaze from a thick bound ledger on his untidy, laden desk. He rose to greet her, a broad smile parting pouty lips in a chubby face, his wide girth knocking items off his deck in his enthusiasm. When he enclosed Seraphina in his arms, she all but disappeared.

"Good fortune smiling at me it's great to see you," he gushed, holding her by the shoulders in front of him as his eyes inspected her up and down. "And as gorgeous as ever." His smile grew radiant, exposing stained teeth from his habit of chewing turko, a mildly narcotic indigenous plant.

"Good to see you too Geb. Was afraid you mightn't still be around."

A sigh rippled the fleshy folds of his cheeks. "Know what you mean. But I'm still hanging in."

"That bad? Looks emptier than the last time I popped in."

"And getting worse," he said, accompanied by another dejected sigh.

"What's going on?"

"Who knows for sure? You've probably heard the talk. Crashed portals. Clickers." He shrugged heavy shoulders before reclaiming his seat. The tortured chair emitted a loud shriek under his weight.

"You here to do some business?"

"Same as usual," Seraphina said. "And as usual for you." She lifted the flap of a leather bag slung across her shoulder, extracting a package wrapped in soft brown cloth. She handed it to the port agent.

"Oh princess. Is that what I think..." the unfinished question hung in the air while the port agent gazed open mouthed at the package, holding it in his hands as lovingly as if cradling a newborn infant.

Seraphina nodded. Her bluish crop of hair bobbed across her forehead.

"You have no idea how long it's been," he said, his gaze shifting between Seraphina and the package. "I don't even want to see it yet," he sighed, opening a lower drawer of the desk, placing the package in it. "I have to wait for the right moment to savor it."

His gaze shifted to Ezekiel, as though noticing him for the first time.

"Never knew you for coupling," he said to Seraphina, a suspicious stare fixed on Ezekiel.

"He's just someone I picked up, offered a ride. Name is Ezekiel."

Ezekiel responded to the sound of his name. The only word he'd understood since entering the tiny chamber. The big man stared at him. He rose and extended a beefy palm toward Ezekiel.

Ezekiel uncertain regarding the gesture, its nature, or significance, though the man seemed to expect something from him.

He heard Seraphina speaking. "Don't mind him. He's not from any of the nearby sectors. Not used to the customs."

The man withdrew his hand. Spoke to Seraphina. "If you say. Still. Doesn't say much does he?"

The port agent reached across his cluttered desk, extracted a sheet of flimsy from a pile and handed it to Seraphina. She reached into her bag and handed him a small square data chip.

"What I have for now," she said, also handing back the sheet after pressing her thumb to one corner.

"Gonna be slim pickins out there though," the port agent said. "And best be careful. Especially if you go into the city. Not as many enforcers on the payroll as used to be."

"I know my stuff's safe with you. But what about the scrubs."

"Not to worry. The rules still apply. And the enforcers pay attention to those. The Guild isn't about to lose their profit, even if it's smaller than it used to be."

"Thanks Geb. I'll see you later when I'm done."

"Looking forward to it princess, maybe we'll break open that package," the wide, tooth-stained grin resurfacing on his face.

Ezekiel followed Seraphina as she wandered the labyrinthine paths of the bazaar. Not in the least concerned by his inability to understand the language, but intrigued by the constant babble. And enthralled by the variety of goods displayed on the stalls, and inside the shops. Flabbergasted such a place existed, pausing to touch, and examine, and smell, anything capturing his interest.

Seraphina amused by Ezekiel's childlike wonder and enthusiasm. Infectious too, as she joined him in examining the various wares, her own enthusiasm growing, enjoying the experience for the first time in her many years of trading. Unconsciously they resumed the familiar pattern established in the cargo hold.

"Crocks," she said, indicating an intricately decorated food bowl Ezekiel held in his hands.

She reached onto an adjacent shelf, lifted a small round transparent jar containing a red powdery substance. She held it under Ezekiel's nose.

Ezekiel's head jerked backward in response to the sudden strong scent. Only for a moment. He leaned forward, his nostrils over the jar. The scent pungent, but pleasant, producing a smile.

"Spice," Seraphina said.

Ezekiel reached for other jars on the shelf. A different colored powder in each. Sampled each beneath his nostrils. Offered them to Seraphina to smell, his smile widening at each new scent.

They ambled on, continuing their peculiar communication.

"Gao," Seraphina said, pausing at a fruit stand. She plucked a yellowish red fruit from an overflowing basket, bit into the fruit, offered it to Ezekiel.

Ezekiel studied her gestures. She bit into the unfamiliar object a second time, offered it to him again. Her chewing recalled the memory of his hunger and apprehension on the ship after he'd decided he hadn't perished. His thoughts had turned to the essentials, food, and water. How he'd be able to meet his basic needs without the masters to provide them. Aware quiri in the wild managed such necessities on their own, but he'd never had to experience it himself. And his surprise at the food the fenori had offered. An unexpected explosion of tastes, pleasant once he'd overcome the initial shock. Like spice.

He accepted the fruit. Observed Seraphina's delicately defined jaw and smooth cheeks manipulating the morsels inside her mouth. The pleasure around her dark full lips, and in her wide oval eyes.

Ezekiel bit into the fruit, surprised again by the rich pleasurable sensation, savoring its taste. The fruit's succulent juice coated the inside of his mouth and ran onto his chin and jaw, now devoid of hair. Seraphina had removed his facial hair during the washing. "Shave" she'd called it.

Seraphina giggled at Ezekiel's obvious pleasure, pushing aside the nagging thoughts of what to do regarding him.

Seraphina paused at a clothing shop. She stepped inside, followed by Ezekiel. His eyes roamed aimlessly over the shelves and racks. Fascinated by the variety of colors and materials. Seraphina more focused, inspecting specific items. One portion of her brain rationalized her decision to purchase clothing a normal part of business. Clothing a desirable commodity, and she always carried a selection for trade. Another section of her brain more attuned to the truth as she glanced frequently at Ezekiel, estimating size, considering color, material, and noting the items catching his interest.

Her fashion sense personal. No idea of his likes and dislikes. Whether such considerations even mattered to him. Fashion in any case irrelevant. An indulgence of a small caste able to afford importation of trendy designs and patterns and colors, like members of the Guild. Everyone else wore an ad-hoc assortment suited to their occupation or climate.

Her purchases, and arrangements for payment and delivery to her agent completed, Seraphina and Ezekiel moved on. Her next task provisioning. They browsed store to store, performing their usual ritual.

"Sweet bread," Seraphina said, breaking a piece from a loaf, biting off a mouthful, handing it to Ezekiel, delighting in his pleasant reaction.

Until they approached the livestock pens. Ezekiel's intense reaction an unexpected shock. His voice raised in anguished shouts, his arms flung in wild gestures. His words meaningless to Seraphina. But Ezekiel's sudden outburst and increasing agitation had attracted attention. And the combination of rage, fear, and sorrow in his eyes, concerned and disturbed her. She hurried him away from the area.

Ezekiel had never seen such animals before. Possessed no knowledge of them or their nature. But he instantly understood their captivity. And the sight of them in the pens had provoked a visceral reaction. A recognized affinity. Captivity, service, and slaughter. His instinctive aversion no longer overridden by an imposed control.

Ezekiel's outburst, and her reaction to it, perplexed Seraphina. Uncertain as to the cause of his upset. Or why it had moved her to want to comfort him. The expression she'd witnessed in his eyes haunted her. She could forgo livestock. In truth, she seldom transported any for lack of facilities aboard to properly feed and care for them, though they were excellent for trade. On rare occasions she'd had a few chickens, or small animals the size of rabbits. But for trade. She had no need for them as food.

She continued shopping for the ship's stores, a wary eye on Ezekiel. His upset, apparently limited to the livestock pens, appeared to have passed. But the earlier childlike wonder and enthusiasm in his eyes no longer present.

Ecibor's solitary G-type sun hung low in the sky, prompting Seraphina to head to the next priority on her list before loss of daylight. The area, on the west side of the market, a collection of spaceship scrap yards and used ships for sale. Seraphina chose her vendors deliberately, trustworthy traders with whom she'd conducted business before. She moved from yard to yard, swiftly completing her transactions. She'd determined beforehand the items she required for Dauphin's upgrades. No need to browse.

At the final vendor on her list Ezekiel erupted into unintelligible speech beside her.

Now what? Seraphina thought. But Ezekiel's manner different, more like the excitable enthusiasm of before.

"Command link." The words repeated again and again, pointing to an object in a pile of discarded parts, his excitement and insistence increasing.

The scrap dealer eyed Ezekiel, a speculative gleam in small, shifty eyes. A cunning smile stretched thin misshaped lips. An abrupt change in his predatory expression when he noticed Seraphina's cold, stern glare.

"That thing? Not sure it's anything you want. Been here for years. Can't get rid of it. No one can even figure out what it is."

"Let's see it," Seraphina said, her intense stare glued on him.

When the dealer returned carrying the object, Ezekiel snatched it from him.

"Command link. Need it for the ship," Ezekiel said, thrusting the object at Seraphina. The words meaningless to Seraphina, but Ezekiel's excitement obvious, his intent clear.

Not understanding why Ezekiel wanted the object, or why she cared, especially if she'd be moving on without him, Seraphina nevertheless told the dealer, "I'll take it."

The dealer's smile returned, a calculating expression in his eyes. Finally able to unload the piece of junk he'd had sitting around for years. Ready to discard it among the other junk. But aware of Seraphina's harsh stare, her reputation, and she a particular favorite of fat Gebediah, who had the power to put him out of business. Not worth the risk.

"See here, you can have it if you want. But it won't do you any good, whatever it is, without this," he said, retrieving a power converter from the stack of shelves behind him.

"Nice try," Seraphina said, the hard stare unrelenting, pinning him.

"No. No. No scam. For whatever reason it only powers up with this converter, on this frequency. But even powered up no one's been able to figure what it does. Tell you what, You pay for the converter, I'll throw in that thing, whatever it is, for no payment. That do?"

The dealer accessed Seraphina's port account on his ledger. He perused the items Seraphina had available and they settled on a trade. Seraphina paid no more than she would have for the power converter. The other item the man had been prepared to toss in the scrap yard. The transaction completed, Seraphina and Ezekiel were headed away from the yard when an object in an adjacent yard captured her attention.

Seraphina's sudden change of direction caught Ezekiel unawares. He trotted back to her side as Seraphina's purposeful stride led them around stockpiles of used ship parts. She halted in a corner of the yard, close to the fence adjacent to the path from the previous dealer's yard. Ezekiel followed Seraphina's gaze as she studied a large transparent bubble sitting on a dirty tarp.

Seraphina had spied the object through the fence. Her keen eye for spatial relationships, an innate talent, assured her it might fit. As she contemplated acquiring the viewport, it occurred to her she'd reached a decision. The decision nagging her since arriving on Ecibor. And once again her instincts had led her, while conscious thought lagged behind.

She'd learned to accept and trust her instinct. Even if the unconscious rationale eluded and confused her. As it did now, contradicting the detached, unemotional lifestyle she'd grown accustomed to and cherished. Self-sufficient and self-contained in her person and her ship. No one to care for, or answer to. But she also trusted the reliability of her instinct's inner unconscious dynamics. Aware a decision delayed by questioning and procrastination meant instinctual misgivings. While her natural inclination invariably proved correct. She'd saved a strange man from the cold dark clutch of space. And while rational thought told her to abandon him and move on, her instinct informed her otherwise.

Seraphina spent the following day receiving her acquisitions and preparing Dauphin for departure. She'd provisioned the ship for a six months stay in space. Ezekiel a constant presence at her side, following her lead as she arranged and stowed the cargo.

Late in the afternoon she returned to Gebediah's office to settle her account. The port agent greeted her in his effusive manner.

"Princess. Wish you were staying longer. Such sunshine you bring to my dreary existence."

"You know me Geb. Always on the move."

"More's the pity. I trust everything arrived in order?"

"As right as star shine. No problems."

"Glad to hear it. Then just give this a look see, ensure everything is to your satisfaction," he said, handing her a flimsy.

Seraphina perused the sheet, nodding as she checked the itemized transactions. The items traded and those Gebediah had converted to credits. The credits paid primarily to the clothing and food vendors. The Guild's commission higher than she'd expected, but satisfactory. She affixed her thumbprint to the bottom of the flimsy and returned it to the agent.

"Now that's done, and seeing I may not get the pleasure of your company for a while, why not celebrate with a tot of the special item you brought me."

Not waiting for an answer he reached into the desk drawer and withdrew a large square- sided bottle containing a dark amber liquid. He produced two small drinking glasses and poured three fingers worth of the liquid in each. He glanced tentatively at Ezekiel, shook his head, produced a third glass, and poured an equal amount into it. Holding a glass in each pudgy hand he offered the drink to Seraphina and Ezekiel.

Ezekiel followed Seraphina's lead, accepting the glass as she did.

"Avidio," the port agent said, emptying his glass and swallowing the liquid in a single gulp.

Ezekiel observed Seraphina performing the same action. He raised his glass, drank, and swallowed. His throat burst into flame. His free hand flew to his neck. His spasmed coughing involuntary, his brain spinning. The burning sensation dissipated, followed by a spreading warmth within his chest, and a sweet fruity aftertaste in his mouth.

Seraphina and the man both laughed in unrestrained mirth. The sound a new experience for Ezekiel. He hadn't known laughter before setting foot on Ecibor.

The man poured himself and Seraphina another small helping of the liquid. They tossed it back in one swallow as before. Ezekiel gulped down the remainder of his glass, now aware and prepared for its strange affect. The burning sensation, the warm flush, the sweet aftertaste. He examined his empty glass, raised it to his nose and sniffed. A satisfied grin spread across his face.

Twilight enclosed the port as Seraphina and Ezekiel strolled toward the ship. The sun a large reddish pink globe low in Ecibor's sky. The bazaar's shops already closed for the night. An unseen, unknown danger pricked at Seraphina's senses, alerting her. A sensation of being followed. Confirmed after three sudden random turns onto side streets on the edge of the bazaar. Two men, not closing, but keeping her and Ezekiel in sight.

Seraphina acutely aware she carried no weapons, a sensation akin to being naked. The port enforcers didn't permit off-worlders to carry weapons into the bazaar. The men following undoubtedly armed, Seraphina surmised, off-worlders or not. Most likely local thugs preying on easy, unwary targets. No matter. Seraphina a seasoned street fighter. Everything around her a potential weapon.

As she turned the next corner, heading again in the direction of the ship, Seraphina had to rethink the scenario. Two other men approached from ahead. Their focused attention on her and Ezekiel undisguised. She the prey. And they'd boxed her in. Not a robbery. More likely a shag gang. A female kidnapped off the street, raped, before being sold to a shaghouse, or aboard ship as a forced companion.

Seraphina had been both in her short lifetime. First as a pubescent in a shaghouse on a backwater mining world. Kidnapped off the streets of her homeworld as a girl. Maybe sold by her destitute mother. She'd grown up a slave to sexual brutality and degradation. And later, a forced companion to a space trader who'd bought her from the house. Another form of sexual enslavement. But from whom she learned the trade business, and how to pilot a ship, before she'd killed him. She'd since learned how to fight, how to defend herself, how to turn the predators into prey.

She continued walking, searching the alley for objects to use as weapons as the men approached from ahead and behind. Her instinct for self-preservation a raging fever inside her. Not only would she not allow herself to be captured, ever again, but she didn't mind gutting these four like the pigs they were. Suddenly conscious of Ezekiel beside her. Shit! He'd be of no use to her. Maybe even a hindrance, getting in her way. She questioned her decision not to jettison him before this.

The men closed the distance. Halted. Seraphina turned to present her profile to them, studying them for the first time. The two behind her dressed in scruffy clothing. Young. Thin. Almost emaciated. Their gaze roamed over her, undressing her, lechery in their bulging eyes. Visualizing and vocalizing the debauched fun they planned to have. No problem, she concluded.

She leveled the same assessing stare on the two in front. One of the men heavier, sturdier, but the same expression in his eyes, joining his companions' gloating anticipatory laughter.

The fourth man a different story. Broad shouldered, muscular, appraising her through one undamaged eye, the other eye half closed by a jagged scar running from his forehead above the eye, along his cheek to his jaw. Cautious. Watchful. No laughter. Not a lecher. A merchant. The clear leader of this shag pack.

Him first, Seraphina decided. The most dangerous. And if she put down their leader the other three might simply fly. In any case Seraphina had no doubt of her ability to handle those three. Her sole concern Ezekiel.

The words spoken by the three men were meaningless to Ezekiel. Their laughter a relatively new experience. Though he observed no context for it. Uncertain regarding the type of transaction this might be. Though unlike any Seraphina had conducted in the past two days. But even in his uncertainty, Ezekiel understood the posture of the men surrounding them. Had already determined the master. Recognized the menace in his eyes. His silent control over the other three. And the palpable tension hovering over the scene. As a quiri checker, he'd experienced such circumstances before. As a scout, he recognized the tactical arrangement of the men surrounding them.

Slowly, imperceptibly, he increased the distance between himself and Seraphina. But his movement had not escaped the master's notice.

Seraphina noted it too. Misinterpreting it as Ezekiel's attempt to remain clear of her business transaction. Relieved he'd not encumber her, and maybe even escape unharmed. She'd also noticed the leader's silent signal.

The men moved in. The leader stood his ground, maintaining his distance. Seraphina flung herself at him. Her flying body tackle landed in his midsection, driving him to the ground, cushioning her fall. She rolled off him onto her feet, in time to see Ezekiel fall forward on both hands as though performing pushups. Supported by his arms he reared and drove both legs up and back into the chests of the men rushing him. The snap of bone echoed in the narrow alley. Both men crumpled to the ground, unmoving.

No time to indulge her amazement. The gang leader almost on his feet. Seraphina aimed a kick to the side of his head. He blocked it in both hands, grabbing her boot. Seraphina spun away before he could apply the twist to her ankle. But he'd gained his feet, facing her. The half- closed hideous eye magnified the malevolent malice in his undamaged eye.

In her peripheral vision the other man unsure who to attack. Deciding his boss could handle a woman, he stepped toward Ezekiel as Seraphina blocked a stiff armed punch and countered with an elbow to the left side of the leader's face. Not sure of his vision from the half- closed eye, but she'd decided to focus on that side. She ducked under a roundhouse swing and moved into the center of the alley, allowing herself room to maneuver. A quick glance at Ezekiel.

The man came at Ezekiel prepared for a fistfight. Arms raised, hands balled into tight fists. Unaware his opponent had been trained by his deadliest enemy, whose anatomy favored the use of legs and taloned feet. As the man closed into range, Ezekiel folded his arms across his chest. His right leg lashed out. The hard-toed boot struck the man in the chest, under the breastbone. Again the crack of bone echoed in the alley, accompanied by a loud anguished shriek.

Seraphina and the gang leader both turned at the sound. A rage filled howl from the leader. He swung at Seraphina. She blocked the blow, again counterattacking to his left side. His confidence waning, his rage overflowing, the leader reached under his coat. Seraphina heard the familiar sound of metal sliding on leather. Stepped back as the first swing of the long double- edged blade sliced the air in front of her. Anticipating a high backswing she ducked as the blade scythed above her head.

She needed to get inside his swing. But the blade kept her at a distance. Alternatively she needed a weapon. Something to parry the blade and get her inside. She searched the alley while dodging her attacker's swings. Nothing close at hand. And he'd been backing her toward the wall. With scant feet to maneuver remaining, she shed her leather coat and wrapped it around her arm. She'd have to take a blade strike on her arm in order to get in close. And once inside she'd have to finish him fast, before the blade found a vital target.

The man smiled as Seraphina finished wrapping the leather coat around her arm, his confidence rising, sensing the kill. He changed tactics, thrusting to stab instead of swinging to cut. The maneuver forced Seraphina against the wall.

Seraphina noted the murderous intent in his eyes. The crooked smile on his lopsided face. His intention no longer to capture and sell, but to kill. Gut her like an animal. Satisfy his bloodthirsty rage. She studied his eyes. Waited for them to telegraph his move. Conscious of the restricting wall against her back. Noted the subtle downward flicker. Braced herself for the parry, the certainty of a wound. But she only needed a tiny opening.

In the moment when time slowed to a crawl, Seraphina followed the approach of the blade's point, timing her parry and counterattack. The man's mouth fell open in slow motion. His eyes bulged, even the damaged half-closed eye, opening to twice its former size. An agonized howl escaped his lips, reaching her ears long after he'd uttered it. A bluish glow lit the dark alley.

Time returned to normal. The leader collapsed to the ground before her. Standing behind him, Ezekiel, the elongated lance held by his side.

Dissidents

Agar awoke rested and rejuvenated. Eager to commence work. He remained roosted, donning a headcap hanging next to the roost. His other possessions hanging around him related to his occupation, weapons, communications, clothing. Nothing of his origins or familial colony.

Like all Borinians, Agar had departed his maternal colony at weaning age. But unlike most, he had not maintained a familial attachment to his mother or siblings. His abilities had been recognized early, and he'd been reared, educated, and trained in the military colony, where he'd spent his entire life.

He synchronized the headcap and recorder frequencies, including his own recorder, and absorbed the recorded images into his mind. He wanted a generalized overview prior to delving into the details. At the last site he'd conducted a mental interrogative survey before he'd destroyed it, leeching the unconscious thoughts of the individuals before they died.

Their thoughts, and the initial pass of the data on the recordings, ominous and disturbing.

The implications spinning in his mind, Agar curbed his impatience to dive into the details. A ravenous hunger distracted him. A long period since he'd last eaten. Placing the headcap and recorders in a briefcase, he released his taloned grip, fell headlong, and flew into a connecting tunnel.

His first stop, a chamber at the far end of the tunnel. The floor of the chamber at the bottom of a deep dark abyss running through the mountain. Agar clamped his talons in roosting position, bent at the waist and grasped his ankles. His still naked posterior pointing into the abyss, Agar relieved himself, a long stream of urine, followed by the meager contents of his bowels.

Agar returned to the roost, retrieving a bag from among the hanging items. He slung the long leather strap around his neck. The bag strapped to his chest, he flew out again.

He stood at the entrance to the cave, unconcerned by his lack of attire. No other living soul within hundreds of echospans. His vision roamed across the long line of peaks and vast stretch of desert below, as he plucked morsels from the bag and fed them into his mouth. Dried and preserved fruit, and preserved preparations of small ground animals inhabiting the gorges beneath the ever present blanket of mist.

No quiri. Not a matter of conscience, but of palate. Agar had simply never acquired a taste for quiri flesh. Perhaps a subconscious recognition of their sentience, but Agar had never given his reasons much thought.

He gazed up at the darkened pink sky. The primary sun now dimmed by the 'Ketu' interval. He turned to gaze at Orh, eclipsed by its smaller companion. The only time staring directly at the sun was possible. In communities around the world loud raucous celebrations were underway. Unseen and unheard at this distance. But Agar pictured it in his mind. Vast swarms soaring across the sky like dark clouds covering the cities. The festival of Orh, the mother, giver of life, guiding the smaller sun back from the underworld where she'd transported the dead during 'Rahu'. A symbolic rebirth of those who'd died. Orh the mediator. The guide between the realms of living and dead. The raucous noise of the celebrations to help guide the reborn back to the living.

Such fundamental beliefs, the founding mythology of the collective's religious concepts of creation, of life and death and rebirth, soon to be shattered.

Agar returned to the roost. Somber thoughts drove his motivation to resume work, parsing the data the second time around, lingering on the details, rewinding when necessary, digging deeper.

A record of numerous sites around the planet. The two he'd infiltrated merely the tip of a hidden mountain. More than he'd imagined. And more than the general's intelligence reports were aware of. The research from the sites spanned the ages, from their earliest discovery. Research successive governing councils had restricted, and banned, deemed classified. And yet, the dissidents had access to it.

And more sites on Nivalinorhnus. The research on the sister world even more widespread and sophisticated. Catalogues of thousands of skeletal fossils, Borinian and quiri, containing detailed descriptions, and analysis of form, structure and chemistry. Catalogues of artifacts dating back many millennia, into the prehistoric past.

The excavated remnants of ancient quiri settlements suggested a once sizable population scattered among many communities, on both Borinorhnus and Nivalinorhnus. The images on the recordings reminded Agar of peculiar markings and artifacts he'd observed on other worlds during his various missions. His penchant for remote, isolated lairs, had led him to explore areas containing such artifacts. Including the lair he currently occupied, which exhibited evidence of prior occupation. Not recent. Ancient.

Agar digested the reports, analyses, discoveries, and conclusions contained in the recordings. Many referenced other research and reports not contained in the recordings. But the accumulated data painted a picture of the evolutionary history and development of both species. Borinian and quiri. Side by side. From the first appearance of both species hundreds of millennia in the past. The skeletal and artifact evidence indicated large scale battles fought at sites now occupied by Borinorhran cities.

Agar reached a level in the recordings where the discoveries, the science, and the conclusions, no longer concerned him. Rather he perceived a widespread pattern of collaboration, stretching across scientific and historical communities. The numbers of individuals and disciplines involved in gathering, collating, analyzing, and distributing the research extensive. In itself, sufficient to strike fear in the Council of Governors. But the idea which truly concerned him, was the central, prominent, and as yet unperceived role, Nivalinorhnus held in an apparent separatist movement.

And one other item. Numerous references to reports emanating from a lone archeologist. A revered figure. Referred to as the father of the movement. An archeologist who'd lived off world for many decades, exploring and conducting research on other worlds. The reports on the recorders indicated he held the key to deciphering the origins of the Borinian species. General Zanth's intelligence reports contained no mention of him.

Agar deactivated the recorder. He removed his headcap. His mind a whirlwind of images as he dissected, analyzed, collated, and connected the staggering implications of the reports.

He needed to see General Zanth.

Fission

General Zanth's sour mood persisted as he waited for Agar. Exacerbated by the length of his journey, and the insistence of his subordinate on meeting face to face. He hadn't heard from Agar since their meeting on darkside, and now Agar wanted to meet on the far side of the world, resisting Zanth's entreaties, almost commands, to transmit his information. Zanth had been forced to squeeze time into his pressured schedule. Agar probably the only individual under his command possessing the temerity to insist, and to whom Zanth might permit such insubordination.

Zanth waited in a private cavern of the funerary. Quiet. Isolated from the swarms gathered for the ritual preparation of the departed, and the attendant burial rites of final passage. Zanth detected movement at the base of the cavern. A lone individual, whose mind touched his in greeting.

"An honor to see you again General Zanthinvolar." Agar ascended to the ceiling, grasped the roost and hung head down alongside General Zanth.

The individual roosted next to Zanth different in appearance and every other measure from the person he'd met in the mining colony. The scent different, as always. The facial hair removed, revealing smooth, almost youthful features. The hair swept back from his broad flat forehead, neatly groomed, as was the collar of rust-colored fur around his neck, a dark brown the last time Zanth had seen it. The individual alongside him also the epitome of a military officer. Taller than the average Borinian, lean and muscled. His bearing erect and commanding. His demeanor direct and disciplined.

"As always," Zanth thought, recovering, although Agar's constantly changing appearance should, by now, be unsurprising. Agar changed his appearance as routinely as he changed garments. "But I am in a foul mood over the necessity for this meeting in the midst of the current pressures attendant on me." General Zanth's mood apparent to Ager, reflected in Zanth's thoughts and vocalizations, a long series of staccato clicks and short snappish screeches.

"Why did you insist on meeting instead of transmitting your information. Our communications are secure."

"I am not as certain general."

"And why this place. Surely there are other secure locations closer to the capital. Why did I need to travel half-way around the world."

"There is a particular librarian in this colony I needed to consult. An ancient and wise individual. In fact general, it might be worth your time to meet him too."

"My time is not my own Agar. And I am under tremendous pressure. The council is increasingly agitated and pressing me for answers I do not have."

"Perhaps as you suggested, the council is aware of more than they allow you to see. If they are aware of even the smallest fraction of the information I have uncovered, they have reason to be concerned."

"Proceed. What have you to report?"

Agar removed a briefcase attached to his chest coat. He handed it to General Zanth.

"There are two data recorders, each one recovered from a different site I visited and subsequently destroyed. And a data chip of my own analysis and conclusions. You may analyze the data yourself, but I have learned this."

Agar's thoughts flowed into General Zanth's mind. The images and perceptions organized into a coherent briefing. Mental images relayed the information, but Agar's insights provided the context.

"At its most basic, this began as an academic attempt to reconstruct the evolutionary history of our species. The quiri an afterthought. A mere curiosity. It has since expanded into much more. The reports indicate our scientists have achieved groundbreaking discoveries of which the public is unaware, and well beyond the boundaries established by the council."

"How can it be? The Governor Supreme has established strict oversight."

"Science knows no boundaries general. Only knowledge and the people seeking knowledge can be suppressed. While conducting studies in approved areas, like the quiri breeding program for example, unexpected avenues of research and discoveries often presented themselves. These advances, particularly in DNA research, have been instrumental to researchers studying our evolutionary history. And has led to even further breakthroughs. And it is not the only area of science where this is occurring. Breakthroughs and discoveries are occurring in every branch of the sciences. For example, are you aware there exists a map of our entire genetic structure, and one for the quiri as well? Are you also aware, according to these maps, the variance between our Borinian gene structure and the quiri, is a mere two percent?

"So it is true," General Zanth thought.

"The evidence is compelling. And it threatens the foundations of the collective."

"Perhaps not Agar. When we took our first steps into space, journeyed to other stars, discovered other worlds, we were able to incorporate the new reality into our belief systems."

"This is not the same general. This will require a fundamental change in our perception of the quiri. And ourselves. Sufficient to upset the social order."

"What is your concern?" Zanth asked, sensing an underlying discomfort in Agar's thoughts.

"Not only the extent of the research. But also the extent of the following, the numbers involved. And the diversity. Some are in it for the science. Some for truth. Some for religious reasons. Some opposed to our current relationship and treatment of the quiri. And some opposed to our military operations and losses in space hunting the quiri. These individuals represent a separate underground colony. And more, I suspect."

"Continue," Zanth prompted. "Give me your thoughts Agar."

"It is more than a handful of dissidents General. Or an infection which can be cured by purging. The process has been developing for quite some time. Decades, if not longer. It has grown beyond a movement. I am perceiving a growing separatist collective within the collective. And I believe it has reached fission. The only options, to allow fission or...."

General Zanth emitted an alarmed series of clicks and screeches as Agar's thought touched his mind.

"...Civil war," the thought echoed back at Agar.

Agar paused, his thoughts absorbing the turmoil occurring in General Zanth's mind. Disparate thoughts coalescing, reflected back at Agar.

"Birth rate in decline, continuing losses in space, the death toll and destruction of a civil war, Borinian against Borinian. A catastrophic event. But can you be certain of this Agar? I cannot imagine a situation as you report, on the scale you believe it to be, occurring without every mind on Borinorhnus being aware of it."

"I believe the center of this separatist movement is located on Nivalinorhnus. The reports on the recorders indicate much of this research and these discoveries, this new manner of thinking, emanates from there. I believe Nivalinorhnus to be compromised, and no longer part of the collective." Agar waited for this further bombshell to penetrate General Zanth's thoughts.

Zanth emitted another series of alarmed screeches, his clicking vocalizations rapid and agitated.

"It is impossible. We have a governor there. A military garrison."

"And yet it appears so general."

"I had hoped after our meeting I might at last have news for the council. Now I am uncertain I am ready to share your report with them."

"The council will be concerned not only by this separatist thinking infecting Borinorhnus, but the loss of resources provided by Nivalinorhnus."

"And perhaps resort to war," finished Zanth, their thoughts in agreement.

"Indeed. And the outcome uncertain in the absence of further intelligence. Especially if the recordings are true, which I believe them to be. The reason I did not want to transmit my report."

"Of course. You were correct Agar. What do you propose now?"

"I will go to Nivalinorhnus to assess the situation. And you general?"

"I am uncertain Agar," allowing his tortured thoughts to reach Agar, unprotected, unfiltered. Borinians lacked certain emotions, but possessed a strong 'manchi', akin to liking, or empathy, but not the same. More an association bonded by intense loyalty. Zanth considered Agar such an associate. Perhaps even a friend, a rare affinity for a Borinian.

"You will do your duty general, as always," Agar sought to reassure him, to ease his troubled mind.

"There is duty, and there is duty," Zanth responded, the conflict between the duty of his occupation, and a higher duty to the collective's wellbeing, conveyed in their comingled thoughts.

"My duty is to follow your orders general," Agar thought, his own 'manchi' for General Zanth a strong presence in him. "There is one other item, a particular archeologist mentioned in the reports."

"If he is as important as you think you must find him."

"It is my intent general. After Nivalinorhnus. I may uncover information there which may lead me to him."

"I approve Agar. And good fortune attend you. I must depart now, if there is nothing further. I have much to consider."

"Not at this time General. I will board the attack cruiser immediately."

"I will alert them of your arrival and inform them to prepare the ship for departure."

"My honor to serve you General Zanthinvolar Abydynus." The parting thought reached Zanth as Agar plunged into the depths of the cavern and spread his wings.

Headcap

The instrument depicted an enormous energy field, at the upper limit of the scale, the portal opening for incoming traffic. An equally strong signal on the navigation console, the destination frequency accepted and locked. Seraphina performed a final scan of the flight instruments as her ship approached the portal.

On the threshold again. Excitement gripped her. Adrenaline coursed through her. On the move. To the next place. The next enticing destination. She and her Dauphin. And now the man, Ezekiel.

The ship had been accelerating, captured by the activated portal's immense gravity well. The portal's ring-like structure visible through the forward ports as the ship rushed toward it at velocities exceeding the capability of its engines.

The portals a mystery. The builders unknown. Discovered by accident as spacing factions travelled farther out in space. The portal's purpose also an accidental discovery. Ships from distant sectors of the galaxy mysteriously appeared through them. Others attempting to travel through them went nowhere, many destroyed as they transited too close to the nearby star.

A few factions had established stations close to a portal, waiting patiently for years for a portal to activate. Vanishing forever when they flew into an activated portal. But such stations had discovered the navigation signals emitted by the portals, and which activated them. More ships vanished, never to be seen again. Until over decades of trial and error, a chart of known portals emerged. The chart grew over time.

Transition through the portals like flying into a thick goo of congealed jelly. Acceleration instruments ceased to register, as thought the ship had come to a dead stop, held in place. The stars and space itself disappeared from view. Until the ship popped out a moment later in another area of the galaxy, an entirely different and distant sector of space.

Dauphin's instruments returned to normal. Seraphina reviewed her ship's orientation, position, and velocity. She trimmed the sails for the ambient solar wind streaming from the nearby star, charting a course to her destination three shipboard days away.

"Ezekiel," she called, diverting his attention from the cockpit instruments and viewports. "Come."

Since their departure from Ecibor, Seraphina and Ezekiel had settled into a comfortable routine. Ezekiel explored more areas of the ship on his own, settling in, as though the ship were his home. Seraphina, to her surprise, unbothered by the arrangement, by his presence, by sharing her personal space and her solitary lifestyle. Such an integral part of her being before Ezekiel.

She scanned the auxiliary control console as they entered the cargo hold. Assured the sensors and controls had been effectively transferred and registering, she headed to the corner of the hold where the little scout sat.

Ezekiel followed Seraphina to the pod. Observed her touching it, drawing her hand along its smooth hull. An appreciative gleam in her large oval eyes, an admiring smile on her dark face.

The stained tarp concealing the pod during their time on Ecibor now covered a crate in front of the pod. Seraphina bent and removed the tarp, revealing the round viewport she'd acquired from the scrapyard. She returned to the scout pod. Her arms circled the smooth round nose. Her glance shifted between pod and crate.

Seraphina retrieved a small handheld object from a compartment on the bulkhead. She activated it. A thin red beam played across the circular end of the viewport. She transferred the beam to the pod. Using an implement she extracted from a pocket of her garment, she placed marks on the pod.

Ezekiel continued to observe Seraphina's actions, uncomprehending, until Seraphina hauled over a machine he'd seen her use for cutting.

"Seraphina?" Ezekiel's sharp tone startled her, and halted her motions. She was still unaccustomed to hearing her name called, though oddly comfortable hearing Ezekiel say it. His eyes questioned her, his expression one of deep concern.

The irrational concern for the pod, his dismay at Seraphina's intention to dismantle it, perplexed Ezekiel. It's presence represented a physical reminder of his former life. A life of enslavement and servitude. A life he'd rather perish than return to. Yet he experienced a strange affinity for the little scout. A 'manchi' for the tiny craft, which had saved his life.

Seraphina was touched by Ezekiel's concern for the scout. She'd react in similar fashion if anyone approached Dauphin carrying a laser cutter.

"Ezekiel, good," she said, attempting to explain her intentions with her touch, her eyes, as much as with her words. Their ability to communicate using language still limited. They'd both acquired a lengthening list of vocabulary, but complete sentences as yet beyond their capability.

Seraphina mimed her idea. She pointed to the cutter, mimed removing the nose of the scout, to be replaced by the viewport. She pointed to her eyes, and Ezekiel's eyes. Mimed peering out into space from the scout, through the viewport. An unexpected warmth flushed through her when his eyes met hers, his vigorous nodding conveying his understanding, his wide appreciative smile aimed squarely at her.

Seraphina's idea excited Ezekiel. His first view of space from inside a ship had been on Dauphin, Seraphina's ship. An experience he'd never erase from his memory, and never cease to enjoy, spending countless time in Dauphin's cockpit.

Seraphina's gaze followed Ezekiel as he turned and strode across the hold. His new garments fitted him comfortably, accentuating his masculine form. The black, collarless shirt tight against his broad chest and shoulders. Its short sleeves displayed his muscular arms. His strong thighs and calves, bulging against the form fitting trousers, recalled memories of the alley, his lethal use of those legs and feet.

And not for the first time since she'd rescued him, Seraphina experienced a lump in her throat, a shortness to her breathing, the inexplicable warm flush flooding her body. And a mysterious, unfamiliar desire.

She continued to observe Ezekiel across the hold. Curious as he paused by the cargo bins, opening them, selecting an assortment of items. She turned her attention to the scout. She gathered tools from around the hold, carefully laying them out at the head of the scout. In no rush. She had ample time prior to planetfall. And she needed to be precise.

All had been assembled, laid out, and prepared by shipboard 'nightfall'. Dauphin's on board chronometers gradually lowered the interior 'daylight' luminosity as time wore on, until only muted 'nighttime' lighting remained.

Seraphina strode over to Ezekiel, busy at a workbench, surrounded by alien objects, including the part he'd insisted she purchase from the scrap dealer.

"Food," she said, using the word from his language, unnecessarily miming the action for eating.

Ezekiel lifted his head from his work. His gaze met hers. The warm smile on his face reflected in his eyes. He nodded.

"Food," he said, in Seraphina's language.

The following morning Seraphina and Ezekiel breakfasted together. Ezekiel fresh and scrubbed clean. His Long flaxen hair, still damp, fell atop his shoulders. He'd acquired a particular fondness for the wet shower, like Seraphina. He used it often, at the slightest opportunity. Seraphina, though amused, recalling his first experience in the shower, needed a way to communicate water storage tanks, limited supply, and conservation.

Following breakfast, they shared the cockpit as usual. Seraphina checked their course, surveyed Dauphin's sensor readings, performed the necessary adjustments. She noticed Ezekiel had abandoned his usual scrutiny of the instruments, and the star speckled view of space beyond the viewports. Instead he'd been busy opening access panels and studying the cockpit's circuitry, relays, and terminals. His attention particularly focused on the ship's command controls.

Seraphina dismissed it as the normal curiosity of a fellow pilot interested in the ship's systems. And Ezekiel had proven himself a fast learner.

"Just don't mess with anything," she admonished in her own language.

They'd established a shipboard routine on the voyage out from Ecibor. In fact Seraphina's long established routine, which Ezekiel assimilated naturally. After the cockpit, Seraphina normally focused on Dauphin's maintenance chores. But she postponed the planned upgrades. Another project she wanted to complete first.

Ezekiel accompanied her to the hold, resuming his work at the workbench. Seraphina focused her attention on the scout.

She'd been working continuously, disregarding time, when her growling stomach interrupted her. Food the last thing on her mind, but the empty growling persisted. She laid aside the grinding tool, removed her protective goggles and gloves, and stepped back to inspect her work. The nose of the scout had been cleanly cut away. The pilot's compartment open and exposed. She'd attached the mating collar and ground it smooth against the adjacent hull. She ran her hand across the joint. The smooth transition elicited a smile.

She turned to summon Ezekiel. Show him her progress. The workbench empty. The cargo hold empty. Engrossed in her work, she hadn't noticed him leave.

Ezekiel lay on his stomach, the access bay to the ship's command controls open below him. Other access panels around the cockpit also open. His mind guided his actions, somehow possessing the knowledge to design and complete his project. His thoughts now a part of him. Not superimposed. Not commanded by an outside presence. An experience he'd grown increasingly accustomed to since awakening on Seraphina's ship.

But his sense of self not yet complete. Still marred by a lingering uncertainty. How did he know to do this? He hadn't been taught. Hadn't been trained. The knowledge and ability a byproduct of years of sharing other minds. The knowledge absorbed and lodged in his memory from having performed it. Now recalled unconsciously by Ezekiel.

Ezekiel completed the final connection as Seraphina entered the cockpit. Thin curved eyebrows rose beneath the crop of blue-black hair. Her eyes widened, her mouth fell open. A horror struck expression on her face.

"What in shagger hell..."

Ezekiel leapt to his feet, his beaming smile radiant. Excitement in his eyes. His eager enthusiasm mollified her. At least a little.

"Seraphina, good," he said, repeating the words she'd used in the cargo hold when she'd explained her idea for the pod.

His words had the desired effect. Seraphina recalled the scene in the cargo hold. Ezekiel's horror when she'd hauled the laser cutter to the scout. She had no idea what he'd done to her ship, but didn't believe he'd intentionally damage it. Her eyes followed him as he moved around the cockpit, tidying up, closing the open panels. She recognized the components he'd installed. All alien. The thing he'd called a command link. The power converter. And another piece of debris he'd called a command relay.

Ezekiel stood before her. His smile locked in place. He reached out, picked up the peculiar headcap he'd worn when she first found him. In her agitation, she hadn't noticed it on the pilot seat.

"Put on," he said, miming the request at Seraphina, offering her the headcap.

Seraphina studied him. His childlike enthusiasm and expectant smile calmed her. When he handed her the headcap, spoke, and mimed donning it, she nodded. She placed it on her head. It's elastic material conformed comfortably to the shape of her head. Ezekiel, still smiling, reached for a second similar cap he'd retrieved from the scout. The scouts always carried two, or more, depending on the mission. The masters never out of mental contact. He placed the cap on his head.

Seraphina reeled backward. Off balance. Almost fell. Ezekiel's strong arms caught her. Held her upright. Her knees like jelly. Unable to support her. The mental shock sudden, unexpected. Images flooded her brain. Ezekiel. Clicker swarms filled the sky. Space battles. Seraphina as a young girl. The shaghouse. Seraphina standing over the unconscious Ezekiel in the cargo hold.

She ripped the headcap from her head. The fleeting images instantly vanished. But deposited an afterglow. A stamped impression on her memory.

Seraphina stared at the thing in her hand. Her mouth open. Her stare shifted to Ezekiel. Time passed. Moments. An eternity, before Seraphina regained her voice.

"This thing can see into my mind?" she said. Her incredulity pitched her voice an octave higher. "What the fuck..."

Ezekiel unable to understand her words. But concerned by her agitated, frightened reaction. Her flustered discomfort.

He nodded.

Seraphina stared at him. Understood his nod. And also noted the deep concern expressed in his eyes. She did not blame him, but the experience had shocked and frightened her.

"We can see each other now," he said, aware she didn't understand his words. But his soft voice, his soothing tone, an attempt to calm her, reassure her. He mimed the act of speaking to each other.

Seraphina understood. He'd installed the apparatus to allow them to communicate. But being in another person's mind, having another person's inside hers. The concept too alien and disturbing. She shook her head.

"No. No. Not good," she said.

Ezekiel understood the words 'not good'. The words deflated him. Disappointment replaced his earlier enthusiasm. His eyes held hers in his stare, searching hers. Searching for the reason. Discovering it in the faint impressions her thoughts had conveyed to his.

Seraphina recognized the disappointment in his eyes. And his hurt. But was unable to accept the headcap's purpose. The concept eerie and grotesque and frightening. She blinked, glanced away, afraid to peer into his sorrow filled eyes a moment longer. Afraid of the emotions they evoked, welling up unbidden inside her. As shocking and frightening as the headcap.

Ezekiel uncertain now whether to show her his other modification. Maybe if he explained it first, instead of demonstrating as he'd done before, perceiving his actions may have been a mistake. The link had disturbed her, creating in him a hurt greater than his disappointment.

Seraphina aware of Ezekiel's hand on her shoulder. She raised her head. Stared again into his clear grey eyes. Experienced their compelling tug on her. Something he wanted to tell her.

He swept his arms wide, encompassing the cockpit. He pointed into space. He spread his arms again, flapping them like wings, circling the narrow confines of the cockpit. He stood in front of her. He picked up the headcap, pointed to her.

Seraphina stepped back instinctively, shaking her head. Ezekiel placed the headcap on the pilot seat. He lifted the second cap he'd worn, crossed to a locker and placed it inside. He pointed at Seraphina. Pointed at his head. Shook his head vigorously as she had.

He retrieved the cap he'd deposited on the seat. Turned it toward her. Pointed at a tiny flat dial on its underside, directly below the small ridge running across its top. Pointed at Seraphina, pointed at himself, shook his head vigorously as before. He depressed the tiny dial, pointed at the headcap again, at Seraphina's head, and repeated the pantomime of arms, and wings, and circling the cockpit.

Seraphina uncertain, but a germ of understanding pricked her brain as she recalled the open access panels. "Can't be," she thought, and said.

Ezekiel noticed the curious tilt of her head. The changed expression in her eyes. He smiled. His first since her reaction to the link.

"Ezekiel...." he searched for a word in their mutual vocabulary. "Say," he blurted the word. "Ezekiel say Seraphina?"

Seraphina's initial confusion turned to comprehension. She remembered their cargo hold ritual. Now part of their normal limited conversational routine. They'd learned the word 'say' in both languages, using it to convey the name of, or explain an object.

Seraphina nodded, producing a wider smile from Ezekiel. Her elation at his smile, the affect it provoked in her, especially after his recent hurt and disappointment, increased her already considerable confusion regarding this man. And the unbidden emotions he effortlessly evoked in her.

Ezekiel sat in the pilot seat, indicating Seraphina sit in the seat next to him. He donned the headcap. His eyes scanned the instruments.

"See," he said.

Seraphina was intimately familiar with her ship. Every nook. Every cranny. Every sound, vibration, and idiosyncrasy. The low, almost inaudible whir of servos and gears changing the angle of Dauphin's sails reached her first. Her pilot's instincts kicked in. She glanced toward the forward viewport, noted instantly the stars beyond shifting position. Her gaze fell to the nav console. Confirmed. A spectral shift, and the artificial course line depicting the ship's trajectory slipped to the left. Dauphin had entered a gentle starboard roll and turn. The low, ever present background hum of Dauphin's engines and harmonic vibration increased.

Seraphina's initial instinct was to grab the ship's controls and steer it back on course. Halted by Ezekiel staring at her, a wide satisfied grin on his face.

"You?" Seraphina said, pointing at Ezekiel, her mouth agape, her eyes wide and staring.

Ezekiel nodded, pointing at the headcap, His arm swept around the cockpit.

Seraphina stunned. Incredulous. Her ship piloted by his mind. Unable to immediately grasp the concept. But she'd witnessed it with her own eyes.

Ezekiel pointed at the headcap, then at her. Nodding.

Seraphina uncertain. Her trepidation at a high level following her recent experience. A pure emotional response. But her intellectual side understood the implications of piloting the ship with her mind. Encouraged by Ezekiel, his every motion gentle, patient, placing the decision in her hands, she accepted the headcap. She held it. Hesitant. Ezekiel observed her closely, not rushing her.

Seraphina raised the cap. Her eyes glued to Ezekiel. A tender expression in his, his smile encouraging. She placed the cap on her head, never letting go of it. Prepared and poised to yank it off in an instant. Nothing happened. No images. No mental shock. No invasive thoughts. Nothing like the previous experience. She relaxed, aware of the unconscious tension in her posture. She'd held her breath. She smiled at Ezekiel.

Ezekiel noticed the released tension in her body. The visible relaxation. The smile as she opened her eyes, shut tight as she'd placed the cap on her head.

"The ship faster when you think," he said, miming his words, pointing at her, and at the cockpit. "You think, Dauphin do."

Seraphina studied Ezekiel's hands. Aware they were attempts at instruction. She recognized enough words in their mutual vocabulary, accompanied by Ezekiel's gestures, to understand whatever she thought, the ship would obey. And react faster to her thoughts.

Ezekiel's smile widened. A gentle touch of his hand on her face. He nodded.

Nodding in return, Seraphina turned to the command console. She studied the displays. Noted the ship's course. Noted the configuration of the sails and the energy readings of the ambient solar wind. She listened to the low hiss of the wind's aural tone as streaming particles from the star impacted the sails. Seraphina had piloted a variety of ships, having different controls and input requirements. From heavy handed to a deft touch. And she possessed sufficient experience to avoid over controlling. Slow and easy until you acquired the hang of it.

She needed to roll Dauphin twenty degrees to gain full advantage of the wind. And turn to port seventy degrees to return to the intended trajectory. She decided to attempt the maneuvers in increments.

Her eyes glued to the instruments, Seraphina thought of a five-degree roll to port. Observed the spectral shift registering immediately on her instruments. And confirmed visually as the perspective through the forward viewport changed, the stars shifting in a clockwise direction.

She turned to Ezekiel, who'd been observing her intently, his ready smile answering hers. On the display the energy collection of both sails decreased. Their configuration inefficient for the ship's current attitude. She'd trim the sails after completing the maneuvers.

She thought, roll ten degrees port. Observed the ship's quick response on the instruments. Roll five degrees port, she thought. Dauphin completed the maneuver.

Seraphina decided to approach the next maneuver differently. She thought, turn port ten degrees. As the ship responded she thought, continue turn, continue turn. Until the nose arched through seventy degrees. She thought, hold course. Dauphin steadied on the new course.

"Wazowee!"

Her sudden outburst alarmed Ezekiel, fearful Seraphina might be experiencing a similar reaction as she had to the mind link. Reassured when he noticed the bright smile on Seraphina's face, the excited gleam in her eyes.

"Wazowee," he imitated her, turning Seraphina's smile into full-throated laughter.

Refocusing on the console, Seraphina wondered if she'd have obtained the same result by thinking of a turn to the specific heading. She'd have to confirm it later. She wanted more practice using this incredible thing Ezekiel had given her. She thought of the optimal sail configuration, observed the instruments as Dauphin's sails trimmed themselves.

Seraphina set a waypoint alarm to alert her when Dauphin intersected the desired trajectory. She turned from the console, removed the headcap, beaming in delight at Ezekiel. She leaned forward and kissed his cheek, the disturbing mind link pushed to the back of her mind. And in her excitement, the uncharacteristic, spontaneous gesture of affection, hadn't registered in her delighted thoughts.

Linked

A day later Seraphina completed a close pass of a gas giant in the system. She'd visited the system and her intended destination a number of times before. Her getaway world, whenever she needed time to think, recuperate, or simply disappear for a while. She'd performed the slingshot around the gas planet each time. The maneuver whipped Dauphin into a trajectory for her destination, at a velocity to intercept the planet by the following shipboard day.

Seraphina and Ezekiel settled comfortably into their shipboard routine. Seraphina completed the modifications to the scout. And spent hours in the cockpit practicing with the headcap. She learned she could control the ship from anywhere on board, except the engine room, which for unknown reasons, blocked the cap's transmissions.

Ezekiel spent the time hunched over the workbench, working on the headcaps whenever Seraphina had not been practicing. On the underside of both caps, beneath the center ridge, he'd opened a small thin panel, exposing tiny electronic components. And other small rectangular panels on the inside of the caps, corresponding to a wearer's temporal and frontal lobes. So flush against the cap's underside, Seraphina would not have suspected their existence had Ezekiel not opened them. His tinkering baffled her whenever she paused to gaze over his shoulder. The headcap remained a marvel. Its function magical. Its technology incomprehensible. Her brief glance into Ezekiel's mind assured her of the headcap's clicker origin. They had woven metal into a flexible elastic material. They possessed technology allowing a person to reach into another's mind, and to control mechanical and electronic systems using thoughts. Seraphina's instinctual fear of clickers grew.

Ezekiel was no coms engineer. His ability to understand the electronics controlling the headcap equally baffling to him as to Seraphina. But he'd had years of experience using the equipment, adjusting its range while scouting ahead, repairing it in the field, maintaining it and the components linking it, and his mind, to the ships he'd served on. All under control of his masters. His actions directed by their thoughts.

Now he scoured his mind for the bits of imbedded memory. His concentration remained intense and focused as he worked. Determined to correct the link. Correct the thing he'd learned during his brief glimpse into Seraphina's mind. A thing so alien to him, so incomprehensible to his experience, he'd not have understood it without the link.

He'd encountered a profoundly imbedded sense of self. An individuality of mind and thought and experience in Seraphina's mind belonging to no one else. He recalled a fleeting moment in which he'd experienced Seraphina's visceral abhorrence to the presence of another mind in her head. Like an attack, shattering her singular self, her essence, her innate being. The loss, the confusion, created madness in her mind.

A phenomena Ezekiel had witnessed often in his former life. Common among quiri captured from the wild. A madness no one, including the masters, had understood. The afflicted relegated to the food processors. Ezekiel understood the madness now.

His glimpse into Seraphina's mind provided the context to cement his own personality. Setting to rest his confusion surrounding the individuality he'd discovered only after awakening on Seraphina's ship.

Seraphina was understandably apprehensive when Ezekiel arrived at their late day meal carrying both headcaps. Her initial reaction to their combined use still raw in her mind. He ignored the food before him, usually devoured with undistracted focus and an enthusiastic delight in the various scents and tastes. Instead he stared at her across the table.

"Ezekiel fix," he said. "Not all of Seraphina in the link. Not all of Ezekiel in the link. Ezekiel will see only what Seraphina want me to see." His voice soft, soothing. "Seraphina do. Seraphina no do. Ezekiel not want Seraphina to have madness."

The last word new to Seraphina. Unfamiliar. It held no meaning for her. But she understood Ezekiel's intention. His desire for her to attempt the link again. And perhaps he also understood her reluctance. Expressed in the calm, compassionate voice, the unmistakable concern in his gentle eyes, his leaving the choice to her.

He'd fixed it he said. How, escaped her. He'd still be in her mind, hearing and seeing her thoughts. A prospect too frightening to contemplate, for too many reasons. Unnatural. An invasion. Similar to every time her body had been invaded against her will. And opening those memories to Ezekiel an abhorrent prospect.

But a change had occurred. To her. In her. A slow, subtle transformation. Imperceptible. Unconscious. It'd crept upon her in the time she'd spent in the company of this man. Ezekiel no longer a mere passenger. A transient episode. A tolerated inconvenience. He'd insinuated himself into her life, her routine. And she'd allowed it. Even welcomed it. Most unfathomable of all, she desired it. His laughter provoked her own laughter. His distress saddened her.

And her prolonged use of the headcap to pilot Dauphin had produced a level of comfort, replacing her initial misgivings. It had altered the relationship between her and her ship, melding them into a smooth, exhilarating symbiosis. Might the cap offer her and Ezekiel the same?

Seraphina stared at the alien objects on the table. Expectant and wary. Hopeful and suspicious. One friendly. The other menacing. Ezekiel said he'd fixed it. How? she wondered again. Seraphina reached for the headcap. She placed it on her head. Her eyes searched his. Her trust in him inexplicable, irrational.

Seraphina's gaze followed Ezekiel's hands. His every motion. Observed him lifting the other headcap to place it on his head. Her hands poised to remove the one she wore in an instant. Relief when nothing happened. No invasive thoughts. No flood of unfamiliar images. Her mind silent except for her own thoughts.

"Seraphina."

Her name sprang unbidden into her mind, Ezekiel calling her. But she'd been staring at his face, his eyes, and he hadn't spoken.

"Can you hear me? The words clear in her mind. The sentence complete. Unbroken. Understood in her native language.

"I can hear you," she said aloud.

"Don't say it. Think it, " the thought loud in her mind.

"What did you do?" Again she spoke the words. But she'd also thought them.

Ezekiel laughed.

"I did not know how to laugh before I met you," his thoughts said. "And I am sorry for before. I did not know how the link would disturb you. On my world there in no one voice in your mind. But many. It is the nature of the masters, and how they control us."

"The masters?"

Ezekiel conjured an image.

"Clicker ships. You lived among the clickers?"

"I was bred and grown to serve them."

Ezekiel perceived a silence in Seraphina's mind. A pause. A thought she did not wish to express.

"How did you do this?" she thought instead.

"The headcaps have many uses. The frequencies can be calibrated to receive and transmit all of only some brainwaves and patterns. Or to block all thoughts. Different frequencies to control the ship and other things, like communications and navigation."

"This is too incredible," she thought.

Ezekiel laughed again.

"I see images," she thought. Things I have no memory of. I don't know them."

"I am showing them to you. You can do the same. I will only see what you want to show me."

"I'm not certain I like this," the thought flowed into Ezekiel's mind.

"I know. And now I understand. I do not wish another mind in mine. Not anymore. I did not know it was possible before. I did not know my own thoughts before awakening on Dauphin. Did not know they were mine, and only mine. But I enjoy hearing your thoughts in mine Seraphina. And I also enjoy learning to make language with you."

Seraphina lifted the headcap from her head. Her gaze fixed on Ezekiel. On his square masculine face, strong and gentle at the same time. On his compelling compassionate grey eyes. His innocent smile. Aware of the unfamiliar longing stirring inside her, the thirst returning.

Shipboard morning. Krilan a large, looming, blue-green sphere in the forward viewport. Dauphin caught in the planet's spell, accelerating toward it. Sensors busy gathering, analyzing, synthesizing, displaying planetary data as the ship approached. Krilan's mass, magnetic fields, radiation densities, atmosphere. The navigation console displayed approach vectors and orbital insertion trajectories.

Seraphina and Ezekiel sat at their usual positions in the cockpit. Seraphina wore the headcap, now acclimated to, and comfortable using it. Confident in its reliability. But she also enjoyed the physical thrill of piloting her ship. The exhilarating pride in her skill and ability. She decided to use both mental and manual control for planetfall, increasing her exhilaration.

Seraphina mentally rolled the ship, and turned starboard ninety degrees. She manually decreased engine thrust as Dauphin's nose swung away from the planet. She continued to manipulate the thrust manually, decelerating to fall into Krilan's gravitational embrace. The ship settled into orbit two hundred and thirty sectares above the world, approximately two thousand two hundred and fifty kilometers, or fourteen hundred miles.

The magnificent globe filled Dauphine's overhead viewport. The northern hemisphere almost entirely encircled by a green and brown speckled continent. The planet topped by a white capped pole. The southern half encompassed in the deep royal blue of an unending ocean, dotted by small, scattered islands.

Seraphina mentally rolled the ship another twenty degrees, exposing the underside of Dauphin's port sail to the sun. The starboard sail pointed at the planet as Dauphin hurtled around the world.

Krilan a familiar destination, charted during her first visit to the system and the planet. Her destination on its surface already chosen and plotted. A small island in the southern ocean, just below the equator. Isolated and far from possible intrusion. Seraphina used the time in orbit double checking Dauphin's systems, ensuring everything aboard had been properly stowed in preparation for atmospheric flight and landfall.

On the fourth pass around Krilan, the large northern continent filling the viewport, Seraphina again activated Dauphin's engines, decelerating further. She scanned the instruments and mentally adjusted Dauphin's flight path. She rolled one hundred eighty degrees, and pitched up seventy degrees, heading into the atmosphere in a slight nose up position, her eyes fixed on the plasma temperature gauge. The temperature reading in the green band as Dauphin crossed the terminator and plunged into Krilan's outer atmosphere.

The ship plummeted through the sky, a red and orange blazing streak, penetrating layer after layer of atmosphere, denser as Dauphin neared the surface. In the cockpit, the glow of red hot plasma surrounding the ship dissipated as Dauphin streaked through the first cloud layer. Hull temperature returned to the yellow zone after peaking close to the red band. Seraphina manually adjusted the ship's attitude. Her hands deftly manipulated the controls. Her first atmospheric flight since she'd acquired the headcap, and uncertain of her ship's response to mental control in atmosphere, she piloted the ship manually. She'd have time to experiment later.

A different set of instruments in play now. She noted wind speed and direction. Atmospheric density and altitude. The ship's airspeed and attitude. Dauphin's outstretched appendages, which served as sails in space, now wings in the dense atmosphere. Wind flowed across them, buffeting the ship. Seraphina adjusted their angle and trim. Sensed the fall of her stomach as Dauphin's wings generated lift. The ship rose and soared in the bright sunlit sky. Seraphina leveled off.

"Wazowee!" Ezekiel erupted next to her, his huge grin matching her own.

Nivalinorhnus

Borinorhnus receded like a fading echo in Agar's mind as the attack cruiser's navigator relayed readouts from the bridge instruments. Agar's distaste for space travel occupied the forefront of his thoughts, shielded from the crew. The confined spaces aboard ship, the proximity of the crew's minds merged into his own, the vast dark nothingness beyond the ship's thin walled hull, all contributed to his discomfort. He'd spent much of his career off world, and still hadn't grown acclimated to space, experiencing the mental anxiety, the sustained sensation of impending doom, common among his species in space. Nor did he relish the multitude minds comprising a ship's colony, its crew. He much preferred the solitude required by his clandestine occupation.

Agar hung head down from his station on the bridge. His crew hung similarly at stations around the cavern shaped enclosure. Their minds linked to his. Only the communications officer and Agar wore headcaps, the frequency linked to fleet headquarters on Borinorhnus.

An image filled Agar's mind. An artificial depiction of Orh and its smaller companion, circling each other in the center of six worlds orbiting around them. The third world out from the paired stars his home, Borinorhnus. Across a dark, empty corridor of space, a fourth world, Nivalinorhnus and its twin moons. And in the distant darkness beyond, two enormous gas giants and their numerous moons, comprised the remainder of the Orh system.

Agar scanned the data on Nivalinorhnus. He had visited the planet only once, many years before, to train prior to one of his earliest interstellar missions. Nivalinorhnus as different from Borinorhnus as dusk and dawn. Two and a half times larger than Borinorhnus, and three times its mass. And alternating night and day sides as it rotated on its axis and circled its parent stars. Its elliptical orbit transited closer to the smaller red star, producing dual sunrises and sunsets, and varied seasons.

A lush world, covered in forested mountains and valleys. In certain latitudes its continental ridges resembled the topography of Borinorhnus, though not as sharply peaked or harsh. And oceans of water, numerous lakes, and rivers. A strange place compared to Agar's home. Full of abundant life. In its skies, its oceans, its forested continents. Able to sustain Borinian life in an atmosphere similar to Borinorhnus, though the air denser, its gravity heavier.

Nivalinorhnus's minerals vital to Borinian industry and technology. According to the historian Agar had consulted prior to meeting General Zanth, Borinian science and technology had been based on discoveries from Nivalinorhnus. Much of it learned from artifacts ancient quiri had left behind on both worlds, providing the earliest indication of the creatures' intelligence and technological superiority. The information had precipitated a rift in Borinorhran society, one of many in their history. An upheaval so destructive to the collective, successive Keepers forbade knowledge of the quiri's intelligence, and curtailed certain areas of scientific inquiry.

History on the verge of repeating itself, Agar thought.

Three shipboard days later, as calculated on the Borinorhran solar calendar, the attack cruiser settled into orbit around Nivalinorhnus. Agar had debated landing by shuttle, accompanied by a squad from among the ship's crew. He opted instead for a single-pilot fighter, allowing him to pursue the operation in the manner he preferred. Alone.

The cruiser skimmed Nivalinorhnus's upper atmosphere, releasing the fighter from low orbit. The fighter dove head first from the cruiser's hanger, plunging toward the blue green and white speckled world. The fighter's sensors alive, feeding data directly to Agar's brain as the dragonfly shaped craft streaked like a blazing meteor through the planet's upper atmosphere. Agar's request for a trajectory to land him on the planet's daylight side, granted by Nivalinorhran controllers.

Hitting the stratosphere, Agar deployed the fighter's wings, held close and swept back against the hull. The craft steadied, diving toward the distant continent at supersonic velocity. Crossing the troposphere, Agar leveled the fighter and deployed its wings outward, arresting his descent and reducing his airspeed. His destination, a roost he'd constructed during his training on Nivalinorhnus, hoping it had remained undiscovered and undisturbed in the intervening years. He'd chosen the area for its remote isolation, allowing him to train and prepare for his mission without having to interact with the local population.

His flight path crossed areas of particular interest he wished to reconnoiter prior to visiting them. The colonies below probably already aware of his presence, alerted to the cruiser's scheduled arrival and Agar's ostensible inspection visit. The real nature for his visit known only to him and General Zanth. He'd chosen to arrive during daylight, roosting time in the capital. It'd allow him the opportunity to rest, digest the over flight data, and reacclimatize prior to his first meeting. The diurnal passage of day and night another off-world feature Agar particularly disliked.

The fighter's sensors swept the surface. Returning echoes and scans painted detailed images in Agar's mind of Nivalinorhnus's surface features and topography. The forest canopy, industrial colonies, and quiri compounds scattered across the continent below rendered in crisp detail. And the pinging of Nivalinorhran sensors tracking his flight. He'd prepared for it. But not yet ready to mask the fighter.

Later, in the twilight between setting suns, Agar departed his roost, a mountain cave in the northern highlands. He'd arrived clean, the tracking sensors deflected as he dove into a deep rift valley, winding his way through its steep canyon walls, releasing the signal decoy before exiting at the trench's northern end. He found the cave as he'd left it years before. Undisturbed. He'd left no indication it'd ever been occupied. Upon arrival he'd explored its familiar interior, resurrecting memories of another time spent in its cloistered caverns.

Agar's nighttime destination the capital city, two hundred fifty echospans, eight hundred kilometers, south of his lair. He was acutely conscious of his increased weight, and the additional effort required of his arms and fingers as he flew in Nivalinorhnus's higher gravity, despite his earlier laps around the mountain to acclimate his muscles and respiratory system. The wide circles around the mountain also allowed him to scout and clear the lair's perimeter.

His first meeting, Nivalinorhnus's governor. Agar wore his headcap, though he didn't require it to communicate or shield his thoughts. The headcap bore the military emblem of the spacer colony and his rank insignia. And contained a customized clandestine frequency scanner. Agar also wore his uniform, cobalt tunic and leggings trimmed in scarlet, beneath a brown leather uniform chest coat, and matte black chest plate.

Agar met the governor on the outskirts of the capital city. The governor above average Borinian height, as tall as Agar, and slim. Young for his office, a governor usually an elder. Small charcoal eyes, wide spaced in a broad flat face, greeted Agar. A full head of flowing brown hair protruded beneath his polished headcap, covering his upper brow and ears, only the pointed tips of his ears visible. The musculature of his tall thin frame undefined, but well toned by the higher gravity. The governor had planned a tour.

"My honor to welcome you Captain Commander," the governor greeted Agar formally. "I of course, received notice from the council of your impending visit, and have been instructed to provide you every assistance and cooperation during your stay on Nival."

"My honor Governor Nakurinmaral Sokhoranus," Agar thought, noting the abbreviated form of the planet's name used by the governor. And the governor's informal attire. The sole symbol of his office affixed to the headcap he wore.

The small entourage departed the tree top rendezvous. Governor Nakurinmaral, Agar, and the governor's aides formed a small swarm among larger swarms heading in and out of the capital. The city center hidden from Agar's view behind a ridge of low-lying hills.

Governor Nakurinmaral's thoughts flowed into Agar's mind. "The council was rather vague concerning your visit Captain Commander. Perhaps if I knew more regarding your purpose here I might be of better assistance." Despite his seer ability, Agar was unable to access Nakurinmaral's unfiltered thoughts, or the thoughts of the headcapped aides and officials accompanying him.

"You are aware we recently had a thorough inspection."

"A courtesy Governor Nakurinmaral." Agar responded. "My main purpose is to visit our garrison. I will be meeting the General Commander following our meeting."

Their flight passed over a teeming transportation hub. Shuttles connected end to end in a lengthy train arrived and departed along rails leading into and out of the complex.

"Processed and refined ore for Borinorhnus," the governor informed Agar.

Agar's continuing attempts to probe deeper into Nakurinmaral's mind blocked by the governor's headcap, which ordinarily shouldn't have hindered Agar's seer ability. The odd circumstance aroused Agar's mental alarms. And increased his perception of an unease, maybe suspicion, underlying Nakurinmaral's thoughts, reflected in the governor's questions. And by his vocalizations, a series of shortened clicks, which may have been his normal manner, but which Agar perceived as deliberate cautiousness.

The tour continued. More industrial complexes, on the edge of the city, Agar noted, their route away from the city center. Unshielded errant thoughts and images floated through the ether, gathered by Agar's mind. Operations, quotas, labor relations, a showcase of Governor Nakurinmaral's administration, and the city's industrial efficiency. No thoughts from the science colony complexes, or commercial, governmental, or residential areas of the city, those areas also absent from the tour's itinerary.

The orchestrated tour completed, the formalities respectfully observed, Agar departed for his second meeting. He flew westward, flexing his fingers and flapping his wings in response to sensory inputs delivered to his brain by sensitive tactile sensors embedded in the skin of his wings. He soared on the cool night updrafts, the ground below shrouded in darkness. Sprinkled lights scattered in the dark indicated quiri compounds. The compounds of particular interest to Agar, an important item on his mission agenda.

Agar arrived at the military garrison's main base, a sprawling complex of interconnected caves, hilltop crevices, and tunneled cavities surrounding long rows of tall buildings. The lower levels of the buildings housed transports, fighters, armories, machinery and maintenance facilities. The peaked A-frame upper levels provided troop barracks and roosts.

The base busy and alive with arriving and departing transports. Troop swarms drilled in the sky above. An aide greeted Agar at a cave entrance in one of the surrounding hills. The base's command headquarters.

"Captain Commander, my honor to welcome you. The General Commander is expecting you."

Agar grasped a moving rail alongside the aide. The rail transported them deep into the mountain. Releasing the rail, the aide swooped toward an opening below, extended his wings to glide into a wide ornate tunnel. Agar followed.

They exited into a crowded cavern. Personnel at their posts, headcaps plugged into an array of sensor, communications, and weapons consoles, collecting, processing, analyzing, and relaying information from orbital and surface stations around the globe. Their voluble clicking and cheeping echoed around the chamber.

The aide swept upward through the cavern. Agar followed. They entered a tunnel above the command cavern, exiting into another cavern above. Four individuals roosted in a group, capped heads close together, surrounded by large glowing screens of shifting data. Their clicking, cheeping vocalizations more subdued than in the command center below.

The group separated upon sensing Agar's arrival. They fell head first, all but the General Commander, and swooped out of the cavern through a separate exit. Their thoughts a fleeting impression on Agar's mind. The surface only.

Agar grasped a roost next to the General Commander vacated by the departed officers. He removed his headcap as protocol demanded, hugging it against his chest. He waited for the General to address him first.

"Captain Commander," the general greeted him. "It is my honor to welcome you."

"It is my honor General Commander Dogarinmaral Korcharnus," Agar responded, aware of the general's probing thoughts attempting to reach deeper into his mind. An adept privy, Agar closed his mind except for the areas he wished the general to see, at the same time searching beneath the surface layer of the general's mind. The general's thoughts shielded by the headcap, which he had not removed as was customary during meeting between officers. Agar also sensed a tightly compartmentalized, highly disciplined mind. The general's unshielded surface thoughts disguised beneath innocuous layers of mundane trivia, shifting frequently, permitting no time for Ager to grasp any single fleeting thought.

General Dogarinmaral was unfamiliar to Agar. They'd never met before. Agar's knowledge of him only from his file and by reputation. A new generation. Like the governor, young for a General Commander. And also like the governor, new to his position, having recently returned from off-world deployments. Dogarinmaral had assumed command of the garrison as part of a routine rotation. Agar also noted the general and governor shared the same matronymic, Maral. Perhaps related. Maybe siblings. Their names indicated they'd been born in different maternal colonies. But their mother may have changed colonies at the time of each birth. He affixed a mental note in his memory to request General Zanth check both maternal lineages.

"I am notified you are on an inspection tour for the council?" The thought innocuous, but Agar perceived an interrogative suspicion in General Dogarinmaral's inquiry.

"Correct general."

"But you report to General Supreme Zanthinvolar Abydynus."

"Also correct general." Agar disguised his surprise at Dogarinmaral's information. Certain now of a subtle interrogation.

General Dogar's thoughts again shifted rapidly, not resting in any one area, eluding Agar's probing attempts.

"You have already met Governor Nakurinmaral?" A question. But Agar sensed the general was already aware of his meeting.

"Yes I have general."

"And your impression of our governor?" Again, Agar sensed Dogarinmaral burrowing into his mind as he considered the question and his response.

"Cooperative and accommodating," Agar thought, his response noncommittal, possessing none of the suspicions already forming in his mind. "A qualified and competent administrator."

"I am happy to know you think so. Though such matters are none of my concern. But we have established an efficient relationship between the civilian and military colonies. An undue though manageable complication were he to be replaced."

"I shall pass on your perspective in my report general."

"I thank you. Though I am sure the council is already aware of my thoughts on the matter."

"I am certain you are correct general. But my report will serve to reiterate it." Agar unable to shake the sensation of a probing interrogation. The General Commander may not have been able to delve into Agar's shielded thoughts, but his questions were cunningly directed at achieving the same goal.

"What is the concern regarding the garrison?" Dogar inquired.

"No particular concern general. A routine follow up to the reports received from the recent inspection. Confirmation of troop strength and requirements. Troop disposition and deployment. Readiness. Supply issues and logistics. All of which I'm sure you have readily available. I need not occupy much of your time."

"And all of which are contained in our regular reports to headquarters." No mistaking the suspicious nature of the general's thoughts. "My executive officer can provide all the information you require." General Dogarinmaral summoned the officer.

The meeting apparently at an end. Agar considered insisting on a briefing from Dogarinmaral personally, deciding against it. The general's suspicions already aroused, and Agar concluded he'd get no farther into the commander's mind than he already had.

The officer who'd greeted and escorted Agar into the complex entered the chamber.

"Brief the Captain Commander on our current status and provide him anything he wishes to see," Dogar commanded.

Before Agar departed the roost, a final inquiry from General Dogarinmaral entered his thoughts. "Communications has informed me our sensors have been unable to locate the fighter you arrived in. And they have tracked your cruiser departing orbit Captain Commander. It has not returned."

Agar now acutely aware of the general's interrogative manner, reflected in his suspicious questions and stare."

"I cannot account for the inability to locate the fighter general. Perhaps a problem with the sensors you may need to attend to. The cruiser is on a routine refueling trip to the gas giant, after which it will return for me." The true position of the cruiser, concealed in geosynchronous orbit behind the larger of Nivalinorhnus's two moons, buried deep in Agar's thoughts.

As Agar prepared to release the roost, he turned the general's tactic back on him.

"A final point, General Commander. It is beyond the purview of my instructions, yet if I may inquire, how is the relationship between the science, military and civil colonies?"

"As it should be," Dogar replied, performing his metal gymnastics as he responded to Agar's inquiry. "Nothing of significance to concern the council. The colonies on Nivalinorhnus enjoy a harmonious working relationship."

"And the quiri?" Agar followed up, now attuned to Dogar's mental mechanizations.

"Status quo. Again, nothing of significance to concern the council."

"Thank you General Commander," Agar's increasing suspicions hidden behind the shielded recesses of his mind.

The formalities observed, Agar donned his headcap and followed the aide from the commander's chamber. They returned to the noisy command center. The aide handed Agar a headcap attached to a console, before swooping away to a station requesting his attention.

Agar donned the headcap he'd been handed. Reports flooded his mind. A steady stream of images depicting the garrison's current status, troop complement, deployment, readiness, equipment, and logistics. The reports clinically routine. Unremarkable. Except in one respect. A perception Agar reserved for later examination, far from the minds in the command center.

His visit completed, Agar departed the complex, flying low, skimming the treetops, in the direction of lights twinkling in the distant darkness. His senses reached out in all directions, while his headcap scanned the range of frequencies used by the civil, military and science colonies. Innocuous, routine thoughts and images reached him. But much less mental activity than he'd normally expect. Especially on a world as populous as Nivalinorhnus. And he noted the background static on frequencies where he'd expected a great deal more thought chatter.

His mind focused on his mounting suspicions, while his echo senses painted the path ahead, rendering his surroundings in detail. He detected insects in flight around him, large birds in the sky above, and small creatures foraging in the underbrush, reminding him of his hunger.

Agar slowed, circled, snatching small flying insects in the air surrounding him. As he ate, he pondered the unusual silence. And the shielded thoughts of Governor Nakurinmaral and General Dogarinmaral, which he had been unable to penetrate. He had sensed a scant few minds during his tour and at the base. The silence of an entire population troubled him.

He detected a large tree bearing a fruit he particularly enjoyed, remembered fondly from his previous stay. The small round fruit hung in bunches, growing from a long central stem. Its juicy nectar never failed to drip onto his neck fur. Circling back toward the fruit tree, Agar sensed him.

Not an animal. The returning echoes unmistakably Borinian, disappearing a moment after the first fleeting pulses reached Agar's ear. An individual following him. Practiced and adept at it. Agar had only detected him by the abrupt turn toward the fruit tree, even though Agar had anticipated the governor, or more likely the general, might have him followed, and had prepared for the eventuality.

Agar perched on a thick middle branch of the fruit tree. The tree's large purplish leaves surrounded him and formed a closed canopy above. Agar reached into a low pocket of his uniform chest coat, removed a round object, not by coincidence similar to the peach sized seed of the fruit he picked and ate. He dropped both seed and object to the ground.

Agar flew a zigzag route around the grove of fruit trees, pausing frequently when he spotted a ripe fruit, plucking it from the stem, eating it while perched on the branch. He discarded the seeds and metallic balls as he moved from tree to tree. His task completed, and his hunger slackened, Agar sought the concealment of an enormous tree trunk. Its circumference the size of a personal shuttle. Agar clamped onto a branch, head down, fingers closed, arms across his chest, cocooned in his wings, the detonator clamped between palm and thumb.

The miniature sonic grenades exploded one after the other in the pattern Agar had laid down, emitting a continuous silent, ear splitting pulse in the frequency range Borinians use to receive returning echoes. Agar had contracted muscles in his middle ear to avoid being deafened. His follower, caught unprepared.

Agar waited in his concealed perch until the pulses subsided. He fell headfirst toward the forest floor, spread his fingers, and soared upward to a tree where his returning echoes located his hapless quarry thrashing in the branches overhead. Still conscious, but disoriented. His inner ear useless. He might eventually return to his base by sight alone, but his echolocating ability had been permanently damaged. His military career ended.

Agar swooped upon him from below, plucking the cap from the disabled follower's head. Agar flew on as the wounded Borinian continued falling through the branches.

Agar alighted on a thick branch high in the treetop canopy. He switched his headcap for the one he'd grabbed from his follower. Silence. The headcap probably equipped with a single dedicated frequency for the mission. Now shut down. And the sophisticated scanner in Agar's headcap had not detected it.

Ager donned his own headcap, his mind receptive as he scanned a wide range of frequencies. Same result. The other headcap's frequency absent from the bands he'd sampled, resolving the problem he'd been pondering. The authorities had been suspicious of his presence from the outset, which didn't explain the absence of every mind among the population. Unless the general population, the governing and military colonies, and perhaps the science colony also, were tuned to a band width outside the standard Borinorhnus frequencies. It still didn't explain the absence of thoughts from an entire population.

Agar flew on, calculating the window of time before the search for him commenced. Even in his distressed mental state his follower may have reported the ambush in the seconds following the first sonic explosion. His handlers would also be aware of their operative's last position. And Agar's actions had been demonstrably hostile.

Agar switched direction, forgoing his intended destination. He'd planned a close-up observation of the quiri compound south of his position. But given the closing time window, he needed to advance his timetable.

He flew east instead, toward the rising suns. His destination a large science colony complex. The science colony comprised the largest population on Nivalinorhnus. More of the population involved in some branch of the sciences than any other occupation. Specialties and sub-specialties Agar had not heard of before viewing the data on the recovered recorders. Ostensibly under the direction of the civil government, a distant second in terms of population size. And protected by the military colony. But if the separatists were centered in the science colony, how had they managed to deceive, or perhaps coerce, the civil and military authorities. The situation perhaps more complex than Agar initially perceived. His suspicions of the governor and general commander, coupled to the secured thoughts and communications, effectively locking out Borinorhnus, suggested not merely a separatist colony, but perhaps an entire separatist world. An ominous development if accurate.

Agar arrived at the science complex during the twilight dawn of the primary sun. A shift change underway, as swarm trails heading in and out of the complex crisscrossed an apricot colored sky. The departing personnel presumably headed to daylight roosts. Individuals parted company from the main swarm, gathering in smaller swarms bound in different directions. One such swarm comprised of females, pregnant and close to bearing Agar's senses informed him. No doubt headed to a maternal colony.

The science complex sat in a valley of tall grassland and small trees south of the capital city, surrounded by a low mountain range. Tall buildings scattered around the complex resembled building at the military base, their function similar, housing transports, laboratories, offices, and roosts. In one building large elevators ascended and descended, ferrying personnel, equipment, and machinery in and out of the complex's underground facilities.

Agar's memory of reports he'd retrieved from the recorders, informed him the science complex had been constructed over the remains of a vast ancient city. One of many such sites around Nivalinorhnus, where the science colony's various disciplines conducted research into technology left behind by the ancients. Ancient quiri. A fact kept secret from the general population on Borinorhnus.

Agar searched the surrounding forest for a suitable hide, a location from which to observe the complex. He needed to determine a way into the complex, aware of the narrowing window to get in and out before the search for him intensified. Not only magnifying the risk of his task, but perhaps trapping him on this world, neutralizing his ability to escape, or transmit a report.

Agar did not underestimate the difficulty he faced. His first priority to shed his military uniform, and procure garments allowing him to blend into the colony. He also possessed no intelligence on the complex's underground layout, nor information regarding the complex's method of information storage and retrieval, whether compartmentalized as the military did, or held by a central library archivist, or some other method he was unaware of. The odds of obtaining such information prior to infiltrating the complex certainly not in his favor. But he'd proceeded on less during more than one operation in the past. He'd have to improvise.

Agar used large trees foresting the perimeter as cover while he searched, hopping from tree to tree, branch to branch. In one tree his echolocating senses detected a shadowed opening. His vision confirmed it. A large open hollow midway up the wide tree trunk. Large enough to conceal him. Probably an animal's liar. Now empty. The animal hunting or foraging during the night. Soon to return. Agar removed his military breastplate and chest coat. He stuffed them into the hollow.

From his concealed perch Agar observed the hillside entrances and exits. Long enough to determine it presented his best opportunity. Following the swarming shift change, he'd observed smaller groups entering and leaving a particular opening. And even smaller groups, no more than four individuals, settling to roost in dark rocky crevices or beneath thick tree branches. Probably staffers from outlying cities, too far from home to commute, or too fatigued. Perhaps on a short break. And couples, seeking the privacy of hidden crevices and thick concealing branches.

Agar identified a likely candidate in a shaded tree close to the hillside entrance. A lone individual, roosting from a thick branch, concealed and shaded from the bright sunlight. The shaded area beneath the canopy of broad leafs almost dark. The individual already asleep. His mind at rest.

Agar perched on an adjacent branch. His own thoughts shielded. He attenuated his seer sense and reached out, a gentle brush of the other's mind. The individual in a sound sleep. Agar moved closer, maintaining concealment among the thick branches. He pushed deeper, slow, careful, insinuating himself into the sleeper's thoughts like a nested part of the sleeper's own dream. His presence natural, unobtrusive, gathering superficial details from the sleeper's memory. His identity, occupation, position in the colony, current projects, the routes he travelled during his daily routine within the complex.

Agar eased out of the sleeper's mind. The information he'd gained not everything he required, but a sufficient start. Probing any deeper presented a risk, perhaps waking the sleeper. The light contact ensured the sleeper might remember Agar, if he did at all, as a mere figment of a dream.

Agar flew for a hillside entrance the sleeper's thoughts had indicated. Senses on heightened alert, Agar slipped into a large cavern, a changing area, like a locker room, where staffers entering and departing the underground complex changed garments.

Back at the hide Agar changed. His uniform replaced by the garments he'd pilfered. The leggings light blue, the shirt top white, the chest coat also a light blue matching the leggings. Ready, Agar flew into the hillside cave a second time.

History

General Zanth had not heard from Agar. He'd noted the attack cruiser's arrival at Nivalinorhnus, following which the cruiser had maintained communications silence. Probably on Agar's orders Zanth assumed, aware of his operative's security conscious proclivities. Zanth continued to receive routine reports from Nivalinorhnus, though nothing mentioning Agar's activities. But following his study of the data Agar had provided, and Agar's briefing prior to departing for Nivalinorhnus, Zanth anticipated the worst.

His own conclusions had prompted him to heed Agar's advice. He'd returned to the Santokh colony, where he and Agar had met. He waited in a cavern at the mountaintop. In reality, a huge crevice, a split in the cliff face, open to Orh's slanted rays. The opening provided a view of the adjacent mountains, stretching to the horizon, their jagged peaks like spears pointed at the sky. And far below, the mist covered gorge. Another world. Unseen. Hidden even to Borinian echolocating senses, the mist absorbing and scattering the sonic pulses.

Zanth sensed the presence rising to roost alongside him. The librarian he'd travelled to the colony to meet. The librarian's formal name, Anokhinonkar Santokhnus. Old, as Agar had described him. Ancient even by Borinian standards. The city his original birth colony as indicated in his name.

Zanth wondered if the old librarian had ever left the city, or had spent his entire life here.

Anokhinonkar's small, onyx like eyes, blank and sightless. His grizzled back and neck fur harsh and stringy. His facial hair thick, hanging to his neck, entwined in his neck fur, the boundary between facial hair and fur difficult to determine. His skin like the gristled desiccated hide of a mummified corpse. The course material of his drab brown garment and chest coat also old, seemingly as aged as the librarian.

Zanth had kept his headcap in place. Aware even given his military training and discipline, he'd be no match for the old librarian, a powerful seer. The librarian's mind already nested inside Zanth's as the librarian settled beside him, probing beneath the headcap's electronic shielding, beneath the mental barriers Zanth has erected.

"There is no need for apprehension General Zanthinvolar Abydynus," his thoughts said in Zanth's mind. "I was told I might expect you. And you may be assured of my discretion. I have kept the oath of privacy for longer than you have been alive."

"I did not know myself I would be here until a short while ago," Zanth thought.

"Your young protégé is a strong and astute seer. And keenly perceptive. He possesses strong 'manchi' toward you. This project you are both working on brought him to me. He knew it would eventually bring you to me too."

Zanth often wondered how much of his mind Agar had accessed in the long span of their association. Maybe even influenced. Like meeting the librarian. Had the idea been entirely of Zanth's own volition? But Zanth trusted Agar. And even if Agar had seen or touched the deep recesses of Zanth's mind, Agar had never provided Zanth reason to question his trust or faith in him.

"Your mind is troubled?" the librarian thought. More statement than question.

"It is why I have come to you. Perhaps you can provide insight allowing me to see a path ahead, which does not end in destruction and calamity.

"I have no insights. I am merely an historian. I can only show you what has been. Not what is to be."

"Please show me."

The old librarian emitted a sound like a sigh. An exhalation of breath as he gathered his thoughts, much of which Zanth was unable to read. Until the images flowed. Unbidden. Unfolding in an unbroken stream as if Zanth were viewing a recording.

A world Zanth did not recognize, but also familiar. The mountain peaks dotted by large luminous domes protruding from cave mouths like bubbles dangling from the tip of a straw. The domes scattered across the surface too. The valleys and gorges open and devoid of mist.

A lone figure stood atop a tall gagged peak, face turned to tiny lights raining through a twilight sky. Like diamond chips, the lights twinkled and sparkled, providing no illumination, splattering into nothingness as they rained against the mountainsides.

The figure on the mountaintop Borinian, Zanth thought initially. But on closer inspection not Borinian. Similar but different. Like the world the figure inhabited. The individual an adult male, half the height of a true Borinian. He stood not completely erect, on a pair of short spindly legs. A single hooked claw grew from the tips of padded feet. On each side of his body, a limb attached to a wing of thin skin, the limb articulated by a muscular appendage at the front, and a ridge of muscle at the back. The ridges formed shoulders, separated by a hard spinal column running from the base of his neck down his back, continuing into a long stout tail. His head flat and pointed, running to a snout of wide flared nostrils. Unlike any creature Zanth had ever seen.

Zanth sensed the creature's mind. Uncertain how the old librarian managed to convey the creature's thoughts. How could he know the creature's mind? The mind mingled in Zanth's was devoid of cogent thoughts. Primitive. Instinctual. Unrecognizable as sentient intelligence. But possessing self-awareness, and a deep foreboding. An instinctive sense of impending doom.

Through the creature's mind Zanth visualized the surrounding peaks as if he were standing upon them. He observed a pass below. More peaks in the distance, stretching to the horizon. Zanth sensed the flutter of wings overhead.

Like smoke from chimney stacks the creatures rose from peaks not occupied by the domes. Long black lines snaked through the twilight sky. Hunter-gatherers. Zanth, the lone creature, followed their passage as they flew westward across the great valley.

The creature leapt, unfolded its wings in midair and joined the swarm. But the creature, Zanth, did not join the hunt. He alighted onto a peak high above the foraging hunters. Again alone, where Zanth observed the hunters from his high vantage point.

The raucous ruckus of thousands filled Zanth's mind. The multitude filled the skies and lined the peaks. Male and female. Young and old. His 'fiel' among them, pregnant and close to bearing. Zanth's mind hoped for a strong and healthy offspring. The numbers of healthy newborns were diminishing. Fewer and fewer as the years passed, not surviving much beyond birth. The once vast swarms weakened and diminished.

Zanth continued to observe the hunt through the creature's eyes. The females and young dove at vegetation in the gorges, snatching fruit and berries, immediately fed into their mouths. The males hunted small animals on the ground, clawed feet spearing their prey.

The lone observer stiffened. Senses alerted. Zanth experienced the sudden alarm in his own mind. The hunters sensed it too. Their hunting ceased. They cloistered together against the cliff, unmoving. They held their positions. Silent.

The images exploded in Zanth's mind, as in the creature's mind, and the minds of all the hunters. Terror and panic gripped them as a whole. Death on a massive scale. An entire colony extinguished. The anguished cries of the dying flooded the assembled minds, pushing all other senses aside.

Until utter silence remained.

The creature's mind screamed in primal rage. Its force overwhelming. An explosion in Zanth's head. And amid the rage a primitive instinctual fear. For in the dying echoes the creatures had glimpsed another mind. A presence they feared. New and unfamiliar. Like them, but not of them. Different and strange. More powerful. Over the span of the creature's lifetime these strangers had slowly displaced his kind, presaging the end of their existence.

The images faded, leaving Zanth shaken, empty, and confused. His mind attempted to process the information the librarian had imparted. Discern its meaning. But before he'd properly assimilated those images, a new set entered Zanth's mind.

Two individuals locked in battle. A fight to the death. And more. For the creature's mind conveyed not only its expected doom, but the extinction of all life. The end of their existence. He among the last of his kind.

Zanth clung to the rock face by his claws, while he bore down on himself from above. Zanth in both minds. Experiencing the battle from each combatant's perspective. The attacker a true Borinian. Also primitive, but self-aware and sentient. Its mind and Zanth's mind pushed through the creature's and Zanth's primitive impulses, carving a path into its innermost consciousness, perceiving its life cycle. Its entire history.

The creature's muscular tail whipped behind, lashing the Borinian's shielded thigh. The stiff legging material absorbed the blow. The Borinian continued his attack undaunted.

The creature unable to escape his attacker. The invasion of its primitive mind a crushing force, as debilitating as physical blows.

Zanth's mind screamed in pain as the creature's did. His tail lashed out in wild desperation, the force of its impact chipping the rock face. The Borinian and Zanth leapt clear of the powerful tail, planting taloned feet into the rock face, but not grasping it. Instead his feet uncoiled, catapulting him from the wall in a backward somersault. He landed on the creature's back, between the shoulders, smashing Zanth into the wall, shattering his shoulders.

The deep, solid hold of his claws prevented him from falling. But his arms were useless, unable to spread his wings. The Borinian dove, opened its wings, and soared to a position above and behind his disabled opponent. The Borinian swooped down, legs forward, talons extended.

Zanth experienced his talons ripping into the creature. And experienced the shock and pain of shredded tissue and bone, dislodging his grip from the rock face. Zanth experienced the pain and anguish, and also the triumph. The creature fell, impacting a lower ledge of the mountain. The impact completed the destruction of its back and shoulders, the thin membrane of its wings ripped and torn. Zanth tumbled toward the gorge below, his death cries ringing in his ears. While also observing his death plunge from high above, a sense of triumphant pride in his mind. And images of a vibrant, expanding population.

The images ceased and faded. Zanth weary and exhausted. His thoughts confused. Though now he perceived an historical context. Memories of history classes from his childhood. Tales of a time stretching back to prehistory. To the dawn of Borinian existence.

Zanth astounded by the old librarian's detailed images of such a distant past. And the memories, as though from actual experience. But before the question formed in his thoughts, the images commenced again, like hallucinatory flashbacks over which he had no control.

Another hunt. The peaks covered by hunters as before. This time the hunters recognizably Borinian. And the world more familiar. The deep gorges between the mountain ranges covered by a mud brown mist like gaseous lakes.

The hunters used tools. The females prepared long lines of woven material, which the males dropped into the shrouded gorges below. The young and other females anchored the lines to the cliff. Other males grasped the lines in their talons, flying between the peaks, dragging hooked buckets along the gorge. The females hauled the lines up the peaks until the loaded buckets appeared above the mist. The hooked debris pounced on by the waiting swarm and sorted. The edible catch devoured on the spot.

The organized hunt followed by a festival. The celebration a product of developing culture. Zanth fascinated by the vocalizations, and the sounds produced by beating sticks, bones, and other implements against rocks and other materials. Primitive sounds, unfamiliar, but rhythmic, recognizably musical. Accompanied by ritualistic dances mimicking hunts and combat, depictions of individual prowess and leadership. Dancers leapt at each other in feigned attacks, wings unfolded, outstretched talons scything the air. Up one peak and down another taloned feet bit into the granite, scratching and gouging the rock as the dancers leapt and climbed and sprang along the cliff face.

The dance also a precursor to mating. A method of choosing and pairing. The females studied and followed the male dancers, erupting in appreciative vocalizations for their favorites. They imitated the movements of their favorites, posturing and presenting themselves in sexually receptive positions.

The tempo rose to a frenzy in Zanth's mind. The dancers a blur of whirling limbs, twirling bodies and outstretched wings. Until a sudden halt to the dancing. An abrupt cessation of all movement. As though the image had been frozen in place in Zanth's mind. He sensed the mounting alarm. Each mind in the swarms covering the peaks sensed it as one. Death on a massive scale. Another of their colonies destroyed.

A social order had evolved among them. They sought out the leader, known as the keeper. Zanth experienced the full onslaught of the keeper's anger, his rage, and his fear. A fear present in the minds of the gathered. A fear born of the threat to their domain. The dome dwellers had to be destroyed, lest the domain perish.

Zanth inhaled a deep breath. His mind struggled to digest the enormous impact of the images, visions, and emotions. Visceral and immediate, though the events had occurred in a time long since turned to dust.

The old librarian not finished yet.

They came by night. Thousands of them. Tens of thousands. Like a dark blanket covering the world. The terrain passed invisibly below, yet navigated with uncanny precision. Through the dark night the flying swarms snaked around towering peaks, swooped into treacherous valleys, skirted the jagged ridges and sheer cliffs. The landscape in Zanth's mind increasingly familiar. Except for the illuminated domes. They lit the dark around the peaks like stars in the night sky.

The swarms soared on slender outstretched wings, approaching the domes in silence. They alighted onto the rock face surrounding the domes, filling the peaks around the glowing globes. Strong, sharp talons protruding from thick padded feet held them against the granite walls. Their wings folded against their bodies. A proud lift to their fur covered chests. They waited.

As though with a single mind they attacked. Short powerful legs launched them through the air. They soared on thin fragile wings, rolling to dive on the domes, caught like tiny gnats in the dome's luminescent glow. The light in the domes grew brighter, obliterating the shadows, turning night into twilight. And the attackers fell, uncontrollably, one after the other, in growing numbers. Until they fell like raindrops in a downpour, dead before they plunged into the mist covered gorges below.

But many remained on target. The velocity of their diving bodes, living and dead, pierced the domes by the hundreds.

A massive explosion split the night. The initial explosion followed by others, and secondary eruptions, splitting the mountain open. The ruptured domes spewed their contents into the night, hissing and belching clouds of smoke, steam, and gas.

The surviving Borinians returned to the peaks. Zanth among them, sharing their thoughts as the swarm passively observed the destruction of the 'sun caves'. But at tremendous cost. Thousands of their brethren dead. Their sacrifice ensured the survival of the colonies, and reserved for them an immortalized place as honored ones in the collective memory.

A sudden terror seized their minds. Reacting as one mind they leapt from the cliffs in a black swarm, thousands of wings beating in a wild frenzy to escape the approaching terror. A terror powerful enough for Zanth to screech aloud in fear, the sound echoing in the cavern he shared with the librarian.

The explosion silent, devoid of light. Waves of energy pulsed outward, enveloping the fleeing swarms. Lasting only an instant. They fell from the sky by the thousands.

Zanth aware of his heavy breathing. The pounding in his chest. His involuntary screeching. His mind shocked and agitated.

"By the fires of Orh..." the thought escaping, beyond his control.

"It was as you have seen for many hundreds of years," the old librarian thought.

"You claim it as such. But I am skeptical. You have shown me memories. But how can you have these memories? How can you know their thoughts from a time so distant in the past?"

"The answer is of no consequence. You have seen our beginning. And also our end."

"Now you present me riddles."

Zanth's mental discipline was overwhelmed by the turmoil of his thoughts. Probably flowing unshielded into the librarian's mind. Zanth unable to care. His thoughts latched onto a memory. Tales of certain individuals, a once in a generation anomaly, possessing the genetic memory of all Borinians since the birth of their existence. Perhaps the old librarian was such an individual. But such stories were considered no more than myth.

True or not, Zanth had no time to ponder the question. His agitated mind focused on the history he'd viewed. And the present. From the archeological reports Agar had retrieved, Zanth concluded the dome dwellers had been quiri. And through the librarian Zanth had witnessed the struggle for survival. The cycle of a species rising to dominance, replacing another. His species had not only survived, it had thrived, and dominated the world.

"We may be dominant now," Zanth heard in his thoughts, "But the cycle, and the struggle, continues." He'd momentarily forgotten the old librarian's presence in his mind. A subtle, unobtrusive, imperceptible presence. Probably much deeper than Zanth had been aware, reading every thought, touching every memory, every experience.

"However the struggle is not the point," Zanth heard in his mind.

"More of your riddles," Zanth thought.

"Observe," the old librarian thought, streaming new images into Zanth's mind.

The world quiet. The Borinian swarms Zanth had observed earlier no longer filled the skies. Their numbers diminished. Ire rose in Zanth as he imagined the decimation wrought by the quiri. But the world scrolling across his mind absent of quiri too. Their domed habitats broken and empty. Long abandoned. Decayed into dust.

Who were the new enemy? Zanth wondered.

He sensed an unseen madness. A catastrophic mental upheaval ripping the fabric of Borinian existence. Images of colossal battles raced through his mind as though on fast forward. One after the other after the other. An endless stream of wars. Fought not against a faceless alien enemy. But Borinian against Borinian. Oceans of shed blood. Mountains of dead. A spasmic screaming bloodletting pitting colony against colony, generation against generation, brother against brother. A species committing suicide.

The images abruptly ended.

"What in Orh's name?" Zanth thought.

"Just so," responded the librarian. "And there is more. A great deal more of course. But I am much fatigued. My stamina is not as it used to be. If you wish to continue you will need to return another time."

"But what does it mean?" Zanth insisted, his displeasure at the unsatisfactory end to the meeting expressed in a string of exasperated clicks. But he calmed himself. He'd lost track of time during his intense focus on the history relayed by the librarian. His internal clock indicated he'd spent upwards of four hours in the old librarian's company.

"The meaning is for you to determine," the librarian thought. "I do not interpret, as I indicated to you before. I merely present what has been."

The librarian departed, leaving Zanth paralyzed and confused. More uncertain than he'd been before the meeting. The fate of the world, two worlds, a crushing burden weighing upon him. He had much to contemplate and process. And he dreaded the prospect of returning to the noisy chaos of the capital. The cavern's cloistered tranquility more conducive to contemplation.

He replayed the nested memories. The distant past experienced through the eyes and minds of individuals who had lived it. As though he'd been transported through time. He compared everything he had seen, and experienced, and learned, to historical accounts generally accepted throughout the collective, passed down through generations. The events, if not the details, matched the collective's common knowledge. The basis of Borinian myths and legends. Stories of heroes and epic battles from the long dead past.

Except for the central lie. The earliest primitive inhabitants of Borinorhnus had been discovered long ago and accepted as a prehistoric truth. To evolutionists, they represented the progenitors of the Borinian species. To deitists, a separate entity put on the world by the creator of all things. To Orhists, a manifestation of Orh's life renewing rebirth.

But according to the old librarian, and the reports Agar had retrieved, the quiri had occupied Borinorhnus before the primitive creatures he'd witnessed in his mind. The illuminated domes preceded the creature's first appearance.

Zanth had never been particularly religious. He'd spent his entire adult life in the military. He trusted science, and the technology it spawned. He accepted evolution as a natural process, and didn't care if it resulted from a creator, or Orh, or some other deity. The definitive link proving Borinian evolutionary history had yet to be found. An intermediate creature which demonstrated a clear transition from primitive to Borinian. Many believed such a creature never existed, its absence the central argument used to refute evolution.

Such arguments never more than an academic curiosity to Zanth. But following his meeting, and the experiences the librarian had shared, Zanth no longer doubted Borinians were genetic descendants of the primitive species still alive in his restive mind, now embedded in his memory. Through the librarian, Zanth had experienced their minds, before the appearance of true Borinians. The experiences had not been imagined or conceptualized by the librarian, but flowed from his memories. Memories he was only able to possess through direct genetic lineage.

Why had librarians like the old man not shared this knowledge before? Zanth wondered. Perhaps they had, he concluded. The knowledge purged and erased during a past upheaval ushering in the dark ages. Its effects lingered into the present. Vast stores of knowledge lost and forgotten. Scientific study and research only recently reemerging from the shadows of blasphemy and sedition. Certain areas still suppressed, certain knowledge still prohibited.

And now a new factor. A quiri evolutionary link. Agar perhaps correct. Such knowledge possessed the potential to fundamentally upset Borinorhran beliefs, exposing a truth unacceptable to many. Perhaps precipitating a similar type of calamitous madness as he'd witnessed. Perhaps the process already underway.

Perhaps the point of the librarian's lesson.

Infiltrate

Deep underground, Agar navigated the passages and tunnels from memories he'd retrieved from the sleeping technician. A general idea of the direction he needed to follow. Amazed at the vastness of the underground complex. And the lack of posted sentries. Another anomalous item to support his conclusions.

The underground complex possessed an unsettling strangeness. An alien quality as though from another world. Its numerous levels accessed by pod-like lifts constructed of a transparent material. And in place of the familiar railways, a different type of rail, along which transparent pods similar to the lifts zipped silently through the tunnels. Staffers inside the pods stood or sat as the pods whisked them to their destinations. Borinian and quiri together.

Other staffers strode through the tunnels, their thoughts silent, touching Agar's mind only in passing greetings. Their heads bare. No headcaps to shield their thoughts. Yet their thoughts silent in Agar's mind.

The tunnels and chambers he passed through were unlike the bored, arched tunnels of Borinorhnus. The walls uniformly smooth, meeting the ceiling in a gentle curve. Chalky blue in ultraviolet illumination. The light source indiscernible, as though emanating from the walls and ceiling itself.

Agar entered an enclosed chamber. Blank walls around him. A dead end. Turning to retrace his steps, he halted. A section of the wall contracted before him, collapsing like a house of cards after the bottom card is pulled out. The wall lost its solidity, transforming into a smoky apparition. Turning less smoky, more transparent, until in place of a solid wall, an opening materialized. The entire process lasted no more than an instant.

Agar stood rooted in place, astounded and confounded. He'd never encountered a technology like the transforming wall in all his off-world travels. The experience focused the uneasiness haunting him since entering the underground complex. A sensed presence. Intangible, yet disturbing. As though the tunnels and chambers were imbued by an alien essence. For the first time in his life, Agar experienced the stirring of an emotion akin to fear.

Beyond the opening a short passage ended on a terraced ledge jutting out into a vast circular shaft. The shaft's features and dimensions discernible only in his ultraviolet visual range, and by echolocation. The floor half an echospan below, equivalent to one and a half kilometers. The ceiling a similar distance above. The shaft perhaps a quarter echospan across in diameter. Other terraced ledges were spaced like dark open mouths along the shaft's length, and around its circular walls. More levels of work chambers and laboratories, Agar assumed.

Long conduits and rails lined the walls, connecting the various levels and terraces. Illuminated transparent pods flitted around the shaft like iridescent insects, ferrying personnel to the terraced openings. Agar wondered why no one flew inside the shaft. The answer lodged in the memory of the sleeper. The conduits supplied power and fresh breathable air to the tunnels and chambers. The immense shaft itself nothing more than an underground thoroughfare, the air between its curved walls lacking the density to sustain flight. The sleeper's memories also provided Agar instructions on how to summon and operate the lifts.

Agar's first objective the main library, from where he'd be able to access the central archive. The colony possessed librarians, but he'd learned from the sleeper the colony also stored information in data archives for quick reference. Agar understood why after entering a library chamber, and accessing the archive from a vacant console. The information contained in the archive vast, spanning research across multiple scientific disciplines and hundreds of years. Too voluminous for any one individual to assimilate and process. The librarians used primarily as historical archivists. The stored information more than Agar had time for. He needed to narrow his search. Focus solely on the pertinent information he required.

The chamber sparsely occupied, and quiet, a half dozen other staffers at various consoles. Including quiri, working silently at their consoles alongside Borinians. The minds in the chamber silent, like others Agar had encountered since arriving underground. The thoughts, which briefly brushed his mind, did so only to acknowledge his greeting, before immediately departing. And his brief mental links to the quiri indicated no other minds occupying theirs, exerting control or direction over their activities.

Agar accessed the library's central index and selected the name Khalinaltani Ogadeinus, the archeologist referenced on the data recorders. An enormous amount of information scrolled onto the screen, including all of Khalinaltani's research, cross-referenced to a multitude of other topics. The information Agar had viewed on the recorders the visible tip of an enshrouded peak. Agar quickly scrolled through the data, not interested in the science. He required personal information on the individual. A lead to track him. He discarded most of the files the search index displayed, leaving him a shorter list to sort through. A biography, and an indexed catalogue of Khalinaltani's most significant findings and reports. Many of the reports recent. And the item which captured Agar's attention, a catalogue of recent archeological sites.

The sites spanned systems known and unknown to Borinorhnus. Areas of space no Borinian had ever travelled to or explored. Except for Khalinaltani. Systems and worlds Agar had never heard of, prompting Agar to ponder who had named them, and how had Khalinaltani's reports been transmitted, especially the most recent.

Agar memorized the pertinent information as he scrolled through the files. His mind already focused on his next priority, communications. A more daunting and dangerous task. Agar had hoped to avoid it. The sleeper's mind had suggested compartmentalized information, similar to the military. Confirmed by Agar's access of the archive. But avoidance of the communication problem no longer an option. The archives provided no information or insight into the mystery. Agar needed to discover how the colony and Khalinaltani communicated, the nature of their communications, and most important, the frequency bands the Nivalinorhrans had switched to.

One portion of his mind had been pondering alternatives while he'd accessed the archives, searching for a suitable workaround. A means of tapping into the communications network without having to physically access it. Accessing the central switching station, or any of the relay stations around the planet, might immediately reveal his presence, and his access, negating his prime operational maxim, infiltrate and exfiltrate, leaving no indication or trace of his presence. And even if he had been able to access the communication net, he expected it to be encrypted.

Agar needed a mind. The complex's administrator, or a close aide. Or a communications technician. He immediately ruled out the administrator. He accessed the archive's personnel roster, scrolling through until he located an individual fitting his required particulars.

Khalinaltani Ogadeinus

Khalinaltani Ogadeinus had devoted his entire adult life to the study of Borinian prehistory. A gifted privy and seer, his early education had been geared toward government, or academia, perhaps a librarian. But he'd rise in government only as far as his lineage and social connections permitted, despite his mental acuity. And anyway, politics held no interest for him. One fateful day his history instructor had scheduled a field trip to an ancient Borinian site. The day Khalinaltani discovered his true vocation.

The ancient ruins of the cave had fascinated him. The scene ravished and eroded by weather and time. His youthful curiosity stimulated by a shaft at the back of the cavern, descending into a black underground void. Remnants of rails and rungs protruded from the rock, along with the ruins of a spherical structure, embedded in the rock, continuous with the rock, having no distinct discernable separation, as though part of the rock itself.

His mind had been captivated by the pock-marked walls, by drill marks and bore holes. By layers of time uncovered, delineated by striations in the soil. And amid the tool marks, other gouges in the rock, indicating tracks, and roosts. Evidence of occupation. Of a community. In that moment Khal had experienced the thrill of discovery. Of history awakening and coming alive.

The instructor's thoughts, recalling events enshrined in Borinorhran history, had held no particular interest for Khal. His mind had envisioned more than epic battles, more than one species triumphing over another. Rather the scene in the cave had sparked an urge to uncover buried mysteries. Decipher a civilization long since absorbed by time. How they lived, their thoughts, their beliefs, their culture. And their demise. Their passage into history. The lessons they'd left behind, which might enlighten and enrich the present.

Khal had sensed from a young age he didn't belong. Didn't fit in. A sense of estrangement and displacement accompanied him, setting him apart. Partly due to his mental abilities, those of a prodigy. But also an instinctual aversion to orthodoxy, to conventional thought and practice, the acceptance of conventional truths unexamined by critical questioning, thought, or reason. An aspect of his personality Khal had learned to hide from his peers and instructors, further setting him apart.

In later years, toward the completion of his education, this fission aspect of his personality manifested and asserted itself, increasing his discomfort in the managed, constricted society around him. He'd discovered a contentment living apart, separated from the minds of his colony and the collective. He'd discovered and embraced his individuality, without the angst and trepidation of his youth. And he'd accepted the concept of his destiny being of his own choosing, uniquely his own.

As Khal embarked on his chosen career he'd developed a determination to uncovering truth, often at odds with the status quo, and the accepted parameters of knowledge and research. He'd sought out opportunities to travel off world, accepting an assignment allowing him to depart his home system for the first time. The experience completed his transformation. He'd set off on his own to explore the fascinating new horizons open to him, and pursue his research unhindered.

Khal focused on his notes as his small ship swept across the void. As always, he embraced the quiet solitude, his thoughts his sole companion as he transformed his notes into a final report. Undecided concerning the final item. Uncertain how the knowledge might be received, or used. Perhaps suppressed and purged. Or corrupted for a self-serving purpose. But perhaps such considerations were not his to decide. And he had been away far too long to have a valid opinion as to the current state of civil society, though he doubted it had improved much in his absence. Khal considered himself a seeker. His primary guiding principle his belief in the universality of knowledge, meant for all.

His ship raced toward the gravitational grasp of the nearby star, and portal. The ship old, but sturdy and reliable. A relic of the past, Khal had stumbled upon it by accident. A fortuitous event, which had saved his life. His Borinorhran ship damaged beyond repair, he'd reconciled himself to spending the remainder of his life stranded, when he'd discovered the alien ship in an enormous natural hanger carved into the side of a mountain. He'd spent two years learning its systems and how to operate it. And another few years adapting it to accommodate his anatomy, converting it into a comfortable home. The result a satisfying hybrid, an apt analogy of the Human-Borinian relationship he'd spent a lifetime studying.

But the ship was nearing the end of its useful lifetime. Khal possessed neither the tools nor the knowledge to maintain and upgrade its systems. And even if he found such a person, which he doubted, the parts no longer existed, the technology to replicate them lost to time. The ship's fate sealed. The inevitable fate of all things. Yet the ship had served Khal well. Had been his home. Had transported him to remote corners of the vast galaxy, and in a way, across time.

The enormous portal visible beyond the view ports represented the end of his search. The culmination of a lifetime of exploration. The memorized images of the world he'd recently departed still fresh in his mind. Davidia, where he'd spent the last five celestial years. He'd discovered the name, apparently a tribute to some revered personage, inscribed upon numerous sites around the now barren world. Its inhabitants and their civilization long gone, a brief waypoint along the cosmic span of time. Davidia had provided the final pieces of the story.

Khal possessed the entire story now. He'd discovered the final piece. A truth so profound it surpassed anything he'd imagined at the outset of his quest. And it possessed equally profound implications for his people.

Once through the portal he'd deliver his final report. His search at an end. But before returning home he had one more world he wished to visit. Perhaps his last voyage in the dying ship. The thought decided the question for him. He'd include everything in the final report. And if he ended up stranded on the lost world, he could not imagine a more fitting place to spend the remainder of his existence. The politics of his home worlds a concern for others. He'd provided the knowledge. His sole purpose.

Khal laid aside his work to focus on the approaching portal. The frequency for the Burude System already transmitted, awakening the enormous ringed structure. The portal's gigantic field generators, connected by thin filaments, formed an enormous circle, its diameter equal to the circumference of a small star. The gravitational force of the activated portal sucked Khal's ship inexorably toward it at a velocity greater than the ship's capabilities. The portal's immense energy output spiked the ship's instruments. Khal had also discovered the origins of the mysterious portals, including the civilization which had built them. Knowledge perhaps he alone possessed.

Khal marveled at the portal's ingenuity. Its science. Its colossal yet simple structure. The thin connecting filaments seemingly unequal to the task of maintaining the portal's shape, or conducting the enormous amounts of energy. As he pondered the herculean feat entailed in constructing and seeding them across the galaxy, the portal swallowed his ship.

Khalinaltanists

Orh slid behind the distant peaks. Its dimmer companion painted the twilight sky pale pink and blue, as a greenish crescent moon rose on the opposite side of the world. The moon also accompanied by a companion, a pale sliver ascending in its wake.

The city below Agar laid out in a neat pattern of streets and broad avenues. A leftover from ancient quiri occupation. The alien design no longer required. Yet Agar noted restoration of not only the street system, but also buildings in ancient quiri sections of the city. Including dim city lights flickering on as the sky darkened. Another unnecessary requirement for a strictly Borinian population.

Attired in casual everyday garments he'd pilfered from the changing cavern, Agar followed a group of flyers who'd split away from the swarm. Their destination a city square below. The Science Director's administrative aide among them. The aide's distinctive ultraviolet markings allowed Agar to maintain visual contact from a discreet distance.

The square, located toward the edge of the city, contained a large bustling agora of garment stores, food venders, and eateries. Adjacent to the square, Agar noted a residential area of tall peaked buildings, emulating the mountainous topography of Borinorhnus. And on the periphery of the residential area, a quiri farm. Agar had not yet been able to observe any of the quiri farms up close, but at his current distance, the farm's lights allowed him to discern a distinctive dissimilarity from quiri farms on Borinorhnus.

The most obvious difference, besides its physical layout and appearance, the compound lacked the breeding, cleaning, and rendering pens common on Borinorhnus. Instead, the compound reflected a residential community of neat streets and dwellings, not unlike the restored sections of the city. The other significant difference, planted vegetable and produce fields surrounding the compound. Not at all like the livestock farms on Borinorhnus.

Agar paid particular attention to the vehicular traffic snaking along the restored streets below. Many of the vehicles operated by quiri, he noted. Others by Borinians. And he noticed groups of quiri working and conducting business in the square. Vendors and shopkeepers hawking wares and foodstuff. Their activities independent of Borinian control. The customers both Borinian and quiri.

The confounding unorthodoxy below also present in the air. Quiri flyers joined the swarm of Borinians aloft, wearing a modified version of the Borinian environmental flight suit used in space, and on worlds lacking a breathable atmosphere. The head, front, and rear enclosures, and the environmental packs, had been removed. The twin-engine pods on the back, and thrusters around the finned tail empennage, retained. Flexible expandable wings mimicked the anatomical architecture of Borinian wings. The quiri wore visor equipped control headcaps.

The modified fliers intrigued Agar. Their light, compact design, and versatility, recognized and appreciated by his tactical mind. He decided if an opportunity presented itself, he'd acquire one before departing Nivalinorhnus. Assuming he departed Nivalinorhnus at all.

Agar noted the increased presence of security forces, including quiri in security force uniforms. Patrols in the air and on the ground. Hover drones crisscrossed the sky, targeting lone fliers separating from the swarm. The search for him under way.

The small swarm Agar had joined descended toward the square, headed for an eatery. His observations at the science colony complex, and in the city, confirmed a conclusion he'd been formulating since his arrival on Nivalinorhnus. And explained why the capital city had been omitted from the Governor's tour. Further confirmation when he entered the eatery. Quiri occupied the main room in slightly less numbers than their Borinian companions. Both ate, drank, and conversed together. And the eatery itself, designed to accommodate both Borinian and quiri. Some Borinians sat at tables alongside quiri. Some quiri hung alongside Borinians from mechanical talons attached to their boots. At a few tables a combination of roosting and sitting, the heads of the hanging and sitting diners level with each other.

The quiri on Nivalinorhnus were apparently free, Agar concluded. Able to conduct their activities of their own accord. Unherded or shepherded by quiri watchmen or Borinian overseers. But more, he suspected, they appeared to be fully integrated into Nivalinorhnus society and culture as equal citizens.

Agar again noted the astonishing absence of other minds reaching his as he inspected the room. Especially in a crowded eatery. The minds surrounding him silent, even as the ebb and flow of human conversation and Borinian vocalizations reached his ears. The peculiar mental silence deliberate, Agar concluded. Mental privacy the norm. A desired, even protected attribute on Nivalinorhnus. Unlike Borinorhnus, where mental privacy was considered rude, and suspicious, except where officially sanctioned.

Agar noticed an empty table against a wall across the room. He headed in its direction, skirting a circular hole in the middle of the floor providing access to a roosting-only room beneath. Behind the table he'd selected, a stairway built into the wall led to an overhead lattice works spanning the room. He observed similar stairways in the wall behind other tables. Agar used the stairway to reach the lattice over his table. He hung from his talons in a comfortable roosting position, his wings folded against his sides.

He studied the dispenser menu while his mind reached across the room. He did not linger in any individual mind. Merely a gentle passing brush. Snippets of thoughts collected before quickly moving on.

"...Haven't determined its function yet..."

"...It cannot have been used in that manner..."

"...Never happen on Borinorhnus of course..."

"...Britahri is ready to bear. She left for the Jadahran maternal colony today."

"...The weather there is wonderful during the late season..."

"...I suspect she wants to mate with him..."

The crowd consisted mainly of science colony staffers, discussing work and plans for their off time. The remainder a smattering of city workers and civil administrators. The bantering thoughts and lively vocalizations in the room reflected a genial conviviality, a pleasant sociability Agar had sensed among other Nivalinorhrans. A sense of well being, of contented, fulfilled lives. Their mental silence a comfort to Agar, accommodating his preference for mental and physical solitude. And a refreshing, pleasant contrast to the dour mood and thoughts of most Borinorhrans, shared by all in an unbroken communal mental link.

"...Another incident at the mine today. When will we be rid of Borinorhran miners?"

"I heard the few remaining who do not wish to immigrate and remain on Khalinorhnus are to be transferred soon."

"And what if they report to the authorities on Borinorhnus?"

"They are being rotated to off-world sites outside the system. Receiving above average compensation. They are not complaining. I believe they are happy not to be returning to Borinorhnus."

Agar had first encountered the name 'Khalinorhnus' in the sleeper's thoughts. And again in the library archives. He'd initially lacked a context to understand it. But the term 'Khalinaltanist' had appeared in his index search of Khalinaltani Ogadeinus. He'd learned the separatists, and indeed the Nivalinorhrans he'd encountered, referred to themselves as Khalinaltanists. And the world had been officially renamed Khalinorhnus.

Borinorhnus unaware of these startling developments.

Agar fiddled at the menu dispenser, as though deciding on a selection and changing his mind. In truth, he did not possess a valid account identity to activate the machine. His mind continued its fleeting eavesdropping as he pretended to study the menu.

"...But it appears they acquired the adaptation..."

"...The results are inconclusive..."

He returned to the small group three tables to his right. All seated instead of roosting, though all were Borinian. The director's aide among them. The aide's features considered handsome by Borinian standards, a strong square face, smooth prominences, round energetic eyes, and a long rounded snout featuring small symmetrically flared nostrils. A lush head of black hair flowed upward from the mid line of his forehead. His neck fur bright amber. His features had not gone noticed by the female sitting across from him. A portelier, revealed an errant thought, amid thoughts of her attraction and desire to mate with the aide.

"We have the coordinates and have scheduled a launch for the portal in the morning," the portelier conveyed to the aide, the thought intercepted by Agar.

The portelier's response triggered a memory in the aide's mind, an earlier conversation. "We have the coordinates of Khalinaltani's next rendezvous," the aide remembered. "A moon orbiting the third planet of the Burude System." An image of an office chamber and the science colony director floated into Agar's mind. A quiri! Nivalinorhnus's science colony director a quiri! Agar fled the aide's mind lest his astonishment betray his presence.

When Agar sidled up to the aide's mind again, the image of the quiri director and the office reformed in Agar's thoughts. He again tapped the memorized conversation. "We'll need to dispatch them immediately," the director advised. "Instruct them to wait at the rendezvous. Governor

Nakur just informed me of another infernal inspection. And so soon following the last one he believes the Borinorhnus Council is suspicious. He believes the real purpose of this inspector they've sent, a military officer this time, a Captain Commander, is to spy on our activities. We need to be especially careful while he is here, and the portelier ship must be off world and preferably through the portal before he departs."

Agar had the information he required. He prepared to withdraw from the aide's mind, cautiously, slipping away as though he'd never been there. On the threshold, he brushed another memory. A response to an inquiry from the director. Recalled now in response to a question from the portelier concerning communications.

"We'll be completely switched over by then. The last relay stations will be reconfigured by tomorrow night, and the new grid will be online by the time you rendezvous with Khalinaltani." A list of stations, and a timetable, impressed themselves on Agar's thoughts as he slipped from the aide's mind.

Agar released his taloned grasp, climbed to the floor and exited the room. But he didn't exit the building. He used the building's peculiar hybrid railway-escalator system to ferry him to the toilet chambers in the basement level. He waited in a private stall until his senses detected a sizable group departing the eatery.

Agar joined a line of fliers snaking through the night sky, heading in the direction of the residential complex. He lingered at the tail end of the line. Once out of the city, passing a small forested area, Agar slipped away from the fliers and landed on the branch of a fruit tree. Not unusual, even for one who'd just departed an eatery. Borinians still foraged at night, mostly for fruit. An ancestral trait. Now more of a social activity than a need to procure food.

The group moved on, dispersing into smaller groups of couples and individuals heading to their respective roosts. Agar resumed flight. Under cover of the trees he changed direction, heading north, his keen senses alert to any presence or movement around him. He circled and backtracked, alighting in forested areas to scan his surroundings, and the skies above. In open areas he flew close to the ground, or walked, after ensuring a clear sky above. Before first light of the dawning suns, his trail clear, he approached his secluded roost in the mountains. He scouted the perimeter before entering the cave. He checked his telltales and traps. Nothing had been disturbed during his absence.

Exhausted, he slept away the daylight hours.

Agar awoke before dusk. The paired suns low in the sky. He ate from the rations he'd carried in the fighter, while he ruminated on the information he'd gathered, and his next move. He'd learned the location of an impending information drop, where he hoped to intercept Khalinaltani Ogadeinus. He'd never heard of the Burude System. But he'd retrieved the portal frequency from the portelier, and rendezvous coordinates from the director's aide.

His first priority, to evade capture and escape Nivalinorhnus alive. Or all he'd learned would be lost. The information he'd uncovered vital to Borinorhnus. He'd prepared a plan in the event the authorities discovered his true mission and were searching for him. But he'd had to factor in the unexpected wrinkles. They didn't surprise or deter him. When had it not been the case on any mission?

The aide's memories had provided an opportunity to gain intelligence on Nivalinorhnus's communications. Information vital to General Zanth and Borinorhnus. It'd entail more time on Nivalinorhnus. Perhaps more than prudent. But worth the risk if his escape worked as planned.

Agar exited the cave as the suns commenced their slide toward the distant horizon. The equipment he required retrieved from the hidden fighter, and strapped to his chest. He flew southwest, following the setting suns, toward a communications relay station among the last to be reconfigured.

The primary yellow giant Orh, sank behind the distance peaks. Its pale red companion lagged behind, casting a dull red and purple glow over the landscape like a full moon. Until it too disappeared below the horizon, leaving a night sky as black as the depths of space.

Agar arrived at his destination as nightfall shrouded the forested mountaintop. He scouted the area, noting the telltale ultraviolet outlines of seismic, sonic, and motion detectors guarding the clearing around the remote antenna array.

Agar selected a hide providing the desired concealment, and waited.

Bright twinkling stars salted the black sky above. The constellations familiar to Agar. The paired suns and his home world invisible on the opposite side of the world. Nivalinorhnus's twin moons yet to rise.

His acute hearing detected it first, an air shuttle approaching from his right. The sound reached him before the glowing ultraviolet hues of its thrusters. The steeple shaped craft cleared the last ridge and crossed a tree-covered valley, racing toward his position.

Agar waited until the shuttle pierced the defensive perimeter around the relay station. As it hovered to land he slipped through the deactivated sensor net. He moved along the ground in a half crouch, wings folded against his sides. He'd chosen his spot beforehand, close to the station's access portal. Reaching the spot, he lay face down on the ground, wings spread wide on either side, his body part of the ground. Uncertain of his next move.

A technician, female, exited the shuttle. Another startling contrast to Borinorhnus, Agar noted. Nivalinorhran females, like the quiri, were more autonomous, independent. Employed in skilled occupations, and holding positions of authority.

The technician wore a control headcap, preventing Agar from reading the electronic key code her thoughts transmitted. Even if he had worn his headcap, he doubted it'd access the clandestine frequency Nivalinorhnus had adopted. And anyway, he'd avoid probing her thoughts, ensuring he remained undetected. Not just by her, but by the authorities. Any indication of his presence at the relay station negated his advantage. The Nivalinorhrans would simply change the configuration again. His only option, to breach the station undetected. A task he still had no idea how to accomplish, hoping his observations of the technician, and the station, might present a solution. He'd have to risk a brush pass at her thoughts. Insufficient to gather much information, merely a sense of her mental awareness and abilities, and perhaps a glimpse of something he might be able to use.

A portal hissed open in the side of the relay station. The technician disappeared inside. Agar waited.

His keen hearing detected the buzzing of insects around him, and their faint scratching as they crawled in the dirt around him and over his outstretched wings. He'd have to carefully groom his fur after this.

Agar sensed the technician's return. His mind reached out to lightly touch hers. She immediately sensed the intrusion. But Agar had already withdrawn, leaving her in doubt. Confused as to what, if anything, had just occurred. Perhaps nervous jitters from being alone on a mountaintop. Or perhaps a fleeting embodiment of the fanciful notion uppermost in her mind. A hopeful wish for the festival she planned to attend. A wish conveyed to Agar, providing his next move, and a change of plan.

As the shuttle hatch closed behind the technician, Agar scurried outside the perimeter before the craft lifted off and reactivated the sensors. He flew a long circuitous route to an area close to the festival ground, scheduled for later in the day. The detour partly to check his trail, but more importantly, enabling a necessary stop on a hilltop south of the destination, where he concealed the equipment he'd carried from the cave. He collected a pocketful of fruit before alighting on a perch among the trees, where he ate, and waited.

He pondered his experiences on Nivalinorhnus, all he had learned, and the ominous impact of his report to General Zanth.

Eclipse

The day dawned bright and clear. Orange and amber clouds floated across a mauve sky, dissipating as the suns rose higher. The sky turned a pale blue, promising a delightful day for the celebration. A festive day on both worlds, though Agar curious to observe how Nivalinorhrans marked the event. The crowd already gathering across the forested mountainside as Agar waited. The site a favored venue to observe and celebrate the eclipse. More Nivalinorhrans arrived as the hours passed and the suns rose in the sky. Many quiri among the spectators, their flight suits winging them from the city and outlying areas, lifting them into the treetops alongside their Borinian companions. Music filled the air, wafting across the valley on a warm breeze. Dancers twirled in the clearings, and in the sky.

The crowd as loud and celebratory as on Borinorhnus, but without the religious undertone and ritual. Rather, Agar noted, and as he'd glimpsed in the technician's mind, the festival a prime opportunity for coupling and mating. An opportunity Agar hoped to use to his advantage.

Males in the gathering crowd, anticipating receptive females, had dressed simply in one piece tunics and leggings. No chest coats or other outer coverings. The short skirted tunics colorful and festive. Females similarly attired, the decorative hems of their tunic skirts hiking up as they dove and hung head down from the branches. Their uncovered genitalia inviting.

Couples already paired off, flying into the valley and semi-privacy beneath the canopied tree cover. Unable to delay their frenzied desire. Others copulated in plain sight. The methods of coupling innovative, festive, carefree; distinct from the staid practices of Borinorhnus. Agar observed the cheerful couples in flight, the male hovering above the female, matching her flight path and speed. Their joyful clicking and chirping carried on the wind, invitation and acceptance. The male descending slowly, covering the female, their palms meeting, thumbs entwined. The male flat atop the female, his legs wrapped around hers as they fell through the sky together. Spreading their wings they soared together, as one, rolling into graceful, gliding turns on combined wings. Cheeks pressed together, the male entered his partner in flight, commencing a thrusting aerial ballet. The music echoing across the valley accompanied by excited chirps and cheeps from the air, and from beneath the canopied tree cover.

Agar's keen sense of smell guided his eyes, locating the communications technician as she alighted onto a branch on a tree to his left. The colorful ultraviolet markings and subtle hues he'd observed during nighttime now illuminated by Orh's brilliant light. Bright amber hair covered her head and ears. Her hair shaped to a point, like the front of a headcap, on her gently sloping forehead. Only the tips of her ears peeked through the long flowing tresses falling to her neck and shoulders. The narrow fur collar around her neck, thinner in females than males, a darker rust color.

She stood upright on the branch, unaccompanied, reminding Agar of the wish he'd glimpsed at the relay station. She observed the dancers, the games in play, the mothers carrying infants clinging to their fur, the couples mating in midair. Her gaze settled on the male dancers, tall, lithe and graceful. Taller than the average Borinorhran, Agar noted, their physical form more slender, their musculature more developed in Nivalinorhnus's higher gravity.

She'd changed from the utilitarian, or perhaps uniform, garments she'd worn the night before. The one-piece shirt and tool studded chest coat, replaced by a bright red and white short-skirted tunic.

Agar landed on an adjacent branch. He surveyed the dancers in the clearings below, and the revelers in the surrounding trees. He feigned the motions of plunging off again, hesitated, paused, his nostrils subtly testing the air around him. He relaxed, closed his wings, turned to the technician. A pleasant rhythmic humming, like a cat's purring, emanated from him.

"Good fortune to you," the thought touched his mind in acceptance of his invitation. Agar was an experienced infiltrator, capable of adapting quickly, as he did now to Nivalinorhran customs. His instincts and observations informed him Nivalinorhrans did not enter each other's minds uninvited. Her greeting an invitation, confirmed by the subtle pheromone scent reaching his nostrils.

"You are not participating?" Agar thought, hopping the short distance to the branch she occupied.

"I prefer to watch." Large liquid eyes turned to gaze at him. The allure of her pheromones stronger as he stood next to her.

"May I share watching with you?" Agar thought. "I am Jiraninogul Chilkikunus, of the military colony. It is an honor and pleasure to meet you."

"The honor and pleasure is mutual Jiraninogul. I am Khulaninchirina of the science colony. You are from off world? We are not as formal in our names here."

"Yes. I am stationed at the base on Bagatur. Visiting the city on a short leave."

"You are a spacer then?" The excitement of meeting a spacer reflected in her pleasant clicking and dark animated eyes. "I have always wanted to travel off world."

"But you are off world. This is not the home planet."

"It is mine. I am Khalinorhran. Born and raised. I have not travelled beyond this world. But I am training for the Porteliers. I am a communications technician."

"I would not wish to dissuade you Khulan, but I do not find space travel a pleasant experience. I cannot wait to return to solid ground below my feet and open sky above."

"I have heard such thoughts from others. And none have dissuaded me. I still wish to experience it for myself. It is not the space travel, But the discoveries awaiting out there."

"The mind of a true explorer," Agar thought, accompanied by amused chirping.

The boisterous celebration fell in volume. Agar sensed the sky darkening. They both gazed skyward as an expectant hush befell the crowd. Orh's small red mate drifted across Orh's face, creating a crescent shape of the primary star. The sky darkened further. The silence of the crowd like an anticipatory lull, the low rumbling of a volcano before the sudden eruption. The small red star slid before its mate, creating a dark circle in Orh's center, and a circular ring of resplendent gold. The crowd erupted.

Agar's thoughts to Khulan suggested not the Borinorhran ritual of death and rebirth, but the sexual coupling of the paired stars. The prevalent theme among the gathered celebrants, including Khulan. It provoked the response he'd hoped for.

Khulan opened her wings, her head moving close to Agar's. She sniffed him. Agar's thoughts receptive to her advance. He followed her lead. She leaned in closer, nuzzled Agar's neck fur, sniffed his neck and face. Agar responded, his head next to hers, sniffing her face, her fur, her skin. He spread his wings. Their palms met, thumbs curled around each other's. Cheeks pressed together, their individual scents stimulating the other, they dove head first from the branch. Their combined wings lifted them as one. Khulan wrapped her legs around Agar's as they soared. They flew as one, spiraling, diving, soaring, spinning in the air to alternate who lay on top and on bottom. The flutter of wings vibrated in the air around them.

Beneath the darkened sky they dove toward the trees in the valley. Alighting onto a branch, they sank their talons. Hanging head down they wrapped their wings around each other, sniffing, licking, nipping each other's skin and fur. Their minds mingled. Their thoughts entwined.

Agar unhooked the straps holding the crotch flap of his chest coat. He opened the seam of his leggings to expose his erection. He untied the skirt of Khulan's tunic. The material between her legs fell away, exposing her crotch. The tunic's skirt fell downward over her inverted torso. Khulan's strong, pungent scent tickled his flared nostrils.

Agar positioned himself behind her, his face nuzzled against hers, cheek to cheek. The thumb of both hands gripped her fur. He pushed his erection into her soft opening. A series of elongated clicks escaped Khulan's open mouth, accompanied by loud cheeping from Agar as the initial sensation rushed through him. He thrust into her. Back and forth. Khulan responded by thrusting back against him, until they settled into a rhythm, forward and backward. Khulan bent upward from the waist, raising her head to her crotch and the thrusting organ between her legs. She leaned forward, Her tongue reached out to curl around Agar's thrusting penis, licking as it slid in and out of her, lubricating it, prolonging their coupling. The sensation produced a long string of pleasurable clicks from Agar. Khulan fell back, hanging head down again, emitting her own pleasured cheeping as her muscles spasmed and grasped and squeezed, milking the appendage inside her of its life giving fluid.

The couple hung beneath the branch in a post coital embrace, licking and grooming each other. Bodies and minds entwined. Khulan unaware how deeply Agar's had delved into hers. Not the first time Agar had used seduction as a tool, or a weapon. The experience usually a detached physical act. Agar to his surprise, had enjoyed the coupling. Had delighted in the sensual eroticism of their coupled bodies and minds, each experiencing the other physically, and in their thoughts.

Neither concerned by the risk of impregnation. Agar aware Khulan had not been seeking a long term mate, but the pleasure of coupling during the festive atmosphere of the eclipse. And Khulan, like all Borinian females, controlled reproduction, possessing the ability to postpone or prevent fertilization until a time of her choosing. An adaptive genetic trait of Borinian females, though whose lineage inheritance and social status flowed.

Agar and Khulan spent the remainder of the day together. Agar not only needed to kill time, but he discovered an enjoyment in her company, a rare occurrence. They parted at twilight, following a long nuzzling embrace. Khulan to her roost in the city to prepare for her work shift. Agar to his lair in the northern mountains. Enroute he stole a flyer from among a stack piled at the foot of a large tree. He flew on, having acquired the information he'd been seeking.

At midnight, Agar prepared to depart Nivalinorhnus. He did not underestimate the danger. The authorities had not reacquired him on the surface. Their last option would be to intercept him in the air attempting to escape the planet. Planetary defenses were undoubtedly on alert and scanning for him. He did not rule out a blockade to prevent his ship returning for him. Agar reasoned their objective would be to capture him for interrogation, but failing to accomplish it, and to prevent him reporting to Borinorhnus, they'd blow him out of the sky, or blast him into cosmic dust in space.

Agar lay prone in the fighter, on his stomach, the normal flight position, sealed into the combination escape pod and environmental suit. His arms tucked against his sides, his fingers closed, his wings wrapped around him like a blanket. The suit pod enclosed him like a cocoon.

Agar maneuvered the fighter to the mouth of the cave, his commands relayed through the headcap to the suit, and through the suit's command link to the fighter's controls. At the mouth of the cave, he waited.

When the timer wound down, the portable transmitter he'd hidden on the mountaintop broadcast its signal. A long burst on a standard military frequency contained encrypted instructions for a rendezvous. Hidden within the transmission a shorter burst, using a personal encryption known only to the commander on the cruiser. Agar's personal cipher. Like any code employed by Agar, used once and discarded.

Agar estimated the time required for Nivalinorhnus Defense to intercept the transmission and dispatch units to its point of origin, and to the rendezvous the signal indicated. Planetary defenses armed and targeted. The blockading ships deployed into position to intercept.

Agar lifted off in the fighter and rocketed away from the surface. He experienced the tug of gravitational and acceleration forces as the suit's internal compensators lagged behind the fighter's tremendous speed. The forces disappeared in moments as the fighter transitioned to space, its velocity ripping it free of the planet's gravity, hurtling it across the void toward the moon. He had instructed the cruiser to break moon orbit and set a course for the portal at full velocity.

His instruments remained clear. No pursuit. No missiles or satellites tracking him. But only a matter of time. By now they'd discovered the ruse, the misdirect, and were busy acquiring his fighter and retargeting.

An echo in his brain from ahead. He focused on the images streaming into his mind. As detailed as the sonic echoes he used in navigating terrestrial terrain. In his mind, the trajectories of the cruiser and fighter rapidly converged.

An energy blast blossomed behind him, quickly dissipating on his sensors. His pursuers not yet in range. The reading not a pursuing missile. An electromagnetic charge. Designed to render the fighter dead in space. His assumption regarding capture correct.

Agar extended the fighter's roosting hook. Moments now. The hulking outline of the cruiser like a hurtling asteroid, growing larger in his mind. The fighter approached it from behind and below. The cruiser matched Agar's speed as he lined up the roost ring hanging in space from the cruiser's belly.

Another energy spike from aft. This time a missile. Long range, tracking, and closing fast. But at the cruiser's current velocity it'd outrun the missile. The fighter's hook clamped onto the cruiser's roost ring, the grasp locked and secure. Agar shut down the fighter's engines. Thrusters stabilized the fighter in a nose down position below the cruiser as the coupled crafts charged toward the suns and the portal. The missile's fuel expended, it fell behind. The cruiser's roost ring retracted, drawing the fighter into the hanger, where it hung nose down, the roosting position, among a dozen other fighters.

"Welcome back Commander. Hanger sealed and pressurized. Portal in twelve hours. Pursuit craft breaking off."

Agar acknowledged the transmission. He was clear. Despite the distance to the portal, and the presence of Nivalinorhran ships transiting to and from it, the cruiser now travelled in open space. To attack it meant Nivalinorhnus exposing its hand, and committing an act of treason in the eyes of Borinorhnus. Agar unsealed the suit pod, opened the fighter's nose, and plunged headfirst into the dark hanger. He spread his wings and soared for the exit hatch at the top of the hanger. Outside the hatch he grasped a waiting rail and rode it through the artificial tunnels of the cavernous ship to the bridge.

He roosted at his station, his command headcap affixed on his head.

"Navigator, input this destination frequency for transiting the portal," Agar relayed through the headcap com.

"Coms, I need a secure frequency to General Zanth."

Agar received their thoughts acknowledging his orders.

Agar organized his thoughts in the moments required to locate General Zanth. His report would be unwelcome news. His observations on Nivalinorhnus confirmed not merely a separatist movement, but a world and a society already fissioning. Already separate in form and function, if not in deed.

"Your channel is secure Commander," the com officer informed Agar. "And the General Supreme is standing by."

General Zanth's image and thoughts appeared in Agar mind simultaneously.

"Captain Commander. It is an honor and delight. I had thought to worry."

Agar mentally checked the com link before responding. The channel isolated, bypassing the com station's headcap and streaming directly to Agar's mind.

"Yet still among the living general, with a bit of good fortune."

"Pleased to hear it. And your report?"

"It is not at all pleasant. Worse than we had expected."

"Give me your thoughts Agar."

"The situation is indeed more than a collection of dissident separatists general. I can confirm Nivalinorhnus is the center of the separatist movement, including the civil and military colonies. The current governor and general commander may be matrilineally related. I am sending you the particulars. The culture has diverged significantly from Borinorhnus. The inhabitants have renamed the planet

Khalinorhnus, and refer to themselves as Khalinaltanists, followers of the teachings of Khalinaltani Ogadeinus. Quiri and Borinians coexist and associate freely in this culture."

Though unable to pry beneath the general's thoughts given the distance and communication via headcap, Agar was sufficiently astute to perceive the subtle shift in Zanth's mood upon receiving the news. The burdened nature of his thoughts.

"I see." A morose irritability accompanied Zanth's thoughts. "And what have you discovered regarding this Khalinaltani Ogadeinus?"

"I have a lead on his whereabouts. I am departing the system in hopes of intercepting him."

"And what then?"

"Uncertain at the moment general. Our options are narrowing. I am certain military action to reclaim Nivalinorhnus will be resisted. I received a briefing on the current status of the garrison, but I am certain it was manipulated for my benefit. The authorities on Nivalinorhnus were suspicious of my presence prior to my arrival. They allowed me to see only such things as they wished me to see. Two items of significance however. The Khalinorhnus have reconfigured their communications net. They are using a frequency band we do not possess and the technology is not one we currently utilize. But I've obtained a partial schematic. Perhaps our engineers will be able to duplicate the technology. Until they do, Borinorhnus is shut out of Nivalinorhnus communications."

"And the other?"

"Following this communication I will record and transmit all I have seen and learned before we transit the portal. You will be able to study the details in my full report.

But for now, as I indicated, I believe the report I received at the garrison had been tailored for my benefit, as I suspect all the reports transmitted to Borinorhnus for some time have been. Both civil and military. It is my belief based on my own observations, and surface and orbital scans, Nivalinorhnus's military posture is not indicative of a homeworld garrison, but is configured for defense against an attack, and for counterattack. The only potential adversary requiring such a posture is Borinorhnus."

"In Orh's name Agar."

"Indeed general. As I indicated, the options are narrowing. Having failed to detain me or ascertain what I have learned, they must assume I have reported to you and will reconfigure and reposition their defenses. And there is the matter of sympathizers on Borinorhnus. Perhaps large groups among whom the Khalinorhrans undoubtedly have informants. You will not have the element of surprise general. Military action to prevent fission will entail a great deal of bloodshed."

General Zanth's silence spoke volumes. Agar did not envy Zanth's position. The decisions he had before him weighed heavily on him. But Agar had his own immediate concerns. A full report to record for General Zanth. A decision and plan of action regarding Khalinaltani Ogadeinus. And the portal, it's effects already registering on the cruiser's instruments. A thing he detested. Unnatural. Once past the threshold, he's have to endure the unsettling sensation of hitting a wall at full velocity, and the equally discomforting sensation of being held in place while an alien device devoured and digested the ship and its crew, regurgitating it out the other end. Hours yet before transit, but the mere thought of it, and the anticipatory wait, only heightened Agar's displeasure.

"We are approaching the portal's gravity well general. I must prepare my report before we are ready to transit."

"Understood Agar. I wish you good fortune on your journey and your decisions. You are aware of the stakes."

"Indeed." Agar possessed no clear certainty regarding the correct course of action. And once through the portal, circumstances dictated he'd remain uncertain until the moment he encountered Khalinaltani Ogadeinus, the moment of decision. The explosive in place. The fuse already set. One individual the key to defusing it, or detonating it. And Agar had no way of determining before hand, which outcome Khalinaltani's death, or survival, might ensure.

Krilan

The sun's bright rays slanted through Dauphin's ports, brightening the ship's interior. No need for artificial lighting, except in the enclosed spaces lacking ports. The light streaming into Seraphina's cabin woke her. She swung her legs over the side of the berth, stretched, and yawned. By habit she strode naked to the head and shower, undeterred by Ezekiel's presence on board.

Seraphina used the head but did not shower. Still naked, she unsealed the starboard hatch and stepped out onto the sandy soil. She'd set Dauphin down in an open area of short sand grasses, and felled branches from palm-like trees ringing the shoreline. A long low sand dune separated the landing spot from the softer powdery sand of the beach. The splash of surf reached her ears. The fresh scent of salt-laden air touched her nostrils.

She scaled the dune, heading for the surf. Ezekiel stood at the shoreline. A solitary figure staring out across the turquoise lagoon enclosed in a horseshoe shaped bay. He wore the simple single-piece tunic she'd first seen in the shower compartment after he'd removed the stiff outer suit. The light garment easy to don and remove, as comfortable and usual to him aboard ship as her nakedness to her. Seraphina stood behind him, not wishing to startle him, or disturb the reverent awe in which he contemplated the scene before him.

"It is called ocean," she said in a soft voice.

He turned to face her. His smile wide and radiant and joyous. His shining grey eyes expressed his wonder. Her nakedness around him by now unremarkable. Customary and usual, no longer evoking his curiosity. If it ever had.

"This, where you are standing, is called beach," she said, digging her toes into the soft sand.

Ezekiel's curiosity not as dormant as Seraphina supposed. Her naked body never failed to provoke an hormonal surge within him, an involuntary flush of heat through his blood. But he had grown accustomed to her wandering the ship without garments.

"I have known ocean before. From worlds I've scouted. But not close like this."

"Need to get closer," she said, her smile teasing as she swept past him, ran through the surf, and plunged into the water.

She surfaced beyond small breakers close to the shore. Water streamed in sparkling droplets from her slick, shiny hair. Her arm waved at him, beckoning Ezekiel to follow.

Ezekiel paused at the water's edge. Curious and apprehensive. The surf washed over his bare feet and ankles, sinking them beneath the sand. The sensation tickling and pleasant. The temperature warm, like the water in Dauphin's wet shower. He stepped farther, the water around his calves, still enjoying the pleasant sensation. He bent at the waist, placed his palms flat against the surface. Sunk them to his elbows, circling his arms, swirling the clear water around him.

Concentrating on his exploration, Ezekiel failed to notice Seraphina gliding toward him. Until she grabbed hold of both his arms and tugged him off his feet. He splashed face first into the water. The unexpected submersion an initial shock, forcing him to inhale. His brain immediately closed his air passages in reflexive defense, but not before he'd swallowed a quantity of the briny water.

Ezekiel reared above the surface, sputtering and coughing. A salty taste in his mouth. A burning in his eyes. Seraphina's hearty laughter in his ears. But concern in her eyes as she gently wiped the sides of his face. Seraphina untied the tunic's fastening around Ezekiel's waist. Pulled the material from between his legs and lifted the soaked garment above his head. She bundled it and tossed it onto the sand. Taking his hand in hers, she led him deeper into the water.

Seraphina halted when the water reached her chest, sandy bottom firm beneath their feet. She had no idea if Ezekiel knew how to swim. She doubted it, based on the dunking.

"Swim?" she said, her brown eyes lively and playful. Their color changeable in the shifting sunlight, from a yellowish fawn to dark reddish umber. "Ezekiel swim?" she repeated.

The word new to Ezekiel. They'd progressed in their ability to communicate. Each possessed a rudimentary understanding of the other's language. Aided by their occasional mind links. But both preferred only minimal use of the headcaps.

Observing Ezekiel's perplexed expression, Seraphina eased her body lower into the water. She raised her feet and drifted away from him. She turned, stroked and kicked, her profile low in the water. As lithe as an eel. She dove beneath the surface, turned, and glided back to him, surfacing in the spot she'd vacated moments before, her sleek hair plastered against her head and shoulders.

"Swim," she said.

Ezekiel smiled his understanding, while shaking his head. He did not swim. Yet he mimicked her previous actions, lowering his torso into the water and kicking off from the sandy bottom. His strokes awkward and ineffective. But he managed to remain afloat, and did not swallow any more water. He ducked below the surface, not swimming underwater as Seraphina had, but spinning in place, his arms spread wide on either side, his cheeks puffed from the effort to hold his breath. He placed his feet on the sand and stood, surfacing next to her. Seraphina laughed in pleasant abandon at his side.

Her laughter like the tinkling chimes of small bells. Infectious. Eliciting his own to accompany hers. The sound of her laughter produced a joy in him. He desired hearing it. Welcomed it. Even if he seldom understood what provoked it.

The sensation of immersing himself in the ocean new to him. A delight. Like the many other new experiences Seraphina had introduced him to. The water tickled and soothed his skin. Enveloped him like a warm cocoon. Flowed through his streaming hair like a liquid comb.

The sensation remained long after he and Seraphina departed the beach, all through the morning meal, and during their maintenance chores aboard Dauphin. A rejuvenating freshness which lingered long after leaving the water.

In mid afternoon Seraphina approached Ezekiel carrying both headcaps. She donned the cap modified to control her ship. Handed Ezekiel the other.

"I want to fly the scout," she said as Ezekiel fitted the cap to his head. "I want you to teach me." Spoken words accompanied her thoughts, Seraphina unable to break the habit of speaking aloud while conversing mind to mind.

Ezekiel's answering smile produced a warm flush inside her, a smile of her own. Seraphina still not entirely comfortable in the mind link, but it no longer abhorred her. Ezekiel's the only other mind in hers, allowing her to understand him, where he came from, his life before. Enslaved. As she had been. She now understood his reaction to the livestock pens on Ecibor. The link drew her closer to him. Even if they'd been able to speak the other's language fluently, the link conveyed insights language alone did not. Raw images and memories shared. His as a child. His captivity. His training for military and space service. His experiences as a scout and 'checker', the term for a clicker spy deployed on Human worlds prior to a hunt. And his absolute servitude to the clickers, the masters. But while Ezekiel shared his past, Seraphina kept the doors to hers securely locked.

The little scout sat in a corner of the hold, squatting on long flat ski-like runners on either side. The runners attached to stout retractable struts. When retracted the runners merged into the smooth sides of the scout without discernible seams.

During a maintenance check after Seraphina had installed the viewport, Ezekiel had demonstrated how to power up the pod and its drive. He'd deployed the landing struts, prior to which the scout had simply nestled on its belly in the hold. He'd shown Seraphina how the pod maneuvered along the ground on a cushion of compressed air expelled beneath the runners. And he'd demonstrated the maneuvering thrusters ringing the drive nozzle in the tail, producing directional steering from the rear, like a rudder.

They headed toward the scout. Seraphina's building excitement touched Ezekiel's mind through the link.

"Seraphina wait," he thought.

"What?"

"Power up Dauphin's command link."

"Why do we need...?"

"You see why," Ezekiel's thought interrupted her.

Seraphina stepped over to the hold's command console and complied. Poised to open the rear ramp she heard his thoughts in her mind.

"Think it."

Seraphina smiled. "I forget sometimes," she thought and said.

She thought of opening Dauphin's rear ramp. The result a pneumatic hiss as pistoned arms lowered the ramp. Sunlight bathed the hold's interior.

They entered the scout through its dorsal hatch, one after the other. Seraphina first, assuming the pilot seat. Ezekiel followed, scrunching his frame into the opening between the cockpit and sensor compartment behind the pilot.

Ezekiel heard her thoughts, bewildered by the lack of physical controls. Only instruments on the panel before her.

"Think of power," she heard Ezekiel in her mind.

She did as instructed. The instruments blossomed into life. She heard the faint whine of the drive spooling up.

"Now think secondary connect and think this frequency." The digits streamed into her head.

Again she complied as instructed.

"You now have command of both ships," Ezekiel's thoughts said. "Now you must clear your mind. I will pilot the scout to the beach. You can fly from there. And you must see images in your mind Seraphina. The scout is clicker and does not understand language. Your mind must picture what you want to do as you do with Dauphin."

Seraphina nodded. She heard the sudden burst of pressurized air. Sensed the scout rising. Confirmed by the view beyond the new port. The little scout rose from the deck. It moved toward the center of the hold. The transparent nose turned. Dauphin's hold pivoted to the left until the open ramp slid into view. The pod moved forward, exiting the hold into bright afternoon sunlight. A swirl of sand kicked at its sides as the craft glided smoothly across the ground, skirted the dune, and hovered at the water's edge.

Another sound reached Seraphina's ears. She peered out the viewport and aft, toward the sound's origin. Observed in excited wonder the scout's wings unfolding. Section after section telescoped out, until the wingspan on either side stretched four times the length of the scout.

Ezekiel's thoughts reentered her mind.

"The screen in the center. How the clickers see and navigate, by sound echoes."

Seraphina stared at the lines on the screen. It depicted a detailed outline of the surrounding terrain, including the ocean, its depth, even the underwater topography.

"The next one on the right, the visual scanner. Since mostly my kind fly the scouts, it is set for our visual spectrum. But can also see in infrared and ultraviolet. The clickers also see in ultraviolet."

The screen's image familiar to Seraphina. Like the visual scanner in Dauphin's cockpit.

"The one on the left show energy and fuel reserves. See the blue line rising, energy from solar collectors in the wings.

Like Dauphin's wings. And in space like dauphin too, indicating solar wind."

Seraphina's initial discomfort at the absence of physical controls diminished as her familiarity with the instruments increased. Clicker technology surprisingly similar to the factions. A prospect she'd never imagined. Her experienced eyes recognized the instruments and their depicted information even before Ezekiel explained them.

Ezekiel aware of her increasing comfort as her thoughts mingled with his through the link. Seraphina distractedly unaware of the leakage, or not caring. While Ezekiel was careful to prevent his streaming thoughts from crowding hers.

"Remember, only pictures in your mind. Picture the drive and amount of thrust. See it only to here," Ezekiel thought in Seraphina's mind, indicating a mark on the thrust meter. "See skimming over the water. Then see flight. The scout will adjust the wings to allow flight. You ready?"

Seraphina nodded, twisting her head around to offer Ezekiel a smile.

The pod had been hovering over the sand. Seraphina pictured skimming over the water, visualized the drive and a moderate amount of thrust. The sudden forward motion pushed her back into the seat as the green lagoon rushed beneath the scout.

"Whoa," the involuntary exclamation escaped her lips as the pod sped toward the mouth of the bay.

Seraphina glanced down at the thrust meter, visualizing the mark Ezekiel had indicated. The drive responded immediately, its low hum pitching higher as it pushed the pod faster across the bay, a curtain of spray arching along its sides. Seraphina imagined the scout taking flight. The response slower this time as the craft adjusted the angle of its wings and sought the lift it required.

The ocean racing past below receded as the scout climbed through the air.

"Wazowee," Seraphina shouted, a joyful grin plastered on her face. The scout rose at a steady pace toward cotton white clouds scattered across the bright sky.

"Picture runners retracted," Ezekiel's thought surfaced in her mind like a lapsed memory.

Seraphina sensed the reduced drag as the runners retracted into the scout's belly. The hull now a smooth sleek shell racing through the sky. Seraphina also in her element. She mentally adjusted the thrust and pictured a left turn. The scout dipped its left wing, arched its right, and banked. A short burst of maneuvering thrusters turned the nose in the desired direction. Seraphina repeated the maneuver in the opposite direction. The smile on her face grew wider, ending in a happy, satisfied grin.

Seraphina leveled the scout below the clouds. She turned in the direction of their isolated island, the long strip of land visible through the view port, surrounded by a vast ocean stretching to the horizon in every direction. She flew across its narrow width, banked, and turned, circling it. Her confidence increased as her 'feel' for the little scout grew stronger.

"Can we fly it into orbit?"

"I am not certain. I do not know if the port can withstand the heat."

"It is the same material as the ports on Dauphin. It is structured for the heat."

"Then you must set thrust power here," indicating a mark on the thrust meter. "And you must see orbiting the world."

"I just want a low orbit. Not too far."

"Then see that."

"What of pressurization, and breathable air?"

"The pod does the adjustments by itself. Or it will abort if there is a malfunction. It is the same with all clicker ships. You only have to image what you want it to do, where you want it to go."

Seraphina did. Observed the thrust indicator increasing toward the mark Ezekiel had indicated. The sudden acceleration again pushed her back into the seat. The nose of the scout pointed at the sky and the tiny craft shot past the layer of clouds. She sensed a slowing of their ascent. Glanced at the panel. Noted the shifting energy readings and the stalled thrust indicator. The energy readings a result of the wings reconfiguring. Sections retracted, folding into each other like the telescoping sections of Ezekiel's lance. The sections closest to the hull retracted into their recess, until delta wings formed on either sides.

Seraphina smiled. Just like her Dauphin. A kick in her stomach as the thrust surged. The indicator moved rapidly toward the mark. The drive rocketed the pod up through the clear sky, the gravitational forces dissipating as compensators kicked in. The sky ahead shifted hues. Lighter. Darker. Merging to complete black.

"Thrust off," said Ezekiel's thoughts in her mind. But Seraphina ahead of him. Already throttling back in her mind, shutting down the drive as the scout settled into low orbit around Krilan.

The world below filled the viewport. An immense green blue and white panorama. The scout crossed the terminator, passing into night. The northern continent dark, except for scattered clusters of twinkling lights.

Ezekiel unable to contain his wonder. His emotional thrill at the sight beyond the viewport flowed freely into Seraphina's mind.

"It is wonderful," she concurred.

"It is not only that. This thing you have done Seraphina. I have travelled to many places of space, to many worlds in this scout and others like it. And never have I been able to see outside like this. No clicker ships have such transparent ports. Never have I seen space or a world from inside the scout, or from any clicker ship. Never imagined it until I came aboard Dauphin. And now from the scout. It is more than wonderful Seraphina. And you made it so."

The sentiment, unreservedly sincere, and intimately immediate when experienced directly in her thoughts as words alone could never express, produced an endearing warmth within her. The emotion overwhelmed her, encompassed her being. She did not deny it, or resist it. Its raw impact stirred a fervent desire in her, like a flame burning her up inside.

The scout circled the world. Their thoughts silent except for the awe and wonder they shared in each other's mind. As the scout crossed into daylight Seraphina scanned the instrument console. The echoscans unable to penetrate beyond the upper layers of the atmosphere. The pulses scattered and dissipated. The instrument depicted only the outer layer and the space surrounding them. But the visual scans imaged the surface, revealing the scattered islands dotting the southern hemisphere.

Seraphina pictured their island destination. Pictured the drive and thrust meter. Imagined a turn to line up the drive. The scout responded to her mind as sweetly and smoothly as though it were her own body.

The braking thrust decelerated the scout from its orbit. The pod plunged into the atmosphere like a small flaming meteor. It transitioned to atmospheric flight in the stratosphere. Slowed and extended its wings in the troposphere. It settled gently on a cushion of air onto the island. Seraphina comfortable enough piloting it to ease it into Dauphin's hold. Her exhilaration unfettered and boundless.

After nightfall, Seraphina and Ezekiel ate outside in the cool night air below Dauphin's folded starboard wing. A small campfire crackled and blazed, spreading a small circle of light and heat. Seraphina snuggled against Ezekiel. The action normal and unconscious. The fire's warm glow merged with the lingering glow of Ezekiel's appreciation, and the afterglow of her flight in the scout. The ember inside her reignited, feeding the unfamiliar desire growing within her since she'd first laid eyes on Ezekiel.

She reached up to cup Ezekiel's face in her hands. She drew it close until her lips met his. The touch of his lips set the fire inside her raging, sent a hot wave surging through her blood.

Seraphina's actions surprised Ezekiel. The peculiar touching of their mouths. But he didn't resist. Another new experience she wanted to show him. Her mouth opened, parting his lips. Her tongue pushed into his open mouth. Flicked against his tongue. Ezekiel tasted her, as he had the fruit and other foods she'd introduced him to. The sensation pleasant, arousing, driving a desire he did not understand. And an urgent stirring between his legs.

Seraphina reached beneath Ezekiel's tunic. Her grasp accelerated his swelling hardness. Ezekiel broke the contact of their mouths.

"You wish to mate?"

Seraphina's response a shushing sound. A finger placed across his mouth. She reached for the ties of the tunic she'd washed and dried earlier in the day. Pulled the garment off him and tossed it aside. She proceeded slowly, wanting to get it right. A first for her too. Her experience had always been forced. Had been rough and painful, brutal and quick. An enslaved vessel for the entertainment of men. The only sexual pleasure she'd ever experienced had been with another woman. The woman had devoted time to the activity, a slow touching and licking, a gentle pressure in places which had aroused autonomic responses in Seraphina. Sensations she had never experienced before. Or imagined her body capable of.

Now she did the same to Ezekiel. Recalling the experience. Kissing his eyes, his nose, his mouth. Bending to kiss the rigid erection between his legs. The remembered unpleasantness of the act absent, her actions under her control, not someone else's. Her mouth enclosed it. Her lips stroked it. She drew her tongue across his stomach, his torso, his chest. She nipped at his nipples, his lips, his ears.

Seraphina lifted the short simple dress resembling Ezekiel's tunic over her head and tossed it atop the discarded tunic. Her mouth returned to its slow roaming kissing and licking, imitating the performance held in her memory.

Ezekiel's soft moaning and gasping inhalations encouraged her. And pleased her. Her actions correct. Eliciting pleasure in him, as it had in her. She pulled his head to her bare chest. Ezekiel imitated her roaming kisses, as she'd hoped.

Ezekiel burned in the heat of desire. Unaware of its meaning, but surrendering to the sensation. He followed Seraphina's example, kissing and licking. His touch soft and gentle. He nipped at her brown erect nipples, as she had his. A soft moan escaped her throat. He licked and suckled. Moved to her stomach, and lower, to the triangular patch of soft fur above her female opening. When his mouth pressed against the soft lips, Seraphina moaned again, longer and louder than before. Deep and guttural. Her hands wrapped around his head, fingers entwined in his long flowing hair. She held him there. Opened her legs and rubbed herself against his mouth.

Ezekiel had wanted to taste her. Had opened his mouth and licked the soft, moist, curled lips, slipping his tongue inside her, slurping her like another newly discovered succulent fruit. He tasted the tangy saltiness of her secreted juice. Her sudden gasping cries surprised him. Perhaps he should stop. But she held him hard against her, rubbing herself against his open mouth, not wanting him to stop.

Seraphina gasped for breath. The heat rose in her. Engulfed her. Consumed her. She writhed against Ezekiel's mouth. His tongue licked and tasted her. When his tongue slid inside her an uncontrollable wave of sensation flooded her, mounting, growing, stronger, more urgent with each flick of his tongue. Until they overwhelmed her. She shuddered and spasmed. Her mouth open. Her breathing ragged. She rode the flood until they subsided, leaving her wasted, and glowing inside.

Seraphina shifted position. Her palms pushed Ezekiel flat against the ground. She did not want to be in the customary positions she remembered while being raped. She climbed atop Ezekiel, straddled him, her knees sinking into the soft sand on either side of him. She reached for his erection. Guided it inside her. She gasped at the fullness sliding into her. She'd expected it. But the sweet sensation unlike anything in her memory, as if experiencing sex for the first time. Her experience of other men an aberration, having nothing in common with the sensations coursing through her now.

A loud moan escaped Ezekiel's lips as a soft slippery velvet glove enclosed him, sliding along his throbbing phallus. Ezekiel uncertain what Seraphina expected of him. But aware he and Seraphina were mating. A mating unlike any he'd ever experienced. As before, he followed her example.

In the dim firelight, he gazed up at Seraphina straddled atop him. His stiff appendage buried inside her. Her head thrown back. Her eyes closed. Her mouth open. Soft humming sounds emanated from her throat. Her thick dark hair bounced on her forehead and shoulders, brushing against his face and cheeks, in harmony to the bouncing mounds on her chest, the hard dark nipples also occasionally brushing his cheek. He captured a nipple in his mouth. Suckled. The taste salty on his tongue. The action produced a soft cry from Seraphina. But Ezekiel now aware the sound arose from her pleasure.

She moved up and down astride him. The motion sliding him in and out. An aspect of mating familiar to him. The back and forth thrusting in the fenori. Though he had never experienced it in this position. He lifted his hips and thrust in rhythm to Seraphina's bouncing motion. The increased friction stoked a fire in his veins, and drove him to the peak.

Ezekiel's sudden thrusting intensified the sensations consuming Seraphina. From the electric tingling in her pelvis, to the surge along her spine, to the exquisite explosion in her brain. A primal state she surrendered to, abandoning control to the autonomous responses of her body. Nerve endings fired, muscles spasmed, involuntary cries escaped her lips. Until a shuddering, ecstatic release swept through her.

Ezekiel too cried out as Seraphina's internal spasms massaged his swollen, sensitive glans. His hands clasped her shoulders in Borinian fashion as his groin tightened and arched, forcing him deeper into her, propelling him over the edge to his own shuddering, trembling release.

Seraphina fell against him. Her skin moist and slick. The heat of their combined exertion greater than the dwindling fire before them. A combined pounding in their chests. They lay unmoving, Seraphina's arms folded on Ezekiel's chest, her head next to his, Ezekiel's arms wrapped around her shoulders.

Until restful sleep enveloped them both.

Burude

Free of the portal's gravitational tug, Khal examined his flight trajectory. He compensated for the minor slippage produced by the star's gravitational influence. His piloting skills proficient, given the enormous amount of time he'd spent in space. But Khal did not consider himself a natural, possessing the innate sense. Rather he placed heavy reliance on the craft's instruments.

Those instruments now increasingly erratic and unreliable. Their sudden random winking scintillation, the fluctuations in stellar wind density, and the shock waves impacting the ship, indicated an intensifying storm.

Khal deactivated the ship's solar wind collectors and generators. Under power the ship generated a small magnetic field, insufficient to protect it and its occupant. Khal increased the field output and increased power to the ship's four drives, hoping to put as much distance as possible, as quickly as possible, between his ship and the star. The storm's effects spanned the entire stellar system, but the farther away from the coronal ejections, the better off he'd be.

The portal's orbit around the disquieted star had placed Khal on the near side to intercept the third of five planets in the system, the location of his expected rendezvous. The massive planet and its largest moon offered some protection from the storm.

The news he'd received over the years informed him of the new thinking his discoveries and reports had encouraged. Particularly among scientists and historians. It had spawned an awakening, a positive development in Khal's opinion. And a movement, the Khalinaltanists, in his opinion an unwarranted, undesired approbation. He supported the cause, but he considered himself neither a founding father nor a messiah. The movement had since grown into a separatist collective on Nivalinorhnus. He held no opinion on that. Except a foreboding regarding its political implications.

The ship's sensors continued their erratic attempts to process data on the approaching planet. To the naked eye it appeared as a small speck, like a star in the night sky. Eight times the circumference of Nivalinorhnus, and a hundred times its mass. Its vaporous surface shrouded beneath a thick atmosphere of deadly gasses.

While the ship devoured the diminishing distance to his destination, Khal contemplated again the ramifications of his discoveries. The unwitting role he'd played in the political developments in his home system, and the potential impact of his final report.

As much as he'd endeavored to maintain an objective distance, insulating himself within the walls of science, and the search for knowledge, Khal had never been naïve concerning the political proclivity to suppress the truth. To maintain the status quo. The echoes of past civilizations discovered in his far-flung explorations, further illuminated his people's speciocentric hubris regarding their superiority and longevity. Blind to the insignificant anthill they occupied, and the brief blip of their existence in the cosmic span of time.

An anthill vulnerable to the falling fruit, or the giant's footstep. Obliterated in an instant. Replaced by a new other.

His explorations and discoveries had led him to the inescapable conclusion of a cosmic matrix connecting everything in nature; everything that had lived, is living, and will live. A matrix his people were unable to perceive, blinded by social convention, religion, and a myopic speciocentrism. The irony being they missed observing the true miracles occurring all around them, the invisible scaffolding binding all of creation, which maintained their world spinning in its place, and perpetuated their life cycle generation after generation. And which must inevitably end. For any species' grand existence constitutes but a small movement in a grander cosmic symphony, occurring along an infinite stretch of cosmic time.

The pale yellow world grew larger in the viewport. An oblate spheroid, flattened at its poles and bulging at the equator. Its face streaked by thin striated bands of icy clouds. Its eight moons also in view, circling like newborn pups around their mother.

The ship's sporadic sensors managed to gather some data. The planet possessed a strong dipole magnetic field, its magnetosphere deflecting the streaming stellar wind, producing auroras visible to the naked eye. Khal focused on the readings from the moons. The largest, his destination, also possessed a magnetic field, though not as strong as its parent. And a thin tenuous atmosphere in which, according to readings from his previous visits to the system, complex hydrocarbon and organic chemical reactions were occurring.

The Burude system held a special fascination for Khal. He'd deciphered the star's portal frequency from a stellar chart discovered early in his explorations. The presence of a portal indicated the system had once been explored, perhaps even colonized, by the portal builders, though he'd discovered no evidence of established colonies, or of long term occupation. But the indication of nascent life drew him to Burude repeatedly, where he'd spend months collecting readings on the celestial bodies orbiting the parent star, especially the moon he now approached.

His ship's trajectory already captured by the gas giant's gravity, Khal adjusted to intercept the moon. The side facing Burude a bright citrine crescent as the moon slid around its gaseous parent, heading toward his ship.

The distance closing, Khal prepared for orbital insertion, his attention focused on the flight instruments, and on the storm's intensity and ambient radiation. The navigation console calculated and depicted a position providing maximum protection. Distracted by his philosophical musing, and his concentration on piloting the ship, Khal missed the significance developing on the sensor display. Already in orbit, awaiting his arrival, not one ship, but two. And two more closing on his position from both sides.

In another sector of the Burude system, Agar's mind pieced together the distorted images communicated by the fighters. The live images winked in and out, forcing him to rely on memory. The Nivalinorhnus ship, and a Borinorhnus fighter, faced each other nose to nose. Two other fighters had maneuvered to flanking positions around Khalinaltani's ship. But the solar interference distorted the moment-to-moment tactical situation.

The cruiser departed the far side of the planet closest to the portal, where it had hidden during Khalinaltani's entry into the Burude system. Agar ordered a course toward the portal, meant to cut off Khalinaltani's escape should he sense the trap. The archeologist hadn't. Khalinaltani's capture easily achieved. Too easy, Agar thought. His habitual caution and skepticism a byproduct of his occupation.

The storm complicating the operation only increased his unease. Burude ejected another massive prominence. The ejections occurring at regular intervals, and growing in intensity, disrupting communications, creating havoc in the cruiser's instruments, and exposing the crew to increased radiation. Important components already damaged by accumulated electrostatic charges. The crew occupied battling minor explosions and fires around the ship.

The storm represented another reason Agar hated space travel, and space itself. Too many bizarre phenomena. Too many opportunities for disaster. Too many variables over which he had no control.

Though in nominal command, Agar possessed little ship command experience. He relegated operation of the ship to his executive officer, an experienced ship commander, while he focused on the mission. A mission the storm now delayed and complicated. The commander ordered increased distance between the ship and the star, abandoning the blockade of the portal.

"Magnetic field strength to maximum." The commander's orders flashed in Agar's mind, as Agar simultaneously queried the fighter's pilots.

"You haven't been able to penetrate the command link?"

"No commander. It does not appear to have one." The response broken, disjointed, disappearing altogether in a burst of static as another blast of super heated plasma erupted from Burude's surface. The charged energy deformed the ship's magnetic field, inducing new electrostatic surges and explosions in the ship's electronic components.

Agar continued to study the memorized image. Khalinaltani's ship of alien design. It's configuration unknown to Borinorhnus. It featured a triangular, pointed forward section, shaped like an arrowhead, connected by a slender neck to the main rectangular body of the ship. Drive nacelles were incorporated into the wing roots on either side. The wings gull shaped, gracefully swept back and angled upward. Another pair of drive units at the ship's rear end.

The Nivalinorhnus ship also unfamiliar, although Agar had seen the type once before at the base on Nivalinorhnus. A prototype he'd surmised. Now aware it hadn't been designed for the Borinorhran fleet. Its wings also gull shaped, and swept forward rather than rearward, unlike the wide wings and long slender body typical of the dragonfly-like Borinorhran fighters. Twin drives incorporated into the wing roots, rather than beneath the main fuselage. A forward protruding cockpit and nose section contained another pair of smaller, canard-type wings. No discernible weaponry, but Agar instinctively convinced the strange craft represented a fighter.

Khal had not expected the ambush. The idea he might be the target of machinations occurring half a galaxy away had never entered his mind. The purpose of the fighters as yet unknown, but their presence ominous.

He remembered he had not activated his communications console, or donned the headcap, a device Khal seldom required in his solitary lifestyle and work. The headcap stowed in a compartment below the com panel, used only during these periodic ship to ship encounters. At his last rendezvous a few years prior, a technician had installed modifications to his communications apparatus. The technical details beyond Khal's understanding or interest. But he'd been informed the modification was necessary to allow communication on a new bandwidth in use on all Khalinorhran ships.

Khal activated the console and donned the headcap, connecting him to thoughts emanating from the ships around him. Or at least one of the ships.

"Esteemed Khalinaltani Ogadeinus, do you hear us?"

"I hear you. Though your thoughts are not clear."

"It...storm...Khalinaltani...interfering...communications ...our honor...greet you Khalinaltani Ogadeinus."

The thoughts reaching Khal fragmented, as though pieces of a broken string. The images faded in and out. Names reached him. Nokhilinaraku Daladnus and Ticeusintutei Daladnus. Born of the same maternal colony, Khal thought. Or maybe the names distorted by the interference. Ticeus, the night hunter, he recalled. A powerful name.

"The honor is mutual. But I do not understand the other ships? Fighter ships if I am not mistaken. It is most unusual. And I am not receiving their thoughts."

"Our...communications...technology...possess...cannot receive..." A sudden burst of clarity. "They are here to detain you. Perhaps to kill you."

"Detain me? Kill me? For what purpose?"

"There is much occurring on the home worlds of which you are unaware esteemed Khalinaltani. You have been away a long time. A crisis may be upon us. A crisis with the potential for war.

"You are referring to fission Nokhil," Khal thought. "I am aware the possibility has been suggested in reports I have received over the years."

"It is inevitable Khalinaltani. The only question is how will it occur? Peacefully or by conflict? The attack cruiser's presence may be the answer."

"I appreciate the circumstances Ticeus. But I will not be the cause of an interplanetary civil war."

"The choice is not yours Khalinaltani. We had not anticipated them finding you, and since they have, it may be a mute point."

"What do you suggest?"

"We will protect you as best we can esteemed Khalinaltani. But we will have to wait out the storm before attempting the portal."

"It is my honor to protect you as well, esteemed Khalinaltani," the sudden thought connecting from a different mind, and on the old Borinorhran frequency.

The fighter facing the Nivalinorhnus ship pivoted in place. A pair of slim missiles leapt from beneath its long slim body at the roots of its retracted wings. The Borinorhran fighters on either side of Khal's ship erupted in sudden simultaneous explosions, the fireballs immediately snuffed in the vacuum of space, leaving seared and blackened hulks amid floating debris.

"I am Ghuladinrahna Jamughanus, a Khalinaltanist. I am transmitting an authentication code."

"Authentication received and verified Ghuladinrahna Jamughanus," the Nivalinorhrans responded. "We are honored by your presence fellow Khalinaltanist. However the cruiser will have seen the destruction of the fighters. They will be alerted and dispatch others."

"The storm has disrupted communications. I timed my attack when the cruiser lost contact with the fighters. I will continue to transmit images of our last tactical situation. They will be unaware the situation has changed. At least providing sufficient time for us to escape. The cruiser has also sustained damage from the storm and has moved away from the portal. Prior to departing the ship I set a timed charge to sabotage the fighter hanger. They will be unable to open the hanger portal to launch additional fighters. By good fortune they may also consider the damage to be storm related."

"What do you propose?"

"We will have to wait out the storm. The planet's magnetosphere will shield us, and also conceal us from the cruiser. The planet's orbit is now moving toward the portal. When the storm clears we break away for the portal. You draw their attention while I protect Khalinaltani. Once he is through the portal, I will cover your run to the portal. We can portal from the system together. Is your craft capable of it? I am unfamiliar with the design."

"Quite capable. It is faster and more maneuverable than the Borinorhnus fighters and cruiser."

"I am pleased to know it."

"We are intercepting your transmissions on a Borinorhran frequency Ghulad. Do you possess a Khalinorhran transceiver?

"I do not. The risk is too great of it falling into Borinorhran possession. However I do possess a skip scrambler.

Khal monitored the communication between both fighters. His own thoughts silent. Uncertain and undecided. Out of his depth. The situation, the destruction of the Borinorhran fighters, the sudden loss of life, still raw in his memory.

"I will not ask you to risk your lives on my account," he transmitted the thought.

"It is done esteemed Khalinaltani." The thought from Ghulad, the Borinorhran pilot. "There is no going back."

"We risk our lives not for you Khalinaltani, but for our world and its people. The future of our children," from Ticeus of the Nivalinorhran ship. "It is a risk we assume every day."

The communicated thoughts a shocking revelation to Khal. He hadn't understood the extent to which fission had progressed. Or the passionate convictions of the separatists. The sacrifices they were prepared to endure. The terrible cost repeated throughout Borinian history. An upheaval he'd never imagined to witness first hand.

Agar's frustration grew moment by moment. His discomfort intensified. Annoyed by the storm driving the ship farther from the portal and disrupting its operations. He'd lost contact with his fighters, receiving only disjointed, garbled images of the tactical situation around the moon. A situation he no longer trusted.

The cruiser now in pursuit of Burude's fifth planet. Another gas giant, its slight elliptical orbit headed away from the star, where they hoped to shelter in its strong magnetic field. The third planet, and the moon around which the fighters orbited, now on the opposite side of the system's orbital plane, circling to intersect the portal's orbit.

"Commander," Agar's agitated thoughts shouted at his executive officer. "Our current course is not optimal. It is taking us farther from the portal and the fighters."

"It is necessary for the safety of the ship and crew commander."

"We need to complete this mission, not prolong it. There must be an alternative."

The commander torn between the safety of his ship and the adamant demands of his commanding officer. The storm still at full strength, and the ship' crew diverted and occupied attempting to repair and remain ahead of the damage.

"If we maintain station between the orbits of the fourth and fifth worlds, at this distance our magnetic field offers some protection. But not much," his thought conveyed to Agar. "We will need to curtail repairs close to the outer hull, including the fighter hanger. Move all personnel to more protected areas of the ship."

The damaged fighter hanger touched a raw nerve in Agar's mind. The damage perhaps a result of the storm. But his inability to launch the cruiser's fighters a coincidence his skeptical nature did not accept.

"And the bridge?"

"We are in the most heavily protected section of the ship commander."

"We must complete repairs to the hanger," Agar insisted.

"It is a priority commander. However we cannot have repair crews in the area if we remain in the storm. And in any case we cannot open the hanger in the midst of the storm."

"Is there nothing we can launch to back up the fighters if they require it?"

"Two shuttles, a transport, and two scouts are housed in a separate hanger on a different level. We can launch any of those. But again commander, to expose the hanger during the storm may damage the ship beyond our ability to repair. And expose the crew to lethal radiation. Also those craft offer little protection to the crews against radiation."

"Prepare an armed shuttle and have it standby for launch on my order. And proceed with the plan you outlined. Just get us back to that world commander."

"As you command."

The Nivalinorhran fighter and its Borinorhran counterpart maneuvered into orbit around the gas giant. Khal followed, the three ships maintaining station in the elongated wake-like region of the planet's magnetosphere, facing away from the star.

"We are ready to receive your report Khalinaltani. I suggest you transmit to both ships to maximize the chance of it reaching home. We also have our own communication relay station at the portal. Our communications are secure from Borinorhran interception. As a last resort we can transmit a com package through the portal."

"You are not confident of escape Nokhil?" Khal asked.

"Ghulad's plan is sound Khalinaltani. But if the cruiser manages to intercept us our chance of escape is poor."

"How long to intercept," Agar thought, his anxious question piercing the commander's busy mind."

"In three hours Commander. The storm has ended. The ship is eighty percent operational. Repair crews are back at work."

"And the fighter hanger?"

"Heavy damage to the controls conduits and actuators. The ports cannot be opened manually. And there are indications the damage may not have been a result of the storm."

The commander's last thought a bolt of lightning in Agar's mind. Followed immediately by anxious calls from the communications and tactical stations.

The tactical situation resolved into an image in Agar's mind. Khalinaltani's ship headed for the portal at high velocity. Followed by one of his fighters. But the fighter hadn't fired on the fleeing Khalintani, or attempted to delay or capture the ship. The other two fighters registered nowhere on the cruiser's sensors. And the strange Nivalinorhran ship, looping around for a close pass to the cruiser.

Agar's instincts had been correct. He'd sensed the mission in jeopardy. If he hadn't changed course when he did, they'd have missed the fleeing ships altogether.

"Launch the shuttle," his mind screamed. "Target the alien ship. Destroy our fighter if necessary, but only disable the other ship if possible."

"But commander, there is another ship on an intercept course."

"It is a decoy, meant to distract us. Concentrate on the ship fleeing for the portal."

Agar's mind registered his orders being relayed throughout the cruiser. Acknowledgment of his orders registered in his thoughts as the crew charged weapons, acquired target resolutions, and launched the shuttle.

"Why have we not fired?" Agar thought.

"We are not in range commander."

"Fire anyway. Throw them off course until we close the range."

On the Borinorhran fighter's sensors, Ghulad noted the flight of missiles and the bursts of charged energy erupting from their warheads. The cruiser out of range, but changing course to intercept, its missiles streaking across the vast empty space at velocities near the speed of the stellar winds. Even a low energy hit might be sufficient to prevent Khalinaltani reaching the portal. Ghulad's mind hailed Khalinaltani's.

Khal followed the staccato instructions streaming into his thoughts. He banked hard starboard, his sensors registering the energy plumes bursting from a distant speck in space. He decreased azimuth, diving before breaking to port as instructed, his ship flying an evasive pattern while maintaining a trajectory for the portal.

Thoughts from the Nivalinorhran fighter also streamed into his mind.

"The cruiser is not accepting the bait Ghulad. They are ignoring us, and their fire appears designed to force you into evasive maneuvers while they close the range."

"Can you delay them?" inquired Ghulad."

"They have launched a shuttle which is following," Nokhil informed him.

"The shuttle is of minor concern," Ghulad responded. "It possesses light armament meant primarily for use in atmosphere. Its purpose may be to follow Khalinaltani through the portal if the cruiser is unable to intercept."

"Adjusting course to target the cruiser," from Ticeus.

Agar noted the Nivalinorhran ship's course change. Its objective to distract the cruiser from the primary targets.

"Any readings of armaments or weapons charging on the Nivalinorhran fighter?"

"None commander. We are unable to determine if it is a fighter, or if it possesses weapons. The ship has changed course. The present trajectory will put them behind us."

"Continue to monitor for weapons and continue pursuit of primary targets. Time to intercept?"

"Approximately two hours Commander. They are approaching the portal's gravity well, which will increase their velocity."

"Have you been able to establish a communications channel to the target ship?"

"I have established an open channel commander," responded the com officer. "I have been passively monitoring all frequencies. But I have not received any thoughts. He may not be wearing a headcap, or he is blocking his thoughts."

Or his ship is equipped with the new communications technology, Agar thought in the guarded recesses of his mind.

"Cease fire for the moment and hail his ship," Agar commanded.

"To what purpose commander?"

"Engage him in conversation. Perhaps distract and delay him. His ship's command link?"

"As before commander, there does not appear to be one on the ship."

"Khalinaltani Ogadeinus. It is my honor to greet you," a new mind reached into Khal's thoughts. The thoughts transmitted on a Borinorhran frequency, from the attack cruiser.

"I doubt it based on your actions thus far," Khal replied. "And whom do I have the honor of addressing?

"I am Captain Commander of the cruiser sent to escort you home."

"And yet I am not ready to return. Your actions suggest you are prepared to escort me by force, against my wishes if necessary."

"I have my orders Khalinaltani. There are circumstances developing on our home worlds which require your presence."

"Circumstances which do not concern me commander. Nor am I subject to your orders or the orders of your superiors."

"There are those willing to fight, to kill, and to die in your name. Such circumstances do not concern you?"

"Any loss of life concerns me commander. Including Human life, which you disregard and treat as livestock. Those who will fight and kill and die may append my name, but the struggle is theirs. For their own freedom, to live as they please, free of the constraints binding them. They only seek the truth."

"Whose truth Khalinaltani. Yours?"

"I agree many may claim to possess the truth. It is why the search in itself is of primary importance. Each individual's search for meaning as important as another's, unconstrained by another's truth."

"Range?" Agar asked, shielding the thought from transmitting through the com link."

"Closing commander. But they are approaching the portal's gravity well."

"I still only wish to disable the ship if we can, but it must not be allowed to transit the portal."

Agar shielded the thoughts racing through his mind, still uncertain of the consequences should Khalinaltani be killed. Agar did not wish to kill him. At least not yet. Not before learning the information Khal possessed. And a martyr might provoke the conflict General Zanth wished to avoid. Agar still convinced of its inevitability, but he trusted General Zanth's wisdom. And Agar's own meeting with the librarian had shaken him. The theoretical analysis of a conflict's outcome entirely different when witnessing its previous devastations.

"Commander!" the anxious thought exploded in Agar's mind, interrupting his ruminations, as an actual physical explosion shook the cruiser.

Agar focused his thoughts on the tactical image streaming into his mind. The Nivalinorhran ship arcing aft, weapons pods slung below its angled wings. It fired again. The sensor image traced a long energy beam lancing from the craft, impacting the cruiser.

"Tactical," Agar's mind shouted, the commander's simultaneous thought reaching the tactical officer as one.

"A high energy directed particle beam. Tightly focused."

"Why did you not see its weapons?" Agar demanded.

"No weapons were detected by our sensors until they deployed and fired Commander."

Damn Nivalinorhnus, Agar thought. His mind occupied by technologies Nivalinorhnus had concealed from Borinorhnus. Their communications. This fighter and its weapons. What else? Agar wondered.

"Evasive action. Target the ship," the executive officer's thoughts intruded on his own.

"They are too fast commander. The ship maneuvers too tightly to obtain a target lock. And their last burst disabled the main drive. We are adrift commander, moving under inertia alone."

The news hit Agar like a kick to his midsection.

"Range?" his mind screamed. His focus on the ships approaching the portal, unseen by the naked eye at their current distance. Mere dots depicted on the tactical array. His executive officer's mind focused elsewhere, his thoughts screaming his own orders for damage control and status reports.

"Target ships in the portal's gravity well commander, pulling away. We are at the limit of our range, and falling back. "

"Fire on both ships," Agar ordered. Outwardly calm, his intense vocalizations the only sign of his agitated thoughts.

"Nivalinorhran ship breaking off the attack," relayed from tactical.

"Only wished to disable us," Agar thought. "Keep firing on the primary targets unless the Khalinorhran turns to attack again.

The thoughts reaching Khal indicated a decisive point in the tactical situation, although he claimed no familiarity of battle tactics in space. But the cruiser's commander abruptly terminating their conversation, and the maneuvers to escape the missiles as the cruiser maintained a steady rate of fire, convinced him his assessment had been correct. The cruiser meant to stop him at all costs, its missiles closing, zeroing their target. Their explosive discharges ripped the space around his ship.

Ghulad's thoughts intruded on Khal's, reporting their status to the Nivalinorhran fighter.

"Khalinaltani's ship is in the portal's grip. Approaching transit. The cruiser has us zeroed. A hit might still destroy Khalinaltani's ship, even at this extreme range. Can you distract their fire? I will attempt to intercept the incoming missiles."

"Commander, the Nivalinorhran ship is turning for another attack." The report directed at the executive officer. The thoughts also reached Agar's troubled mind.

"Spread pattern from all dorsal aft batteries if we are unable to target the ship," the commander ordered. "All forward batteries continuous fire on primary targets."

Agar followed the battle in the tactical images streaming into his mind. Khalinaltani's ship a streaking spectral blur caught in the portal's gravity. The Borinorhran fighter in a rearguard position, covering the fleeing Khalinaltani, firing at the cruiser's incoming missiles. The Nivalinorhran fighter an elusive target, a pesky gnat flitting around the cruiser, avoiding its missiles, returning fire with devastating effect. Under different circumstances Agar might have admired it.

"Forward batteries one, three, four and six disabled commander. Aft batteries unable to bear on primary targets. Forward dorsal battery two and forward ventral five still firing."

"A hit commander," the excited thought focusing Agar's mind.

"The Borinorhran fighter hit and breaking up," relayed the tactical officer, confirmed by sensor images relayed to Agar's mind.

"The other target?" Agar asked.

"Approaching the portal and ready to transit commander."

"The shuttle?"

"Out of range commander."

"Forward battery five disabled," reported tactical. "The Nivalinorhran ship is breaking off its attack. Battery two still operational and firing."

"Blow that damn Nivalinorhran out of space," Agar's forceful command eclipsing every other thought on the bridge.

"Registering a hit on primary target commander, unable to access the damage. The ship is still moving under power and close to transit."

Agar's thoughts bypassed the com officer, linking directly to the shuttle commander through the com link."

"Follow the ship when it transits the portal. If you are able to intercept detain the occupant on board without harming him. I repeat he is not to be harmed. Acknowledge. We will rendezvous at...commander?"

"The Korochar system," the commander finished for Agar. "Navigation is relaying the portal and com relay frequencies."

"Acknowledged commander," from the shuttle.

"The Nivalinorhran ship?" Agar demanded.

"Moving away commander, on a trajectory for the portal. We have used maneuvering thrusters to reposition the cruiser, aft batteries bearing on target but unable to lock. The craft is too quick and agile commander."

Ghulad's death weighed on Khal. He hadn't known the Borinorhran beyond their fateful encounter, but the Borinorhran had given his life to protect Khal. And the other lives he'd witnessed snuffed into nothingness. How many more? How many others he hadn't been aware of? How many more to come?

Intellectually he understood fission to be a natural process involving passions and yearnings beyond him. Beyond the knowledge he'd uncovered. But they had adopted his name for their cause. Based their beliefs on his discoveries. Had the cruiser's commander been correct? Might his presence change the course of events? Be the difference between war and peace?

His troubled introspection interrupted by a loud concussive boom reverberating through the ship. The aged craft shuddered. Alarms blared their shrill urgent summons. A dissipating charge had impacted the ship's aft section. Sufficient to damage it. Insufficient to destroy it.

The thoughts of both Ticeus and Nokhil reached him. "Khalinaltani, your ship has been hit. Are you injured? What is the extent of the damage? Are you able to maintain flight?"

"I am uninjured. I am uncertain of the damage. The number two drive is disabled. I've shut down number three due to a fire. The wings close to the drive cones have sustained damage. I am not certain of the extent. I am being pulled into the portal and uncertain of the ship's flight capability."

"You must return with us Khalinaltani. Once in the home system we can tow your ship if necessary."

"No. See to yourselves. Are to able to safely reach the portal?"

"We are in no immediate danger Khalinaltani. We can outmaneuver the cruiser's batteries and their drive is disabled. They are unable to follow. However there is a shuttle following you toward the portal. Shall we intercept it?"

"You have done enough. See to you own safety and deliver my last report. I have one more journey I must complete before returning home."

"As you wish esteemed Khalinaltani Ogadeinus. It has been an honor. Good fortune attend you."

"The honor is mine dear comrades. Indeed I owe you my salvation. Good fortune attend you also and be safe."

Khal confirmed the destination frequency he'd transmitted to the portal, aware it may be the final journey in his wounded ship, stranding him. A prospect he'd already contemplated and accepted. But what of the shuttle following him? Scenarios raced through his mind. Options considered and discarded. Recent events a jarring new reality he needed to consider. Not too late. He nulled the current portal frequency. Entered a new one from memory.

Agar noted the spiking energy readings on the cruiser's sensors as the portal opened. Khalinaltani's ship vanished from their sensors and their screens.

An impassioned screech escaped Agar's lips.

Clicker

Ezekiel awoke, not of his own volition. Vaguely aware an external force had pulled him from the depths of blissful sleep. From a peace and contentment like he'd never known before. The fenori, Seraphina, still wrapped in his arms. Her warmth soothing. Her long silky hair tickled his flesh. Her musky scent inhaled on each breath.

An image brushed his mind. A desperate plight. His half-closed eyes searched the star-filled sky. Close to dawn. The first hint of the new day a lighter shade of grey low on the horizon.

The object flashed across his vision. A momentary flare. Followed by a blossoming glow and an elongating tail.

"Seraphina. Seraphina," he called, gently shaking her shoulder.

She moved against him. Her soft smooth skin pleasant against his. She mumbled as he continued to shake her.

Seraphina aware of the warmth against her bare skin. The comforting strength embracing her. The taut firmness upon which she nestled. Not her berth. Memories of the previous night slowly surfaced as consciousness awakened.

Ezekiel. The only man she'd ever willingly allowed to penetrate her. The afterglow of the experience a warm flush lingering inside her.

Opening her eyes Seraphina followed his pointing finger. A meteor falling through the sky. A common sight in this latitude on this world. Recalled fondly from earlier visits. Shooting stars and spectacular meteor showers, like sparkling diamonds raining in the night sky.

Not a meteor she concluded in sudden awareness. Unless unusually large. The fiery descent lasted longer than any she'd ever witnessed. And the illuminated tail indicated a change of direction. Controlled flight.

She sat upright. Fully awake, joining Ezekiel in following the object's fiery descent.

"A ship," he said next to her.

"A ship," she agreed. "Come."

Seraphina stood. Almost fell. A pleasant wobbly weakness in her knees. She noticed her nakedness. And Ezekiel's. Memories of the night flooded her mind again. She searched the ground for their clothing. The small fire had long since burnt to ash. Her crumpled dress lay atop Ezekiel's tunic. She bundled both garments into her arms.

"Come," she repeated to Ezekiel, his eyes still fixed on the fiery plume in the night sky. Seraphina's customary caution sensed danger in the unusual event.

Seraphina headed directly to the cockpit, dumped the garments on a console, and powered up Dauphin's sensors.

"A ship," she confirmed. "I do not know the type. Not any faction ship I have ever seen. Damaged."

"We must see in the scout," Ezekiel said.

Seraphina turned to face him. Hesitant. Uncertain. Her first instinct to hide. Remain invisible. Not involve herself in an uncertain situation.

"Why we must see?"

"May need help. Like when you find me."

"I not know you in the scout when I find you."

"We not know what we find in ship. Maybe something for Dauphin. Or the scout."

A rationale Seraphina understood. Ezekiel's awakening scavenger spirit overrode her usual cautiousness. At least for the moment.

They paused mere moments to grab clothing from their cabins, tugging the garments into place as they headed for the cargo hold. Seraphina in a maroon blouse, tight green leather pants, and unlaced boots. Ezekiel also in green leather pants, a shade lighter than Seraphina's, the legs tucked into knee high boots. A red leather skirt he'd designed himself belted around his waist, open at the front, the side flaps hanging to his knees. The skirt a weapons carrier, like Seraphina's belt, containing pockets, pouches, holsters and sheaths.

As Seraphina inspected her weapons they prompted an idea. She paused in her stride across the hold. "Ezekiel," she said, turning to him. "We take Dauphin. May need her weapons. I cover while you scout."

Seraphina circled five thousand feet above the island on which the object had crashed. The largest in the archipelago, twelve times the area of their little hideaway. It stretched east to west in length, its western end rising to a volcanic-like peak. A line of low hills inland from the shoreline formed a perimeter around the island, surrounding a central valley of grassland and forest.

The wreckage lay in a forested area close to the southern hills, on the edge of open grassland, as though it had overshot the open field and crashed into the trees. The wreckage, the surrounding area, and the skies above, under the probing scrutiny of Dauphin's sensors. The ship's ventral cannon locked on the wreckage. Its dorsal cannon pointed at the sky.

The scout plunged nose first from Dauphin's hold, diving toward the indigo sea. Its slender wings unfolded, biting into the crisp morning air. Ezekiel prolonged the dive, pulling out a scant thirty meters above the undulating surface. He approached the island from the south, low against the ocean, a winged creature in search of its morning meal.

The images painted by Dauphin's sensors relayed in crisp detail in Ezekiel's mind. Accompanied by the detailed echo rendering of the surrounding terrain as the scout moved inland. The same picture streamed into Seraphina's mind through their headcap link.

The unidentified ship had ploughed a long wide furrow in the soft soil. A swath of shorn and stripped trees on either side. A trail of debris in its wake. A torn and crushed section of wing, ripped and mangled bits of hull plating, the burst innards of a drive. Leaves and branches festooned the crumpled hull.

A pointed nose section lay some distance ahead of the main wreckage. Severed at the neck like a decapitated animal. Its canopy sprung open. Empty.

Seraphina's thoughts entered Ezekiel's mind. "Sensors show no organic signs in or around the ship."

"See this," Ezekiel responded, cycling the scout's visual scanners between infrared and ultraviolet. The images depicted heat plumes still radiating from sections of the crashed ship. And the dull glow of residual energy in many of its systems. But no life signs. Or any indication of a crew. No bodies.

"Maybe they abandoned ship before it crashed," Ezekiel thought.

"I'm not sure. Came down like a controlled crash," Seraphina responded.

"I will land and see."

"Wait for me. We go together so we can cover each other," she said. "There is a clearing beyond the trees east of the wreck. Do you see?"

Ezekiel acknowledged.

"I meet you there. Then we go together."

When Seraphina stepped from Dauphin's hatch she reminded Ezekiel of the first time he'd seen her. A fenori warrior. Her tight garments, black leather coat over the maroon blouse, and skin tight leather pants tucked into laced calf high boots, accentuated her female form.

Her weapons belt fastened around her waist, its black webbed straps fastened between her crotch and around her thighs. A projectile weapon tucked into cross draw holsters on either hip, and a kukri shaped blade in a sheath next to the pistol on her left. A short double edged dagger in a leather sheath strapped on her left forearm, and a longer single edged combat blade sheathed on the outside of her right leg.

Two leather straps crisscrossed her chest between each breast, a strap over each shoulder. On one strap across her back a scabbard contained a long forward curved pattah sword. On the other, a long barreled projectile weapon.

The final item new to her combat ensemble, the headcap. Her thick blue-black hair flowed from beneath the smooth snug fitting cap, below the rim across her forehead, from the sides onto her shoulders, and beneath the nape, down her back.

She reached behind her right shoulder to grab the barrel of the projectile rifle. As she pulled on the barrel, the attached strap slid across her torso, until the weapon lay across her chest. The strap already adjusted to her size, allowing the weapon to hang in easy reach of her hands.

Seraphina glanced at Ezekiel, her gaze studied his preparedness. A nod upon noticing the shokra lance tucked into a holster of the leather shirt. A short blade enclosed in one of its sheaths. Still not satisfied, she drew one of her pistols and handed it to him.

"Do you know how to use this?"

Ezekiel shook his head no. "Show me in your mind. Quicker," Ezekiel said.

Seraphina pictured the hand pistol's operation in her mind. A shorter version of the rifle. Its lethal explosive projectile propelled by an electromagnetic charge. Ezekiel nodded as he hefted and turned the weapon over in his hand. He tucked it into a holster of the skirt. Seraphina held the rifle in the ready-fire position as she and Ezekiel set off for the wreck.

They crossed the open patch of tall grass and entered the tree-covered woodland which stretched to the foothills of the western peak. The destructive path of the crash lay around them, amid sheared treetops tangled in the bush. Damage to the trees lower on their trunks as Seraphina and Ezekiel neared the crashed ship.

Seraphina more convinced of a controlled, or at least partially controlled crash, as she approached. The ship had overshot the open ground to end up in the trees. Her conviction heightened her alertness. She moved among the mangled tress slowly, cautiously. Her head swiveled side to side and front to back. Her senses probed ahead like the sensors of her ship. Her hands tightened their grip on the rifle.

Ezekiel aware of Seraphina's heightened alertness. He followed her lead. He unholstered the pistol, held it in his right hand.

The furrowed ground detected by the sensors now before them. Frightful and distressing up close. A gagged laceration of gouged and ejected soil. The scent of raw earth and torn vegetation hung heavy in the air. They approached the shattered remains of a once elegant ship, buried in the trough. They detoured around a main drive section, three times the height of either Seraphina or Ezekiel, with enough space for both of them to walk around inside the twisted housing.

Approaching the severed nose section, Seraphina more certain than ever she'd never seen this type of ship before. Or anything resembling it. Maybe a faction she'd never encountered before. The thought heightened her caution and alertness. Her mind unable to concentrate on the wreckage or salvage. Her attention instead focused on the surrounding trees, the terrain, any area providing concealment, while Ezekiel poked around the cockpit's interior.

The sudden alarm in Ezekiel's mind alerted Seraphina. She stiffened. Raised the rifle. His thoughts a mixture of cautious confused curiosity and surprise. An image sprang into her mind, a long rounded object, shaped like a pea pod. Open like a clamshell and empty. Ezekiel sniffed the air, turning slowly, his nostrils sampling each new direction.

"Clicker environmental suit and escape pod," Seraphina heard in her thoughts.

The single word froze Seraphina in place. Her feet braced. The stock of her rifle jammed firm against her shoulder. The barrel moved as her eyes moved. Her finger poised on the trigger.

"Where? How many?" This time Seraphina had not spoken aloud while questioning Ezekiel.

"Not certain. Only one suit. But this is not any type of clicker ship I have ever seen."

"Maybe a clicker faction you've never met before."

"No clicker factions. Not like Humans. They live on only two worlds of one system. They travel into space, but only to hunt. They have off world bases but do not colonize other worlds."

"Why do you think there are clickers?" Seraphina not caring if her thoughts also conveyed her exasperation, and her fear. She no longer minded such emotions travelling through the link. Perhaps she'd grown sufficiently comfortable in the link. Or maybe she'd have expressed such emotions to Ezekiel anyway, a byproduct of her acceptance of him.

"The scent," Ezekiel replied, aware of the hair trigger tension building inside her, seeking release. He'd detected a direction for the scent. Faint amid the strong odors surrounding the crash, but distinct.

"Come," edging away from the crash site, sniffing the air like a blood hound as he moved deeper into the trees.

Ezekiel paused before a large tree, its trunk broad enough to conceal them both. Seraphina aware through the link of Ezekiel's anxiety. His caution. His fear.

"You go around that side. I will take this side," his thoughts said.

Seraphina nodded. Ezekiel held the charged pistol in front of him. In his left hand, the lance he'd pulled from the skirt's holster. The lance elongated to its full length. Seraphina readied the rifle.

They stepped around the tree from opposite sides. Seraphina's eyes searched among the surrounding trees until her mind registered Ezekiel staring up into the branches of the tree they'd skirted.

Seraphina raised the rifle, finger already squeezing the trigger.

"No." Ezekiel shouted in her mind. His hand knocked the rifle aside and down as it discharged. A shower of dirt erupted from the ground where the projectile struck.

"Great shagging stars that's a clicker?" Seraphina's thoughts and words a simultaneous exclamation. Her eyes opened large, staring up at the creature hanging head down from a thick branch, almost entirely concealed in the tree's foliage. Her first up close and personal sighting of the dreaded creatures. Loathsome and bewildering. Fascinating and fearsome. She raised the rifle again.

"No," Ezekiel repeated in her mind.

"Why not? It's a shagging clicker."

"Yes. But strange. He is alone. It is not common among clickers. Only a few can survive living outside a colony. And the ship he came in. It is not clicker. And he is not trying to reach into our minds to control us. He may be dead."

"A good thing," Seraphina said.

"Seraphina. Remove your headcap. He should not be able to reach our minds through the headcaps. But if he can he will not capture both our minds through the link. Put your weapon on him. If I say he is trying to take my mind, you must kill him. If I think he is trying to take your mind I will kill him."

"You are certain you want to do this thing?"

"Yes."

Seraphina pulled the cap from her head. She fell to one knee, the rifle steady in her hands, butt firm against her shoulder, her cheek pressed against the stock. She lined up the hanging clicker in her sights. Her aim steady and true.

"You. Borinian of Borinorhnus. Do you hear me?" Ezekiel transmitted through his headcap.

Khal had been aware of the human presence approaching. A male and female. Perhaps a mated pair. And aware their discovery of him meant his death. His only hope they'd pass him by, unaware of his presence. A faint hope. The male had sensed his precise location, as though attracted by a homing signal. Khal intended them no harm, even to preserve his own life.

He'd survived countless sectares of space on his own. Had survived uninhabited worlds long forgotten in time. And inhabited ones where he'd had to conceal his presence, working in secret solitude. He'd survived the battle of Burude. Had not expected to survive the crash on this world. He'd been reconciled to his impending death. Had accepted it, prepared for the passage into eternal rest. His work done. His purpose complete.

His miraculous survival of the crash a short respite Khal reasoned. His inevitable death not far off without food or water. Or when they found him. Either the inhabitants of this world, or his pursuers.

He had no fear. His time in the intricate matrix connecting his brief existence to everything, to all who had lived before, and would live after, provided comfort, and peace. He had welcomed death when the female attempted to fire her weapon at him. Aborted by the male. Whose thoughts now called to him. Who recognized him as a Borinian of Borinorhnus. As astonishing to Khal as the fact he still lived. Who were these Humans? Simple enough to determine, but Khal had foresworn such methods.

"I hear you Human," Khal's thoughts reached out to the male. "It is my honor to greet you, and I mean you no harm."

Ezekiel recognized the formal Borinian greeting, though it had never in his life been directed at him.

"How do you know my kind?" Khal asked.

"You cannot see for yourself?"

"I will not."

"I am, or was, Borathquiri. I am now free and wild. And we will kill you if you attempt to capture our minds. But I do not hear you in my thoughts Borinian."

"I enter your mind only to respond to your thoughts, to communicate. Your mind is your own. Not for anyone else to possess or control. You alone decide who may see your thoughts."

"It is not the Borinian way."

"It is my way. It is the correct way."

"What is happening?" Seraphina asked, a perplexed stare directed at Ezekiel as he holstered the pistol and lance.

"Not kill. Not yet," Ezekiel said verbally in her language. The fluency of communicating through the headcap absent from his speech. "Headcap," he said, indicating she wear it again.

"I do not believe he will harm us," Ezekiel's thoughts flowed from the cap settled on her head.

"How can you know? He is of your masters. The ones who enslaved you. Who hunt our kind. Maybe he is controlling your thoughts."

"He is not. I am aware now which thoughts are mine, and which are not. And he is not like the masters. He does not seek to enter our minds and control our thoughts."

"He knows we will kill him," Seraphina argued.

"We will see."

Ezekiel directed his thoughts at the clicker. "What are you called?" Seraphina heard in her mind.

"I am Khalinaltani Ogadeinus. What are you called?"

"Among my kind I am known as Ezekiel. The woman is called Seraphina," indicating Seraphina at his side, her wary, suspicious stare fixed on the clicker, the rifle still aimed at his hanging body.

"Do you hear him in your thoughts Seraphina?"

"No," she said in a quiet breath, a perplexed frown fixed on her covered brow, a wary suspicious squint in her eyes. "The moment I do he is dead."

"He does not require the headcap to access our thoughts. It is strange we do not hear him except when he wishes us to. It is unlike the masters."

"I do not trust him. How did he come to crash here? Maybe his ship was damaged during a hunt."

"Ask him if you wish."

Seraphina spun to face Ezekiel, her eyes wide, her mouth open. She fixed a questioning stare on him. His suggestion the last thing in the galaxy she expected. Her eyes, her expression, her posture, her thoughts, all screaming, "Are you shagging me?"

Seraphina lifted her gaze to the treetop. She studied the hanging clicker.

"Why are you here?" she asked, words accompanying the thoughts sent in the clicker's direction. "How did you come to crash on this world?"

"Attempting to escape. My government wishes to capture me, or kill me I suppose. They sent an armed ship to intercept me. My ship was damaged during the battle, but I managed to escape through the portal and came here." Images of a space battle, exploding fighters, a desperate dash across space, the portal, accompanied the thoughts entering Seraphina's mind, relayed through her headcap to Ezekiel.

A sensation akin to being knocked off her feet gripped Seraphina as the string of thoughts and images streamed into her head. But she did not rip the headcap off as she had the first time she'd experienced it. She stared at Ezekiel, undecided whether to be annoyed, appalled, or afraid.

Seraphina continued to stare. The situation incredulous. Surreal. She'd spoken to a clicker. Not spoken. Exchanged thoughts. An experience she'd never thought possible or even imagined. And if not for Ezekiel, she'd have killed the clicker on sight.

"You may come down Khalinaltani," she heard Ezekiel convey to the clicker.

Seraphina stared in wide-eyed astonishment as the clicker's feet released the branch. He plunged head long from the treetop, spreading thin wings moments before crashing into the ground. The wings lifted him in a tight spiraling circle around the enclosure formed by the surrounding trees. He landed on his feet before them.

Seraphina continued to stare. The figure before her strange and alien. Repulsive and intriguing. His full height reached only to her chest. The skin of his face dark and leathery beneath coarse stringy hair on the sides of his face, and below his chin. Thick, coarse hair flowed back across his head from a lined, sloping forehead, falling to his shoulders and back. His neck concealed beneath a thick ring of muddy brown fur encircling it, covering the upper portion of his chest. Large leaf-like ears on either side of his head. A long flat nose, and large flared nostrils. Small pointed teeth in a round mouth.

Seraphina captivated by his blank expressionless stare. His eyes small and round, like black marbles. His eyelids flickered. Unlike the way Humans blinked. Instead a rapid flickering series between long unblinking intervals.

Wide shoulders. His strong arms similar to Human arms, Seraphina noted. Its skin a continuous membrane enclosing and connecting long flexible fingers, forming his wings. His hands no more than a palm, and a single articulating clawed thumb. His legs also similar to Human legs. strong, covered in leggings like those worn by Ezekiel when he'd removed the hard, outer suit in the shower. Boots covered his feet. The front open, exposing toes tipped by sharp extendible talons.

And his scent, which had led Ezekiel to his location. More like a stench. Strong and pungent. Overpowering. Also like her first encounter with Ezekiel.

"You are not perished Khalinaltani," Ezekiel informed him, recalling his own confused befuddlement upon awakening on Dauphin. "And we will not harm you unless you attack us or attempt to control our minds. What is your intent?"

"I am uncertain. I had not thought beyond death. And you may call me Khal. Before Burude, I had planned one more journey. A visit to a world to culminate my life's work, and perhaps my life itself."

"I do not understand," Ezekiel thought. "What is your work? And how is it you are separated from you colony."

"I have no colony. I have spent much of my life in space, exploring many worlds. How is it you are here Ezekiel. Separated from Borinorhnus?"

"I was adrift in space after a battle which destroyed the Borinorhran fleet I served in. Certain I had perished. The woman found me."

The mention of a battle stirred Khal's interest, particularly after his recent experience.

"A battle? What sort of battle?"

"A hunt for quir..." Ezekiel squelched the thought before thinking the name he no longer wished to use in referring to his kind. "Humans," he thought instead. "But the Humans fought back, as they are doing with more frequency and ferocity."

"As they should. And must," Khal thought. "But my inquiry is due to curiosity regarding another battle. One involving your people and mine, setting Borinian against Borinian. Do you have knowledge of this?"

"It cannot be. How can such a thing be possible?"

"Yet it is so. And if you will permit me Ezekiel, I will show you another thing many considered impossible."

Images streamed into Ezekiel's mind, with his consent. Large communities, whole cities, of Borinians and humans living and working together, side by side. The humans uncontrolled and free.

Seraphina had been following the conversation through her link to Ezekiel. Experienced Ezekiel's astonishment alongside her own. But unlike Ezekiel, the images only heightened her suspicion.

"It is not true Ezekiel," she said. "It cannot be. He is only trying to trick us so we do not kill him."

"I do not believe so Seraphina. The images are from his memory and his experience. I not only see them I also feel them. And imagined thoughts are not the way of clickers."

"You said he is not like the others. We cannot trust him. He is a clicker," she said. "We see what we can salvage and leave him."

Her thoughts passed from Ezekiel to Khal.

"There may not be much time," Khal thought.

"What does he mean?" Seraphina asked Ezekiel, not addressing Khal directly. The unsettling sensation of clicker thoughts entering her mind gripped her again.

"A shuttle from the warship followed me when I transited the portal. They may have tracked me here. I cannot be certain. And if they did, I am uncertain how long it may be before they find me. But there are many things in the ship I am certain you will find useful.

"Shagging scrugs. More clickers," Seraphina's thought also uttered in words.

They returned to the wreckage. Seraphina in the rear, maintaining a close eye on the clicker ahead of her, her suspicious gaze fixed on his movements, the rifle casually cradled in her arms, unwaveringly pointed at him.

The clicker's reaction to the wrecked ship provided another astonishing event in a morning already filled with an accumulating list of weird, unusual events. More than Seraphina could have imagined when she'd awakened to the new day. The clicker emitted a low soft clicking and chirping, a mournful sound as his eyes surveyed the wreckage. He leaned forward, placed his cheek against the hull. A rhythmic humming replaced the clicks and chirps. Seraphina stunned by the unexpected display.

"The ship saddens you," no hesitation as she projected her thoughts at Khal. "But you are not saddened by enslaving and slaughtering my kind."

"That is not my doing. And it is an aspect of my culture I abhor and wish to see changed. Just as there are aspects of your culture which results in misery, death, and destruction, which you may abhor and wish to see changed."

Seraphina flinched at his thoughts. Not only the truth they contained, but also the possibility he had seen deeper into her mind than she'd been aware. Had witnessed her past. She dismissed the notion. There'd been no indication of his mind in hers. But it heightened her resolve to remain vigilant.

"And you are correct," his thoughts continued. "I am saddened. Though its demise had been approaching in any event, I had not considered such an end as this. This ship has been my home these many long years. We have journeyed across an endless expanse of space together, and explored many worlds. I had established a strong manchi toward this ship."

"A magnificent ship," she expressed in his thoughts, as she gazed across its torn and deformed body. She imagined its graceful beauty when alive, its head proudly thrust forward on its sturdy neck. Odd shaped wings majestically swept outward, slipping effortlessly through space, or soaring regally through an atmospheric sky. "I have never seen a ship like it. Do you know its origin? Which faction built it?"

"It was built by your ancestors. Over sixty thousand years ago."

The response rendered Seraphina speechless. Her thoughts incoherent.

"There is much I can tell you," Khal continued. "About you, and where you come from. The shared history of your people and mine."

"How can it still be after so long a time? How could it still function?"

"I discovered it in a sealed cave. Protected from the environment and time. Perfectly preserved."

As they toiled into the afternoon, Seraphina was unable to dismiss Khal's response concerning the ship's origin, or his thoughts regarding a shared history. She filtered it through her suspicious skepticism, but returned to it again and again as Krilan's sun arced across the sky, and as the pile of salvaged components grew.

Khal contributed to the pile, including a communications component he indicated Seraphina's ship might require. He'd also salvaged a small collection of tunics and other personal possessions, as though remaining in their company had already been decided. Ezekiel dragged the combination environmental suit and escape pod to the pile.

By nightfall they'd hauled their treasure to Dauphin's hold. Khal still in their company, as Seraphina prepared a small cooking fire under Dauphin's folded wing. She drew Ezekiel aside.

"It is one thing to be around a clicker, which I tell you is uncomfortable and maybe dangerous. But he is not stepping a foot aboard my ship. And he needs to wash. You were bad enough. He is ten times worse."

"Not like me," Ezekiel said. "It is natural for them. And they do not use water. They are afraid. Even of rain. But how is he to wash or cleanse his scent if he cannot go aboard the ship?"

Seraphina reluctantly allowed it. Her instinct again overruling her overcautious self. She needed to think in solitude. Sort through this new development. Ezekiel seemed comfortable around the clicker. More at ease than she. Perhaps understandable considering he'd spent his entire lifetime among them. But she wished to hear his thoughts regarding this new situation. And she did not wish to argue or disagree. Her emotional uncertainty new and unsettling. As alien to her as the clicker. Her unease partially the result of a bewildering fear, of having to choose between Ezekiel and the life she once knew. She did not wish to leave Ezekiel. But she also did not wish to be the rescuer and keeper of every stray they chanced upon.

It was not the only emotion confusing her. The clicker had also triggered something inside her. Seraphina at once appalled and intrigued by a dormant curiosity awakened by hints of knowledge the clicker possessed. She busied herself preparing the evening meal, lost in contemplation.

By the time she'd completed preparing the meal, Ezekiel and the clicker emerged from her ship. The clicker dressed in an old, worn, and frayed one-piece garment covering his legs, midsection and furred chest. At least it appeared clean, Seraphina thought silently. And he no longer smelled. His obnoxious odor replaced by a subtle scent, reminding her of fruit trees.

Seraphina uncertain if the clicker might find the meal palatable. She possessed no knowledge of their diet. Or anything else concerning them beyond stories she'd heard. Khal the first clicker she'd met face to face. A situation still befuddling her brain. He sat on a raised mound facing her and Ezekiel, feeding small morsels of fruit into his mouth, his rapid chewing accompanied by a string of low clicks and hums.

"You say you know of us. Our history and where we came from," Seraphina said, her thoughts accompanying her words. She no longer wore the headcap, curious to experience communicating without it.

"My search is complete," Khal's thoughts responded in her mind. "The story of our history complete."

"What is this history?" Seraphina asked. "Tell us."

"There is much to tell. More than can be related in one night," aware his thoughts had been both true and a device. Khal recognized these Humans represented his salvation, and his only chance of reaching the world he wished to visit, the culmination of his life's work. At least his chance to leave this world as a first step toward that goal. And he did not forget his Borinorhran pursuers.

"Also much to show you," Khal continued. "Therefore I must ask you a question."

"What question?" Seraphina asked.

"Will you allow me to give you a dream?"

Seraphina's reaction reflexive denial. "I do not think so. I do not wish to have you in my mind, especially when I'm sleeping."

"I will not need to be in your mind. I merely put the memories there. When you are asleep your mind will access those memories on its own."

"How can you do that?

"He is seer," Ezekiel said, who'd been following the conversation through Khal's thoughts. "And a privy too, I believe."

"What is that? Seraphina asked.

"Is why we not see all of his mind when he is in ours," Ezekiel explained in a combination of his and Seraphina's language. His syntax broken but understandable. "Only see what he sends. And he can give you thoughts you do not see or hear."

"Ezekiel is correct," she heard in her mind.

"Well what can you tell us now?" Seraphina thought, her suspicious misgivings regarding the dreams not dispelled. If anything, increased.

"Your people came from a great distance. From a world orbiting a main sequence type star midway between the center and outer edge of this immense galaxy. Millions of years ago your form of life evolved on this world, though it may not have been the first appearance of your form. Your ancestors may have been the second evolution of this type. The seed perhaps transported to that world from some other origin. Or it may have been two separate but parallel developments. The world your people came from has long since been forgotten and lost to time. But I have discovered many references to it on other worlds your ancestors explored and colonized. I have been searching the galaxy for it. And I believe I have finally found it. The destination to which I was headed after Burude. Before the battle disabled my ship and I crashed here. I wish it to be the final stop in completing my life's journey."

"Why do you spend your life searching for a thing lost and forgotten? A thing of concern to no one else?" Seraphina asked.

"Each individual searches for meaning in their lifetime. Even if they are not aware of it. And no one's search is more important than another's. We differ only in the degree of importance we place on the search. I am a seeker of knowledge, of the legacy of time and the past. In this manner I attempt to understand my own existence."

Seraphina remained uncertain, but more intrigued. Especially regarding Khal.

"All clickers like this one?" she asked in a whispered aside to Ezekiel.

"No. I say you before, he not like any Borinian I know. That is how they are called. Like Human. Not like clicker or chirper, or quiri."

Seraphina rolled the word around her tongue, practicing its pronunciation. Ezekiel coached her, as they did each day practicing each other's language. He formed the word, pronouncing it slowly for her.

"Borinian," Seraphina said, mimicking Ezekiel, producing a smile. His face bronzed by exposure to Krilan's sun.

"Many hundreds of thousands of years ago, perhaps more," Khal continued, his thoughts streaming to both Seraphina and Ezekiel. "Your people learned the science of traveling among the stars. They journeyed beyond their home world, exploring vast areas of this galaxy, and established colonies on many worlds they visited. You and the other factions, as you call them, are what remains of a species who once numbered as many as the stars you can see in the night sky."

The three conversed past completion of the meal. And into the night. Until the weariness of the day's exertions overcame them. Following their mating, Seraphina had decided to share her cabin with Ezekiel.

"We sleep in my cabin," she said to Ezekiel after dousing the fire. "Where Khal sleep?" The first time she'd used Khal's name instead of referring to him as the clicker. Though still not wholly comfortable by his presence, especially aboard her ship.

"He not sleep," Ezekiel said. "Is nighttime, when Borinians awake and active. Is normal for them. He maybe explore island. Then find a tree to roost when daylight comes.

As they had the night before, Seraphina and Ezekiel fell asleep in each other's arms. Soft naked flesh nestled against each other.

Borinorhnus

Agar's report increased Zanth's depressive mood. A morose brooding pervaded him, a permanent fixture of his personality since receiving Agar's report regarding Nivalinorhnus.

Compounded by Agar's report on the Burude encounter. Zanth replayed the images in his mind. Khalinaltani Ogadeinus's escape, aided by a Khalinaltanist aboard the attack cruiser. How many more in the military colony, and in other colonies? He wondered. And the astonishing Nivalinorhnus fighter, a craft Borinorhnus's military intelligence had been unaware of. What other surprises did the Nivalinorhrans possess? The image of the attack cruiser limping toward the portal nested in his thoughts, the passage requiring days under jury-rigged power.

Agar had forwarded the report from the Korochar system, where Agar had expected to affect repairs and replenish his fighters at a Borinorhnus base. Only to discover the facility recovering from a devastating quiri attack. The base's ability to quickly repair the cruiser compromised, even given priority, requiring a lengthier layover than expected. Agar had received the portal frequency his shuttle had intercepted from Khalinaltani's ship, but his ability to follow delayed, if not in doubt altogether.

Zanth pondered the feasibility of continuing the pursuit given the circumstances at home. Containing the volatile situation a dwindling option. In any case an option which silencing or prosecuting Khalinaltani Ogadeinus might no longer affect. And may in fact worsen if Khalinaltani were elevated to the status of martyrdom.

Zanth had ordered certain actions since receiving Agar's reports. He'd increased patrols and inspections at the portal, short of a blockade. He did not wish to alert the council to a situation beyond his cover story of routine military exercises. And a blockade might spark a confrontation with Nivalinorhran ships entering and leaving the system. In response, Nivalinorhnus had also increased their presence around the portal. For the time being Zanth had to be content monitoring the number and types of Nivalinorhran ships transiting the portal.

Zanth also secured his military communications, including the portal relay station. Though he remained uncertain whether Nivalinorhnus hadn't already penetrated their communications, including Agar's reports, while Borinorhnus remained deaf to Nivalinorhran transmissions. Borinorhran technicians toiled feverishly to duplicate the Nivalinorhnus communications technology. Without success. Zanth had also recalled three mother ships.

He'd researched Nivalinorhnus's governor and general commander. Perplexed by the notion of such high-ranking officials turning against their government. Both were of the same birth mother, as Agar suspected. Both had been reared and trained on Nivalinorhnus. They'd spent their formative years and adult life there. General Dogarinmaral had been deployed off-world to other systems through much of his career. Neither had spent any significant time on

Borinorhnus. Both were products of the culture they'd been reared in.

The degenerating strategic situation, the imponderable variables, the waning options, had haunted Zanth for days. And Zanth still struggled to grasp how the situation on Nivalinorhnus had gone undetected. Such a cultural divergence had not occurred overnight. How had Borinorhnus intelligence failed so spectacularly?

As Zanth entered the citadel, he prepared his thoughts for the council meeting. He'd need to maintain extraordinary mental discipline. The consequences of armed conflict, of all out civil war, unsettled him. His discomfort informed by his visit to the librarian, the images still vivid in his mind. In his morose contemplations, Zanth had been pondering a plan. One he dared not formulate and keep in his thoughts. Not until he'd taken the council's measure, gauged their reaction to his thought as a nascent unformulated idea, without his thoughts betraying how far he intended to pursue it. Or the specific means by which he might achieve it.

Zanth entered the familiar chamber. The governors already assembled and waiting.

"General Supreme Zanthinvolar Abydynus," they greeted him as he settled at his roost amongst them.

"Esteemed governors," Zanth addressed them. "At our last meeting I outlined a plan to discover the extent of the dissident movement, and possible means to crush it. I must report to you the situation is more severe than we thought. We are not dealing with a dissident movement, but a society on the verge of fission."

Loud excitable clicks and chirps accompanied the alarmed, dumbfounded thoughts bombarding Zanth's brain.

"Impossible."

"Preposterous."

"Must be mistaken."

"Governors. I assure you my report is accurate and the situation is grave. There is no turning it back." Zanth allowed selected portions of Agar's report concerning Nivalinorhnus to flow into the assembled minds. "The question now is, how do you intend to manage it?"

"This treason must be stamped out. It must not be allowed to spread further," thought Governor Supreme Khorabinjolen. "Fission must not be allowed to occur, whatever the cost."

"You risk a civil war, Governor Supreme," Zanth responded, provoking another round of agitated clicking and chirping.

"Surely you exaggerate general," from Mokharinsephin, Governor of Information and Culture.

"You have seen the report of my agent Governor Mokharinsephin," Zanth replied. "There is however a way to be certain," Zanth continued, providing a partial glimpse of his idea.

"The idea is intriguing. How do you propose proceeding?" asked Science Governor Tovarinkara.

"By meeting the leaders seeking fission and determining their intentions," Zanth responded carefully, maintaining his mental shield against Governor Tovarinkara's probing thoughts. Tovarinkara's small raven eyes fixed Zanth in an equally piercing, perceptive stare.

"Who are these leaders?" asked Khorabinjolen. "If we know who they are we can detain them and put an end to this nonsense."

"Such a course of action will be resisted, perhaps precipitating the conflict, provoking an escalation resulting in all out civil war," Zanth responded. "I suggest we obtain further intelligence regarding their intentions and capabilities before deciding on a course of action."

"Your report must be mistaken," insisted Governor Supreme Khorabinjolen. "It cannot be possible events have transpired to the extent you report without the council being aware of it."

"And if your report is correct," interjected Zepharinlenar of Law and Security, "the fault for this criminal omission must lie with you and the military," his charcoal eyes expressing a malicious intent to deflect culpability for the failure of his intelligence colony. A failure as colossal as Zanth's own military intelligence.

"Perhaps Governor," Zanth responded, shielding his intense distaste of Zepharinlenar from his thoughts, if not from his glaring eyes. "But now we are aware the Nivalinorhrans support their culture, their council's policies, and the desire for fission. And will fight to defend it. There are indications they have been preparing for this eventuality for some time. There is also the question of uncertain loyalties here on Borinorhnus," Zanth continued, shielding Agar's report on the Burude encounter. Zanth did not need Khorab, or Zephar, mounting a purge in the military. "There may be sympathizers to the Nivalinorhnus cause here on Borinorhnus, more than we suspect. Again I must urge caution and the need for further information before we proceed."

"Something has to be done," Antrozinpanar of Farming and Industry echoed the thoughts of his colleagues. "We cannot afford to lose Nivalinorhnus's vital resources."

The discordant discussion and anxious arguments racing through the governors' minds obscured Zanth's mental polling. Science Governor Tovarinkara's silence, and that of Space and Technology Governor Laskarinadya, telling. The anguished thoughts of Health and Habitats Governor Sorkahringorol an indication of his indecision. Zanth uncertain which side he might settle on. Information and Culture Governor Mokharinsephin similarly undecided. Antrozinpanar of Farming and Industry in the Khorabinjolen column. And of course Zepharinlenar. The latter three preoccupied discussing arrest of the rebel council and seizing Nivalinorhnus, the notion of a seditious rebellion already established in their thoughts.

Governor Nakurinmaral of Nivalinorhnus was technically a member of the council, having a voice in their deliberation. Under the circumstances, a voice Governor Supreme Khorabinjolen would nullify by branding him a traitor, appointing a loyal Borinorhran to replace him.

The council's discussion proceeded, heated at times, their animated thoughts accompanied by vociferous vocalizations. Zanth remained silent, a spectator to the mental arguments surrounding him.

"I consider General Zanthinvolar's proposal prudent under the circumstances," declared Laskarinadya of Space and Technology. Seconded by Science Governor Tovarinkara.

"I also agree," Health and Habitats Sorkahringorol joined them. His decision dictated by a trepidatious prudence rather than acceptance of their position. "Surely Nivalinorhnus does not wish to engage in a destructive war."

"One of the things I intend to determine governor," Zanth replied. "If the council will consent to my meeting the Nivalinorhran council."

"If the council consents it is only to determine their intentions, and affirm our intent to preserve the collective against rebellion by all means at our disposal," Khorabinjolen stressed in their thoughts.

Zanth reflected on the meeting as he departed for his headquarters. He'd achieved his primary objective, relieving him of the burden of committing a treasonable act. Despite his performance in the council meeting, Zanth had already determined to meet the Nivalinorhnus council, or Khalinorhran as they called themselves, regardless of his council's decision. Preparing for such a meeting occupied his thoughts as he navigated the teeming swarms traversing the city.

Zanth's life and career had been molded by a structured hierarchy. A hierarchy of leaders and followers. Of orders given and obeyed. Of subservience to a collective will. A collective now fractured. Its will no longer cohesive or rational. And a government corrupted by a self-preserving instinct to maintain the status quo. An instinct driving their civilization toward the edge of a precipice.

A signal from Zanth's communications officer intruded on his thoughts. "Governor Tovarinkara wishes to connect with you General," the officer informed him.

"Connect him," Zanth instructed. A moment later the Science Governor's mind touched Zanth's. Their thoughts merged.

"Is there a matter requiring further discussion governor?" Zanth inquired, though he suspected the purpose of the governor's call lay elsewhere. He had not perceived any other matters requiring discussion before the council dismissed him. And if there had been, he'd have been summoned by the Governor Supreme, not an individual member of the council. He'd sensed Tovarinkara's perceptive probing during the meeting, seeking the silent thoughts beneath the surface. "I shall return if the council wishes." Zanth offered, disguising his suspicion.

"Not at all General Zanth. I rather wondered if we might meet privately prior to your departure for Khalinorhnus."

Governor Tovarinkara's use of the name adopted by the Nivalinorhran fissionists had not escaped Zanth's notice. He had not provided the name in his briefing to the Council.

"My honor Governor Tovarinkara. When and where?"

"I appreciate the time constraints and pressure you are currently under general. At your convenience. However, I must stress upon you the importance of meeting prior to your departure. I will be at my maternal estate awaiting your call."

Khalinorhnus

General Commander Dogarinmaral Korcharnus sat at the marble table in the compact, comfortable council chamber. Sitting not the most comfortable posture, but he'd long ago grown accustomed to it. The cultural customs of Khalinorhnus natural to him. Khalinorhnus his home since separation from his mother at weaning. Its people his people.

Though Khalinorhnus retained a hierarchical social structure, they'd forsaken the trappings and ceremonial posturing of rank. The circular conference table reflected that culture, symbolizing an assembly of equals, including Khalinorhnus's Human Council Members. The chamber, indeed the entire citadel, including its facilities and furnishings, designed to accommodate both Borinian and Human citizens of Khalinorhnus.

Dogar waited for the council to assemble around the table, beneath dim artificial illumination emanating from fixtures embedded in the walls and arched ceiling.

Unlike Borinorhnus, Khalinorhnus was not governed by a Council of Governors appointed by a Governor Supreme possessing authoritarian power. Rather Khalinorhnus elected its governor by popular consent, for a specified term in office. The elected governor appointed ministerial directors and administrators, performing duties similar to the governors on Borinorhnus. On Khalinorhnus however, such appointments were subject to the consent of an advisory assembly consisting of local officials elected in districts around the world. These officials' primary duties the administration of their local districts and communities. But they assembled periodically to provide advice and consent on matters of worldwide concern.

On Dogar's right sat Governor Nakurinmaral, his maternal brother, older by three years. The familial resemblance limited to their physical build. Both tall. Both slender, although Dogar had acquired a more defined musculature from his military training. And both covered in mustard brown fur. There the similarities ended. Nakur's face flat and broad, Dogar's rounded, his cheeks defined and his jaw pointed. Nakur's dark eyes lively and animated, Dogar's lighter, impassive, and searching.

Nakur opened the meeting, his thoughts imparted in a free and consensual exchange among the assembled members, including the two Human directors. Unlike their Borinorhran cousins, Khalinorhrans did not maintain a continuous merging of minds. Their thoughts solicited and accepted by invitation, at the consent of the recipient, as in a conversation.

"Before we get to the Borinorhnus situation," Nakur thought, "What is the assessment of Khalinaltani's last report?" His question received by all around the table, but his attention directed at Dogar.

"As you are all aware," Dogar thought, his gaze lingering on each of the directors as his thoughts touched their minds. "An incident occurred at the rendezvous in the Burude System. An exchange of fire between a Borinorhran attack cruiser and one of our long range fighters. We believe the cruiser is the same one that visited here recently. We now believe its presence here was to gain information on the location of Khalinaltani, which somehow they achieved.

Perhaps to detain him. Perhaps to kill him. We are not certain. Khalinaltani managed to escape through the Burude portal, but not before his ship sustained damage from the cruiser's weapons. We are unaware of Khalinaltani's current location, or status. All off-world bases, research sites, and colonies have been placed on alert. None have reported Khalinaltani's ship entering their systems, nor has there been any communication from him."

The mention of off world research sites the cue for Life Sciences Director Jeremiah, a Human, seated two down on Dogar's left. He projected his thoughts through a headcap to the assembled directors. Jeremiah's clean shaved face pale pink from a career spent underground. In stark contrast to the bronzed brown, leathery textured skin of the other Human council member, who'd spent his career bathed in Orh's brilliant glare.

"Khalinaltani's last report indicates he had completed his research on the common origins of both species," Jeremiah reported. "A conclusion he requested we corroborate and verify before releasing it publicly. He also believes he has discovered the location of the origin world, and planned to journey there."

"Assuming he is still alive," Nakur thought. "Did he provide any indication as to the location of this world? Perhaps it is where we may find him."

"Unfortunately no. He did not. And he also wished us to remain focused on the so called catalyst which triggered the transformation."

"We are still certain such an event occurred?" Nakur inquired of the assembled minds.

"Excavations at the site here on Khalinorhnus, and the site on Kheralincygninus, indicate ancient Humans believed such a catalyst existed. The search for it was a primary focus of their research on many worlds. Including the last world explored by Khalinaltani. However we are no closer to identifying this catalyst. We are not even certain what it is we are searching for."

"It may require greater effort director, considering the circumstances we face," Nakur advised. "Have you all the resources you require?"

"Up to this point governor, yes. But perhaps now our secret is out we need not exercise the customary precautions and can allocate additional resources to hasten our efforts."

"Assuming we can spare the resources. As you correctly suggest the secret is out. We may have less time than anticipated before a conflict is forced upon us." Nakur turned to face his brother. "What is the current status Dogar?"

"We have been contacted by General Supreme Zanthinvolar Abydynus. He requests a meeting. His purpose is undoubtedly to determine our intentions and assess our strengths and weaknesses, our determination, and our military capabilities. Perhaps confirming information reported by his spy. We have received reports the general has already reported to the council, but other than the increased patrols around the portal, we have observed no significant change in security activities, or in their military posture. This is unexpected in Khorabinjolen, but perhaps the general has been able to exert some restraining influence. We cannot be certain. I do not know General Zanthinvolar personally. Only by reputation. I believe he will be a reasonable but shrewd interlocutor. For our part, we need to assess the intentions of

Borinorhnus's council. Left to Khorabinjolen, I'd anticipate forcible invasion, but the council may be divided."

"Our information is in agreement," Nakur concurred. "My informants have indicated a divided council. However, I am certain it will not deter Khorabinjolen for long. If it is to be war Dogar, has our assessment, or our preparations changed?"

"Not significantly. We reconfigured our defenses following the Captain Commander's escape. We can defend our command and control infrastructure. And resources have already been prepositioned to carry out plans to destroy theirs. We've also recalled a number of squadrons from off world, including both mother ships. One will arrive in the system in time to escort the general's mother ship. In terms of troops and technology, we can defend our world, and even take the fight to theirs. But I cannot stress enough the need to avoid hostilities unless we are directly attacked."

"Hostilities may be unavoidable," advised Ishmael, the bronze complexioned Director of Human Affairs seated next to Jeremiah. Ishmael represented Khalinorhnus's Human population. His large liquid grey eyes twice the size of Nakur's, but just as lively, intelligent, and impassioned. His emotions always close to the surface, often producing unease among his Borinian colleagues, whose emotions did not span the range or depth of Humans. His gaze darted among the seated directors.

"Even if Borinorhnus agrees to fission, they may not accept terms to free the Human population held captive on Borinorhnus. Conflict may be our only resort to free them."

"Conflict may not accomplish what you seek Ishmael," Dogar cautioned, his Borinian stare pinning the Human. "Win or lose, an all out war will be devastating to both worlds. And such a war only ends of its own accord, when no one is left to wage it. There may be no Human survivors to free."

Silence enveloped the chamber. The clicking vocalizations of the Borinian members ceased. The Human voices and thoughts quieted. Each in silent contemplation of the image deposited in their minds by Dogar.

"We must stick to our strategy," Dogar's thoughts reentered their minds. "The Borinorhrans must leave the meeting convinced an attack will not go unanswered, and an all-out war will assure their destruction. We use their dependence on our natural resources to leverage our freedom, and the freedom of the Human population on Borinorhnus."

Dreams

Seraphina awoke in an irritable mood. Despite the comforting presence of Ezekiel nestled against her. And despite the soothing afterglow of her dreams. She performed her morning routine in an abrupt, perfunctory manner, her thoughts disquieted, unsettled. Her irritation not directed at anyone in particular. Rather a nebulous restlessness. An instinctual need to be on the move. Spurred by the annoying interruption of their idyll, hers and Ezekiel's, by Khal's unexpected arrival and continued presence. A Borinian, a clicker, who until yesterday she considered an enemy to be killed on sight. And by the anticipation of more clickers on the way, searching for Khal. Real enemies this time.

Her irascibility also a product of continuing confusion surrounding Khal. Her perplexing inability to reach a decision regarding him. She'd only recently grown comfortable having another person on her ship. And in her life. And now Khal, in all likelihood a continued presence for the foreseeable future. From her perspective, the ship unnaturally crowded.

Ezekiel, dressed in his loose comfortable tunic, entered the galley, driving the irritable thoughts from her mind. They sat at the galley table sipping a hot tea brew.

"We must leave this place now," she said, giving voice to her restlessness. "Before other clickers come."

"May not be near yet. Still searching. And depends how far behind Khal when his ship transit portal. But when search this world from orbit will see crash, and search for Khal. Maybe find Dauphin. But find or not, we must stop them returning through portal."

"What you saying?"

"They see Humans live on this world. They will return to hunt. We must stop them. If fight in space I think Dauphin faster and more powerful than shuttle."

"And if they find us here?"

"Must fight them here. They will come only at night."

"And Khal?" Seraphina voicing her silent concern.

"You have sleep vision?" Ezekiel asked instead.

The question startled her. And forced her to concentrate on more than the muddled thoughts swirling in her head.

"A dream? Yes."

"What you see in dream?"

Seraphina focused on the images nesting in her conscious mind since awakening. Vivid and real. As though observed and experienced moments before in wakeful reality. Close enough if she reached out she might touch them. Their serene afterimage calmed her otherwise troubled thoughts.

Her dream had been a mixed montage of birth. A nebulous pillar of gas and dust swirled in a black void, coalescing, condensing, breaking into fragments. The fragments condensed further into rotating spheres of gas and dust, the embryos of future stars. In Seraphina's dream one such sphere collapsed upon itself, until its center burst into bright burning light, its heat and luminosity increasing with the birth of a star.

A flattened disk of unused gas and dust rotated around the newborn star. Particles in the swirling debris collided, coalescing, clumping together in larger masses, growing like a snowball rolling downhill, giving birth to planets around the new star.

In her dream she saw tiny thin strands of string. Seraphina did not understand these strings to be nucleotide molecules, but in her dream they swam in the gas clouds, regurgitated into the cosmos by stars that had lived and died before the newborn star. The newborn's fiery birth transformed the strings, spitting them back into the swirling gases surrounding the newborn planets. Embedded in one of the new worlds the strands acquired an ability to replicate, to reproduce itself. The isolated strands interacted, accumulating complexity, mimicking the coalescing birth process of the star, and the worlds orbiting the star.

A seed emerged on the nascent planet, dividing, replicating, multiplying, growing. Forming anatomical structures, appendages, internal organs and structures. Offspring develop, assuming the structure of their parentage, and a new life emerges.

"I do not know your words," Seraphina said in awe and wonder, recalling the dream. "And you do not know my words to see it. I must show you in the link."

"I see birth." Ezekiel said. "The beginning."

Seraphina's brows arched beneath the crop of blue hair covering her forehead. Her eyes wide, mouth open, registering the impact of his words.

"A star?" she said.

"And worlds," he said.

"Beginning of life," she said.

"New life," he finished. Both stared open mouthed across the table at each other.

"Khal," Seraphina said. The single word emphatic. "He give us dream. Same dream. Where Khal?" she asked in Ezekiel's native tongue, her tone accusatory and apprehensive.

"Maybe sleep," Ezekiel said.

At that moment, Khal hung roosting in a tall tree on the edge of the clearing. Enveloped in the dark shade of the tree's thick branches and leaves. Unable to sleep. His mind active, focused on images and reports summoned from the depths of his memory. Time to complete his final task perhaps running out. And he no closer to a solution. The answer perhaps awaiting discovery on the origin world. But he had no idea the nature of the solution. Or where to search. He had the story. The complete history. Except for the single elusive final proof.

A transformation had indeed occurred. Ancient Human researchers had been aware of it. Had documented the result and devoted enormous resources to determining, and perhaps reversing, its cause, the catalyst which had initiated the process. Khal was convinced the ancient Humans had discovered the solution in the long abandoned laboratories he'd excavated and explored. Convinced the information he required to point him in the correct direction had to be contained in data already accumulated. But the memorized images scrolling across his mind continued to conceal their secret.

Khal aware of an unconnected thought intruding on his contemplation. A summons. The Human female.

He released his grasp on the branch. His wings lifted him on a rising current or air, heated by a sun rising full and white hot in the bright sky. The Humans waited next to the serenely nesting ship. The female stepped forward to address him as he landed. Her manner stern, perhaps angry. Khal uncertain of the Human emotion seemingly directed at him.

"We must leave this place," she informed him, vocalizing her thoughts. The words and thoughts abrupt, reflecting her demeanor. "We find another island away from your crashed ship. After we find another island, we see how to go from there."

Her thoughts ended abruptly. She turned and marched into the ship. She did not wait for a response.

Seraphina's attitude not directed at anyone in particular. Her earlier mood returned. An anxious apprehension regarding the developing situation. A restless instinct to be on the move amid unsettled thoughts regarding Khal. And the implications for the relationship developing between her and Ezekiel. And maybe something else. Seraphina recognized the familiar signs preceding her bleeding. By her calculation the time drawing close. As regular as the cycles of the sun. Preparing and moving Dauphin provided a welcomed distraction from her thoughts.

Later in the evening, the three gathered in Dauphin's lounge off the galley. Seraphina's disposition had improved as the day wore on. She hadn't resolved the issues troubling her. But they weighed less heavily on her thoughts and her mood. As night settled over their new island location, she'd decided against an outdoor campsite. And she had shut down as many unnecessary systems aboard Dauphin as possible. But the ship still radiated small amounts of energy from the systems its three occupants did require. Perhaps enough to be detected by sensitive sensors.

Seraphina eyed Khal. Her stare suspicious and unwavering on the figure sitting across from her on a backless stool. More comfortable for him, he'd explained. His back held erect. His arms at his side. His closed fingers wrapped the thin translucent wings close around his body. Eyes closed, a low rhythmic murmur escaped his parted lips.

"What he doing? Seraphina whispered in Ezekiel's direction.

"Thinking." Ezekiel said.

"Thinking what?"

"You ask him."

"What are your thoughts Khal?" Seraphina asked, the aggressive tone of the morning no longer present, but a suspicious glint still present in the eyes scrutinizing him.

"A solution I am searching for and have been unable to find," his thoughts entered her mind. Thin, hairless, closed lids opened to reveal opaque glass marbles staring back at her.

"But I have considered a solution to another issue. There is a world in the Ghulbaran system I explored some years ago. There is now a colony of Nivalinorhrans on this world, both Human and Borinian, continuing to excavate and study the ancient sites I discovered there. I will be able to acquire transport there for the remainder of my journey. I will have no need to impose on you further if you will agree to deliver me there."

Seraphina turned to Ezekiel seated next to her, recalling the images of Humans and Borinians together. Ezekiel's face impassive, his eyes expressing his customary child like curiosity. His unchanged demeanor a blank reaction to Khal's thoughts. She wondered if perhaps Khal had not shared the thoughts to Ezekiel.

"You hear his thoughts too? She asked him. What you think?"

Ezekiel's gaze rose to meet hers. His enticing grey eyes stared deep into hers.

"I go where you go," he said.

Her heart seemed to pause beating. Stilled by his response. Emotion welled within her, rising to constrict her throat, strengthening her connection to him, her desire for him. Aware of a quickened strumming inside her chest. His simple response answered her troubled questions, and laid her silent fear to rest.

Seraphina turned to Khal. "Tell about the dream you gave us. Tell us what it means."

"It is where the history begins," Khal replied in their minds. "The beginning of all things. The journey we all share with each other, and also with the Universe around us. In the dream you saw the scaffolding which binds us all. From interstellar cloud to life-giving star, orbiting dust to life-bearing planets, insemination of the seed to birth of a new generation."

"Why show us this dream?" Seraphina asked.

"To teach you. To provide you the knowledge in a manner you can understand. These things have been known before. Much of it inscribed and recorded so it may be passed on. On my world my people have no need for writing. We keep all knowledge in our memory, or recorded as images. And your people have not been taught to read or use inscriptions as your ancestors did. In any case the language of the ancients is forgotten. Even on the worlds where Humans still read and inscribe, the language in which this knowledge is told is unfamiliar and unrecognizable."

"You say there is more. You will show us?"

"If you wish to learn more I can give you more dreams. But some of what you will see is not pleasant."

"What will we see?"

"Wars. The deaths of millions upon millions. Catastrophic upheavals. The extinction of entire species. Our journeys have had their gloriously enlightening periods, and dark destructive periods. But it is who we are and where we came from. It is my belief if we can understand ourselves and our shared cosmic connection, we may avoid the destructive behaviors of our past. Unfortunately it is not a universally shared belief among my people, or yours. And I fear this ignorance may precipitate yet another upheaval. Perhaps having cataclysmic consequences. But perhaps that too is part of the cycle. Who can know how many times, on how many worlds, this has occurred before, or will occur again? As species we must all inevitably return to the dark from which we came, as stars and planets also do."

"Must it always end?" Seraphina asked, unexpectedly enthralled by the thoughts Khal imparted, edging toward another unconscious decision. Another resolution to another set of confounding emotions.

"It is the natural cycle of life. But as long as the Universe continues, there will always be new beginnings."

"What about afterlife," Ezekiel asked, breaking his long vocal and mental silence. The word unfamiliar to Seraphina.

"Afterlife?" she repeated, mimicking Ezekiel's pronunciation.

"Another life after death," Khal translated in her mind.

"Yes. What about afterlife?" she repeated Ezekiel's question, using the word of her language, recalling stories among some factions regarding a transformation to another life after death. An expectant eagerness for Khal's response in her voice.

"I cannot teach you of the afterlife as a scientist. I have no empirical evidence an individual's life continues in another form after death in another realm, or on some other plane of existence. Which does not mean it does not exist. Such beliefs are the realms of philosophy, religion, and mythology, based on faith rather than science. All I can convey to you is all cultures appear to have such beliefs, even if the beliefs are different from culture to culture. Ancient texts I have translated indicate your ancestors had many different beliefs regarding an afterlife. Some believed in a spirit, which after death of the physical body is transported to another place to live an eternal existence. Others had a belief similar to one among my people. Of a rebirth after death. Repeating the life cycle. On my home world, Borinorhrans believe the cycle of death and rebirth is mediated by the twin stars, manifested during the eclipse. That is all I know concerning the afterlife. I cannot prove or disprove its existence."

As they had the previous night, the three conversed until weariness beckoned sleep. Seraphina rubbed the back of a hand across her drooping eyes. She stood, reaching out to Ezekiel. Her motion frozen by the expression on his face, hardened, as though chiseled from stone. His jaw clamped and set. His eyes, liquid and innocent and beckoning whenever she stared into them, now cold and fierce.

"Weapons," he said. "Must hide Khal."

"They have found me," she heard Khal's thought, reporting a fact. Her gaze shifted between Khal and Ezekiel.

"You have sensed them," Khal inquired of Ezekiel. "Remarkable you, a Human did, and I did not."

Ezekiel sprang from the cushioned settee. "Must hide Khal. They come."

"No." Khal's thought rang in their heads. "I must go to them. It is my fight. Not yours."

"You can fight?" Ezekiel asked.

"No," Seraphina heard Khal's response. "But I cannot allow you to be harmed on my account."

A fighter ship in space erupting into a fireball scorched Seraphina's mind. Only for a instant. The image vanished as abruptly as the fires engulfing the vessel.

"No. You hide," her response as much a surprise to her as to Khal. She hadn't contemplated it. Hadn't considered another course of action. Her decision, as always, instinctual and final.

They hid Khal in an equipment locker on the way to the cargo hold. There Ezekiel and Seraphina striped to bare skin and donned new garments. Seraphina the tight fitting pants and upper coat she'd worn at the crash site. This time she included a hardened Borinian style chest plate Ezekiel had fashioned for her from a suit salvaged in the wreck. The front and back halves fastened at the sides. Her weapons harnesses she strapped around her waist and across her back.

Ezekiel donned the hard shell-like outer garment he'd been wearing when she'd first discovered him. The rigid material like armor. The weapons skirt belted around his waist. The shokra he pushed into its holster. Seraphina drew and handed him both pistols. Ezekiel gazed at them in a cursory examination. Perhaps not skilled in their use, but his practical knowledge of their functioning complete. He tucked them into holsters on either side of the skirt. Finally each donned a headcap.

"The headcap not only allow us to speak together, also keep the clickers out of your mind. They will first try to control our minds. But they do not know the caps are modified. We use it to draw them out. When I say, activate the transmitter we modified. And remember, they prefer to attack from the air. Watch for them there. And they use their feet to strike, their talons as sharp as your blades."

"I remember," Seraphina assured him, recalling their conversation during the trip from their island. She'd initially sought an island providing overhead tree cover, intending to conceal the ship. But Ezekiel had convinced her otherwise, explaining if the clickers found the ship and attacked, they'd use the trees to their advantage. Providing the heights they preferred when attacking, and for concealment. "Out in the open is better," he'd explained.

Seraphina opened the cargo hold's disposal chute. They exited below Dauphin's belly, close to the ground. Dauphin's bulk provided cover and concealment. They waited.

A soft flutter in the night drew their attention. And another. Two Borinians landed in the clearing, flanking the ship. They approached from both sides.

"I sense their thoughts," Ezekiel informed Seraphina through the link.

"So do I," she replied. "Can they hear our thoughts too?"

"No the frequency is blocked to them. But I will allow them to see my thoughts. It will draw them in. You ready?"

"I have the one on the right," her silent answer.

Ezekiel emerged from beneath the ship, straightening his tall frame. He opened his thoughts to the approaching Borinians, allowing their thoughts to invade his mind.

"A quiri."

"Must be wild. Be careful."

"Perhaps not. He is wearing the flight suit of a scout."

"Come to me quiri. Where is your overseer?"

"Unable to see his thoughts regarding his purpose here or any knowledge of our target," the two conferred as they approached. Ezekiel fought to prevent the invading minds from overriding his, the thoughts he recognized solely as his own directing his actions.

The Borinians closed on Ezekiel from both sides. Their weapons high energy particle rifles held rigid along their outstretched arms, pointed at him. A shot at their current range would burn clean through his suit.

Seraphina, crouched on one knee, shuffled into position. Her target in the rifle's optic sights. Her appreciation of Ezekiel's capabilities enhanced since the night in the alley on Ecibor. And from memories he'd shared through the link of his service in the clicker military. His knowledge of clicker tactics an advantage, and his plan for defeating the clickers sound. She recalled his face and eyes in the lounge, an expression she had never imagined him capable of.

The Borinian on Ezekiel's left shifted his focus for an instant. Ezekiel aware they'd been searching the area with their sonic senses. And others, still concealed, covering from above, their thoughts faint images in the minds of the two approaching him. Perhaps the Borinian had detected Seraphina. The distracted Borinian's weapon wavered off target. In the same moment Seraphina fired.

The sharp crack of the rifle's discharge split the still, silent night. The recoil against Seraphina's shoulder cushioned by the stock's shock absorbing rod, and padded butt plate. The smell of explosive enveloped her nostrils. On impact the rifle's explosive projectile opened a gaping hole in the clicker's chest plate and body, pulverized his internal organs, and drove him three meters through the air onto his back.

Seraphina swung the rifle left, centered its sights on the second target, when the dull clap-clap of her pistols reached her ears. Ezekiel held a pistol each hand, firing straight ahead at the advancing clicker, and already moving toward the cover of Dauphin's folded wings before the dead clicker hit the ground.

Ezekiel had waited for Seraphina to fire. The sound of the rifle shot had startled the Borinian advancing on him. The momentary hesitation allowed Ezekiel to draw both pistols and fire. Not pausing to witness the results, Ezekiel moved for the cover of Dauphin's wing. The air where he'd stood crackled and sizzled from bright lances of charged particles. He'd anticipated it. He sent Seraphina the silent mental signal.

Following Ezekiel's plan Seraphina had not moved from her position after firing. As Ezekiel predicted the air around her sizzled as clickers covering from above in the dark night opened fire. She heard Ezekiel's signal in her thoughts, and remotely activated the transmitter using the headcap's command link. She heard nothing. But the firing abruptly ceased.

"They're deaf now" she heard Ezekiel in her mind. "They cannot locate us by sound. They must rely on vision. Time to use your light shell to blind them. It will bring them to the ground."

Still beneath the ship's belly, Seraphina did not see the flare launched from one of Dauphin's dorsal tubes. She heard the whoosh as it soared skyward. Observed the blinding glare as it burst bright in the night sky. Stepping from beneath Dauphin Seraphina raised her rifle, unleashing a rapid rate of fire into the lit sky. Ezekiel firing from the other side.

Ezekiel aware of Seraphina's fire finding targets. The death shrieks of falling clickers heard amid the rapid repeated crack of the rifle. But his eyes were not focused on the sky. Instead on her, around her, above her, as he moved toward her position. His ears strained for the flutter of wings, anticipating an attack from above. They'd be heading for ground now. Of the six man shuttle crew he'd seen in the mind of the Borinian he'd shot, two remained.

Seraphina reacted instantly to Ezekiel's warning. She did not turn for a glimpse of her attacker. Not hesitating, she dropped to the ground and rolled in the direction of the attack. A rush of air brushed her as the attacker sailed over her. His legs stretched forward, wicked talons protruding from booted feet.

He landed in the sand ahead of her, right arm swinging around in her direction. The weapon like a gleaming hollow tube stretched along the arm. She raised the rifle, parrying the swing. The combined force of his swing and her parry ripped the weapon from his thumbed grasp. It spiraled through the air, burying itself in the sand.

He swung a booted foot at her. She rolled away, discarding the rifle encumbering her hands, wishing she had her pistols, searching for an opening to use her blades. She dodged his feet attacking from the left and right. In her peripheral vision she observed Ezekiel firing both pistols non-stop, closing on another landed clicker.

The pistols ceased firing. The soft clicks of their firing mechanism landing on empty chambers signaled their depleted ammunition. The clicker swung his right arm in Ezekiel's direction. The charged particle weapon along his arm targeted on Ezekiel. Ezekiel flung the empty pistols at the Borinian, racing forward as the first pistol struck the clicker's breastplate, the second his right wing below his wrist, impacting his closed fingers, throwing the weapon off target as it discharged. The bright flash and crackling sizzle of charged particles singed the air next to Ezekiel as he advanced on the clicker. Ezekiel grasped the weapon's barrel in his right fist. He rammed it forcefully against the Borinian's shoulder, breaking the Borinian's thumb and releasing his grip. As the weapon came free in Ezekiel's hand he swung his left leg in a powerful leg sweep, striking his opponent behind the right knee, sweeping the leg out from under him.

The clicker thudded to the ground flat on his back, creating a depression in the soft sand. He recovered quickly, rolling to escape Ezekiel's reach. The Borinian gained his legs. His left thumb grasped his second weapon against his palm. The barrel sprang free of its spring loaded holster as Ezekiel hefted the slim particle rifle, left hand under the barrel, right hand around the grip.

Seraphina allowed the clicker to close on her while she timed her move. His arms held at his sides, fingers closed to protect his fragile wings, he lashed out with clawed feet. Loud animated clicks turned to open mouthed grunts as he advanced. His sharp teeth barred. His eyes small black beads focused malevolently on her.

Each time he swung a foot at her, hooked talons sprang forward like spring loaded blades through his open toed boots, retracting after each pass. Seraphina waited. His right foot snapped forward. She shifted to her right. His left foot came at her. Seraphina shifted left. As he planted his left foot, preparing to swing his right, Seraphina reached both hands behind her right shoulder. The Borinian's right foot swung in, hooked talons snapped out. Seraphina's arms swung down to meet his kick, the pattah's hilt in a tight two fisted grip. Sword and leg met in their combined swing.

A harsh ear splitting shriek rent the night as the Borinian's severed leg cart wheeled through the air. The blood stained blade whoop-whooped as Seraphina's practiced hands twirled the long curved sword, ending in a two-handed grip, the blade pointed down. She stabbed downward, the force of her shoulders, back, and hips, behind the blade, plunging it through the writhing clicker's chest plate, body, and into the sand below.

She released the sword. Left it standing impaled in the body. She retrieved her rifle and turned toward Ezekiel as he discharged a long cylindrical weapon he held in both hands. A crack and sizzle like lightning split the air and the breastplate of the Borinian before him. A sharp anguished shriek reached her moments before the odor of burnt flesh.

Seraphina rushed over to Ezekiel. His thoughts informed her the dead clicker at his feet the last of them. She threw her free arm around his neck and drew him close. Held him as though she'd never let go.

"You tell Khal it is finished," he said. "I will attend to these."

When Seraphina returned, Khal at her side, Ezekiel had already dragged the bodies to the edge of the clearing, near the tree line, busy digging a hole in the soft sand.

"I am honored by the actions of you and your mate on my behalf," Khal said in her thoughts. "May I ask why you risk your safety for me?"

"They would not stop with you. They would have captured us or killed us too, and returned to hunt the Humans of this world," recalling Ezekiel's warning. Seraphina paused, examining her response. Her reasoning valid, but also containing a sudden realization, recalling the moment in Dauphin's lounge when her decision had revealed itself to her.

"And you have more to teach," the unexpected thought conveyed to Khal, sealing her decision.

Seraphina approached Ezekiel, now standing waist deep in the hole he continued digging.

"Why Ezekiel?" she asked. "Why we need to hide dead clickers?"

"Not hide," Ezekiel said without pausing in his labor. "Perished must have proper burial for afterlife."

"Why? They are clickers who wanted to kill us."

Ezekiel had no answer for her. No reason for his actions. At least none he understood, or could explain. He hated the Borinian enslavement and treatment of his kind. But he held no hatred for them. No animosity toward them. His attitude regarding them an emotional blank. He simply wished them to go away. To disappear from the lives of his people as they'd disappeared from his mind.

A loud screeching drew their attention. Khal hopped from foot to foot. He leapt in the air, wings folding and unfolding at his side as though attempting to fly. His excited shrieks long, rhythmic, and musical.

"Now what he doing?" Seraphina turned to Ezekiel. Her face scrunched in anxious perplexity. "Does he need to fly? Is it part of Borinian burial?" Concern in her eyes.

"Not to fly," Ezekiel said. "Borinians not able to leap high enough off the ground to fly. Is why they roost high up. They must fall to fly. And not Borinian burial either. I think maybe he is excited."

"Excited by what? The fight is finished. They are dead."

"I do not know."

Ezekiel's mind summoned Khal. But before he had posed the question an excited string of thoughts flooded his mind, and Seraphina's.

"I have found it. Right in front of me all the time. How did I not see? Now so obvious. Ezekiel. Seraphina. The solution lies in the ground The catalyst must be in the ground."

Ezekiel and Seraphina gazed at each other in perplexed bewilderment. Ezekiel still in the deepening hole, Seraphina approached Khal.

"Khal. You think nonsense. What is the meaning of your thoughts?"

Ezekiel perceived a subtle change in Seraphina regarding Khal. In her attitude, her voice, her thoughts. No longer suspicious or apprehensive. No longer irritated by Khal's presence.

Khal ceased his hopping dance. His lyrical shrieks continued, but at a lower, less excitable volume.

"It is the burial. And the bodies," he explained. "Seeing them lying on the ground. The blood leaving their bodies, seeping into the ground. It is the solution I have been searching for. It explains the data I've translated from the ancient texts. It explains my own observations. The process which initiated the transformation occurred in the ground. After death and burial. The notion of death and rebirth not so far-fetched after all. An apt metaphor for the transformation. The catalyst must therefore also be found in the ground. I cannot understand how I did not see it before. The similarities between our two cultures continue to astound and amaze me."

"I still do not understand," Seraphina's exasperated thought also possessing an eagerness to learn.

"I plead for you forgiveness, and your patience. It is difficult using merely my thoughts," Khal explained, the quality of his thoughts less excitable, more instructional, as a teacher to a pupil, responding to the curiosity he sensed in Seraphina's mind. "And I have much to do to prove my hypothesis. We have a saying on Borinorhnus, which I am certain your people originated. 'From the ground we came and to the ground we must return'. This has more literal significance than anyone understands. And that our shared funerary practices should hold the key is quite astonishing. This means I must forego my journey to the origin world and return to Borinorhnus. For the answers lay there. We must depart without further delay."

"First I must complete the burial," Ezekiel said. "And I wish to examine the shuttle. There may be much in it of use to us," his glance resting on Seraphina, aware of the continued confusion in her thoughts. But also a patience, as requested by Khal, and a heightened curiosity sparked by Khal's thoughts.

By afternoon of the next day they were on the move. They'd hadn't slept. The rising Krilan sun painted the sky pink by the time Ezekiel had completed burying the Bodies. He'd glimpsed the shuttle's location in the first Borinian's mind, and they'd spent the morning searching it. Ezekiel scavenged items of particular interest, eliciting frequent smiles from Seraphina. In their short time together Ezekiel had transformed into a scavenger worthy of her pride, although none of the salvaged items were familiar to her. Before departing for orbit, Seraphina destroyed the shuttle using Dauphin's particle beam cannons.

The three day passage to the portal provided time to contemplate, to sleep and dream. Dreams provided by Khal. Their human history. Dreams of a world teeming with abundant life. Also of wars, death, destruction, and rebirth. Of far-flung forgotten worlds spread across the galaxy. Worlds of dusty plains, magnificent mountains, and overgrown forests. Human civilizations arose and disappeared in time lapsed succession. Descendant remnants scattered into small isolated pockets struggling to survive, the knowledge of their forebears and origins forgotten.

Seraphina delighted to be on the move once more. On the threshold of a new place, a new world. Her excitement palpable and alive. Her thoughts settled. Content in the comforting embrace of her accustomed shipboard routine. A routine she'd established during a long solitary existence. Her ship her entire world. Much like Khal, the thought a startling recognition of their similar experience.

Seraphina also at complete ease using the headcap, as though it'd always been part of her. The cap had facilitated and strengthened the bond between her and Ezekiel. Had allowed a new perspective, understanding, and grudging acceptance of a species she'd considered an enemy her entire life. Perhaps best of all, an exciting symbiosis between her and her ship. The sensation of being an organic whole with her beloved Dauphin. A combined creature of flight.

The portal mere hours away, Ezekiel and Khal joined Seraphina in the cockpit. Khal's presence aboard no longer strange, but accepted. During the three day passage from Krilan Ezekiel had modified areas of the ship to accommodate Khal, using materials salvaged from the shuttle, including a roost in a secluded, darkened section of Dauphin's cargo hold.

"Teach me about the portals," Seraphina's thoughts reached out to Khal. "What do you know of them? Where did they come from? Who built them?"

"I believe you may already surmise the answer to your question Seraphina."

Seraphina turned to gaze at him. What might pass as a Borinian smile crossed his short round face. A twinkle in the small sable eyes gazing back at her. A series of soft vocal clicks she interpreted as encouragement. There'd been no visions of portals in her dreams, but an unexpected understanding dawned in her consciousness.

"Humans built them," She said and thought in awe. "My ancient ancestors as you call them." Seraphina noticed the mixture of surprise and expectation on Ezekiel's face as they awaited Khal's response.

"You are correct Seraphina. Many hundreds of thousands of years ago."

"Many factions believe they were built by your people," she said.

"Not so. It is how your ancestors travelled from the origin world to eventually settle all across the galaxy."

"Do you understand how they work?"

"No. Unfortunately we have discovered no inscriptions or records detailing the science behind their function. It appears the engineering aspects were more important as Humans explored farther into the Galaxy. We have uncovered many references to where and how the portals were to be constructed, and the materials used in their construction. As each expedition transited a portal into an unexplored region of space, they carried the materials and blueprints to construct a portal. Otherwise they had no means of returning to the point from which they departed."

Khal paused as Seraphina turned her attention to the ship. She scanned the instruments visually as a cross check to the headcap. The destination frequency provided by Khal had been transmitted to the portal, the Ghulbaran System, unknown to either Seraphina or Ezekiel. The enormous energy output of the portal's activation registered on Dauphin's sensors. Its gravitational tug sucked Dauphin inexorably toward it.

"But how did they know where the portals would send them?" Seraphina thought.

"Ah. It is the genius of the portals. And the genius of your ancestors who discovered and calculated the solutions. Besides the physics of course. At first they did not know. The destinations random accidents, with sometimes tragic consequences according to the records. Many ships and crews were lost. And they were focused in an unrewarding direction. Searching toward the center of the galaxy, a much older and barren region, rather than the more fertile outer spiral arms. Those who believe the portals draw energy from their host stars are correct. But more than this, the portals are tuned to unique characteristics in their host star. Once the physicists learned to engineer this into the portal's design, they would study a star in a region of space they were interested in, using long-range telescopes and instruments, program the particular characteristics of the star into the portal, and use a generated frequency to have the portal lock onto the star. Absolute genius."

"Then there does not need to be a portal at the other end?" Seraphina reasoned.

"Correct again Seraphina." Seraphina sensed an underlying appreciative pride in Khal's thoughts and vocal clicks, like a teacher's pride in an extraordinary pupil.

"The portal at the other end is primarily for the return journey, or to journey somewhere else. From the texts I've examined it appears exiting through a destination portal is an accidental coincidence. A portal will send you to the destination star system whether there is a portal already there or not, or even when the destination portal is active. However, if there is no portal at the other end, or a non-functioning one, you will be stranded."

A smile crossed Seraphina's face as the portal swallowed her Dauphin.

Tovarinkara Pharaxnus

Zanth exited the transport, stepping into the enormous dark cavern housing the governor's and his family's personal transports. Zanth strode toward the open maw of the cliff face, soaking in the view of the twilight lit mountain range and valley below. Gently sloping hillsides covered in lush vegetation emerged from mist-shrouded gorges. His ultraviolet vision detected subtler hues of blue and purple along the slopes. The forested slopes gave way to bare granite walls rising grey and black into the dimly lit sky.

The peaks of the Pharax Range, 50 echospans, 160 kilometers, east of the capital, comprised Governor Tovarinkara Pharaxnus's matrilineal estate. By tradition and law inherited and passed down through the female lineage. Generations of Karan had been birthed and reared in the Pharax mountains. Bordered by the Ghizanar Range father east, on the edge of darkside, its dark uninhabitable peaks rising into the lower stratosphere.

The relative quiet of the few minds Zanth perceived a peaceful respite from the harsh bustling capital. Mostly quiri minds he sensed. Probably a small household herd. And several Borinians. Zanth recognized the thoughts of Tovarinkara's coupled mate, and members of the family, as their connected minds merged seamlessly into his, their individual thoughts mingling. But only the surface of his accessible. Zanth's mental disciple clamped shields around his deeper thoughts.

He studied the carved decorated terraces adorning the nearby peaks. Governor Tovarinkara had provided instructions on which one to use, ensuring their privacy. And Zanth had devised his own precautions upon departing the city to disguise his movements and destination.

Zanth leapt from the cave opening. He savored the rush of sweet perfumed air as he dove. None of the city's noxious fumes. He spread his arms and opened his fingers. His spirit soared in harmony to the lift generated by his outstretched wings. The forgotten serenity of flying for its own pleasure a soothing balm to his troubled thoughts.

He adjusted his wings, banking in a graceful curving arc toward the target terrace. He landed gently on soft shod feet. He'd dressed in civilian attire. No uniform or solid military boots. He'd surmised the governor might not mind. Tovarinkara's subtle invitation indicated he desired an informal, low key, discreet off-the-sonar meeting.

Governor Tovarinkara had been awaiting Zanth's arrival. He strode to the open terrace portal, careful to remain inside. His elderly frame held erect, his bearing regal, as befitting his aristocratic station.

"Please come in General Zanthinvolar Abydynus. It is an honor to have you in my home." A string of pleasant welcoming clicks accompanied his thoughts. The mind entering Zanth's strong, disciplined, despite the governor's physical age. Its intellectual vibrancy never failed to impress Zanth.

"The honor is mine Governor Tovarinkara Pharaxnus," Zanth responded formally.

"May I offer you a drink? Tea? A nectar? Perhaps something stronger?"

Zanth on the cusp of a polite refusal, changed his mind when he perceived the governor's disappointment. Their minds, strong enough to probe deep into the other, politely skimmed only the surface of the other's thoughts.

"Perhaps a Bahquava," Zanth thought instead.

"Appropriate choice. I believe I will join you."

Tovarinkara indicated a ledge high in a corner of the smooth carved chamber. The area provided a roost next to a drink dispenser. Around the dim chamber other carved outcroppings and ledges provided other roosts accessed by stairways carved into the chamber walls. Around the roosts hung personal items and various accoutrements of the governor's office. At one roost a com headcap and data recorder. The chamber evidently utilized for work and relaxation, Zanth concluded. He followed the governor along a series of stairways to the roost. Zanth waited for Tovarinkara to distill the appropriate mixture in the dispenser before they both hung head down from the roost.

"I am of course pleased you agreed to meet me general," Tovarinkara thought, sipping on a tube connected to the dispenser. A pleasurable chirping accompanied his ingestion of the alcoholic beverage.

"Your call did stir my curiosity governor."

"I believe more than mere curiosity was aroused general."

"Indeed."

"Share with me your thoughts regarding our recent council meeting. I am aware there is much you did not share with the council."

"I am uncertain to what you refer governor."

"Let us not be politely coy general. Too much is at stake. I asked you here, because despite your performance at the council meeting, I perceived a premeditation underlying your thoughts. Am I correct in this perception?"

Zanth sipped from his tube. A delaying action while he pondered the direction of this exchange. Governor Tovarinkara perhaps reading those thoughts as well. But Zanth did not sense the governor attempting to dig beneath his mental defenses. Rather he sensed a desire in the governor's thoughts for a mutual sharing.

"You are correct governor," Zanth admitted.

"Then acquiring our consent to meet the Khalinorhrans merely pro forma for a course of action you had already decided to pursue?"

"You are perceptive." Zanth noted Tovarinkara again used the name adopted by the Nivalinorhrans.

"And I also assume, such a decision, such a drastic course of action which our esteemed Governor Supreme might consider treason, is based on your desire to avoid a war at all costs?"

"Correct again governor."

Zanth sipped again. The strong beverage burned his throat and chest. The prerequisite preliminaries answered to Tovarinkara's satisfaction, Zanth expected him to proceed to the heart of the matter. Governor Tovarinkara did not disappoint.

"Please understand general, I am firmly loyal to Borinorhnus. But I am a scientist, and I disagree with many of the council's policies, particularly as they pertain to the advancement of scientific inquiry. Recent discoveries and emerging truths may not be acceptable to everyone, but I believe it must be a choice. Present the facts and allow individuals to choose as they will. To accept or not accept as they will. To believe or not believe as they will."

"I tend to agree governor. Though such issues are not within my purview or my immediate concern. Such matters may be sorted out later, assuming there is a later."

"Well put. Indeed. And your point is well taken. What is your candid assessment of the military situation?"

"In my judgment an all-out war will result in devastation to both sides. The council must be made to understand Nivalinorhran weaponry and capabilities are as formidable as our own. Perhaps even more than we are aware. You should know governor, I redacted certain portions of my reports to the council, particularly a recent operation carried out by a trusted operative. My intent was to prevent an overreaction by the council based on fear. In truth, Nivalinorhnus has developed military capabilities our intelligence were not aware of. Capabilities which may surpass our own in some respects. There is no guarantee regarding the outcome of a conflict.

"But you believe they can be reasoned with."

"It is my hope governor. The General Commander of their military is young, but from my reports of him a brilliant, capable, veteran commander, with an exemplary record. I do not believe he would welcome a war. This contributed to my decision to meet him mind to mind. Yet I despair of convincing the council to reverse the course they appear set upon, especially if Nivalinorhnus is intent on fission regardless of the council's resistance."

"The problem is not the council, general. As I suspect you have already surmised, based on your surreptitious performance at the meeting. The vote may currently be three against and three for, with Khorabinjolen the deciding vote. Since the requirement for war needs more than a simple majority, he will attempt to sway the weaker undecided members. And failing to accomplish it, I do not put it beyond him to constitute a new council, appointing replacements he can control. It places his opponents in and outside the council in a precarious situation. He has already instructed Mokhar and Zephar to quietly prepare a propaganda campaign against the fissionists. And Zephar's security forces have been instructed to round up and detain all dissident influences within the collective. Communications between Borinorhnus and Khalinorhnus are quietly being shut down, particularly interpersonal communications."

"Is there no way to persuade him away from such decisions? To even delay him until I can report to the council following my meeting?"

"Dissuade him? I think not. But delaying him until your return may be possible. Khorabinjolen is by no means a war monger general. But in his mind he cannot countenance fission, even if it means waging a war to prevent it. His mind is captive to an obsolete dogma incapable of recognizing who we are, where we came from, and where we need to go. I'm afraid our collective fate rests in you general, and the other young general on Khalinorhnus."

And perhaps one other Zanth thought, as he contemplated the implications conveyed by Governor Tovarinkara.

Enroute to the spaceport following his meeting, Zanth formulated his plan B, composing a message intended for Agar.

Motherships

The military spaceport, normally a bustling hive of concentrated activity, even busier than usual. Long dark lines of Borinorhran military personnel swarmed into the embarkation caves like fast flowing rivers. The port drowned in the roar of shuttles blasting into the heavens. They rose from the sheared open tops of the port's jagged peaks. One after the other. A continuous barrage of self propelled projectiles streaking upward through the twilight sky.

Zanth's command shuttle, large enough to fit three personal sized transports, lofted him into orbit amid the swarm. Its luxurious accommodations included private quarters, a private wardroom, a command office, and briefing room. More space than required by his small entourage of two adjutants.

Zanth's mind linked to his aides, theirs to his. Also linked to the shuttle's cockpit crew, and through the cockpit to the assembled fleet. Zanth relayed a continuous stream of orders through the aides, his thoughts wholly occupied by the task of positioning his forces. The true purpose of his visit to Nivalinorhnus shielded from them, and the fleet.

The fleet deployment explained as a military exercise. The garrison on Nivalinorhnus the opposing force. Though Zanth perceived in the minds of certain fleet commanders suspicions and rumors regarding the nature of the deployment. Perhaps planted and spread by Zepharinlenar in an effort to gather intelligence independent of Zanth. His aides also aware of the rumors, but refrained from sharing those thoughts with their commander. Instead the aides relayed his constant stream of orders, their vocal clicking echoing around the cave-like office.

An image of Orh's system appeared in Zanth's mind, depicting the planets and their positions around the twin stars. Also depicting the deployed fleet, and their changing positions in response to his orders.

He'd chosen one of two motherships in high orbit above Borinorhnus as the flagship for the mission. The mothership enormous and intimidating. His arrival at Nivalinorhnus in a mothership intended to project a show of strength. Enough to convey the proper impression.

"The flagship is preparing to depart orbit as soon as the shuttle is aboard General," one of his aides reported."

"And the other?" Zanth asked.

"As ordered it has deployed its squadrons in high and low orbits around Borinorhnus to provide force protection and planetary defense.

"Excellent. And the blockading squadrons?" Zanth had ordered a blocking picket line of ships into the interplanetary space separating Borinorhnus and Nivalinorhnus.

"Moving into position general."

Zanth had also deployed sentry ships to guard the portal and communication relay station. One of those ships had transmitted Zanth's coded message through the portal to Agar, disguised as a routine request to the orbital mining station in the Korochar system. A detail Zanth shielded in his thoughts.

Reports from the fleet filtered into Zanth's mind. The routine types he pushed to the back of his thoughts. He focused instead on the sensor scans and scouting observations of Nivalinorhnus's fleet deployments. The pictorial overlay of the stellar system and the relative positions of both fleets perceived like a chess board in his mind. The young Nivalinorhran commander positioned his forces in a pattern similar to Zanth's.

A static standoff. Acceptable under the circumstances. And as previously agreed to between Zanth and the Nivalinorhran General Commander.

Concentrating on the larger strategic picture Zanth missed a detail in the flood of reports streaming to him through his aides. The images instead reached him through the unfiltered minds in the background, increasingly more anxious and intense, capturing his attention. The Nivalinorhrans had deployed Borinorhran type vessels in non-critical sectors. But scans of more significant strategic areas had detected a different type of vessel.

"It cannot be," the thoughts of his aides now focused in his mind.

"Is this vessel known to you general?"

"Has it been under secret development on Nivalinorhnus?"

Zanth struggled to control and shield his astonished thoughts as the sensor images bombarded his mind. His surprise matched the stunned reactions spreading through the fleet.

The size of a Borinorhran battleship, the resemblance ended there. Instead of the oblong shaped, asteroid like homogeny characteristic of Borinorhran battleships and attack cruisers, the Nivalinorhran vessels boasted a sleek elongated forward section and a large square-shaped aft section. The sides and corners of the aft section gracefully curved. An array of spiked sensor and communication antennas lined the aft section's dorsal surface like a spine. Transparent ports illuminated by interior lighting dotted sections of its hull. And scattered around every surface, hundreds of closed ports. Their scans had not been able to penetrate the Nivalinorhran ships, but the most logical purpose of the ports to house weapons, Zanth suspected. And if correct, the vessels possessed a withering amount of firepower.

Attached on either side below the aft section hung two rectangular modules, each the size of the aft section, creating the impression of spread wings. Sensors depicted open portals fore and aft in each of the wing-like structures, their gaping maws revealing cavernous fighter filled hangers within.

Zanth paused, reassessing the situation. Not only the appearance of the strange vessels, but the fleet exercise cover story. The deployment of unknown, alien vessels in the opposing fleet considered by some confirmation of the rumors and suspicions. His aides' thoughts an onslaught of questions. The same questions being asked across the fleet.

Zanth unable to answer their questions. Not yet. And his shielded thoughts returned to a nettlesome question he had shelved for later consideration. Now spotlighted by the new situation. Whom to trust?

"The mission remains unchanged," he responded instead. "The new Nivalinorhran vessels are deployed to test their capabilities and ours. And we may assume there will be other surprises. It will all be explained at the appropriate time.

Pass that on to all fleet commanders, and repeat to all commands the order to maintain weapons uncharged and housed."

Zanth perceived the skepticism in their thoughts. He did not expect the story to hold for long. But he relied on military discipline to carry out his orders. The primary preoccupation of his shielded thoughts at this point, the complete intelligence failure. Agar's report following his visit to Nivalinorhnus, and the encounter in Burude, had been a forewarning. But no one, including Zanth, had imagined the existence of such vessels.

The images in his mind replaced by the looming bulk of the approaching flagship. The epitome of Borinorhran technology and engineering, possessing the means to devastate entire worlds. The ship itself a self-contained world. Its enormous size and tremendous power comforted Zanth's thoughts. It restored his equilibrium and faith in Borinorhran military superiority, erasing the shock of the Nivalinorhran vessels. Borinorhnus still held the military edge.

Designed to mimic the home world landscape, the mothership consisted of a circular base housing its propulsion reactors, engineering spaces, and hangers. Its powerful engines ported along one arc of the circular base. The hangers allowed the ship's hundreds of attack fighters, orbital bombers, scouts, and other attack and support craft to fall from beneath the ship during launch.

Mountainous peaks rose from the circular base, the tallest peak in the center, ringed by smaller peaks of varying sizes. The peaks housed primary and secondary bridges, battle command centers, living quarters, wardrooms, and other facilities for the crew, pilots, ground forces and quiri pens. In total, close to ten thousand souls.

Zanth's mind absorbed the mesmerizing enormity and power of the mothership as the shuttle lined up on final approach. The ominous Nivalinorhran vessels pushed aside in his thoughts. Nothing more ominous than a mothership he reasoned. Yet Zanth tempered his prideful admiration. Sobered by embedded images of motherships destroyed in far-flung systems by marauding fleets of wild quiri, supposedly no match for Borinorhran technology and power. The motherships, their crew, and all their sophisticated attack craft and weaponry lost to fiery deaths in the cold, suffocating depths of space.

Powerful but not invincible, Zanth conceded, reaffirming the necessity of a careful examination and assessment of Nivalinorhnus's military capabilities. His gambit to present a display of strength already producing results, forcing the Nivalinorhran to show their capabilities, even if those capabilities proved astonishing. But he had the mothership, intended to affirm Borinorhran power and resolve. Zanth's decided intent to avert a war. But a war he'd wage none-the-less to defend his home against attack.

Yet the intelligence failure continued to haunt him as he boarded the flagship. The unknown vessels perhaps a moderated response to his gambit. A calculated display, designed to unsettle the Borinorhran fleet while disguising other surprises the Nivalinorhrans had yet to reveal.

Zanth settled into the ornate office chamber aboard the mothership as it broke orbit and swept into the dark interplanetary space between the home worlds. His thoughts returned to his preparations for the meeting. He had yet to

select the squadron commanders for his delegation, raising
again the question of who to trust. He'd decided the smaller
the contingent, the better.

"What is it?" he demanded of the aide whose thoughts
interrupted his concentration.

"A message from the bridge general. They have been
informed the Nivalinorhran escort has departed the planet
and headed for our rendezvous."

"As expected. Inform the flagship commander I wish
him and these officers to accompany me to the surface for the
duration of the exercise." His shielded thoughts recalled the
secret arrangements he and the Nivalinorhran General had
agreed to. Accepting a Nivalinorhran escort, though an
implicit nod to Nivalinorhran independence, a small gesture
in the service of peace. And easily explained to his fleet
commanders.

Zanth thoughts had not heard his last order relayed.
"What is the delay? Why have you not relayed my orders?"
Zanth immediately contrite at his impatience. Not the time for
a foul mood. Though it appeared to be his perpetual state of
late.

His order still not relayed. Both aides appeared
transfixed. Dumbstruck. Zanth probed their thoughts, at the
same time conscious of an increasing anxiety among the
flagship's crew, their agitated thoughts beckoning to be heard,
an anxiety spreading like a wildfire throughout the fleet.

"General, are you aware of this?" the shocked, startled
inquiry emanating from the flagship's commander, bypassing
Zanth's aides, demanding his attention.

Zanth opened his mind, lowering mental shields he'd
fixed into place upon boarding the flagship, the enclosed

proximity of thousands of disparate minds like a small city. Those minds now bombarded his, overwhelming him. Not by their number, but by their nature. A tsunami of bewildered, confounded, horror-struck thoughts. Zanth focused on the bridge, pushing the chaos to the background.

Zanth's thunderstruck mind almost shut down entirely, joining the frightful paralysis gripping the ship and the fleet. His mind unable to process the images relayed from the bridge. Unable to accept the unimaginable, inconceivable input. His mind searched frantically for a recognizable point of reference, without success.

Imponderable details impacted his shocked brain. Perceived as incomprehensible flashes of disconnected bits of data. One and a half times larger than the mothership. Yet half the mass. Faster. Its velocity intercepting his flagship five times faster than a Borinorhran mothership at maximum velocity. It's energy output equal to a small pre-fusion protostar.

Its shape an oblate spheroid, bulging out at the sides, flattened at the top and bottom, like an inflated tire lying on its side. Forty stories, or decks, high. Interior illumination spilled from thousands of transparent ports around its circumference. A multi-colored panoply when viewed in the visual spectrum.

On its bottom rim another multicolor display of reds, blues, ambers, and star hot whites from engine ports arranged in three concentric rings.

A central hub protruded above and below the sphere. The hub a bristling complexity of antennae, collectors and weapons.

Zanth stood aghast. The alarmed chirps and shrieks of his aides registered for the first time. Their vocalizations animated by fear. Zanth unable to fault them. His own reaction similar to theirs, and the entire fleet. Outwardly he remained impassive, but acutely aware his gambit to display power and strength had been rendered mute and nullified.

The Nivalinorhrans had displayed theirs. And won.

Korochar

The base orbited one of five moons, around one of three gas giants on the outer edge of the Korochar System. The moon the size of Borinorhnus. The base's orbit placed it between the gaseous world and the moon every three planetary days, forty two celestial days, seventeen Borinorhran days, when scoop ships skimmed the outer atmosphere for hydrogen and other fuel gases.

The moon's atmosphere and surface unsuitable for life. But the continual volcanic activity which toxified its atmosphere, also spewed minerals and other raw materials from deep beneath its surface. The base obtained these ores from the surface without the dangers and expense of mining, although the moon's toxic atmosphere, volcanic eruptions, and volatile surface, presented their own set of dangers. The base's refineries produced materials enabling the base to remain self-sustaining, while also supplying the home world and off-world fleets.

Agar waited in the wardroom for the base commander. The cabin designed to emulate a natural Borinorhnus roost. But the artificial materials, sounds, and smells, reminded Agar of a ship, of living in space, of his dislike for both, and of other places he'd rather be. He sipped from a nearby dispenser. The hot tangy liquid warmed him inside, momentarily warding off the wardroom's chill. The base's environmental controls still undergoing repair, with areas of the base as cold and inhospitable as the darkside of Borinorhnus.

Repairs to the cruiser almost complete, but proceeding at an agonizingly slow pace. Many of the base's systems required repair in order to provide repairs to the ship. His crew often diverted to assist the base repairs. The base's personnel grateful for the extra hands. But for Agar, it meant more frustrating delays.

Agar was anxious to resume his mission. But uncertain how to proceed amid unsettling unknowns. He'd received no communication from the shuttle. Its destination and current status unknown. And no communication from General Zanth since transmitting his report. His mission status also unknown.

The wardroom's upper portal whooshed open. The scent, ultraviolet outline, and thoughts, identified the arrival as the base's commander, a Sub-Admiral. His rugged muscular frame, similar in build to the miners he supervised, leapt the distance between the portal and a roost next to Agar. On the sides of his face and jaws a patch of unkempt facial hair, almost a beard. His eyes expressionless, as usual, but the drooping lids indicated his fatigue. His uniform soiled by lubricants and soot. He'd been working non-stop to save his base and crew.

"How are the repairs progressing admiral?" Agar greeted him, noting the sub-admiral's weary appearance and distraught countenance.

"As before captain commander. Progress is slow. We have been able to reactivate some critical systems, other will require more time. And a few will remain off line until we receive the necessary parts from home."

The sub-admiral's thoughts and demeanor betrayed not only his fatigue, but his lack of enthusiasm for his posting. The isolated and often ignored base, a transitory supply and repair facility for Borinorhran military vessels, perhaps the final rung in an otherwise undistinguished career. His deepest thoughts reflected a fatalistic resignation. But Agar admired the effort he'd expended for his command and his crew, despite his undesirable posting.

The sub-admiral's preliminary report contained details Agar wished elaborated. But following their initial briefing, every opportunity to meet had been repeatedly delayed by interruptions from either the base or the cruiser. Matters requiring their personal attention. Agar now eager to complete their conversation before another 'urgent' interruption. But he waited for the admiral to choose a drink and settle.

"I wished to know more of your report regarding the attack," Agar prompted after the admiral's deep thirsty slurping from the dispenser.

"As I indicated before, The attack was well coordinated. The first ships through the portal destroyed the communication and sensor arrays. I dispatched scouts and fighters, and placed the outer defense perimeter and the base defenses on alert. But they managed to destroy our outer defenses."

"Did it appear as if the attackers had foreknowledge of your defense placements?"

"Not specifically. But it does appear they had knowledge of our defensive strategy. They divided their attack into waves, each wave targeted a section of our defenses. One wave engaged our fighters while another engaged the base directly."

"How many ships?"

"Approximately fifty."

"And you are certain the attackers were quiri?"

"Quite certain. Our sensors were able to confirm that."

"And no indication of minds controlling the quiri? Even after the arrival of the other ships which came to your aid?

"None. They were wild quiri. From the ship markings probably a faction known as Tau. We have received intelligence reports of these Tau actively searching for our bases and ships. Many have been attacked as we were. Apparently these quiri are no longer content to wait until Borinorhran ships appear in a system. They are hunting us as we have hunted them."

"I require more regarding these other ships which came to your aide."

"For what purpose captain commander? What is your interest? Agar sensed a probe into his deeper thoughts. The sub-admiral's efforts to no avail against a privy as strong and adept as Agar. And Agar's equally strong seer ability easily penetrated the deepest layers of the admiral's mind.

"It may be pertinent to my mission admiral. There are questions for which the Governing Council and General Supreme Zanthinvolar Abydynus, who personally assigned me this mission, require urgent answers. Particularly in light of these increasing attacks as you have observed. It will not bode well for you if I were to report of your less than full cooperation."

Agar not one to drop names, seldom invoking his chain of command. But in his cover as captain commander, it might be useful in rattling the sub-admiral.

"If it will get me off this accursed base and back home I don't mind at all," provoking an amusement Agar shielded from the admiral. "As I conveyed earlier, the battle had waged for several hours and the quiri had gained the upper hand, when an unidentified fleet arrived. The ships unfamiliar. Not Borinorhran. We thought it must be more quiri, and given the new wave we stood no change of survival. But the arriving ships fired on the quiri. And were much faster and more maneuverable than the quiri ships. Eventually the quiri ships abandoned the attack and retreated. The ships were of Nivalinorhnus, but none like I have ever seen. Crewed by both Borinian and quiri, or Human as they insisted. Another thing I have never seen or even imagined. Called themselves Khalinaltanists of Khalinorhnus."

"How do you know this?"

"We exchanged thoughts. Given the combined shock of the attack and these Khalinaltanists, and the damage to the base, much greater than we'd initially suspected, we did not refuse their aid. Without their assistance we might not have been able to stabilize the base. We would be falling toward the moon and burning up by now. The Khalinaltanists also accepted our critically wounded into their medical wards. Are these people known to you captain commander?" the sub-admiral again attempting a probe into Agar's mind for further information.

"To a degree, though we do not know much regarding their bases," Agar's thoughts designed to entice further information, and peer beneath the Sub-Admiral's response.

"Rumors have reached even this forsaken outpost of mysterious ships which protect both Borinorhran and quiri ships from raiders. And defend quiri worlds against our hunts.

They do not appear to takes sides in preventing attacks. We were not aware they were Nivalinorhrans. From the little information we shared there are apparently fleets deployed among many systems."

Rumor perhaps, but the thought struck an ominous chord in Agar's mind.

Agar intercepted the thoughts summoning the sub-admiral. Heard the status report regarding replacement of the communication relay station, and receipt of a communication packet for the captain commander.

"I will receive it aboard the cruiser," Agar informed the sub-admiral, unconcerned by the revelation of how deeply he'd entered the admiral's mind.

Boarding the cruiser enclosed in a repair slip, Agar proceeded directly to the command bridge. The bridge a hive of activity despite the motionless crew at their roosts. Their mental activity bombarded Agar upon entering the bridge. Repair assignments, orders, instructions, status reports, flooded his mind, orchestrated by the cruiser's commander at his command roost.

Agar pushed their thoughts to the back of his mind as he hung at his station and donned a headcap. He tuned out the crew's comingled thoughts, relegating them to white noise in the background, his increasing nostalgia for his accustomed solitude never far from his thoughts.

"Ready to receive," he informed the communications officer.

The message not transmitted from the shuttle as he'd anticipated. Instead from General Zanthinvolar. The message in Agar's personal code. He'd been fortunate to receive it. Probably dispatched prior to the attack and destruction of the previous relay station. Agar contemplated the many stages where the message might have failed to reach him. The time stamp indicated it'd been transmitted three celestial days before. The transmission capsule, small enough to escape sensor detection during the attack, had probably defaulted to standby when it had not received the relay station's signal. Its hardened casing and small magnetic field protected the electronics inside. It had reactivated itself upon receiving the proper coded homing signal from the new relay station, and transmitted its message. Once it had completed the transmission, the capsule had traversed the distance to the relay station, where it had been retrieved, stored, and recycled for its next message.

The message itself prompted Agar to clamp his mind shut, as though he'd vanished from the crew's midst. His involuntary vocalizations stifled before escaping his lips.

"Commander, how soon before we can get under way?"

"We are flight capable at this time Captain Commander. However thrust is only at eighty percent. Weapons are back on line but only three batteries remain intact. Repairs to the hull are ninety percent complete."

"It is good. Secure the repair crews and prepare for departure."

"With respect commander, we are not fully capable of resuming the mission "

"We're headed home commander," Agar informed him.

A groundswell of relief accompanied the thoughts flowing into Agar's mind. Every mind on the bridge joined the commander's pleased reaction. The welcome news travelled as a single thought throughout the ship.

Generals

Unlike Borinians, who carved their dwellings in mountain peaks and caves, the ancient Human inhabitants of Nivalinorhnus, now Khalinorhnus, had dwelt in the valleys and low-lying hills, erecting their cities upon the planet's bedrock. The ancient world had been known scientifically as Beta Cygnus, more colloquially among its Human inhabitants as Canaan.

The ancient cities now no more than archeological ruins, reclaimed and overgrown by the world from which they'd been hewn. But the ancient Humans had also constructed vast underground complexes, protection against the Borinian invasions of the first space era.

Ancient Borinians had been aware of the existence of these creatures, who had also colonized Borinorhnus. And who had been driven from the Borinian home world during the devastating purification wars.

Following the Human disappearance from Borinorhnus, Borinians had lived an insular existence, creating an era of reformation and transformation which produced a belief in their own uniqueness; a higher order of being, at the center of all creation. Until discovery of artifacts left behind by the departed Humans. The revelations of technologically superior creatures resulted in the first or many bloody upheavals throughout Borinian history. But also inspired wondrous technological leaps, which carried

Borinians into space, and led to the discovery of Nivalinorhnus, and its Human inhabitants.

The intertwined histories of both species had come full circle, precipitating another upheaval. One possessing the potential to destroy both civilizations. Such thoughts occupied Dogar's mind as he gazed across the valley at the new city rising in the distance. A blend of Human and Borinian architecture. Its buildings and facilities designed to accommodate the physiological needs of both species. A city reflecting a culture spawned of two species and the recognition of a shared history. And more, each now understood, possibly a shared ancestry.

The possibility recently uncovered. The history of Human civilization had been lost in time, suppressed and eradicated by Borinian fear, and an irrational speciocentrism. The quest for knowledge had been stifled, crippling Borinian intellectual and technological progress for generations. The deleterious legacy still embedded in Borinorhran culture.

The arrival of his aide diverted Dogar's thoughts. Dogar turned from the open air terrace overlooking the city. He strode toward the center of the spacious reception gallery. The capital citadel newly constructed. Another blend of Human and Borinian architecture, like the new city rising around it. The citadel's multilevel columned façade contained reception halls and offices built out from the mountainside. The remaining structure, five times the size of the visible façade, built inside the mountain, containing meeting halls, conference rooms, and the private offices of civil, military, and science administrators and their staffs.

The reception gallery's smooth stone walls interrupted by tall decorative windows. Their thick tinted transparencies allowed subdued natural light into the room. The spaces between the windows decorated by art works of both Borinian and Human artisans. Elaborate, colorful paintings, and intricate sculptures. The Borinian pieces utilized materials producing subtle hues when viewed in ultraviolet vision. And a few of the Human pieces too. Designed under ultraviolet light with materials to produce effects appreciated by Borinian viewers.

"General Supreme Zanthinvolar and his delegation have arrived," the aide informed him.

"Show them in," Dogar instructed. "And has the council been informed of their arrival?"

"The thought has been relayed general. The council await your instructions."

The aide's military boots slapped the polished stone floor as he crossed the room to a tall, ornately carved set of double portals. The portals swung open silently in response to the aide's thoughts. General Supreme Zanthinvolar Abydynus entered, followed by an entourage of four senior military officers. No civilians among them. General Zanthinvolar taller than the average Borinian, his robust frame well muscled for an individual his age, who'd spent much of his career in space and currently roosted in an office. A thick ring of immaculately groomed bright amber fur circled his neck, resting along the top of a uniform chest plate polished to an iridescent metallic shine. His uniform shirt, leggings, and chest coat, also meticulously tailored, fitted and brushed. His feet covered in spotless open toed dress shoes rather than boots.

As Dogar had informed the council members, he'd met General Zanthinvolar only briefly on two previous occasions.

They had never served in the same unit, and the general had been at headquarters during Dogar's off-world deployments. But Dogar had respected and admired both the individual and his career. Admired his tactical acumen, and his regard for the preservation of life, whether his troops, or the enemy, who were Human. During his own off-world service Dogar had devised many ruses to avoid hunting Humans. And he had imitated General Zanthinvolar's strategies and tactics to defend his ships and crew from Human attacks, while ensuring a minimum loss of life on either side.

Dogar approached the esteemed general, their individual minds shielded beneath smooth polished uniform headcaps. Small obsidian eyes in a broad flat face studied Dogar, as a soldier might study enemy positions or terrain on a map. Dogar stared back, taking the general's measure.

General Zanth inspected the officer before him. Well groomed and immaculate. But he noted the altered colors of the chest coat's banded hem and broad legging stripes, indicating a distinct military organization separate from the one to which Zanth belonged. And the sights he had witnessed on the journey across Nivalinorhnus, including the citadel he now stood in, indicative of a separate and distinct culture.

Dogarinmaral Korcharnus was young for the rank he'd achieved in the Borinorhnus military. But despite his youth, Zanth did not underestimate him, and had prepared for their meeting by assiduously studying his counterpart's record. A record surprisingly similar to Zanth's during his off-world fleet service. Many of Dogarinmaral's battle tactics recognizable as Zanth's own. And Dogarinmaral had garnered a reputation as a seasoned veteran, possessing a keen analytical and strategic mind. A leader commanding much 'manchi' among his troops. To Zanth's surprise, the officer before him reminded him a great deal of Agar.

They met as equals, but despite Dogarinmaral's change of allegiance, Zanth did not fail to notice the once subordinate officer waiting for him to communicate first, as military protocol required. This small attention to tradition portended an amicable meeting, Zanth decided.

"It is my honor to meet you General Dogarinmaral Korcharnus," Zanth greeted the younger officer formally.

"It is my honor General Supreme Zanthinvolar Abydynus," Dogar responded, also using the formal greeting, "As I perceive your greeting is sincere."

"You may be assured of it, as I am of yours."

"Then may we proceed to the urgent matter which concerns us both."

"First, if I may make a request?"

"Please do General Zanthinvolar. If it is in my power, I shall endeavor to accommodate whatever you require."

"I do not require the members of my delegation to accompany me into this meeting. I wish to share my thoughts with you freely and openly, soldier to soldier, without the encumbrance or constraints of military requirements and politics. If you find such an approach acceptable, will you agree to do the same?"

"It is eminently acceptable general. I had proposed a similar arrangement to our council and they did not object."

"In that case general, shall we proceed."

"Allow me to notify the council," Dogar thought, summoning his aide. "My aide will arrange accommodations for your officers and escort you to a chamber more suitable for an intimate meeting, soldier to soldier."

Zanth observed Dogarinmaral passing instructions to his aide. Instructions shielded from Zanth's mind. The routine thoughts of his hosts none of his concern, but the unimaginable closed privacy of the Nivalinorhran mind a culture shock. And an unaccustomed respite. One Zanth grudgingly welcomed and luxuriated in. He'd never experienced a time when his mind had not been crowded.

Zanth followed his escort through an elaborately decorated tunnel. The passage subtly illuminated by panels which appeared part of the wall itself. The walls adorned in art, like the reception chamber. Borinians possessed the ability to appreciate beauty, especially in art. But had no need for art to decorate their chambers, the images carried in their minds, available to all in the communal link.

At the end of the passageway Dogar's aide indicated an unfamiliar conveyance, shaped like a pea pod. Its entire surface transparent. Zanth stepped into its comfortable accommodations as instructed. When the aide joined him, the pod closed around them and slid silently into a dark tunnel. Slow at first, accelerating as it moved deeper into the mountain. Zanth experienced the slight inertial effect on his body as the pod's speed increased. At an intersection the pod slowed, and changed direction. It rose, its interior illumination reflecting off the black granite walls surrounding it.

The pod slowed to a stop and opened on a ledge in a dark cavern. Zanth's senses reached out, echolocating the chamber's dimensions, its decorative roosts, the paraphernalia for food and drink. The air subtly scented, and cooled by a draft sucked through the tunnels from an unseen ventilation source.

"You may roost here General Supreme," the aide thought. "General Commander Dogarinmaral is on his way to join you. May I offer you refreshment? A drink perhaps?"

"Most kind. But no thank you," Zanth responded.

"The general is here," the aide informed Zanth unnecessarily. Zanth's sonic emissions and ultraviolet vision had observed his host's arrival from a lower tunnel of the chamber. Dogar dismissed the aide, who departed in the transport pod.

"Forgive me if I have kept you waiting general."

"Not so. I arrived a mere moment before you. First, allow me to thank you for meeting me in this manner. And here," a sweep of his arm indicating the cavern. "A touch of home."

"We are still Borinian general. But many of our citizens are Human, and their needs must also be respected and accommodated."

"As I have observed. It is however quite a culture shock."

"Indeed. May I offer you refreshment. A drink perhaps?"

Despite his earlier refusal, the expectant tension he'd carried inside him eased. Perhaps the Borinian familiarity of the chamber. Perhaps the amicable demeanor of his host, who Zanth noticed, no longer wore his headcap.

"Perhaps a calming beverage," Zanth thought to Dogar. "A nectar tea if you have it."

"By all means. Please follow me."

Dogar dove headlong from the ledge to alight upon a roost on the far side of the chamber. While Dogar mixed the tea in the dispenser, Zanth removed his headcap. Their minds met in a fleeting touch. Zanth retreated, unwilling to fully enter his host's mind uninvited. And Zanth did not sense Dogar in his mind except when Dogar addressed him directly.

Zanth sipped from the dispenser, savoring the sweet sedative tea.

"I must admit general," Zanth thought, "not only to astonishment, but to being impressed. By this citadel, your capital city, the people. Truly by all I have witnessed. And particularly your technological progress. Your ships provided quite a shock. Truly astounding how this world has changed and diverged without Borinorhnus being aware. The distance in space separating both worlds, physically and symbolically, more profound than any on Borinorhnus could imagine."

"Space and time General Zanthinvolar. Our culture is the result of many generations reared on Khalinorhnus. Most have never spread wing on Borinorhnus. And Borinorhran immigrants are individuals who desire to reside here. We have devised our own form of representative government, enacted our own laws, revel in our thirst for knowledge and discovery. When Borinorhnus dispatched governors many chose to assimilate. Those who did not were given a harmless illness mimicking a histological reaction to the planet's atmosphere. And when Borinorhnus changed its policy to permit local governors, it only enabled us to further develop a culture free of outside interference. For us, the concept of a colony subject to the old collective has been obsolete for quite some time. A mere pretense we now wish to officially discard. But we have no wish to forsake our heritage. On the contrary, we wish to embrace it. All of it. Including the history Borinorhnus would wish to deny. We wish to maintain our ties to Borinorhnus. It is unfortunate the prospect of fission evokes such passions.

Hopefully calmer minds will prevail and lead us away from the path of mutual destruction."

"Your thoughts are most eloquent general. And happen to reflect my own."

"I am pleased you think so. I must admit to being an admirer of you and your career general. I may venture to consider I might not have survived my many off-world deployments were it not for you. I did not believe you would welcome a war between our worlds."

"You are correct in your belief. But understand, I am a loyal soldier of Borinorhnus, and though a war between us is not a prospect I wish to contemplate, Borinorhnus will be obliged to retaliate if attacked."

"And you must understand the same general. We have no desire to attack Borinorhnus. But we are prepared to defend ourselves. We would be content to continue upon our present course without a formal recognition of fission, so long as we were left alone and free from interference. Whether Borinorhnus will allow it, fission or no, is one issue. The other issue is of grave concern to Humans and Borinians alike here on Khalinorhnus. The Human population on Borinorhnus must be freed from captivity, and the off-world hunts must cease."

"An issue it had not occurred to me to address. And frankly my primary concern remains the prospect of armed conflict and how to avoid it. Once we have resolved that issue, these other issues may be discussed in their proper context."

"You are correct of course, general. However such issues, including the resources Borinorhnus will continue to require from Khalinorhnus, must be considered and discussed if the peaceful solution we hope to achieve is to be a lasting one."

Zanth did not need to probe Dogar's mind to recognize the underlying implications. The issues around which a solution must be crafted, adroitly introduced by his host.

"I will keep it in the forefront of my thoughts," Zanth conceded. "We are of like minds General Dogarinmaral, as I suspected. And it increases my confidence we at least, will see a path to avoid conflict. Therefore I must ask you. Do you speak for your council?"

"We are in complete agreement general."

"Unfortunately I must inform you the same is not true of my own council. I do not speak for them. Indeed if they had not agreed to this meeting, I had planned to pursue it on my own, at the risk of committing treason. It is one reason I wished to meet you alone. There are certain mechanizations occurring in the Borinorhnus Council which are contrary to the ends both you and I seek. Mechanizations I have devised steps to disrupt. But should my activities be discovered Dogarinmaral, or should they fail, the consequence will be the very thing we hope to avoid."

"I will not require details from you. I will admit we are aware of these matters to a certain degree. We have noted the preparations for war. I am pleased it is not the consensus of the council, and more importantly, that you disagree."

"I thank you Dogarinmaral. But you must understand my position is precarious. And I fear we may have overplayed the game with our mutual displays."

"Please explain."

"The deployment of our respective fleets. The use of a mothership to journey here. As much a display for

Borinorhnus and the council as for you. But the pretense of a military exercise is no longer viable. And the appearance of your mothership and others in your fleet may strike a fear provoking some, including Governor Supreme Khorabinjolen, into a war to reestablish the balance of power and Borinorhnus superiority."

"You must attempt to dissuade them of such a hope general. It is unrealistic. The notion of Borinorhran superiority is an illusion. A thing of the past. Borinorhnus has existed for too long in darkness, and has too far to journey to catch up scientifically, technologically, intellectually and culturally. This is not a vain boast general, but a reality resulting from Borinorhnus's failure to embrace scientific inquiry, and acknowledge certain truths. Particularly concerning Humans, with whom we share a history, from whom we have learned much, and with whom we have built a shared society. It is our true strength. The ships you have seen, cities such as this one, new technologies, and much more Borinorhnus is unaware of, will survive general, even if Khalinorhnus does not. Borinian and Human will continue learning together, working together, building together, on our off-world bases, research centers, and colonies. We will not permit this knowledge, or this relationship, to perish again."

Transformations

Seraphina had travelled to many faction worlds possessing large communities and bustling cities. Savvy to their inherent dangers. Always anxious to complete her business and return to the comfortable quiet of her ship, and space.

None of those worlds prepared her for Kheralincygninus, the long Borinian name for the planet ancient Humans called Signi Canaris, according to Khal. And nothing in her experience had prepared her for a city of Humans and Borinians living and working together, despite recalling the images Khal had deposited in her mind on Krilan.

Seraphina stood in awe on the balcony of a tall A-frame structure overlooking a plain of gently rolling hills, Ezekiel beside her. The plain ringed by a low mountain range in the distance. The buildings dotting the city similar to the one she gazed out from. Tall and peaked, like mountains. The vegetation among the structures varied in height from short grassy knolls, to shrubs and woody plants, and tall willowy trees. In many areas the vegetation had been removed, the soil excavated to reveal the foundations of ancient buildings beneath. And many deep shafts leading underground were scattered across the landscape.

The flutter of wings startled her each time a Borinian leapt from balconies above. Seraphina still unaccustomed to their unthreatening, friendly, and abundant presence. The sky above the city a busy thoroughfare of soaring individuals. Including Humans, who flew on the artificial wings of light atmospheric flyers strapped to their bodies. A device Seraphina determined she must try before departing Kheral, the abbreviated name she'd adopted for the planet. The sound similar to the abbreviation of Khalinaltani, a fitting tribute she decided.

Her opportunity arrived sooner than she'd imagined. Khal joined them on the balcony. His sudden arrival on Kheral had been greeted with all the excitement and enthusiastic approbation accorded a guild celebrity. His esteemed status also encompassed her and Ezekiel, granting unfettered access and acceptance. She and Ezekiel the recipients of curious stares and pleasant greetings from everyone they encountered, Borinian and Human.

"This was a city of ancient Humans," Khal explained, a sweep of his arm indicating the plain below them. "One of many I discovered on this world. But this site appears to have been a center of research. Nivalinorhrans who followed me to continue the excavations have uncovered many libraries and repositories of information and artifacts. There is much to be learned about your ancestors from this world. But come, I wish to show you something."

"Were you able to procure transport?" Ezekiel asked in Khal's mind. The question also spoken for Seraphina's benefit.

"The Administrator is attempting to arrange it. However there are developments in the home system which are extremely volatile at present and may dictate a delay. How long, he cannot know at the moment."

"Explain," Ezekiel asked.

Khal conveyed his thoughts to both Seraphina and Ezekiel. "Both worlds are on the verge of war. The Nivalinorhrans, like those you see here, wish to be independent of Borinorhnus. And wish to free all Humans held captive on Borinorhnus, so they may live as these Humans and Humans on Nivalinorhnus do."

Ezekiel and Seraphina glanced at each other. The expression in their eyes conveyed similar thoughts, understood without the link. Both experienced a similar reaction to Khal's thoughts.

The prospect of Humans freed from Borinorhran captivity, and Borinian mental enslavement, occupied Ezekiel's thoughts and enlivened his imagination as the three flew above the city toward the distant hills. Except when Seraphina experimented, her abrupt maneuvers drawing Ezekiel's attention. He coached her through their headcapped mental link. Though she required little instruction, acquiring an instant intuitive understanding of the flyer, controlling it through the cap. Headcaps now as normal to her as any other piece of her clothing. The one she wore contained a tinted visor, protecting her eyes as she flew through the air.

Kheralincygninus a revelation to Ezekiel. Unlike Seraphina, he'd been accustomed to Borinians. Had spent his lifetime surrounded by them. Constantly in their presence. Constantly under their control. His every action since his birth subjugated to their will. Until the battle in space had freed him. The sudden disappearance of their minds from his, of their mental control, and the gradual reclamation of his own mind, his own thoughts, his own free will, had transformed him.

Kheralincygninus inspired a further transformation. A transformation began perhaps from the moment he'd met Khalinaltani Ogadeinus on Krilan. Culminated by his observations on this world. Humans and Borinians living and working in peaceful coexistence. The experience compelled him in a direction he'd never imagined, indicating a purpose to his life. The reason for surviving the battle, and the dark cold clutch of space.

Seraphina exhilarated by the wind in her hair. Thrilled by its rushing passage over her body. Ecstatic at her buoyant lightness as she banked and rolled, dove and soared on currents of air. Her arms positioned the artificial wings, controlling her flight. Swept back close to her sides to dive. Stretched out forward to climb and soar. Pulled up to an acute angle to slow. While the soft hiss of thrusters on her back pushed her through the sky. Ezekiel flew next to her, following her maneuvers, providing instruction. The bucolic landscape flowed beneath her as in a dream.

They flew past the city to a large flat plateau raised above the surrounding terrain. The plateau formed by a hundred meter wide trench excavated around it. Ancient columns and foundations stood unearthed inside the trench. On two sides of the plateau tall entrances led inside. And at one corner a tall tower rose above the ground. Workers from underground rose in an elevator to the top of the tower, from where they leapt, spreading their wings to fly.

Khal adjusted his arms and long flexible fingers, banking in a graceful arc. The trailing edges of his wings fluttered in the breeze as he descended toward the nearest entrance. Ezekiel and Seraphina followed. Seraphina lowered her right arm, raised her left, entering a curving right bank toward the entrance. Leveling, her outstretched arms slightly forward of her sides, she slowed her flight. She lowered her arms as she descended, shoulder height, chest height. She drew her feet together, unhooked her boots from the empennage-like tail section and prepared to land. On her mental command the vertical fin folded and the tail section retracted into the main body of the flyer on her back. Seraphina swung her legs down and forward beneath her, her head and torso rising. The ground rose to meet her. Forward flight diminished, and the lift of her wings ceased altogether as she lowered her arms. Her feet touched the ground, her momentum carrying her forward in less than half a dozen steps. The smile on her face radiant, like varnished teak. Her entire being suffused in a rapturous euphoria.

"I want to do that all the time," the dominant thought in her mind.

"This was the main research facility," Khal informed them, indicating the entrance.

The sides of the plateau much higher when viewed from ground level. Seraphina gazed at her surroundings in wide eyed wonder as the flyer completed its transformation, its wings telescoping inward and folding against the sides of the thruster pack. The flier no more than the size and weight of a lightly loaded backpack. Lifting her hands to remove the headcap Khal advised her to keep it on.

"You will need it inside. This type of headcap can be switched from control to communication, or both. And the visor adjusted for a wide spectrum. From ultraviolet, which Borinians normally use in the dark, to infrared. You will be able to observe the site in greater detail as a Borinian would, and also exchange thoughts."

Seraphina nodded. She followed Khal through the entrance, Ezekiel in the rear. They entered an immense open space, the interior of a building. Its perimeter walls intact, thought only remnants of the interior structures partitioning the once large rooms remained. The building buried by soil and time. The curved arched ceiling overhead formed the underside of the plateau. The floor rested unseen in the darkness below.

Seraphina experimented shifting the visor's visual spectrum, controlled by her thoughts. Her comfort in using her thoughts to communicate and manipulate objects complete, as though she'd done it all her life. In ultraviolet she observed the building's floor far below. The darkness perceived in illuminated patterns of blues, purples, and whites. The wide ledge on which they stood a trail of grayish white. The ledge ran around the periphery of the large room. Striations created in the substrate by excavating machinery perceived as bright jagged splashes of color.

Crude steps hewn into the rock led down into the excavated pit. They entered a short smooth bored tunnel, exiting into a large chamber. Long tables joined end to end lined the chamber's perimeter. On the tables lay rows of artifacts. Unrecognizable to either Ezekiel or Seraphina. The objects cracked and broken, encrusted in layers of yellowish earth.

Seraphina and Ezekiel moved along the tables, staring at the collected items. The staff paused in their work to greet Ezekiel, Seraphina, and the esteemed Khalinaltani in polite excitement, explaining a particular object, how and where it had been found, and its probable function. Occasionally Seraphina reached out to touch a particular object, drawing her fingertips lightly over it. The touch produced a profound, visceral, inexplicable connection to ancestors she'd only recently learned about. Ancestors who had inhabited the facility hundreds of thousands of years before. The touch transported her back in time. The sensation transformative.

"All of the artifacts found on this world are of Human habitation," Khal explained. "We have seen no evidence of Borinian habitation, or any other species. But of particular interest to us is in the next chamber."

Khal led them to a wall at the back of the chamber. "This I am sure will interest you both. And Seraphina you may wish to see this as a Borinian would. When you are ready think open portal."

Seraphina had not changed the visor's ultraviolet setting, the underground passages and chambers dark and dimly lit, as Borinians preferred. And she observed no portal in the blank blue hued wall before her.

"I see no portal," she thought.

"It may appear so, but open the portal anyway."

Seraphina complied as instructed, her mind commanding a non-existent portal to open, expecting no reaction to her thoughts. Her eyes widened and her mouth fell open as the wall before her shimmered. Its dull bluish hue brightened. Its solid texture softened, dissolving before her eyes. The wall transformed into a misty white cloud. The cloud's opacity cleared, leaving behind a diaphanous transparency, which eventually dissipated, revealing a round arched opening where solid rock existed moments before.

"The researchers here had been tunneling through this accursed rock for years before opening a chamber containing digitized blueprints of these portals," Khal explained.

"Fortunately the data was remarkably preserved, along with much other valuable information regarding this facility, allowing the technicians to reactivate the portals. Not all of them still function, but some, like this one, still do. The exploration of the complex proceeded much faster following this discovery. From reports I have read such portals are quite common on Nivalinorhnus now. Ingenious your ancestors," Khal's amusement conveyed in his thoughts and vocal clicks.

The chamber revealed by the opened portal stretched into the distance. Father than their capacity to visualize in the dim lighting, even in ultraviolet. A long stone table ran down the center, disappearing into darkness at the far end. The end closest to the portal illuminated by dim work station lighting. Each work station occupied by a Borinian or Human technician, busy cleaning, examining, cataloguing and arranging pieces of artifacts. Broken shards, and crumbled bits encrusted in rust and dried earth littered the center of the table along its length. Like their colleagues in other chambers, the technicians paused in their work to greet the three visitors.

"I know this place," Seraphina thought, wandering along the table.

"I too," she heard Ezekiel in her mind. "I have seen this place before. But I have never been to this world. How can it be?"

"In a dream," Seraphina remembered. "We have seen this place in our dream," recalling images of a recent dream now percolating into her conscious thoughts. A long narrow room. Soft white illumination bathed its walls and a long table running down its center. Humans in tight fitting one-piece garments stood alongside the table where Khalinorhrans now stood. The Humans busy at their tasks. The dusty disintegrated fragments on the table bright shiny instruments, and functioning machines, performing delicate biological experiments.

Seraphina reached across the table, lifted a dull encrusted shard, placed it in the center of her palm, visualizing a small orb of shiny transparent metal, shaped like an egg. A jelly-like substance inside. Chemical molecules imbedded within the jelly, replicating, morphing, transforming. Hundreds of the orbs around the laboratory. On the table, on shelves along the wall, in refrigeration units, beneath radiation lamps.

"According to records we have translated," Khal explained to Ezekiel and Seraphina, "The scientists working in this laboratory were studying an apparent spontaneous transformation of a life form on a world they called Cygnus Prime. A world the indigenous inhabitants call Borinorhnus."

Seraphina and Ezekiel both spun to face Khal, their widened eyes and open mouths expressing their stunned reaction.

"Indeed." Khal thought, an amused quality in the single thought, in his twinkling slate eyes, and short series of vocal clicks. Perhaps the Borinian version of a chuckle.

In the fresh open air above ground the three inhaled deeply, clearing their lungs of musty underground air. They stood at the top of the tower, overlooking the excavated trench and the rolling plain beyond.

"I have fond memories of exploring this world," Khal thought, gazing at the distant mountains. "A special quality I cannot explain, which touched me in ways like no other world, except for one. The last one."

Seraphina heard Khal's thoughts as she too gazed into the distance. At the low undulating hills silhouetted against a soft pink sky as Kheral's pale yellow star slid toward the horizon. And she experienced a fervent desire growing inside her. Not the type of desire she held for Ezekiel, but an intense determination, fueled by an innate, awakening passion. The same as when she'd decided, against all odds, to escape her captivity. And when she'd learned the ways of trading, or how to pilot a ship, or how to fight and kill to survive. Now that fierce desire burned inside her again, feeding a hunger for knowledge she hadn't been aware of before. The type of knowledge Khal had introduced her to.

Comfortable, spacious accommodations had been provided for Seraphina and Ezekiel. Though Seraphina would've preferred remaining aboard Dauphin. As they prepared for bed Seraphina handed Ezekiel a headcap and donned the one she held. Ezekiel by now aware it signaled Seraphina had something important to say to him. Something she didn't wish lost in translation.

"I wish to mate with you Ezekiel, but we must wait."

"I wish it too. But you know I do not know the customs. What is the reason we must wait?"

"It is my time of rachtnal. It means shedding, and during this time I bleed. I am aware of females who mate during their rachtnal, but my memories of it are not pleasant. In truth, mating with you is the only pleasant experience I have had with a man. And I wish for more, with you Ezekiel."

"You are injured?"

Seraphina smiled. Her large brown eyes stared into his.

"No. I am uninjured. It is normal among females. You do not know of the bleeding? Does it not occur among your fenori."

"I have heard it spoken of. But do not understand how or why it occurs. What causes it?"

"When Humans mate the seeds of the male and female join to form a new life. If there is no mating, or mating without the joining, the female's body sheds what it has stored to nourish the new life growing inside her. The cycle continues until the female no longer produces her seeds."

"Does it hurt when you bleed? Like when you are wounded?"

Seraphina smiled again at Ezekiel's childlike and endearing innocence. "Sometimes it does, but not always. And there are remedies. What do you think of this place?"

Ezekiel perceived the question to be Seraphina's true reason for wishing to share thoughts. The matter of her bleeding secondary. A ploy to initiate the conversation. He allowed his perception to flow unimpeded into Seraphina's mind, which produced a smile, and she opened her thoughts to him regarding Kheral, and the desire building within her.

"What do you wish to do?" she asked.

"I wish to help Khal," Ezekiel said. "I wish to help free the Humans on Borinorhnus. I wish to remain with you, as your mate."

"Then I think we must take Khal home in Dauphin."

"You wish to go to Khalinorhnus?" In his surprise, he voiced aloud the words in his thoughts.

"I wish to learn more of Khal's teaching. And I go where you go."

Fallen

The council meeting did not go well. No surprise to General Zanth. During the seven day journey to and from Nivalinorhnus, including a day spent on Nivalinorhnus meeting General Dogarinmaral, the prospects for peace had diminished. Governor Supreme Khorabinjolen had dug in his heels, and accelerated his preparations for war. Zanth had not transmitted his report regarding the Nivalinorhnus meeting, preferring to report to the council in person. But reports from the fleet had reached the council. Nivalinorhnus's show of force prompted the Governor Supreme to choose the reckless option rather than the cautious one. Even subtly accusing General Zanth of cowardice.

The council still evenly divided. Governor Sorkahringorol of Health and Habitat sided with his colleagues from Science, and Space and Technology, against war.

Zanth also not surprised by another invitation from Governor Tovarinkara for a second private meeting. Zanth arrived as he had for their previous meeting, alone, without his customary pilot and aide. He used his personal transport, and flew a circuitous route to disguise his destination.

"My honor to have you in my home again General Zanthinvolar," the governor greeted Zanth when they'd settled in the same chamber as their previous meeting. "I only wish the circumstances were more pleasant."

"It is my honor, Governor Tovarinkara.

"And I am certain we will not have an opportunity to meet again in this manner. I have received information Governor Supreme Khorabinjolen, as I suspected, is seeking to constitute a new Council. If he succeeds, we will surely be at war. It is a precarious time general. You may also be vulnerable. He may have been laying the foundation to replace you by using such an absurd and appalling accusation at the council meeting."

"I have given certain orders in such an event governor. Private orders to a private operative known only to me. He is outside the normal chain of command and cannot effect orders to military commanders. However there are other options to which he may avail himself. It is possible he may seek to contact you."

"There is considerable danger to anyone attempting to contact me general."

"Do not concern yourself governor. His orders are to protect you and your like-minded colleagues on the council. And you can trust him completely."

"I am confident you are correct. Though I am not as confident regarding our options at this point, or our chances for success. Even by your operative. Khorabinjolen is intent on Khalinorhnus remaining within the collective. Even if it means war, and despite your report regarding their capabilities and desire for peace. He will certainly not agree to their proposal regarding the Borathquiri."

"It is more than a proposal governor." Zanth relayed Dogal's exact thoughts from his memory of their meeting.

"Indeed. The point is, from Khorabinjolen's point of view the idea of fission, and freedom for the quiri, is blasphemy, sedition, and treason. Which prompts me to ask again general, you are quite certain of the assessment you reported to the council?"

"There is no doubt. Borinorhnus cannot hope to win a conventional conflict. The Nivalinorhrans are more advanced technologically than we imagine, and my brief observations may not have included capabilities we are still unaware of. A war between us will inevitably escalate to the use of weapons which will ensure our mutual destruction. This war cannot be allowed to start."

"There is much we have not learned and much we have neglected due to of our own shortsightedness. And when I refer to 'our' I do not mean this council, but a long line of governors who have perpetuated policies crippling to our society. I am a scientist general, and I can assure you I have spent a lifetime as if my mind had been chained. Fastened to an immovable past, flying in the dark deafened and blinded."

Zanth sensed the vehement passion expressed in Governor Tovarinkara's thoughts, a sentiment reflecting his own, especially following his visit to Nivalinorhnus.

"I cannot disagree governor. And unfortunately, we have not learned the lessons of our history. A history I recently had an opportunity to see. And which it grieves me to contemplate repeating."

"We have only ourselves to blame, as I intimated a moment ago. Our ignorance is a function of proscribed knowledge. What is deemed acceptable and what is not. The criteria for which is inflexible dogma. Such as our insistence on our own superiority, and the inferiority of Borathquiri. All evidence to the contrary. Our continued conceit will be our demise."

"I perceive governor, you share the views of those called Khalinaltanists? I have noticed you use the name Khalinorhnus when referring to Nivalinorhnus."

"My position may not extend to such a degree general. But to deny demonstrable fact is ignorance. The Khalinaltanists have embraced an enlightenment where we have not.

"The coexistence on Nivalinorhnus is quite astonishing A phenomenon beyond imagination. It has to be seen to be believed."

"No doubt. And I would wish to see it myself."

"Suppose we are able to escape this path to war, how do you contemplate proceeding toward this future you envision?" Zanth asked, formulating an idea he shielded in his thoughts.

"Such progress requires meticulous planning and much time general. Time we may not have. It cannot occur overnight, or even in a single generation. The chasm is too wide to leap in a single bound. Such progress must be slow, and commence early in each generation if it is to gain acceptance. Yet at a pace sufficient to create its own momentum."

The wisdom of Tovarinkara's response impressed Zanth, cementing his notion. Tovarinkara not only a suitable replacement for Khorabinjolen, but the type of Governor Supreme Borinorhnus needed if it hoped to close the gap Tovarinkara alluded to. The implementation of such a change in leadership nothing short of treason. But Zanth reasoned he had already crossed that line in his conscience, if not in deed.

The notion, and the actions necessary to achieve it, occupied Zanth's attention and thoughts in the headcapped privacy of his transport. He flew a route through the Tamun pass, where the stratospheric Ghizanar Range curved south. Halfway through the pass the transport's instruments winked out, blinding Zanth to the hairpin twists and turns through the mountains. Zanth attempted to slow the transport, to halt it and hover while he sorted out the malfunction. But the transport's controls were unresponsive to his mental input. He attempted control override. Also unresponsive. And he'd been unable to open the hatch, either by mental command or manually. Zanth had lost control of the transport.

Homecoming

The sights beyond the viewports held Seraphina enthralled. Her mouth agape at the sensor images flooding her awestruck mind. A bewildering variety of ships occupied the space around the portal. A single ship, the size of a small moon, captured her attention. A kaleidoscopic sphere, spinning around a central hub, raced toward Dauphin on an intercept course. The ship's immense size dwarfed the hundreds of fighters, transports, and other small vessels buzzing around it like bees around a hive.

"Welcome home esteemed Khalinaltani Ogadeinus," Seraphina heard in her mind, relayed through the headcap she wore. The headcap new, custom fitted and modified on Kheral, among other modifications and upgrades to Dauphin. The modifications had included upgraded integration of the ship's controls, communications, and sensor arrays through the headcap.

"Maintain your course. The fighters will escort you to Khalinorhnus."

The ships converging on Dauphin sleek and streamlined. Graceful creatures of flight as Seraphina observed their approach. True wing structures designed on many. Others possessed engine pods resembling wings embedded in outstretched appendages on either side. Seraphina marveled at their simple symmetry and grace, and their innocent lethality.

Dauphin's enhanced sensors depicted a three dimensional image of the system in Seraphina's mind, as if she were floating outside the ship, viewing from above the twin stars and its six circling planets. Its two habitable worlds currently on opposite sides of the paired stars. Borinorhnus's lit half a rusty brown. Khalinorhnus green and blue like the beaches of Krilan.

Shifting her thoughts, Seraphina focused on the deployment of both fleets scattered in the interplanetary spaces separating the inhabited worlds. And around the portal orbiting the primary star. Both fleets faced each other, as though poised for attack. But both maintained a discreet distance.

Three shipboard days later Dauphin settled into orbit around Khalinorhnus. The space above the majestic blue-green world crowded corridors of orbital stations, and grids of sensor and defense facilities in high and low orbit. Military and civilian vessels arrived and departed the planet in a continuous stream.

Dauphin's sensors collected data on the planet as Seraphina prepared her ship for landfall. Atmospheric pressures, temperatures, and densities. Wind speeds and directions. Continents and land masses and their topographic features. Approach vectors from Khalinorhnus controllers streamed into her thoughts and into Dauphin's navigation console via her headcap.

The reception on landing, and as she, Khal, and Ezekiel rode to the capital in a transparent transport, overwhelmed her, dwarfing the reception on Kheral, which Seraphina had considered an enormous display. The cheering crowds on Khalinorhnus many times larger. The effusive, celebratory welcome many times more festive, despite the looming threat of war. Long lines of fliers snaked through the skies above the capital city, like streamers blowing in the wind.

Followed by equally festive formal receptions and celebratory dinners. Khal, Ezekiel, and Seraphina, the center of attention and approbation. An uncomfortable role for all three, who attempted polite escape whenever possible. Khal appeared overwhelmed and discomforted by the spotlight and attention. He yearned for the silent solitude of his work. Impatient to continue his research. Seraphina disquieted and restless among the large crowds, only wishing to resume her learning alongside Khal. Ezekiel observed the activities with curious aplomb, exalting in the free existence of Khalinorhnus's Human population.

Khal's impatience further strained by an endless schedule of meetings convened by the science directors and other members of the science colony. Clarifications of his last reports. Questions concerning recently discovered sites and artifacts on Khalinorhnus and worlds he'd recently explored. Plans to establish a science academy having Khal as its director.

"I appreciate the generous welcome and I admit to considerable interest in many of your proposals," Khal responded politely to their entreaties. "However my work is incomplete. And I believe the final piece is to be found here, which is the reason for my return at this unfortunate time. Please do not allow me to distract you from your more immediate and relevant concerns given the ominous circumstances we all face."

"Of course you have complete access to the research facilities Khalinaltani" said Jeremiah, Khalinorhnus's science colony director. "What is it you need to complete?"

"Identification of the catalyst which has eluded our research thus far. I believe I have identified the search parameters which may facilitate success."

Seraphina was also occupied by a busy schedule of meetings with ranking officers of Khalinorhnus's military and intelligence divisions, and a Human named Ishmael, to Seraphina's astonishment, an official of Khalinorhnus's governing council. They sought information on Human factions she'd encountered in her travels as a trader. Their worlds, cultures, and technology. Seraphina instinctively guarded and reticent in her responses, despite no indication the information she provided might be used in a harmful manner. The Borinian and Human minds she touched, and who touched hers, politely curious and deferential. Her relationship to Khal afforded her an esteemed position in their midst.

Ishmael and his military and civilian colleagues also held several meetings with Ezekiel. Ezekiel's knowledge of human captivity on Borinorhnus mainly confirmed, supplemented, or expanded information they already possessed. But his information on Borinorhran military utilization and deployment of Humans, deemed of particular interest. Their discussions produced various strategies to thwart possible deployment of human spies on Khalinorhnus, by jamming or disrupting the mental control link. Of crucial value, Ezekiel's knowledge regarding how such Borinian-Human teams operated.

Lavish accommodations had been provided for all three, but Seraphina and Ezekiel preferred returning to Dauphin after their crowded days. The ship had been moved to a secluded base outside the city in case of an attack on the spaceport. Dauphin was Seraphina's home, and now Ezekiel's too, providing the solitude and quiet comfort Seraphina sought following their busy days in the city.

Her bleeding period passed, Seraphina and Ezekiel mated in the silent confines of her ship. Their minds and thoughts and flesh meshed as one in mutual desire and satisfaction. Ezekiel's presence, his arms enclosing her in their strong embrace, more satisfying than the sexual thrusting itself, pleasant as it also happened to be, much to her surprise. The sexual act had never been an activity connected to pleasure in her experience, but something she'd learned to disassociate herself from. Until Ezekiel. And not only the mating, she reflected, recalling her experiences since salvaging him in space. Her entire world had been rearranged.

Her recently discovered passion for learning exhilarated and inflamed her. Like a hunger. An unquenched thirst. Her eager enthusiasm to accompany Khal each day like the powerful thrusters of a battleship, driving her to ask more, learn more. Her frustration and impatience evident at the endless meetings he was called upon to attend.

She reveled in the use of the headcap. Unimaginable only a short time before. Now a mere accessory, like the leather coat or boots she wore. It allowed her to learn at a rapid pace. Allowed her to assimilate information in a manner words alone could not convey, providing instant understanding. Bits and pieces of knowledge flowed into her mind in an endless stream, introducing her to rudimentary chemistry, biology, physics, mathematics, and history. Particularly Human-Borinian history, interpreting and filling voids in the dreams Khal continued to deposit in her mind. The headcap also allowed her to manipulate the world around her. Her hands replaced by her mind.

Seraphina entered Khal's lab, hoping to find him working rather than away attending a meeting. The circular chamber illuminated in dim diffused light, with muted directional lamps at the Human work spaces. Other dark, shadowed areas occupied by Borinian technicians. The odor of chemical reagents scented the air as soil, tissue, plant, air, rock and water samples were analyzed. In another chamber of the spacious lab complex provided to Khal, others poured over ancient texts and recordings.

She greeted Khal as he flitted from one chamber, headed to another, supervising the staff, checking results, designing experiments.

"I still do not understand this thing you are searching for," projecting her thoughts at him.

"It is the substance needed to explain the gap," Khal explained. "You have seen the history?"

"Yes. In the dreams."

""There is one more dream I must give you to complete the story. Something I myself discovered only recently. But I must await corroboration and verification. The dream will allow you to understand this discovery in its historical context. In the meantime I search for what we call the catalyst."

"What is this gap. And this catalyst you seek?"

"Assuming our understanding of evolution is correct, you would expect to see an evolutionary progression linking all the stages of development of a species. In the case of the

Borinian species, there is an unexplainable gap between the earliest proto Borinian species, and true Borinians. We have been unable to discover a connecting link in the fossil history. Instead, it appears a sudden and rapid evolutionary event occurred, a genetic transformation, which gave rise to the Borinian species. We see this in the fossil record, and the DNA data."

"What is DNA?"

Khal not in the least perturbed by Seraphina's constant questions. On the contrary, he delighted in her enthusiasm, deriving a satisfying pleasure in teaching her. He'd spent his entire adult life learning. His far flung explorations and discoveries a means to answer his questions. The answers transmitted homeward in dry technical reports. Now he'd discovered a pleasure in conveying those answers to a mind eager to soak them up like a dry sponge.

"It is the blueprint of all life," Khal explained. "Present in every cell of every living Human and Borinian," transmitting images of DNA's structure and function directly to Seraphina. She nodded as her mind assimilated the incoming images.

"We discovered DNA a little more than two hundred years ago. As with many other discoveries, as a result of our research into the ancient Human colonists on Borinorhnus and Nivalinorhnus. It required many years for us to understand this discovery, and its significance. Not until we had learned to translate texts and recordings left behind. We learned something astonishing, which produced a violent upheaval in our society."

"What is this thing you learned?" Seraphina's curiosity captivated and enthralled by Khal's thoughts, and images of a human ancestry she had never been aware of, or even imagined.

"We discovered Borinian and Human DNA is closely similar. The variance less than two percent

"And this difference though small, is what makes Borinian borinian, and Human human?" Seraphina asked, her eyes focused inward as her mind processed the information, and its implication. "And otherwise we are the same."

"Excellent. Seraphina. Yes. You are correct. Excellent."

Seraphina turned, her gaze surveyed the Human and Borinian technicians busy at their work stations, side by side, as her thoughts processed this new and startling reality.

"And you are seeking the thing which caused the transformation creating Borinians," she thought, her gaze returning to Khal. "And by finding it, you will be able to explain the gap, the missing link."

"Correct again Seraphina," undisguised pride underlying Khal's thoughts. "It has been a fruitless search for many decades. Many even question the idea of the transformation, claiming the solution must lie in our theories of evolution, and proposing variant theories.

"How are you certain your theories are correct?" Her thoughts reflected her faith in Khal, but also questioning. The trait of a true seeker, Khal acknowledged, his thoughts again conveying immense pride in his Human pupil.

"Texts, recordings, artifacts from many archeological sites, including the one you visited on Kheralincygninus, indicate Humans were also aware of this unexplained occurrence, devoting much research to understanding and explaining it. But we have yet to understand why this was of such importance to them. And it appears they were as unsuccessful as we have been."

"But now you understand where you must search for this, how did you call it," Seraphina hesitated, searching her thoughts, "This catalyst?"

"It is the purpose of these current experiments. The idea arose from witnessing the burials on Krilan."

Duty

Agar's return home less joyous and celebratory than Khal's. The cruiser exited the portal unceremoniously, without fanfare, a day after Khal's arrival. During the four day journey between the portal and Borinorhnus, Agar had attempted unsuccessfully to contact General Zanth. He wished to deliver his report in person, and obtain further clarification of the general's orders.

By the time the cruiser slipped into orbit around Borinorhnus, word had reached him of the general Zanth's death. The general's body discovered in the crashed wreckage of his personal transport in the Ghizanar Range. The crash attributed to sabotage. The unidentified perpetrators suspected to be subversive agents directed by Nivalinorhnus.

Agar's rage grew like the subterranean pressures of a volcano seeking release. An eruption which would wipe his mentor's killers from existence. Without mercy or remorse. There'd be no resurrection in the underworld. No afterlife for those upon whom he'd unleash his vengeance.

The depth of Agar's anguish and loss indescribable. Unimaginable. Like nothing he'd ever experienced. The general closer to him than anyone he'd ever known. The manchi between them stronger than any familial bond. And more, a deep unspoken devotion which surpassed manchi.

That devotion tempered Agar's rage, focusing his mind on the last message received from his perished commander, mentor, and friend. A message which ordered Agar to protect certain individuals while at the same time creating obstacles to others. Zanth had provided the names of the former, all members of the Governing Council. Governors likely to oppose a war with Nivalinorhnus. The latter, unnamed individuals Zanth suspected Governor Supreme Khorabinjolen might seek out in an effort to pack the council. "You will need to identify those individuals and dissuade them by whatever means from accepting the governor's nomination," the message had instructed. Agar uncertain how he might accomplish it. And aware such actions constituted treason. But his general's last orders and wishes overrode all other consideration. Agar was determined to honor his commander's last wishes.

In contrast to the celebrations on Nivalinorhnus, the atmosphere on Borinorhnus subdued and tense. The metaphorical drum beat of war in the air. The population incited by continuous broadcast images of Nivalinorhnus's secret military buildup, its intention to overthrow the Governing Council, and conquer Borinorhnus in order to spread its blasphemous philosophy. The news of General Supreme Zanthinvolar Abydynus's death, undoubtedly at the hands of Nivalinorhran agents, used to further persuade Borinorhrans of the enemy's murderous treachery.

But Agar remained unconvinced of Nivalinorhnus's involvement given General Zanth's last message and orders. The message echoed in Agar's mind as he traversed the capital headed for a safe lair on the city's outskirts. The massage had alarmed Agar, and hastened his return. In hindsight, Agar perceived Zanth's awareness of the danger surrounding him. Perhaps foreseeing his death as it closed in on him. A perception Agar might have sensed earlier had he been in touch with the general's thoughts. Perhaps in time to ensure his safety. But Agar had only the electronic thoughts transmitted in the message.

"Regardless of your personal loyalties, I am not the central issue in this situation. Rather the survival of our people. You possess a highly developed intellect Agar, and though you've spent your life in the military, you are not a blind follower of orders. You do not aspire to be led as most do. For much of your life you have lived apart, unwilling to cede your individuality to others. You do not follow the herd mentality. Such constrictions do not apply to you. And those qualities will be particularly required in our current situation. You are aware of the stakes, and I am certain you will accomplish not only that which is required, but that which is right. Good fortune attend you."

Agar sought time to think. To develop a plan if he were to honor the general's final orders. And he'd probably require assistance. Other than Zanthinvolar, Agar trusted no one. But he knew of a handful of capable individuals, retired military who had served under General Zanth. These individuals currently engaged in nefarious activities, but possessing strong manchi for their ex-commander. The general had steered Agar to them on previous occasions when he'd required certain information and skills. Agar might again need their services in the coming endeavor.

The following day Agar strapped on his purloined Nivalinorhran flyer and flew to the crash site. His decision to procure the flyer before departing Nivalinorhran vindicated. The light machine not merely a modification of a Borinorhran environmental flight suit, but an inventive lightweight machine based on the design. Its ability to fold and contract ingenious.

The wrecked transport had already been removed by the authorities. The site marked by a garish scar upon the rock face, and scattered bits of debris too insignificant to collect.

Agar visited the site to pay a final silent tribute to his commander. He did not wish to attend the official memorials, and final rites of passage planned by the authorities. Not his place. And perhaps also not his beliefs. The planned grandiose show of pomp and ceremony perhaps befitted the general's stature, and eminently deserved. But also manipulative, to further stoke the fever for war. A spectacle and purpose the general would neither condone nor countenance, and in which Agar refused to participate. And as a practical matter, Agar did not wish to be seen.

Agar's next objective, a long range reconnaissance of Governor Tovarinkara's estate. Agar had concluded the Science Governor, the first name on General Zanth's protect list, warranted a visit as a primary source of information. Information Agar desperately required in order to devise a plan. Such a plan, and its desired outcome, as yet unclear.

On the day of General Zanth's Mahgdi, or remembrance, a memorial rite performed for the perished, Agar infiltrated Governor Tovarinkara's estate. The military and civil security forces assigned to guard the governor distracted by the ceremonies broadcast from the city.

Borinians had retained the ancestral ability of rock climbing. Not used much in modern culture, except among a few enthusiasts. But Agar had cultivated his ability, a useful tool in his occupation. A tool he now used to approach the governor's chambers undetected.

His sharp talons dug into the peak's granite walls, pushing him higher along its steep ragged face, while his thumbs curled around cracks and fissures, steadying his ascent. Agar uncertain of the governor's precise location in the mountain complex, but his earlier reconnaissance had indentified the chambers the governor used most frequently. He'd observed Governor Tovarinkara on a particular entrance terrace on a number of occasions. Agar climbed toward it.

Agar halted at the rock terrace, his senses alert, probing the environment around him. Aware of a patrolling hover drone high overhead approaching his position. The portal to the terrace open. A presence in the dark chamber beyond. Agar pushed higher, maneuvering beneath the ledge. His talons gripped the ledge's rocky underside, thumbs hooked into its cracked surface. He waited.

A figure approached the terrace portal, responding to the fleeting call of Agar's thoughts, perceived perhaps as an imaginary figment. The individual stepped onto the terrace. Agar reached out again, a quick subtle touch in order not to startle the individual, and also confirm his identity.

"Governor Tovarinkara Pharaxnus, do not be alarmed and do not respond. I am friend to General Zanthinvolar Abydynus." Agar sensed the Governor's sudden gloom as the name entered his thoughts. And his surprise at the term 'friend', an appellation rarely used in Borinorhran language, denoting an affinity rooted in, but surpassing manchi. Agar perceived in Tovarinkara's thoughts a deep and genuine respect for Zanthinvolar.

"I cannot be certain how closely your thoughts are being monitored. In any case possessing my thoughts in yours may prove a danger to you. I can obtain the information I require without leaving my presence in your thoughts. I only require you to open your mind and allow me to access your thoughts. If you agree I will know."

Agar heard Tovarinkara's agreement, and pushed deeper into his mind, aware of the governor erecting mental shields as Agar delved deeper. Tovarinkara a strong privy Agar noted. The governor's personal memories and life experiences Agar ignored, instead tapping into the memories of the council and private meetings attended by General Zanthinvolar. Agar retrieved the answers to his questions. Governor Tovarinkara's thoughts conveyed his conviction Governor Supreme Khorabinjolen had a hand in General Zanth's death, not the Nivalinorhrans, using Governor Zepharinlenar to arrange the assassination.

"I will leave you now," Agar conveyed to the governor. "There will be no memory of my presence in your thoughts, which others might see. I have also deposited instructions for you to follow. They will appear to be your own ideas and thoughts. And it is my honor to be of service to you Governor Tovarinkara Pharaxnus, as it was to serve General Zanthinvolar."

During the following two days, Agar completed his preparations for the plan he'd devised. He'd contacted General Zanth's retired compatriots and enlisted their help. Reluctant at first, arguing increased security obliged them to lay low and maintain their invisibility, Agar had appealed to their manchi for the general. Their assistance would be in service to the general, in pursuit of the true assassins responsible for his murder. Agar also offered substantial compensation for their time.

Even before meeting to enlist their help, Agar had noted the increased security sweeps and surveillance drones around the capital city. The indiscriminate roundups of individuals and their associates suspected of harboring thoughts and sentiments contrary to the prevailing propaganda.

He'd procured and modified the necessary equipment. He'd prepared a location north of his remote mountain lair. He'd preplaced equipment in the gorge below the governor's terrace, cleared a path through the vegetation hugging the lower slopes, and set sonic emitters to prevent predators wandering into his perimeter. Finally, he'd hacked the hover drone monitoring the skies and peaks around the governor's estate, bypassed its encryption, and accessed its control frequency.

Borinorhnus's zone of permanent twilight shrouded the peaked landscape as Agar exited the thick cloud like mist covering the gorge. He removed his face mask, and commenced his climb. He retraced the route he'd climbed two days earlier. Now laden by the weight of equipment and gear he carried. A closed flyer strapped to his back. Redundant, but Agar prepared for every contingency. A customized chest coat, the equipment he required clipped to its snap rings and carried in its pouches. Two charged particle rifles carried in low slung holsters. A round drum strapped to each thigh, unspooling a pair of strong synthetic lines as he climbed. The thin lines disappeared into the mist below, attached to mechanical winches anchored on the far side of the gorge. A headcap, one frequency to control his equipment, the other tuned to the circling hover drone. The drone currently on the opposite side of the mountain, providing Agar his window to climb.

Agar scaled the terrace, climbing to the cliff face above it. He unfastened the drum from his left thigh, placed it against the cliff wall. At his metal command sharp talon-like hooks sprang from the drum and anchored it to the cliff. Agar repeated the procedure for the drum from his right thigh.

Agar crouched at the portal. His senses reached out, scanning the interior, the chamber's shape and dimensions rendered in sharp three dimensional detail in his mind. An hourglass shaped rock formation rose from the chamber's floor. Governor Tovarinkara, the sole occupant, roosted in an induced hibernating sleep below the hourglass's flared upper end.

Agar entered the chamber. His mind and his thoughts shielded by the headcap. He unspooled a line from one of the drums, leapt across the intervening space, grasping the hand rails and talon rungs of the stairway on the side of the hourglass formation.

Hanging next to the hibernating governor Agar set to work. He embedded a small mechanical winch into the rock next to the governor's feet. From his chest coat he unsnapped a short harness, which he strapped to the governor's feet, attaching it to a hook on the winch. He also attached the line he'd carried into the chamber to the foot harness.

The decoy next. Agar unfastened a folded package held flat against his chest, fastened to his chest coat. He unsnapped a small device from the chest coat and attached it to one end of the folded package. He fastened the device into the rock next to the governor's feet. He attached another device from a chest coat pocket to the opposite end of the package. At his mental command the device activated, inflating the package. As the package unfolded, section after section, Agar bent upward at the waist, reached up and pinched a nerve in the governor's legs between his calves and ankle. The governor's talons retracted in response to the stimulated nerve. His body hung free, swinging by the leg harness attached to the thin filament housed in the winch.

Another mental command and the winch silently unspooled as the decoy dummy neared full inflation. Agar halted the winch when the governor's head hung level to the terrace. The fully inflated dummy replaced the governor. Its outer material designed to reflect sonic pulses in the same manner as a Borinian body.

Departing the roost Agar climbed to the terrace. Coordinating the action of the small winch in the ceiling, and another in the drum embedded above the terrace, Agar maneuvered the governor's prone dead weight to the terrace floor. Agar removed another folded package on his chest coat, a full body bag when unfolded. He detached the cable from the governor's foot harness and attached it to a hook at the foot end of the bag. The other line from the terrace he attached to the head end of the bag. He rolled the prone governor into the bag, the governor's arms folded across his chest, his wings wrapping him like a blanket. Agar placed a small air bottle he'd carried clipped to one side of his chest coat into the bag, activated it, and placed a face mask from another chest coat pocket on the governor. He connected air bottle and mask before sealing the bag.

Agar again activated the winch above the terrace, hoisting the governor off the terrace floor. Agar retrieved three aerial rollers, attaching one possessing a breaking device to the head of the bag. He connected the remaining rollers to rings at the center and foot of the bag.

Agar checked his mental clock. His countdown indicated the hover drone on the last segment of its route on the far side of the mountain. Sufficient time for his final tasks. He returned to the roost in the chamber, retrieved the small winch from the vacated roost, and activated the decoy's transmitter. He located the garment bag the governor had packed prior to drinking the dosed tea. The governor's condition, and the packed bag, increased Agar's confidence the final item to complete his ruse had been prepared. When he'd first arrived in the chamber, Agar could not be certain Tovarinkara had completed the instructions implanted during their first contact, recalling the governor's strong and adept mental abilities. But whether or not Tovarinkara had been aware of his actions, he'd performed as Agar instructed. Including a looped recording of sleeping thoughts. Agar located the recorder and adjusted the output frequency to match the inflated decoy. Agar clipped the bagged garments to his chest coat, and commanded the winch to wind in the line and release its anchor. Agar departed the chamber, confident a scan inside would reveal the governor asleep at his roost.

On the terrace Agar secured the garment bag to the governor's descent line. The hover drone due in moments. The riskiest phase of the operation about to commence. Agar's access of the drone enabled him to increase the drone's speed during this segment of its patrol. He'd also commanded it to transmit images of the empty peaks recorded during previous passes. But he'd be unable to spoof its heat, motion and sonic sensors, the reason Agar had prepared this mode of escape instead of a transport or flyer. He'd decided against an escape pod hoisted from below for similar reasons.

Agar waited for the drone to pass out of view. He activated the winch in the gorge far below, observed the Governor's descent line straightening, hoisting the Governor from the terrace. The line stretched taut, descending at an angle toward the opposite side of the gorge.

The drone out of view. Their small profiles insufficient to trigger its heat or motion sensors. But the descent visible to any guard observing from above, or from nearby peaks surrounding the estate. Agar doubted the few guards assigned to the governor paid much attention to the peaks, relying instead on the patrolling drone. At their last check, the governor had been soundly hibernating in his private chamber, no indication in his thoughts of escape, or rescue. And their minds, indeed the minds of all Borinorhnus, currently focused on the "Rahu" eclipse, during which General Zanthinvolar's final passage had been scheduled, ensuring Orh's guidance to the underworld and the next life.

But Agar left nothing to chance. He checked the flyer strapped on his back, elongated its tail, and placed his feet in the tail clasps. He hooked himself to his descent line and activated its winch. The line tautened, lifting him from the terrace in a head down position, his back to the cliff wall, his eyes and other senses scanning the peaks and sky above. The rifle butts jammed into his armpits, their muzzles aimed upward. Ready to spread the flyer's wings if necessary, providing him the advantage of flight while firing, his arms unhindered by his natural wings.

Agar fitted his face mask and commanded the brakes to release. Agar and the bag containing Governor Tovarinkara slid along the taut lines, their speed increasing as they fell, plunging toward the gorge in a rapid descent. The skin of Agar's closed wings fluttered in the air rushing over him. He slowed their descent when he sensed their approach to the mist covered gorge. They pierced the thick veil, falling through layers of toxic gas. Breathing from his air bottle, Agar slid into the darkness below.

The world beneath the gaseous shroud alien, inhabited by strange exotic plants and creatures. An ecosystem unlike the one above, existing according to its own natural laws. The light and heat received from Orh and its companion sparse. The energy and sustenance required by the world beneath the mist, provided by the invisible portions of the stars' electromagnetic radiation.

The landscape eerily magnificent to Agar's ultraviolet vision. His surroundings rendered in a fluorescent glow. The colors subdued, yet striking. Agar's echolocating senses depicted large rock formations, and broad trees twisted into grotesque shapes in the wide meandering plain between the bases of the mountains. The gentle slopes at the bases covered in strange vegetation, before rising black and bare above the shrouding mist.

Agar sensed the falling drums his mental command had released from the cliff far above. Their lines slack, they fell along the cliff wall, bouncing their way almost straight down, not at an angle into the gorge as he and the governor had. The battered drums landed in the twisted tree branches at the base of the mountain, the lines hopelessly entangled. Agar gathered as much line as ran free, cut away and abandoned the remainder. The gear invisible to anyone searching from above. But only a delaying tactic, like the inflatable decoy and recording. By the time anyone discovered the governor's absence, the clues indicating the escape route, and organized a search of the gorge, the governors on his list would be out of the Governor Supreme's reach, safe in the roost Agar had prepared.

A strange sensation enveloped Agar as he stood on the alien landscape. An affinity and closeness to General Zanthinvolar, whose body, at perhaps the precise moment, was being laid to rest beneath the ground on which Agar stood.

Agar gathered his equipment from the gorge, loading them into his transport, which he'd used to anchor the winches on the far side of the gorge. The hibernating governor he loaded onto an air stretcher. A blast of compressed air disturbed the layer of fine black dirt beneath the stretcher, depositing a powdery coating on Agar's leggings and boots.

The stretcher loaded and secured, Agar departed the area. He guided the transport along the gorge below its opaque shroud, his thoughts already contemplating the rescue of two more governors.

Destiny

"It is out of the question Khalinaltani," implored General Dogarinmaral. "The situation is extremely tense and volatile. Particularly following the death of General Zanthinvolar. The Borinorhnus council is using his death to incite the population, accusing us of assassinating the general. Your presence on Borinorhnus might provide the spark which ignites this war."

"Or provide the means to diffuse it," Khal responded.

"Please explain," thought Governor Nakurinmaral.

Khal surveyed the individuals gathered around the table, Governor Nakurinmaral, General Dogarinmaral, and Director Jeremiah. Their thoughts somber and subdued. The prospect of imminent war weighed upon them. The meeting had been convened to consider Khal's alarming request to travel to Borinorhnus.

"Am I correct in suspecting a decline in fertility and population growth on Borinorhnus?" The three council members around the table turned to stare at each other, their thoughts confirming Khal's suspicion.

"We have received such reports from our contacts on Borinorhnus. The population has been in steady decline over the past decades. It is a concern of the Borinorhnus council. But this information is not widely known Khalinaltani, and no one is certain of its significance. How is it you come to know of this?" Nakur asked.

"I do not possess this knowledge. I suspect it. The phenomena has occurred before in our history. Accompanied by a concurrent decline in the Human population. The most precipitous decline occurred in the era following the Purification Wars, after Humans departed Borinorhnus. We have seen the pattern repeated in the historical record, but its significance has escaped us until now. My current research may provide the solution."

"Do you believe you have discovered the reason behind this phenomena?" Nakur inquired.

"While I am unable to infer a direct cause and effect, or even explain the relationship, the historical data indicates a strong correlation between both phenomena."

"I cannot see how this information, even if you were to prove a causal relationship, might impact on our current situation," Dogar thought. "And how does it pertain to your current research?"

"They may be one and the same. The solution to my first question may provide the solution to the other."

"Even if you are correct Khalinaltani," Dogar thought, "it must wait until this crisis is resolved, one way of the other. The situation on Borinorhnus is chaotic and dangerous. They have not yet fired a shot at us but have been killing their own citizens at an alarming rate. The purges have decimated our networks. We no longer possess the means to communicate with or protect you on Borinorhnus."

"I am neither requesting nor do I require your protection general. I am a free agent and the decision is mine."

"Yet you are here discussing it Khalinaltani. You are not naive and cannot be unaware of the situation's volatility. And as I observed before, if you are discovered on Borinorhnus it may provide the provocation they seek. As it is, I am surprised they have not yet launched an attack. They may be waiting for a provocation. One your presence on Borinorhnus will provide."

Experience and patience tempered Khal's increasing frustration. He'd been stymied before. Had experienced blind alleys and dead ends. Had spent weeks and months uncertain what his search might uncover, if anything, delighting in unexpected discovery. Now he possessed a defined objective, a path directing him to it, and the means to achieve it. Yet it continued to elude him.

He did not fault the governors. The situation indeed precarious. Discontinuing the search on account of a war a first in his experience, but eminently reasonable and justified. And he needn't discontinue his research. There was still much to occupy him on Nivalinorhnus. Other answers he needed to find. But the ultimate answer, the one underpinning all others, lay on Borinorhnus, or rather beneath it.

Twilight faded to night as Khal exited the citadel, his mind unsettled. An uncharacteristic restlessness pervaded him. He flew through the night sky, no fixed destination in mind, his general direction toward his quarters in the science colony's residential section. His flight wobbly in Khalinorhnus's higher gravity, like an infant's first attempts, not yet accustomed to its wings.

Sharp pangs in the pit of his stomach reminded him he hadn't eaten in over a day. Too absorbed in his work, the excitement of his findings. Now he had time, the prospect of a war interrupting his work not as harsh as his disappointment.

He approached a tall A-framed agora, selected an entrance and landed on the terrace. Stepping inside, the sights, sounds, and smells of a bustling marketplace greeted him. The building's top floor an eclectic assortment of stores and vendors' stalls, offering a variety of fruit, vegetables, spices, and drinks. Human and Borinian.

An enclosed hallway around the building's perimeter contained transport rails. The system designed from both Human and Borinian use. He stepped onto a square section of floor as it passed in front of him. The floor sections, designed for standing, alternated with open sections spanned by a bar, designed for hanging upside down. Either method used by both Humans and Borinians, Khal observed. Borinians stood on floor sections as he did, and humans hung from the bar alongside Borinians by means of mechanical talons affixed to their boots.

Khal remained undecided on a destination as the rail slid along the hallway past portals to specialized shops and eateries. His thoughts preoccupied, he may have been on his second circuit of the building when a familiar scent grabbed his attention. A faint flowery scent, subtle and unique to one person. Seraphina.

Khal wondered if he'd forgotten an appointment to meet her and Ezekiel. His indelible memory for historic and scientific detail often failed him in personal matters. It had not been a requirement in his solitary existence. He followed the scent, stepping from the moving floor into a softly lit eatery. The large, open space contained circular tables, around which Borinians and Humans sat and conversed while eating and drinking. In the center of the room, a circular hole provided access to the roosting space directly beneath, where Khal sensed Borinians and Humans hanging from a metal lattice works around food and drink dispensers. The room below also accessible through a hallway portal for individuals hanging from the railway's bars.

The eatery sparsely occupied, many of the tables empty. Seraphina and Ezekiel occupied a corner table, providing a view of both entrances, the one from the hallway and the hole in the center of the room. Seraphina's cautious habits ingrained, even when unnecessary, Khal thought. And though he didn't discern their presence, he suspected Seraphina carried one, perhaps two, bladed weapons concealed on her person. From Khal's perspective again unnecessary, but as normal to Seraphina as the garments she wore.

Seraphina and Ezekiel focused on bowls of Vrechi, a lentil-like vegetable soup, as Khal approached. Their gazes rose to meet his. Welcoming smiles greeted him. Seraphina's smile spread across her creamy brown face, a pastel ochre in Khal's ultraviolet vision. He marveled, as he often did, at the pleasant expression Human faces were capable of, a smile absent from the repertoire of Borinian facial expressions.

Neither wore headcaps, and Khal waited for an invitation before entering their thoughts or their personal space.

"Welcome Khal," Seraphina thought and said in her native language, although she'd been rapidly learning the Human language spoken on Khalinorhnus, much of it similar to Ezekiel's. "We did not expect to see you until tomorrow."

"Then we did not agree to meet here? And this is a most pleasant coincidence? I fear I had forgotten. My stomach had to remind me I haven't eaten."

Seraphina laughed, another Human trait Khal considered pleasing. Unlike the long cheeping vocalizations

Borinians used to signal amusement. Seraphina's soft chucking reminded Khal of water flowing through a brook.

Khal drew a cushioned backless stool from an unoccupied table and sat. His stubbed tailbone hung over the stool's rear edge, his wings gathered at his side. He manually activated the mechanical waiter in the center of the table, studied the menu, and entered his order while Seraphina pondered the alien before her. A species she'd once despised, now a friend. And the man next to her, once an unfathomable stranger, now her mate. And the unexpected, once unimaginable path, life had set her on, now her destiny.

"How did the governors respond to your request? Seraphina asked in Khal's mind, also voicing the question for Ezekiel.

Khal responded in both minds, "They will not approve such a journey. And I cannot blame them. Also, under the circumstances I do not see how it will be possible. Either world will prevent any ship of Nivalinorhnus approaching and landing on Borinorhnus."

"You mean Khalinorhnus?"

"I am uncertain I will ever be comfortable using that name," Khal replied.

" It is named for you."

"An approbation I do not deserve and have not sought."

"Among some Human factions things are given a person's name to honor their status or position. Among others to honor what they have done. Perhaps it is the same here," Seraphina said.

"Thank you Seraphina. I had not thought of it in such a manner."

"And although it is true Khalinorhnus is unlike any world I have ever seen," Saraphina continued, "I have never known a world that did not trade in contraband, and did not have its smugglers. I am certain they must know how to avoid the guilds of Khalinorhnus and Borinorhnus. But in this instance I ask you not to consider it Khal. I too am concerned for your safety."

"Seraphina is correct," Ezekiel said, his thoughts simultaneously streaming into Khal's mind. "I have been meeting many who recently fled Borinorhnus. They tell of an underground, a network which provides assistance and transportation in secret to those seeking to flee Borinorhnus. Borinian and Human. I have been attempting to contact this underground, to help them if I can. But Seraphina is also correct concerning the danger Khalinaltani. Especially now."

A soft chime drew their attention overhead. The mechanical waiter hung from tracks concealed in the ceiling. Telescoping sections lowered a tray bearing Khal's order to the table. Khal lifted the place setting from the tray, set it on the table before him. From the waiter's tray he removed a small bowl containing an aromatic mound of a pasta-like stew, and another small bowl of desiccated fruit. A button dismissed the waiter. Its telescoped sections retracted, and it returned silently along the ceiling to a dispenser where it awaited its next delivery.

Khal lifted a twin tined fork, its handle a flattened shape on one side, a ring on the other. He wielded it between the bowls before him and his mouth, his thumb hooked through the ring, holding the flat side pressed into his palm. The fork's design, like all the utensils, accommodated either Human or Borinian hands.

Khal ate in obvious pleasure, and hunger, spearing morsels into his mouth. His eyes closed, his gnaw like chewing accompanied by his characteristic low rhythmic humming. He slurped his drink through a shorter, thinner version of a dispenser tube attacked to the bottom of a closed half liter container.

"What do you wish to do Khalinaltani?" Ezekiel asked during a pause in Khal's concentrated chewing.

"I am uncertain. What I seek is important, but not so important as to risk lives, many lives. Even if it may also possess the potential to halt this insane march to war. Though I suspect such a hope is born of my own vanity. If Borinorhnus cannot yet see the true path as Nivalinorhnus have, one more piece of truth will not persuade them. They are constrained by leaders and belief systems which have governed their lives for too long. Religious, political, cultural, and behavioral. They, we, cannot help ourselves. We are social creatures, conditioned by learned behavior to follow leaders and the accepted social order. Under enlightened circumstances, this may be beneficial to our individual lives, and to our species as a whole. Under other circumstances it can lead us off a cliff without wings, as is happening now, and has happened before on Borinorhnus."

"What if war comes?" Seraphina asked. "You cannot remain here Khal."

"It will be necessary to safeguard all we have learned, " Khal replied. "Ensure it is not lost again. Ensure we do not continue to repeat the same mistakes. Our libraries and archives are being transported to off-world bases and colonies."

"This knowledge also belongs to all the factions," Seraphina said.

A sudden, startling understanding coalesced in Khal's thoughts. His attention during a lifetime of exploration and research had been exclusively focused on the implications his work held for his home system and his people. But in Seraphina's thought, simple, and yet profound, he recognized the universal implications it also held across the galaxy.

Khal streamed his thoughts into Seraphina's mind. Not as in conversation. Instead permitting her to perceive a tangible manifestation of the cosmic interconnectivity he deeply believed in. Two separate life paths, yet their destinies connected and intertwined from the outset. Delivered to the same world by the unpredictable chaos of cosmic serendipity. One to teach, one to learn. She the seed, fertilized by his knowledge, planting it beyond the confines of Orh's tiny corner of space. Enormous pride and satisfaction bloomed within him, perceived by Seraphina, banishing his disappointment, and strengthening his resolve.

"I have not yet decided," he thought. "I must know if what you propose is a viable option Ezekiel. Will you seek this information for me?"

Ezekiel nodded his ascent, his thoughts conveying the same. His clear grey eyes stared hard at Khal's small marble-like eyes, piercing them, searching behind them, as though probing behind Khal's thoughts.

"If war does come you both must leave this world," Khal conveyed to his companions. "Leave this system for one of our colonies where you may continue to learn Seraphina," his small eyes focused on her.

"I cannot abandon these people," Ezekiel said.

"I go where Ezekiel goes," Seraphina said. "And you must come too. You cannot remain here."

"You are the seed of the future Seraphina. I understand that now. Your destinies," including Ezekiel in his expressionless gaze, "Lay elsewhere. You were meant to spread this knowledge to your people."

"I cannot spread what you have not yet taught me. You must come with us in order to continue teaching me."

"You do not need me. You have acquired the thirst to learn on your own. You have the means, and it is your destiny, to seek your own knowledge. Far more than I can ever teach you Seraphina."

Coup d'etat

Agar waited in a warehouse cave, in an industrial district on the edge of the city. The area straddled the line between twilight and daylight. The bases of the peaks on the sun lit side sloped onto a vast desert plain, the mist covered gorges absent in this part of the world. Stretching into the distance, an enormous field of slim pyramid like towers pierced the sky. An ocean of them. Telescoping arms on their sides held wing like panels collecting Orh's rays, the converted energy transmitted along a distribution grid to the city.

The warehouse was attached to a transport repair facility sharing the same complex of caves and tunnels. The hiss and whir of tools and machinery, the odor of solvents and lubricants, surrounded Agar as he waited.

Two individuals entered from a tunnel on his left. They'd waited and watched, ensuring the clandestine meeting remained unobserved and undisturbed.

"Your guests are secured and unharmed?" Agar's thoughts inquired as they approached.

"As you instructed," responded the taller Borinian standing before him. Muscled and rugged despite his age. Much older than Agar, perhaps four or five years younger than General Zanth, with whom he'd served. Scars on his leathery flat forehead and bristled cheeks, on his arms, and lighter patches of regenerated skin on his wings, reminders of battles he'd fought. His mind disciplined, his thoughts harsh and uncompromising. Agar had not asked for a name, and hadn't provided his own. Instead he'd decided to refer to the big Borinian as the 'minder'.

"We questioned them before inducing hibernation. They do not appear to possess useful information. The Governor Supreme had not advised them of his plans. The Librarian Director awoke from hunger, but we dosed the food we provided him to induce another hibernating sleep. If others awake we will do the same."

"You have done well. And the final package?"

"Being transferred to your transport at this moment. How is your plan progressing, and how else may I assist you?"

"The initial phase is now complete. All I require is for you to keep your guests secure, and they must remain unharmed."

"Then I will wish you good fortune and success in your endeavor. There is no profit to be had from this war, except for the weapons dealers. But what good is profit if all is destroyed in the end. Destruction is bad for business. And as you have shown, the esteemed general was against it. His life sacrificed for his belief. On that subject, my inquiries have identified an individual known to our circles as Nyctiquiri Rafinvelir, the passage maker. His birth name is uncertain, but he is also called Lasiurinceris. He is a frequent operative of Zepharinlenar, though it is believed he is a free agent whom the governor contracts when needed. The one the governor uses for his dirty work. If the governor wished the general's death, Lasiurinceris is the individual he'd have contracted to carry it out."

Uncharacteristically, Agar did not conceal the raw emotion aroused by the minder's information.

"What do you wish me to do concerning him?" the minder asked.

"Nothing. If he is indeed the one, he is mine to deal with. But you can provide me all the information on him you possess, or can acquire."

"I will convey all I am aware of at this time," the minder's information already streaming into Agar's mind. "And I will continue to press my associates concerning his activities. But it will require time. He is not an individual you casually seek information on. How will I contact you when I have more to give you, or if I need to reach you regarding my guests?"

"As before. Use the frequency I provided. It is secure. Nevertheless only a time and location in the message. Nothing more. Or I will assume you have been compromised and I will not respond. When I receive your transmission I will contact you."

When Agar returned to his transport, it had been washed and serviced. In the rear passenger compartment lay the final 'package'. The last governor on his list, Sorkahringorol of Health and Habitats

Agar, ever cautious, inspected and swept both the transport and governor for tracking transmitters or other undesired surprises. Satisfied, Agar launched and dove for the plain at the base of the peaks. He flew a circuitous route on the daylight side of the mountains. Borinians seldom ventured into the harsh sunlight, dispatching quiri for outside maintenance around the power plant.

The skies above clear. The remote hovering eyes focused on the plant, a likely target. Agar flew a route in the opposite direction. His destination the Yahsoldis mountain range, a little over four hundred echospans north, thirteen hundred kilometers, where he'd roosted following his aerial encounter with the dissident. Isolated and secluded. Far from the city and its interconnected minds. And bathed in daylight, a deterrent to any Borinians searching for him or his guests.

The trip long and tedious, due primarily to Agar's evasive route. But it assured he hadn't been followed, either from above or below, as he approached the Yahsoldis range.

Agar continued north another nine echospans, thirty kilometers, past his mountain retreat. His destination another set of peaks containing a warren of caves and tunnels more suitable for his purposes. He maneuvered the transport between two facing peaks, more like a fissure enclosed in the wall of the main peak. The wide entrance to the cave complex, capable of accommodating the transport, concealed between the walls of the fissure and beneath an overhead outcropping. Invisible from above or the adjacent peaks.

Agar navigated the wide tunnel, travelling deeper into the mountain. He landed the transport on a wide ledge. He unshielded his mind and received the thoughts of the other governors already his guests.

"He is arrived," he announced in their thoughts. "You may attend to him."

Agar had used the air stretcher to transport Governor Tovarinkara, his first and longest guest, to the comfortable chambers he'd prepared for the governors' accommodation. Governor Tovarinkara had used the stretcher to transport the second guest, Space and Technology Governor Laskarinadya, who'd arrived a day later. Now they'd transport Governor Sorkahringorol, who still lay in a drugged sleep in the transport.

Agar dove into the dark depths of the enormous cavern before spreading his arms and fingers. His flew in the direction of another large tunnel lower in the cavern's wall. He'd greet the newest arrival after the governor revived, and been settled. Awakening in strange surroundings had been a disorienting process for each of his guests. Agar had eased Governor Tovarinkara through it from concealment. Governor Laskarinadya had awoke agitated and combative until he recognized his colleague, who'd explained the situation and calmed him.

"Where am I? What is this place and what has been done to me?" Agar heard the agitated thoughts of the newest arrival. "It is Khorabinjolen," the awakening governor's mind screamed in fear, blocking out the thoughts of both governors attempting to calm him.

"Calm yourself Sorkah," Tovarinkara urged him, pressing his thoughts into the governor's mind.

"Tovar?" And Laskar? You are here also?

"This is not of Khorabinjolen's doing, Sorkah. And you are in no danger. On the contrary, we are all quite safe here."

"Governor Tovarinkara is correct Governor Sorkahringorol," Agar greeted his latest guest, once the governor's mind had calmed and settled. "As I have already done to your colleagues, allow me to apologize for the manner in which you were transported here. It was necessary under the circumstances. Your colleagues will explain. But as I have cautioned them, and now you, you must remain here under my protection until this crisis is resolved. You are free to leave if you wish, but to do so will place your life, and the lives of your colleagues in jeopardy. Beyond these mountains I will not be able to protect you, which were the last instructions given to me by esteemed General Zanthinvolar Abydynus, who it has been my honor to serve for many years. His last wish, and hope, was the three of you might conceive a plan to avert this war."

"Then I am grateful to you," Governor Sorkahringorol responded in Agar's thoughts. "And I will attempt to honor the departed general, whom I respected and admired. But why do you conceal yourself from us?"

"Without foreknowledge of how all this might conclude, it is necessary to protect you, and myself."

"Sorkah," Tovar interrupted. "We three represent a shadow council. In anticipation of your arrival Laskar and I have been exploring proposals aimed at preventing this war. However, friend of Zanthinvolar," the thought addressed to Agar. "Cut off as we are from the outside, we are uncertain of the current situation, and Khorabinjolen has surely proceeded in his plan to reconstitute the council."

"While still in the city I received rumors he had been unable to appoint any of his candidates," Sorkah informed them. "However I am uncertain whether this is fact or not. Yet the military has not launched any attacks, which they will not do without a declaration from the full council."

"I have been able to secure you some time," Agar responded in their thoughts. "How long I cannot say. Candidates the General Supreme intended to appoint to the council are missing. Others have been persuaded it might not be in their best interest or health to accept the appointment. But time is the enemy governors. The military is on a hair trigger and any small incident may spark this war. The Governor Supreme may also possess a ploy he has yet to play."

The governors' responses to Agar's thoughts a mixture of astonishment, dismay, and hope. The government of their world paralyzed. The unconscionable, even inconceivable act, a fait accompli. One individual had effectively engineered a coup, declared Sorkah. To disrupt a coup, responded Tovar. Necessary, all three concluded. Though still disquieted and unsettled by the events, they turned their thoughts to how best to capitalize on the situation.

"We have already crossed the threshold," Tovar reasoned. "The next logical step, and perhaps only solution, is removing Khorabinjolen."

"How can it be accomplished?" Laskar asked. "Removing him requires impeachment. His warmongering does not constitute grounds for impeachment. And we possess no evidence of wrongdoing. On the contrary, we are the ones he can prosecute and execute for treason during a time of war."

"If you possessed evidence of conspiracy to murder, and perhaps complicity, even foreknowledge, might it be sufficient for your purpose," Agar asked.

"You have such evidence?" Tovar asked, astonishment in his thoughts.

"I do not. However I believe the Governor Supreme ordered the assassination of General Zanthinvolar. Such a murder could not have occurred otherwise. Permission had to have been granted from the highest authority. I am also certain Governor Zepharinlenar orchestrated it, and I may know the individual who performed it."

"If you can demonstrate a connection involving all three in the death of General Zanthinvolar, it will be sufficient," Tovar replied. "It need not be direct proof, but evidence sufficient to require further inquiry. The Governor Supreme, or any other implicated governor, can be required to temporarily vacate the position while the matter is investigated.

"Provided the other members of the council agree," Sorkah thought.

"In the absence of a new council we still constitute the council," Tovar reminded them.

"With only Antrozinpanar and Mokharinsephin remaining, since Zepharinlenar will also be required to step down," Laskar thought.

"They can be persuaded," Agar assured them.

"Indeed," thought Tovar. "But allow that to be our concern. "You have much to do, and as indicated, not much time in which to accomplish it."

Agar returned to the city the following day. His first task, a sense of the time remaining to him and the governors. He contacted the attack cruiser, ostensibly to check in and receive an update on the ship's readiness and any recent orders. Agar had no intention of returning to the ship, but technically he remained its captain. General Zanth's orders to the effect had not be changed by the fleet commander. Agar's real purpose to gather information on the fleet's current status, current orders, and get plugged into the military's communications net.

He learned the fleet's current orders remained unchanged. The fleet on ready alert, but on no timetable for a planned attack. The fleet continued to monitor Nivalinorhran deployments, countering changes in the positions of the opposing fleet. The military High Command increasingly exasperated and impatient toward the Governing Council, aware any small incident in the tense atmosphere might spark a disaster. The Governor Supreme had not consulted the new General Supreme, or explained the delay. The commanders in the field, staring at sensor displays of unfamiliar Nivalinorhran warships, not so anxious to engage a battle.

Agar's next destination the citadel. He entered attired in his Captain Commander's uniform, blending in and invisible in the crowd of military uniforms bustling around the complex. His innocuous presence also aided by an atmosphere of confused chaos surrounding the citadel's administrative offices.

The military and civilian leadership at a loss for direction. A ship of state without a captain. And a paranoid siege mentality pervaded the thoughts of every mind in the city. The thought restricting headcaps worn by military and civilian leadership no deterrent to Agar's powerful mental probing. Around the complex, outside the offices, and particularly around the office chambers of the Governor Supreme, Agar collected useful intelligence indicating he had more time than he'd expected.

The offices around the security section of the citadel another matter. The siege mentality also pervasive, but possessing a focused purposefulness and malevolent intent. The marching orders of the law and security colony clear. Locate the missing governor candidates, and the missing purged governors. Discover the individuals responsible, assumed to be Nivalinorhran operatives. And continue to dismantle dissident networks. Detainees to be pressured by any means for information.

The minds Agar touched in the security colony disciplined, like the military, and accustomed to secrecy. But also possessing a paranoid suspicion. While other minds Agar had probed ignored the intrusion, even expected it under the circumstances, the security officers zeroed in on the prober. Agar more cautious and circumspect in how deeply he probed, and how long he lingered in any one mind.

For most of the workday Agar moved unobtrusively through the ornate halls, and around the office caverns and chambers. Loitering yet invisible, camouflaged amid small groups of military and civilian staffers. No one paid particular or undue interest in him.

Riding a rail through a tunneled hallway to an exit, prepared to depart the citadel, Agar touched a thought containing the name Lasiurinceris. The thought had emanated from a pair of security officers also headed toward the exit.

"I will deliver the message," thought the officer on the left, upon whom Agar focused his attention, memorizing details of the individual's head and neck from behind, the color and cut of his fur, the fall of his shoulders and the drape of his wings. Agar particularly memorized the scent.

Agar exited first, dove and rose to circle above the tiered terrace. When his quarry exited, Agar committed the remaining features to memory. Wide flat forehead, and a heart shaped face. Eyes sunk below deep brow ridges. Flat wide nostrils and pointed jaw. Large leafy ears rather than sharp and pointed.

Agar noted the dark blue, gold trimmed chest coat over the paler blue shirt and leggings. And he noted the weapon concealed in a holster on the side of the chest coat.

Agar followed from behind and above. Returning echoes of his sonic emissions provided details of the swarm around him, and the positions of individual patterns in the swarm, while his eyes maintained visual contact of his target, headed for a public transport station. Agar followed him onto the transport, a section behind. Visual contact lost, but Agar periodically brushed against the mind, like a passing stranger. The target's thoughts concealed by the headcap, but the contact sufficient to verify his exact location.

An hour later, Agar's quarry exited the transport in an outlying town, midway to darkside. The twilight covering the town a shade darker than in the city. Agar followed his target to an area of low peaks housing public eateries and entertainment. His target did not enter, instead the security officer waited on a low crevice, at the side of an establishment offering females for coupling at a price. Agar alighted on a rock outcropping on an adjacent peak, above his target.

He waited.

Agar almost missed the other's arrival. Not sensing him until he appeared as though materializing from the rock. The other's approach shielded by the jagged twists of the crevice. And his movements cautious. His sonic emissions subtle, utilizing a low undulating frequency, which did not produce the characteristic tingling impact on the body. His pulses had almost touched Agar an instant before Agar concealed himself behind the rocks.

In his brief ultraviolet glimpse, Agar sighted a short, solidly built and proportioned figure. His coloring and markings atypical for a Borinian. And his scent absent from the air reaching Agar's nostrils. Artificially masked, Agar concluded, as he routinely did to his own.

Agar peered around the side of the rock formation concealing him, not exposing enough of himself to reflect an echo. Alarmed to notice the new arrival staring in his direction. His eyes unable to locate what his senses informed him might be there. He had the instinct, Agar concluded, probably acquired through military experience. A quarry not to be underestimated.

Agar suspected the new arrival had to be Lasiurinceris. Agar was convinced of it. But following him would be a futile exercise. It'd only expose Agar's presence. Agar required a less sensitive mind, an instinct less developed, to lead him to Lasiurinceris in a manner which would not alert him. Agar decided to focus on the security officer who had delivered the message to Lasiurinceris. The message itself, from whom, and its contents, a matter of more than mere curiosity. One Agar was now determined to learn.

The security officer departed. But Agar maintained his concealment. In Lasiurinceris's position, Agar would wait in the shadows to visually and sonically sweep his trail, ensure his senses had not provided a false alarm. He might attempt to flank the position to positively rule out an unseen intruder. But given their relative positions, such a maneuver might expose Lasiurinceris. Agar would not risk it. He suspected Lasiurinceris would not either. The better option, to wait and watch. Which Agar did, settling behind the rock to outwait General Zanth's probable assassin.

Underground Railroad

The tanker's captain, short, hairy, including a full beard covering his lower jaw and flowing onto his neck fur, displayed a pleasant, polite cordiality toward his passengers, despite the wary caution in his darting glances. He ushered Khal, Ezekiel, and Seraphina into a tiny cramped compartment in the bowels of the tanker's main control section, forward of the long chain of connected tanks. The compartment cleverly concealed behind a false bulkhead.

"The passage is expected to be ten celestial days," the captain informed Khal, who relayed the information to Ezekiel and Seraphina. "We are not as quick as those fancy military ships, or as nimble when lugging a long tail of filled tanks," his cheeping a measure of his amusement. "Unfortunately you will need to remain here during the passage. The less interaction you have with my crew, the less they can have you in their thoughts. Our thoughts will necessarily be more accessible on Borinorhnus, or to any Borinorhran military boarding the ship. By good fortune this ship often avoids inspection, but boardings have been more frequent in the current crisis. Even a fleeting unguarded thought concerning your presence will mean disaster for us all. Everything you require for the journey is provided here. The food dispenser has been stocked, and sanitary facilities are on the other side of that hatch."

"I appreciate the risk you must endure to assist us captain. And I thank you.

"It is nothing we are not accustomed to. And it is my honor to have the esteemed Khalinaltani onboard. I am a great admirer, as is all my crew. It is a pity they cannot be informed of your identify. We all have relatives on Khalinorhnus. The captain of the Khalinorhran tanker which transported you here is my cousin. We do not want this war, and we are loyal to the cause. However it is you who are at risk. If you and your companions are discovered on Borinorhnus, especially when they discover your identity, there will be no help for you."

"I appreciate your concern captain. But this I must do. For the sake of all of us. And I have already put too many lives at risk for my sake."

"As you wish Khalinaltani. If there is nothing further I must return to the bridge."

"Thank you again," Khal thought, as the captain departed and sealed the compartment.

Seraphina's gaze wandered the compartment, noting the food dispenser on the aft bulkhead, and the small circular hatch capable of accommodating a single person at a time. A dozen bunk style berths had been crammed into the tight space. Overhead bars provided roosts. A twinge of claustrophobia clutched at her throat. Seraphina not a true claustrophobic. Rather her incipient anxiety the result of surfacing memories of a childhood and adolescence spent in confined captivity. Perhaps why the vast, empty, openness of space provided her such consoling comfort.

Khal selected a corner of the compartment and climbed to hook his talons around the overhead bar. He hung head down in the roosting position, his head almost touching the deck in the low ceilinged compartment. Khal able to spend the entire journey in hibernated sleep, his mind subconsciously working on his research. But his companions were risking their lives to accompany him, against his long and futile objections. He could not simply ignore them. And he welcomed their insights into the knotty questions his research presented.

He possessed no laboratory, no equipment, and not much time. The tanker scheduled to return to the gas giant after only three days at Borinorhnus. The imposed deadline to complete his task frustrating, but given the circumstances, perhaps a positive incentive. The longer they remained on Borinorhnus, the greater the chance of discovery and capture, not only halting his task, but perhaps precipitating the outbreak of war.

He wished he had sufficient time and leisure to sample a larger area, and to continue sampling until his search proved successful, or fruitless. But under the circumstances he'd narrowed his search area to three specific sites, based on his intimate knowledge of Borinorhnus history and prehistory. One site marked the location of the earliest Human colony on Borinorhnus. Another an early colony of pre or proto Borinians. And the third, a burial site used over the centuries by both Human and Borinian inhabitants at one time or the other. Their task, to collect samples from each site and return them to Khalinorhnus for analysis.

Seraphina still not entirely accustomed to the Borinian upside down roosting posture. Despite her recent proximity to Borinian culture and habits, it remained a curiosity. Yet her destiny, a concept she'd only recently been introduced to, and still struggled to grasp, had been inextricably tied to them, even before she had been aware of it. A people she once loathed and feared. Now in the solitude of her thoughts, in a tiny compartment in the bowels of a ship transporting her to a hostile world and an uncertain future, she contemplated her connectedness to all things, and a cosmic predetermination as Khal believed. That every occurrence in her life, good and bad, had conspired to prepare her for this precise point in space and time.

Ezekiel also, in silent solitude, pondered his purpose, and the unlikely, fortuitous salvation which permitted it. A mind, a body and soul, held in captivity from the moment of his birth, set free to discover thoughts generated of his own consciousness. Free to discover his own unique individuality, and free to explore his existence and purpose.

Mid-point through the passage Seraphina and Ezekiel shared another dream, witnessing the spread of humanity across the galaxy, exploring and colonizing world after world. The colonists carried with them their culture, their science and technology, and the seeds of life from their home world. For hundreds of millennia the expansion continued. Their life adapted to new worlds and new environments. Colonies grew into thriving civilizations. Civilizations withered and died. The cities and edifices crumbled into dust, overgrown and buried by time. To be rediscovered and unearthed.

In a portion of the dream, Seraphina and Ezekiel stood in a laboratory among other Humans, examining a creature in a tall transparent enclosure. The creature bilaterally symmetrical, bipedal, but not ground walkers or dwellers. The creature vaguely resembled a Borinian.

Seraphina's perspective in the dream abruptly changed. Now she was the creature in the transparent container, staring out at the strange dark brown eyes examining her. Her naked body registered for the first time. A nascent self-awareness emerged. She experienced the inhalation of air as her lungs expanded. And the beating of a heart, pushing blood through arteries, veins and capillaries. Her mind not empty as the human observers supposed. Primitive emotions stirred, familiar to Seraphina. Captivity, and fear. And a primal rage.

The dream shifted to another chamber. Her essence, among many varied essences, contained in a seed. The seed transported across the vast void of space, existing without form or substance. Altered to survive on strange alien worlds. But developing within the seed, a capacity its creators had not foreseen.

The dream vivid in Seraphina's and Ezekiel's conscious minds. Seemingly as real and solid as the bulkhead an arm's length away. And viscerally disturbing, for reasons they were unable to explain. They turned to Khal to interpret and explain.

"You have seen the complete story. And though I may attempt to explain it, your questions will be better answered when you discover the answers yourselves, which I hope you will at the places we must explore on Borinorhnus."

The days passed in routine tedium. Their seclusion preyed on their nerves, despite the familiar ease each possessed in long solitary voyages. But on her ship, Seraphina had room to move, to wander different sections and cabins as the days wore on, maintenance tasks to occupy her hands and her mind. And there'd been external references. The inability to gaze out at the star sprinkled infinity of space frustrated her. But her internal clock had not been off by the amount she feared, given the absence of external references. On the day she estimated their arrival, the tanker's captain returned.

"We are in orbit around Borinorhnus," he informed them. "The inspectors detected no indication of your presence aboard. I will show you to the tank intended for the Chokhara refinery."

The three gathered their meager possessions. Khal donned a headcap, the kind typically worn by Borinorhran overseers. Ezekiel and Seraphina wore soft wide brimmed hats similar to those worn by quiri working in the bright sunshine on Borinorhnus's sunlit hemisphere. The hats had been modified with wire thin transceivers hidden beneath the sweatband.

Their attire the same simple garments they'd worn upon departing Khalinorhnus. Seraphina and Ezekiel in soiled grey tunics, leggings, and boots befitting their disguise as working quiri. Khal clad as an overseer. Seraphina's loose fitting top occasionally fell from a shoulder, exposing the curved smoothness of the top half of a breast.

A moving rail system transported them through long tunnels in each of the tanker's coupled sections. Each section contained a gas filled spherical globe the size of a miniature moon, accessed through a system of hatches and airlocks. Khal and the captain hung from their talons, Ezekiel and Seraphina from harnesses fitted around their torsos.

A few tank sections had already been decoupled, piloted to their destinations on the surface when the tanker reached specific locations in its orbit around Borinorhnus. When the three travelers arrived at the section which would transport them to the surface, the captain repeated the plan and timetable to Khal.

"The transport will dock with the tank on the dark side after you enter atmosphere. The area is known for atmospheric and electromagnetic anomalies sensor surveillance cannot penetrate. The pilot will fly you to Bakalornus as you requested, and leave you and the transport there. By good fortune, he will have succeeded in procuring the items you requested. They will be in the transport. Once on the surface you will be on your own. Do not attempt to contact any associates you may have on Borinorhnus. The security forces are monitoring and questioning everyone. Our networks have been dismantled, and many of our associates have disappeared in the purges. We are uncertain regarding the extent of their intelligence, as so many have been taken. You must exercise extreme caution while on Borinorhnus, and you must be at the pickup rendezvous in three days. We cannot wait for you if you are not there. If you miss the rendezvous you will be stranded."

"I understand," Khal acknowledged, "And again I thank you."

"Good fortune attend you on your journey Khalinaltani, and permit me the honor of seeing you again."

"And you captain. It is my honor."

The captain departed, leaving Khal, Ezekiel, and Seraphina in the tank's access chamber. Seraphina surveyed her surroundings, facing a curved section of the giant storage tank. Umbilical tubing and pipes connected the tank to machinery and monitors lining the bulkheads.

Before long they heard the pneumatic hiss and mechanical thuds as the tank decoupled from the tanker, the only indication of movement toward the surface. Until they entered the turbulent atmosphere.

"Seraphina," Khal called to Seraphina's mind. He waited for her response before proceeding.

"The frustration in your thoughts during the journey has not gone unnoticed. I perceived your distress at the lack of view ports. I myself have missed that aspect of my beloved ship, and your Dauphin. Do you care to see our destination?"

Khal's offer invigorated Saraphina. Despite his and Ezekiel's company, and the dreams which had occupied her mind, the confinement and inability to view space outside the ship during the long passage, had induced a bored, dull despondency.

"Show me," Seraphina's enthusiasm expressed in her eyes.

"I can show you only from memory. I am unable to access the ship's sensors, and even if I were able, the readings are not rendered in visual images as on Human ships."

"It is more than I have now, and will end the sensation I have had since departing Khalinorhnus of flying blind."

Not for the first time Seraphina perceived the Borinian equivalent of empathy beneath Khal's thoughts, as images of a world floating in space streamed into her mind. One half lit by its primary sun, the other half in perpetual darkness, a band of twilight between them, the result of Borinorhnus's tidal lock to its primary parent star. Beneath the world's thin, cloud speckled atmosphere, lay a gagged and harsh landscape. Vast interconnected mountain ranges stretched like tendrils across its surface. An unchanging vista of sharp pointed peaks, some small, some tall, some gigantic spires, reaching hundreds of sectares into the sky, their white speckled caps piercing the lowest cloud levels.

On the sunlit side vast stretches of empty rust colored desert, low mountains, and bodies of water, including lakes surrounded by mountains, and oceans separating the continents.

The dark side of the world shrouded and hidden. A faint, foreboding, almost invisible presence against the black of space.

A loud pneumatic hiss and a grating sound drew their attention, interrupting the images being passed from Khal to Seraphina. The portal to the air lock passage slid aside, revealing a short, thin Borinian. His small black eyes studied the control bay's occupants. His sonic emissions searched the chamber surrounding them, the impact on their bodies a prickling, pulsing sensation on their skin. His uninvited thoughts flooded their minds. Seraphina recoiled as though attacked.

"My apologies. I did not intend to startle you. You must come quickly. There is not much time."

Seraphina shaken by the mental contact, despite her increased familiarity and comfort with the link. Somehow the sudden contact felt different. Like another mind grafting onto hers, rather than the light communicative meld she'd grown accustomed to. He'd accessed her thoughts uninvited, as she'd accessed his in the brief contact. His occupation, his colony affiliations, his likes, and dislikes, his darkest fears. As familiar as though they were her own.

Other thoughts entered her mind. "Do not get lost in his thoughts," Khal coached. "It will only open yours further. Remember your exercises. Concentrate on your cover persona. Think only those thoughts. Forget who you are and your true nature. As I explained on Nivalino... Khalinorhnus," Khal quickly corrected himself, "I cannot completely block your thoughts or Ezekiel's. Or use the transceivers in your hats to block others from your mind. It will arouse suspicion. And it will be worse on the surface. Many more than his single mind having access to yours. I will deflect their thoughts as much as I am able. But you must do the rest."

Seraphina nodded her understanding, recalling the arduous mental exercises she'd practiced in preparation for the trip to Borinorhnus. She'd been surprised by the pilot, she rationalized, caught unawares, like the first mental link through the headcap with Ezekiel.

No amount of forewarning or exercises prepared her for an entire world of interconnected minds and thoughts. The mental onslaught threatened to overwhelm her as the transport crossed population centers enroute to the first site. She sat in the passenger compartment, head hung between her knees, her hands crushing her ears in a futile attempt to stem the invasive flood. An unsettling, nauseous bubble rose in her stomach, threatening to erupt.

Ezekiel's concerned eyes held Seraphina in a steady gaze, never leaving her. His hand rested on her shoulder. His mind, attempting to reassure her, just one among millions, unable to reach her without shouting, exacerbating her mental distress.

Seraphina focused her concentration on pushing the others minds away. To summon the strength to hear only Ezekiel. His voice spoke to her, guiding her thoughts to the surface as she pushed through the chaos, until she heard his thoughts, only his thoughts. Aware of his voice, his comforting hand on her shoulder.

Ezekiel also disturbed by the multitudinous minds entering his own, roiling unfamiliar emotions. Not like his captivity, when the minds of overseers had controlled his thoughts and actions. Now the thoughts and memories of the city's inhabitants intertwined, exploding into his own. Mixed images and memories of normal daily routines, of family relationships and personal experiences. Of overseers directing Human life stock. Of culling on the farms, who for the labor pool, who for breeding, who for specialized activity training, who for the slaughter pen and food processors.

The transport touched down. Khal, Ezekiel, Seraphina, and the pilot, exited onto a mountain ledge on the cusp of light and dark. Seraphina, always more at home in space, welcomed solid ground beneath her. Her mental discomfort diminished as she stepped onto a world she'd never seen before.

She stared into the distance, and inhaled a heavy, musk-scented air. The sensations intense and powerful following the artificial recycled air she'd been breathing for the past ten days.

Bright sunlight bathed the landscape ahead of her. Behind her the mountain peaks disappeared into a night as dark as space. On her left a vast lake, half in daylight, the other half in darkness. On the sun-lit shore a large processing plant, belching long white plumes into the air from tall stacks. The sprawling complex connected to adjacent peaks by enclosed overhead tunnels.

"This is the location you wished to be landed, and where I must leave you." The thought surfaced in her mind, amid the pilot's non-ending mental stream, and the ocean of Borinian thoughts in her head.

"I thank you," Khal replied to the pilot. "Good fortune attend you."

"And you," the pilot's final thought before leaping head first from the ledge. His wings rustled and snapped open in the heavy air close to darkside.

"What is this place?" Seraphina asked Khal.

"A mineral and ore processing plant. One of the oldest continually occupied areas on Borinorhnus. The first inhabitants were Humans, who used the lake and its minerals to support a colony established here when they first arrived many millennia ago."

"I have never seen water that color before," she thought.

"The result of centuries of mining and processing operations," Khal explained. "Industrial pollution has rendered the water unusable without purification and reprocessing. The air too, as you can see and smell."

Ezekiel aware of the plant's function. And of the human stock farms located close by, providing food for the complex, and labor for the dangerous mining operations in frequently flooded tunnels and gas filled caverns. His discomfort, wrought by returning to Borinorhnus, and the sight of the processing plant, conveyed to Khal and Seraphina by his thoughts.

Seraphina's initial enthusiasm at encountering a new world, despite the danger, replaced by caring concern. Images Ezekiel had shared of his former captive life resurfaced in her memory, evoking a strong empathic response.

"We must go Khal. Our time is limited," she prompted, responding to Ezekiel's discomfort, his unspoken haste to depart the scene in front of them, and the attendant memories.

"Of course you are correct," Khal responded. Seraphina perceived an underlying concern for Ezekiel in Khal's thoughts, matching her own.

The equipment Khal had requested lay in the transport. Ezekiel and Seraphina each donned a backpack containing tools, ultraviolet torches, and rations. They'd carried sample containers from Khalinorhnus, Khal not confident in the underground's ability to acquire containers to his specifications. And since Seraphina refused to travel into danger unarmed, she'd carried three of her bladed weapons. She wore the double-edged short dagger, and the kukri shaped blade, beneath her tunic. The combat blade she'd given to Ezekiel, to accompany his charge lance, both also concealed below his tunic.

Seraphina and Ezekiel also donned headcaps they had carried from Khalinorhnus, replacing the wide brim hats. The hats to be worn only in the open. The chaos in Seraphina's mind, which she'd managed to push to the background, instantly disappeared, though they remained imbedded in her memory, as if they were her own. The war anxiety and depressive gloom, the patriotic fervor and zeal, the apprehension and fear.

The path inside the mountain led downward, the footing uneven amid sharp rocks. Their ultraviolet torches illuminated the dark walls around them in a kaleidoscopic patchwork of reds, oranges, and greens, as the torchlight played across embedded minerals and other elements.

They continued into the mountain's depths. Passed through caverns bearing unmistakable signs of excavation.

Signs Seraphina had learned to recognize. Her thoughts reached out to Khal.

"You are correct Seraphina. It is true to consider my quest commenced here. In these mountains. These caves produced the first evidence of Human habitation on Borinorhnus. But as exciting a discovery as it was, more astounding was the discovery these Human artifacts preceded the appearance of my species on this world."

"Shag a putard," Seraphina said aloud, halting in her tracks. Ezekiel, in the rear, collided into her. Khal, in the lead, his echolocating senses probing ahead, turned toward her, his eyes shiny milk dots caught in the beam of her torch.

"Your expression is probably similar to my reaction when I observed the results of my analysis. This has since been corroborated at many other sites in proximity to this lake. Apparently the first Human settlement on the planet. And it is where my interest in Humans first sprouted. Of course, official Borinorhnus policy now considers this fact blasphemous."

Khal turned and continued ahead.

"Why did they live in caves, and deep underground?" Seraphina asked.

"They did not always. The earliest artifacts were found closer to the cave openings, and on the surface. I can only assume the caves, given Borinorhnus's geology and topography, provided natural shelters, as they do now. But the Human inhabitants also erected large domes across the cave openings, remnants of which can still be seen in our time. The authorities have destroyed many of the sites where such domes were excavated, but a few remain."

"Why do the authorities want to suppress this knowledge?" Seraphina asked.

"It might upset accepted beliefs and the social order, which considers Humans nothing more than livestock. But to continue answering your previous question. When the Borinian species spread across this world, multiplying in vast numbers, a series of conflicts occurred between Humans and Borinians, spanning many millennia. The conflicts characterized by long periods of calm, hundreds of years in some instances, and equally long periods of destructive conflict. During the peace the Borinian populations increased, as did the Humans. Followed by precipitous declines during the fighting. The Humans moved deeper underground for protection. Eventually they departed Borinorhnus altogether, leaving the world to the Borinians, following which a peculiar phenomenon occurred."

"What phenomenon?" Seraphina asked, never at a loss for the next question to further her understanding.

"It is logical to think the Borinian population would then thrive and rebuilt as it had during the peaceful intervals. Instead the population declined, and did not increase again until Humans were once again present on Borinorhnus. And we have seen this pattern repeated. Though we have yet to explain it.

"Where did the Humans who are here now come from?" Ezekiel asked, his first contribution to the mental discussion streaming between Khal and Seraphina.

"Captured from Nivalinorhnus, I mean Khalinorhnus, which Humans had also colonized. When Humans first abandoned Borinorhnus, after the conflicts we call the purification wars, or purification era, they returned to

Khalinorhnus, where the first colonies in the system had been established. The Borinorhnus settlements established later. When Borinians learned to travel into space, the science and technology learned from the facilities and ships the Humans abandoned on Borinorhnus, they encountered the Human colonies on Khalinorhnus, and a new series of conflicts, known as the first space era, occurred."

They'd arrived at a narrow passage, more a crevice, or crack in the cave wall. Khal indicated they needed to access the chamber at the other end. Khal still in the lead, Seraphina in the middle, and Ezekiel in the rear, the three shimmied sideways through the tight passage. Seraphina and Ezekiel removed their backpack and carried them in their hands, holding the bags down at their sides in order to fit through. Toward the far end, the passage narrowed more, the hard granite walls pressed against their chests and backs as they squeezed their way to the other side.

The passage opened onto a narrow protruding ledge overlooking a large circular cavern. The sound of running water at the bottom. A bottom the beam of their torches did not reach.

"The air is thin but I can fly down." Khal assured them. "Though I will have to climb back up. It is where I need to collect the samples. You do not need to go any farther, or you will also need to climb."

Ezekiel and Seraphina stared into the dark abyss. But they heard the water clearly. The distance perhaps not too great.

"It is not far," Khal answered their distance calculating thoughts. "I will show you."

An image floated into their minds, like a sensor image on a ship's instruments. The cavern rendered in crisp lines and shapes. Its dimensions delineated. Its floor defined, including an amorphous grey mass flowing along it.

"What if you require assistance?" Seraphina asked, concern in her thoughts.

"I will request it. But do not be concerned Seraphina. Until I met you and Ezekiel I did this and more on many worlds by myself."

Khal patted the closed pouches of his chest coat. "I believe I am carrying everything I require to complete the task."

Khal flexed the elongated fingers of both hands, opening his wings. He stepped to the edge, and leapt into the dark abyss.

Ozikarinaren

Swarms of arriving and departing residents masked Agar's presence among the commuters flying across the peaks. He joined a smaller stream descending toward the residences. A large number of flyers in the swarm wore headcaps, shielding their thoughts. Not unusual for the area, populated by residents of high social status in government and industry.

Agar had been observing the governor's residence for the past two days. The residence located in an affluent northern section of the capital. Two mountain ranges ran through the area, separated by a wide meandering mist covered gorge. The eastern peaks contained private dwellings, including the governor's. The western peaks multi-level roosts, like apartments.

Agar had clocked the guard schedule and routine. He'd studied the governor's personal security detail. He'd have preferred a longer period of surveillance, but time a pressing factor. He needed to obtain his objective sooner than later. He needed to force the issue and access Zepharinlenar's unguarded thoughts. Zepharinlenar's headcaps, both official and personal, the obvious choice. But Zepharinlenar's headcaps were seldom left unsecured or unattended. And Zepharinlenar, like most Borinians, carried them on his person in a long vertical chest coat pocket designed specifically for the purpose.

Agar supplemented his surveillance with intelligence obtained by infiltrating the residence, and mentally interrogating the household's quiri. The governor maintained a small domestic herd, and also owned a small farm on the sunlit outskirts of the city. He hired out small groups to households and merchants unable to afford their own. The governor's quiri, housed in subterranean pens beneath the complex, performed the dangerous maintenance and construction tasks in the dwelling, boring tunnels, excavating chambers, carving ledges and terraces, maintaining sanitation and utility tunnels and equipment.

Agar had easily infiltrated their blank minds, devoid of individuality, or distinct personalities and desires. Not the natural state of the species, Agar's was aware. His encounters with wild quiri, his observations on Nivalinorhnus, and the history he'd been shown by the ancient Santokh librarian, had taught him otherwise.

He'd learned the interior layout of the complex, its tunnels, passages, and facilities, allowing him to plot entry into and around the governor's chambers. His intelligence on Zepharinlenar's eating, working, roosting, and sanitary habits, his dietary preferences, and mating habits, including a perverse appetite for young quiri females, aided Agar's planning.

Agar observed the transport's arrival, its timing indicating delivery of Zepharinlenar's sexual entertainment. Agar set a mental countdown. The minimum and maximum time his intelligence indicated Zepharinlenar spent in sexual activity, in a private chamber designed solely for that purpose.

Agar's method of entry through the ventilation shafts bored through the peaks to the outside. Some too small to squeeze into. Others large enough to accommodate a quiri maintenance crew. Most unprotected against intrusion, the circulating fans, flues, and diverters providing sufficient deterrent. Except the few individuals concerned with personal security, like Zepharinlenar, who might deploy sensors and alarms to detect intruders.

Agar removed the mesh screen preventing large airborne objects and flying animals from entering the shafts. At the large circulating fan, he shorted out the power relay, a not uncommon maintenance problem. He squirmed between its large curved blades and encountered the first of Zepharinlenar's sensors. Agar had prepared for those.

Agar peered into Zepharinlenar's sleeping chamber from a shaft opening high in the wall. The shaft narrower and tighter than the main shaft, producing a venturi effect. A slight breeze passed over Agar as the walls pressed against his sides. His head brushed the surface overhead as he crouched on one knee. His senses reached out. Echolocation defined the chamber's shape, dimensions, and roosts. His eyes registered the stairways and handrails in the walls, the personal items and garments hanging at the roosts. His nostrils detected Zepharinlenar's scents deposited on areas around the chamber and on the garments.

Agar located the chest coat Zepharinlenar had worn. In the long vertical pockets, he found the headcaps. Agar hung head down from the roost and set to work, opening a long seam on the underside of the cap beneath the raised antenna ridge. Using a precision tweezers-like tool, Agar removed an electronic chip the size and thickness of a mosquito's wing. He replaced the chip using one from a tiny case he carried in a chest coat pocket. Agar repeated the procedure on the other cap, and returned both caps to their chest coat pockets.

Ager departed the chamber and the residence. He'd left no trace of his presence behind.

During the course of the following day, Agar navigated the labyrinthine maze of insecurities, personal ambitions, conflicted memories, byzantine plots, and self serving desires of Zepharinlenar's mind. But much of the governor's thoughts also focused on the current political and security situation, including the disappearances of the governors, and the governor candidates. His unsuccessful efforts to locate them produced mounting frustration and scornful displeasure at his officers and operatives, who had nevertheless been thorough. They'd discovered Agar's escape routes, and searched the gorge below Tovarinkara's chambers. But the evidence recovered at the missing governors' last known locations all proved dead ends. No connection to the governors or individuals in the governors' circles. No results from their databases. No indication of any individual, or individuals, who may have assisted the governors, and of course, no indication of the governors' current whereabouts.

Still, not the information Agar sought. Agar force pushed subtle suggestions into Zepharinlenar's mind, amplified by the modified headcaps, producing responses of thoughts and memories closer to those Agar required. When such thoughts surfaced, Agar recorded them.

The impatient thoughts of Agar's guests rushed at him the moment he entered the mountain and lowered his mental shields. Eager for updates on his progress, and news of the outside world. Agar had briefed the governors each day on his progress, careful to shield the specifics of his activities, his contacts, and his methods.

"What progress this day friend of Zanthinvolar?"

"What have you learned?"

"What news from the city?"

"Are we at war?"

Agar waited until he'd settled into the small cavern adjacent to the chamber occupied by his guests. The chamber they occupied a common area, surrounded by smaller caverns providing private roosting quarters for his guests.

"I have a recording which may provide the ammunition you seek," his thoughts informed them. "Please access this frequency so you may receive it." The Governors retrieved the frequency from Agar's thoughts.

Their eager inquiries stilled as the recorded thoughts and images flowed into their minds. Agar viewed the familiar data through their thoughts, processing their reactions as they assimilated Zephar's recorded thoughts and images. Their vocalizations increasingly agitated as they viewed Governor Zephar's private assessments of each of them, and especially the methods of their demise he'd devised should it be necessary.

"Disturbing as this is, it is not proof," thought Tovar. "In the absence of verifying corroboration these might be merely mental ramblings."

"I agree," from Laskar. "It is insufficient to justify an accusation of conspiracy or complicity necessary to convene an inquisition."

"Although I have no doubt of Khorabinjolen's and Zepharinlenar's complicity, I must also agree," thought Governor Sorkah.

"The issue is not arrest and prosecution of Khorabinjolen and Zepharinlenar," Agar's thoughts interrupted. "At least not yet. The immediate concern is preventing this war. Can you not see a method of using this information to that purpose?"

"He is correct. And there may be a way," Tovar responded, his thoughts pondering the possibilities. "It may be sufficient to cast doubt on the accepted version of the General's death, requiring closer examination and investigation. And also cast doubt on Khorabinjolen and Zepharinlenar, who have adamantly advocated the version reported in public. If we can cast doubt, particularly in the military, it may be sufficient to turn the high command against Khorabinjolen and Zepharinlenar, or at least give them pause. In either event achieving the primary objective.

"My concern is how to accomplish what you propose Tovar," Sorkah's cautious nature guiding his thoughts. "It will require time to present a persuasive argument, all the while under attack from accusations of treason mounted by Khorabinjolen and Zepharinlenar. And we must also persuade Mokharinsephin, who controls the apparatus of information."

"And the matter of Zepharinlenar's security forces," Laskar reminded the others. "After viewing the measures he is prepared to contemplate, there is no assurance we may survive to voice our concerns and doubts."

"You remain under my protection governors," Agar assured them. "I have completed certain arrangements to ensure your safety in the city and the citadel."

"What are these arrangements?"

"You need not be aware of them until you are ready to proceed. However I urge you to decide quickly. Khorabinjolen has not been idle, and the obstacles I have placed in his way will not hold him much longer."

"We are ready to proceed now," Tovar decided. The concurrence of the other governors relayed to Agar, accompanied by animated clicks and chirps.

"There is the matter of the assassin," Tovar thought, before dismissing what effectively had been a council meeting, and halting Agar. "While he is not necessary for our immediate objective, if he is not apprehended quickly and questioned, he may disappear, as will any hope of establishing a case against Zepharinlenar, and in turn Khorabinjolen. We cannot trust Zepharinlenar will not attempt to warn him, or perhaps silence him."

"Do not be concerned," Agar replied. "The assassin is being attended to." Agar turned and departed the cavern, ignoring the urgent questions streaming at him from the governors to explain his parting remark.

Agar returned to the city, the assassin uppermost in his thoughts. He'd intercepted a message sent by Zepharinlenar, again through the security officer, scheduling a meeting with Lasiurinceris. Zepharinlenar's reason for the meeting carefully concealed. Even when Agar attempted a gentle force push, Zepharinlenar deliberately skipped to other mundane thoughts, refusing to focus on the matter. But Agar used the little information he possessed, a time and place, to position himself long before either participant arrived at the rendezvous.

Prior to the rendezvous, Agar met the minder in the same warehouse complex as their first meeting.

"You have completed the necessary arrangements," Agar asked.

"All is in readiness as we discussed," the minder informed him.

"I will deliver the governors at the agreed time and location. They will be unconscious when they arrive, but they are aware of the plan and should awake without anxiety. They will have garments and other essentials of their offices. However if there is anything else they require you will see it is made available. You and your men will escort them from the location to the council chamber."

"They will be well cared for comrade. And we will see them safely to the citadel."

"The day after the council meeting you may release your other guests. And I thank you again for your assistance."

"Think no more of it. You have compensated us generously. And it is my honor to serve General Zanthinvolar Abydynus one last time."

"In honor of General Zanthinvolar Abydynus," Agar responded. "On the other matter, have you obtained further information on Lasiurinceris?"

"Indeed. His real name is thought to be Ozikarinaren Goraghudnus. If he is indeed Ozikarinaren, he is an extremely dangerous individual. Ex-military, rumored to have been the ringleader behind the Dahlintraxima gang. But the High Command was unable to charge him when key witnesses met curious and coincidental accidents. Ozikarinaren disappeared, and if this is the same individual, he has learned to maintain his invisibility while pursuing his activities as Nyctiquiri Rafinvelir. Perhaps protected by Zepharinlenar and his corrupt colony."

Agar aware of the incident. And if Lasiurinceris was indeed Ozikarinaren, Agar also knew more than enough of his personal resume. Agar had been responsible for exposing and dismantling the gang, a mission undertaken for General Zanth.

Agar lay on his stomach, on a flat rocky ledge close to the peak's summit. The sun blazed bright and hot in the clear sky. The heat uncomfortable. And dangerous following long exposure. His species ill adapted to the environmental extremes of hot and cold. And Borinians despised rain, avoiding it, or any water wetting their bodies. The water itself harmless. But the confused clutter of returning echoes rendered echolocation in the midst of a rain shower useless, and confused the sensile hairs in their wings during flight.

Agar wrapped his folded wings close to his sides, leaving little of the thin skin exposed. His body conditioned to the extremes of operating off-world in alien environments. Heat and cold, and the diurnal regularity of day and night an annoying nuisance, but neither deterred him. Nor did rain. In fact Agar often enjoyed the soothing, cleansing waterfall, standing in its midst, wings spread wide as the rain shower washed over him. He'd even immersed himself in lakes and oceans, and learned to swim. A rare ability in a Borinian, used by Agar on occasion to gain a tactical advantage.

Agar focused his long-range visor on the peaks rising from the opposite side of the dry valley gorge, less than half an echospan away. Scattered in the valley between the mountain ranges he observed quiri stock pens. The farm small by industrial standards, but satisfying Governor Zepharinlenar's domestic needs, while also providing another source of compensation. Zepharinlenar had set the meeting at his farm outside the city, on the sun lit side of Borinorhnus, ensuring privacy. His mental privacy assured by distance from the city and his headcap, unaware his every thought reached Agar.

The transport approached from the north, flying low in the valley, hugging the slopes. Non-descript. Ordinary. Perhaps one used by the farm's overseers. It might go unnoticed by security patrols, but Agar aware of its true nature, and its passenger. Zepharinlenar had also cleared regular patrols from the vicinity of the farm. The transport entered a cave opening close to the ground, disappearing from view. Agar refocused on a terrace above the cave the transport had entered. He switched the visor to infrared view.

Zepharinlenar and Lasiurinceris appeared in the chamber as bright yellow and scarlet spots in a blue outline. Zepharinlenar's infrared and ultraviolet outline already familiar to Agar. The new image Lasiurinceris. Both images approached the open terrace. Ever cautious, Lasiurinceris stepped onto the terrace and inspected his surroundings, visually and sonically. Agar switched the visor to the visible light spectrum.

A familiar image filled Agar's sight. Ozikarinaren Goraghudnus. Squared face, pointed jaw. A flat, lined forehead, and prominent brow ridge above wide spread eyes. The snout long and rounded. The nostrils wide and flared. The cheekbones also wide, and prominent. His large round ink-black eyes expressionless, but the entire face projected malevolent menace. The hidden face behind the Dahlintraxima operation. Indelibly imprinted on Agar's memory.

Ozikarinaren had commanded a brigade, but for motives scarcely of interest to Agar, he'd built a criminal enterprise within the military for personal gain and profit.

He'd stolen, smuggled, and sold military equipment and weapons to wild quiri factions, in exchange for quiri prisoners, who he'd smuggled and sold on the black market, bypassing the merchant middlemen and their fees and official taxes.

General Zanth had tasked Agar to investigate reports of missing weapons turning up in the hands of wild quiri. And a series of accidental deaths the general deemed suspicious, questioning their accidental nature. Agar had penetrated the unit and conducted surveillance identifying the members of the gang. He'd tracked a cache of stolen weapons smuggled aboard a utility freighter to a transfer point in the Dahlintraxima system.

Agar had followed the pipeline, from the arms depot to the Dahlintraxima quiri, and the captured quiri back to Borinorhnus. He'd reported to General Zanth, who had mounted a raid capturing the gang members, who'd been subsequently cashiered from the military and imprisoned. All except Ozikarinaren, who'd escaped and covered his tracks by murdering anyone capable of corroborating and verifying his involvement. He'd commandeered an attack cruiser and destroyed the freighter, the quiri ships, and bombarded the quiri settlement from orbit, destroying every living soul. An incident which the general believed incited the quiri's increased aggression, attacking Borinian ships on sight, resulting in the destruction of two mother ships and their battle groups. And increased attacks on Borinian bases, requiring the urgent retasking of Agar, discontinuing his pursuit of Ozikarinaren.

As Agar observed through his scope, he also heard Governor Zepharinlenar's thoughts. Zepharinlenar pressed

Ozikarinaren regarding the missing governors. Did Ozikarinaren possess any new information to report.

"Whoever is behind this left no trace and is well hidden. I know no more than your own forces, and my contacts know even less."

"I am certain Tovarinkara is behind it," Zephar thought. "But no matter. The Governor Supreme has bullied sufficient acceptance to constitute a new council. It will be installed in two days and we can proceed. We can forget the missing governors. They will eventually be found and dealt with. There is another matter I need you to attend to. I've received information regarding three Nivalinorhrans recently smuggled onto Borinorhnus. A Borinian and two quiri. They have been careful in shielding their thoughts from the population, but we have seen enough small references to be certain of their presence, and to suggest they may be of extreme importance. They must be located and captured."

"I do not foresee a problem, provided we can agree on compensation."

"It may not prove as easy as you suppose Lasiurinceris. And it is too important for you to fail a second time, as you have regarding the governors." Zepharinlenar's thoughts expressed a malice equal to Ozikarinaren's.

"As I conveyed a moment ago, they have been careful in shielding their thoughts. We are uncertain of their whereabouts, or their purpose on Borinorhnus. But if our information is correct regarding the identity of the Borinian, it is of primary importance we capture him."

"I understand."

"Understand he must be captured alive Lasiurinceris. He may prove a valuable hostage we can use against the Nivalinorhrans."

"And his quiri?"

"They are of no consequence."

Agar's access to Ozikarinaren's mind flowed through Zepharinlenar. He'd obtained no direct thoughts from Ozikarinaren regarding General Zanth's murder. And it had not been a topic uppermost in their thoughts. But Agar had no doubt Ozikarinaren had committed the act. Ozikarinaren had blamed General Zanth for the destruction of his operation, and for turning him into a wanted fugitive. He had vowed vengeance on the general. But Zanth had been too important a figure to kill if Ozikarinaren hoped to remain invisible and continue his activities. Until Zanth's death had been sanctioned by the highest authority on Borinorhnus.

Ozikarinaren finally within Agar's reach. But acquiring him entailed a race. To catch Ozikarinaren in the tactical position Agar wanted, Agar had to locate the three Nivalinorhrans before Ozikarinaren, or Zepharinlenar's security forces.

Escape

The second site fascinated Seraphina, reminding her of underwater landscapes she'd explored on Krilan. The notion of being an explorer, compared to Khal, amused her. But their close association had prompted her to reexamine her aimless wanderings, her joy of exploring new worlds, in a new light.

The gorge covered by a thick milky veil. Submerging beneath it reminded Seraphina of diving below the surface of an ocean. Another world within a world. The air breather she wore performed a similar function to the air breather she'd worn beneath Krilan's oceans. The ultraviolet visor covering her eyes revealed a strange, surreal, shadowy landscape of bright and vibrant colors. The soft soil spongy beneath her boots, like sand. The trees twisted into fascinating bizarre shapes.

The site a traditional burial ground, used by both Humans and Borinians in ancient times, according to Khal. Still used by Borinorhrans. A wide plain stretched between the bases of surrounding mountains. Borinorhran funerary equipment sat idle like lonely sentinels amid unmarked graves.

Ezekiel stood on the periphery of the graveyard, cradling a low frequency sonic emitter to deter predators. The emitters harmless to Borinians, even less to Humans, but in the hearing range of predators inhabiting Borinorhnus's gorges.

Khal's sonic senses penetrated the soft soil, careful to not disturb the buried remains. The ground reflected a pattern of reds, yellows, and pinks, depending on when the soil had been turned. The bordering trees faint grey outlines, blotches of color along their gnarled trunks and branches. Their unusually large leaves splashes of iridescent hues.

The gravesite samples collected, they arrived at the third and final site on Borinorhnus's dark side on schedule, despite a long circuitous route north to bypass the city. They landed at the base of a mountain, its spired peak disappearing into the dark sky above. The black night surprised Seraphina as she emerged from the transport, which lacked viewports. As did the sudden drop in temperature. The crisp cold air a shock as it penetrated her thin garments. In the distance, a sliver of light on the horizon. The edge of twilight, like an approaching dawn which never arrives.

The site located in a valley between mountain ranges, like the previous one. But this gorge open and uncovered, like valleys on Borinorhnus's sun lit side. And the sound of flowing water reached Seraphina's ears, as her eyes visualized the colorful panorama through her ultraviolet visor. The ground beneath her invisible, except for thin streaks of ochre, purple, and yellow mineral veins running across it. The vegetation fluorescent pink, yellow, and deep purple. A wide blue band of water snaked through the valley.

In her mind she observed the sonic images relayed by Khal. The broad valley, boulders the size of transports, the base of the mountain, and the wide meandering river, rendered in three dimensional detail as thought she were visualizing it through her own eyes.

"Another burial site?" Seraphina asked Khal, as he set to work boring beneath the soil for his samples.

"Not in recent times. However, it may have been used for the purpose in ancient times. I have excavated Human, proto-Borinian, and Borinian remains from areas around this valley. Also the river flowing through here originates high in the mountains, and passes through many areas once containing populated settlements along its banks. I require water samples from the river Seraphina. You may collect those. And I also require samples from beneath the river bed."

As usual, Ezekiel stood guard against predators, the sonic emitter cradled in his arms. Seraphina walked to the banks of the river, careful of her steps as she stooped to the fluorescent blue water rushing by her.

The samples collected and properly stored, the three settled to wait for the pilot who'd fly the transport to the tanker rendezvous. Khal suggested waiting in the transport, but Seraphina opted instead for the open outdoors. She built a small fire next to the transport to ward off the chill, and heat the remains of their rations.

The intense white-hot plume of the fire created by smashed cinder crystals provided comforting warmth, and a circle of light around their makeshift campsite. But to Seraphina it lacked the magic of a natural fire, the crackle and scent of burning wood, and the mesmerizing dance of flickering flames.

"We have not had more dreams," Seraphina thought to Khal.

"The dreams you have from here on are your own. I have shown you the entire story."

"But you have not explained it."

"Perhaps you can explain it to me," Khal thought.

"I understand the birth of the stars, and the worlds circling them. And the life which formed on the worlds, including Human, Borinian, and all other life. I understand our Human ancestors discovered the secret of travelling among the stars and built the portals to reach and explore and settle on many worlds. Their civilization flourished for much time, but eventually ended, returning to the beginnings of all things. I wonder, if Humans once numbered as many as the stars in the night sky, and are so few now, maybe we are reaching the end of our time."

"You already think as a scholar Seraphina, and I am pleased." Seraphina recognized the low rhythmic humming Khal used when her thoughts and questions pleased him. "Perhaps you are correct. It is the natural and normal order of existence. But where there are endings, there are also new beginnings. Perhaps a species like yours will appear again. I have long suspected it is not the first evolution of your kind. I have explored worlds containing evidence of civilizations predating Human habitation. Yet the fossils appeared to be of the same species, with minor variations. This confused me for many years."

"Have you ever seen it possible your kind may have existed before, in some other place? Seraphina asked.

Khal's humming vocalization resumed as his thoughts responded to Seraphina's question.

"An astute question Seraphina, and a central one. Indicating you are closer to understanding your dreams than you are aware. I wonder why you ask it."

"It is logical if it occurred in one species it may occur in others. I have learned the manner in which life evolves depends on the conditions of the world if forms on and adapts to. Have you not encountered worlds similar to Borinorhnus?"

"Not close enough to produce a species such as ours. I have only encountered evidence of a species close to my own in one other place. But you get ahead of yourself Seraphina," Khal interrupted the question forming in her thoughts. "You are skipping past an important point."

Khal aware of Seraphina's thoughts processing memories acquired and stored since their meeting on Krilan.

"The similar DNA Humans and Borinians share," she thought.

Khal's humming resumed, accompanied by the thought, "I am indeed proud of how you have learned Seraphina."

Ezekiel also shared Khal's pride in Seraphina. Not as her teacher. Indeed much of the discussions between Seraphina and Khal beyond his understanding. But as his companion, and his mate. She had saved him, and helped to free him. And had accompanied him to a world inhabited by a people she'd once considered a mortal enemy. Yet here she sat, discussing the origins of their species. To Ezekiel it signified the possibility of all things, including freedom for every Human on Borinorhnus.

"I will be at your side to help you when you do," he heard in his mind. He'd forgotten the headcaps they both wore as his thoughts wandered.

"We have seen in our dreams the manner in which one civilization replaces another. It has occurred many times," Ezekiel thought. "This is also a natural order of existence?" he asked.

"Indeed it is," Khal replied. "It is seen throughout nature. An established order of preference. Your ancestors called it natural selection."

"But it occurred differently on Borinorhnus, Ezekiel observed. "The stronger, more advanced civilization displaced by a weaker emerging one."

"It is not always strength and technological superiority which establishes the order of preference Ezekiel. In the case of Borinorhnus, something else appears to have occurred."

"Which is the question we hope to answer my Ezekiel," Seraphina said in his thoughts. "Khal hopes these samples we collected will contain the solution."

"Precisely Seraphina. As you have both seen in your dreams. If the solution is indeed contained in these samples, it will also contain the explanation of your dreams."

Seraphina's next question interrupted by a sudden alertness in Ezekiel. Followed closely by a similar tenseness in Khal. An image entered her mind, the outline of an approaching transport."

"It appears our pilot has arrived," Khal thought.

"How can we be certain it is him?" Seraphina asked, her thoughts expressing the suspicion she sensed in her mate, heightening her own caution.

"Borinorhrans seldom venture to the dark side. Except hunters, Khal explained."

Khal's explanation did not ease Ezekiel's wary scrutiny of the approaching craft.

"Can you not see inside?" Seraphina asked Khal.

"The materials used in construction of the transport and our ships do not permit sonic senses to penetrate."

"You are unable to reach their minds?"

"Normally it is possible, but the pilot's thoughts appear to be blocked."

Khal's thoughts, and more importantly Ezekiel's increasing unease, heightened her own. She had grown to trust Ezekiel's instincts, as much as she did her own. But it was too late to douse the fire or conceal themselves. The transport landed next to theirs, beyond the pale circle of light cast by the white fire. Not one, but four individuals exited the transport and approached them.

"This is not right," she thought to Ezekiel.

"I know. The one heading to Khal walks like military."

"The others are walking to flank us," she thought.

"I can see," Ezekiel replied.

Khal's suspicions now raised, especially since he'd still been unable to reach the approaching Borinorhran's mind, despite his strength as a seer. But he hadn't yet dismissed the notion the Borinorhrans had transported their pilot and were there to assist them. Until the one approaching him released the shield blocking his thoughts, and their minds merged.

"Good fortune smiles on me for it is indeed Khalinaltani Ogadeinus."

"You are called Lasiurinceris, but it is not your true name," Khal thought.

"I am told you are a Priviseer. I must be careful not to allow you too deep into my thoughts. But first you will have your quiri remove their headcaps."

Khal glanced over at Ezekiel and Seraphina. The other three Borinorhrans formed a close semi circle around them, charged lances held in their palms.

"They are not my quiri, and not subject to my commands."

"Such nonsense may pass on Nivalinorhnus. But here they will do as you and I command. Command them to remove their caps or I will kill them where they stand. It will mean a loss of profit, but I may still make something from selling their bodies to a food processor. They are of no consequence Khalinaltani, you alone are the prize."

Khal had been transmitting the exchange to Ezekiel and Seraphina. All three of their headcaps tuned to the same Khalinorhran frequency, one Lasiurinceris's headcap would be unable to acquire or penetrate. Ezekiel spoke out loud, but in an undertone, while slowly removing his headcap.

"Remove your headcap slowly Seraphina and listen to my voice," he said in their human language. "Only my voice. Think only of me. See only my face in your mind when their thoughts enter your mind. They will attempt to command you, control you. But your mind is stronger. Your self is stronger. They will not expect it. You must fight their minds just as you fight their bodies."

As Seraphina removed the cap she steeled her will against the expected invasion. A jumbled mix of disparate thoughts flooded her mind. She did not focus on them. Instead she closed her mind and her senses to the onslaught, as she had learned to do as a young girl. And she waited.

One image surfaced above the others, like a shout, shoving her to the side. Another image of her hands being shackled.

"Do as they command Seraphina," she heard Ezekiel say. "Allow them to believe they control you."

"We cannot fight if they shackle our hands Ezekiel," she told him. "We must act before."

"I am fearful for Khal," he said. We cannot allow them to carry us away from this place alive.

"I know. And I am happy if we must die we will be together."

A sudden burst of light erupted overhead, like a dark star exploding, bathing the valley in a bright white bloom. All heads, Borinian and Human, snapped upward toward the source.

Seraphina the first to recover. Her attention diverted for a mere fraction of a moment. She reached both hands behind and beneath her tunic. Her right hand emerged grasping the dagger. In one fluid movement her arm swung forward in an underhand throw. The snap of her wrist propelled the blade as if shot from a bow. The blade met its target, imbedding itself to its hilt in the throat of the Borinorhran directly in front of her.

Ezekiel reacted a moment after Seraphina. The death squeal of the Borinorhran to his left reached him as he advanced on the one to his right, the activated charge lance in his right hand, the combat knife in his left. The Borinorhran reacted to the screech of his dying companion, thrusting his lance at the charging Ezekiel. Ezekiel parried the thrust using his own lance. The Borinorhran swung again for Ezekiel's left side. Ezekiel parried. Another forward thrust. Again Ezekiel parried.

The Borinorhran's frustration evident in the rising volume of his screeches and grunts. He aimed a wild angry swing at Ezekiel's right side. This time Ezekiel parried using the combat knife in his left hand, anticipating a familiar Borinian combination. As Ezekiel parried, the Borinorhran unleashed a left foot kick at Ezekiel, his vicious talons snapping forward. Ezekiel stepped inside the kick's arc and pinned the Borinorhran's leg between his right arm and waist, his charge lance held wide, careful not to touch the lance to the Borinorhran's body while he held him. Continuing forward Ezekiel threw his opponent off balance. The Borinorhran's arms flew outward to his sides to steady himself. The opening Ezekiel sought. Ezekiel's left arm swung inward and up, plunging the combat knife's entire blade beneath the Borinorhran's rib cage, thrusting it up into his heart. Ezekiel pushed the dying Borinorhran away, wasting no time, the blood covered blade withdrawing as the body fell backward.

As the first Borinorhran hit the ground, the hilt of the dagger protruding from his neck, Seraphina continued turning in the direction of the throw's momentum. Her right arm swung to her left side as she pirouetted on her left foot and stepped inside the third Borinorhran's startled swing. Her right arm blocked his arm swinging the charge lance. She completed the turn, now inside his swing, her back pressed against his torso. Her left hand, gripping the kukri shaped blade's bound leather handle, swung backward and up, the force of her turning hip behind it. The blade sank into the Borinorhran's left side, penetrating flesh and bone, its curved edge ripping through internal organs. The high-pitched shriek close to her left ear almost deafened her as she arched her hip against the Borinorhran's waist, her right arm simultaneously tugging downward. The blade, its handle gripped firmly in Seraphina's fist, exited the Borinorhran's body as it flipped over her right shoulder. And reentered through the sternum as Seraphina stabbed forward at the body tumbling over her shoulder.

In the moment Ozikarinaren turned toward the light, he sensed danger from another direction. From behind and above. In an instant he drew his particle pistol, turned, and fired.

Agar landed behind Ozikarinaren, knees bent, head bowed, arms stretched out ahead, palms flat against the ground. Wings spread on either side. The wild snap shot passed harmlessly over his head. He used his forward momentum to roll into a somersault. His descending feet, talons extended, struck Ozikarinaren's shoulders before he had the chance to re-aim and fire. Agar's talons ripped through flesh and muscle, tearing wing skin and cracking thin fragile fingers. As Agar's right foot hit the ground he half twisted, his left leg pistoned forward, talons retracted. The kick landed on Ozikarinaren's exposed chest, lifting him off his feet and propelling him backward to land with a sprawling thud on his back.

Agar vaulted to his feet, closed the distance to the fallen assassin. He sensed Khalinaltani's Human companions moving toward him, placing themselves between him and Khalinaltani, weapons at the ready, blood dripping from the blades into the dry sand.

"I mean you no harm," his thoughts reached out to them. "You can see the truth in my thoughts. But first I must complete an important task."

Ozikarinaren's blank slate eyes stared up at Agar, helpless, his useless arms limp at his sides, wings open between splayed fingers. Agar bent, removed Ozikarinaren's headcap, and the pistol still grasped between unresponsive thumb and palm. Agar pushed into Ozikarinaren's mind.

"We finally meet Ozikarinaren Goraghudnus."

The assassin's thoughts registered his surprise. And his fear. But mostly confusion. Bewilderment at the sudden turn of events. He'd been in complete control mere moments before. And this stranger, aware of his true identity. He sensed the strength of the mind pushing into his. A seer. Helpless to prevent the memories being sucked from his mind.

"I am the one responsible for uncovering your Dahlintraxima operation so many years ago. I provided the information to put you out of business. We should have met then, a missed opportunity I will long regret. But now we have met, and I have obtained the information I required, it is time for you to honor the life of General Zanthinvolar Abydynus. He was not only my commanding officer, he was also my friend."

The assassin's thoughts screamed in defiance as he stared into the barrel of the pistol pointed at his head. Aware of his impending death. An end his mind refused to comprehend, and did not welcome. His thoughts screamed in disbelief, accompanied by loud vocal screeching. His panic-stricken thoughts ceased abruptly when Agar fired. The discharge transformed the assassin's head into a smoking hole.

"You are the Captain Commander of the attack cruiser," Seraphina and Ezekiel heard in their thoughts as Khal addressed the strange Borinorhran."You attempted to kill me in the Burude System. I recognize the quality of your thoughts."

"I am he Khalinaltani Ogadeinus," Agar responded.

"And yet now you save us."

"As you have seen in my thoughts. Though I have observed your companions appear quite capable of saving you and themselves. Especially the female. Astonishing. The male I believe has had Borinorhran military training."

"I do not wish to appear ungrateful," Khal thought. "But I do not understand your purpose here. Or your wish to kill that individual in such a manner."

"I was sent to detain you at Burude, not to kill you. At least not until we had learned the role you might have in this war. General Zanthinvolar Abydynus, who commanded me to locate and detain you, did not believe in this war. He wished me to discover the means to prevent and avoid it. In this instance it meant preventing this assassin from capturing you, and turning you over to a faction in the Borinorhnus council who wish this war to occur. He was also hired to murder General Zanthinvolar."

"And what do you intend for us?"

"I am aware of your scheduled rendezvous. I will transport you to your rendezvous and ensure your safety. Inform the tanker captain not to be alarmed by the attack cruiser I will dispatch to escort the tanker from orbit and through Borinorhran space."

"In that case I am indebted to you. But I do not know your name. You did not give it to me during the Burude encounter, and you have not given it now."

"You have no such obligation Khalinaltani. Indeed, it is I who owe a debt to General Supreme Zanthinvolar Abydynus I can never repay. He was a valued friend, and an admirer of yours, convinced of your truth. As for my name, it is of no consequence. I have been known by many. And indeed it may be safer for you if you do not know any of them."

"I wish I had known your general," Khal thought.

"Indeed. Under other circumstances I am certain you might have been friends. But we must go now if we are to arrive at your rendezvous on time."

Summit

The docked ships, one Borinorhran, one Khalinorhran, served as neutral ground for the summit. The meetings to alternate between Borinorhran and Khalinorhran territory as symbolized by each ship. The initial meeting aboard the Khalinorhran vessel, a new design incorporating accommodations for both Borinian and Human, a symbolic show to the Borinorhrans of Khalinorhran culture.

Acting Governor Supreme Tovarinkara Pharaxnus stepped through the portal hatch into the conference room, followed by an aide. At one end of the long rectangular cabin, an oval conference table faced a large transparent viewport. Dark, empty space visible beyond. In the center of the cabin four plush armchairs faced each other. The armchair's design provided a space between the soft cushioned seat and back to accommodate the vestigial Borinian tail bone. Recessed stairways on the bulkheads led to lattice works in the A-frame ceiling, providing roosts above the conference table, and at the opposite end of the cabin above a raised circular dais.

Waiting for Tovarinkara Pharaxnus in the center of the cabin, Khalinorhnus Governor Nakurinmaral Sokhoranus, accompanied by a single aide. Nakurinmaral a head taller than Tovarinkara. His eyes typically small, but lively and observant as he studied his guest.

Tovar on the verge of entering Nakur's mind when he recalled the protocol briefing he'd received in preparation for the summit. As the host for the initial meeting, it fell to Nakurinmaral to invite the first sharing of thoughts.

"My honor to welcome you Governor Tovarinkara Pharaxnus," Nakurinmaral greeted him. "I trust you had an uneventful journey and the accommodations are to your satisfaction."

"It is my honor Governor Nakurinmaral Sokhoranus. And yes, the accommodations and preparations of both our delegations have been more than satisfactory."

"I am pleased. Do you prefer to sit or roost?"

"As you are my host I shall defer to Khalinorhran culture and sit."

"As you wish. Before we begin governor, is there anything you require beyond the refreshments provided here?"

"Not at this time Governor Nakurinmaral. All indeed appears satisfactory."

"Then may I suggest we can dismiss our aides and proceed."

Both aides escorted their leaders to armchairs in the center of the conference room, ensuring both were comfortably seated and required no further assistance, before withdrawing and exiting the cabin.

"I must admit I am most impressed," Tovar thought. "I have followed developments on Khalinorhnus with more interest than most Borinorhrans. And the late General Zanthinvolar provided his own remarkable impressions during our private meetings. But the actual experience is quite a revelation indeed." Tovar's low humming betrayed his surprise at the comfort the curious furniture provided for his seated posture and folded wings.

"My honorable condolences on the loss of General Zanthinvolar. The news of his passage quite upset the entire Khalinorhnus Council. Particularly General Dogarinmaral, who had established a mutual rapport in their short time together. We had invested our hope for peace in the general. Have you learned who was responsible?"

"The matter is currently under investigation," Tovar's response intentionally vague.

"Do you still maintain contact with your mother?" Tovar asked instead, surprising Nakur by the unexpected and personal question. "I only ask since I have a distant connection to her. An aunt of mine resided in the Sokhora maternal colony at the same time as your mother. They developed a relationship. She requested I inquire as to your mother."

"She is well," Nakur thought, recovering from his initial surprise. "She resides on the southern continent in a marine science colony. She is happy in her work and her life."

"I am glad to hear it, and I shall pass the news to my aunt."

"And I shall pass your aunt's greeting." Nakur responded.

"They are among the reasons we must succeed at our task Governor Nakurinmaral. To renew the free association of our two societies separated by Borinorhnus's xenophobic policies."

"It is a hope and a goal we share governor," Nakur agreed.

"As to the other issues we must resolve. The Borinorhran council has agreed to the agenda as proposed by your delegation. However, apart from the immediate issue of establishing a viable and lasting peace, discussion of the others items may be premature."

"Premature in what manner?"

"The political situation on Borinorhnus is yet unresolved, and volatile. I cannot guarantee anything we may agree to will survive changes in our government."

"I appreciate your position governor," Nakur thought, a shrewd gaze observing his guest, his mind evaluating the thoughts reaching him. "I also appreciate you did not consider our summit premature under the circumstances. If you cannot guarantee agreement regarding the items on the agenda, you also cannot guarantee agreements regarding a peace between our worlds. I do not underestimate your position governor, and will consider it in our deliberations. But am I correct in considering, as long as your investigation continues, Governor Supreme Khorabinjolen will remain sidelined. And even if he were to be reinstated on the council, his power and influence diminished?

"It is an accurate assessment."

"Then I am confident the reconstitution of your government will proceed as you planned Governor Tovarinkara. And also confident Borinorhnus will abide by these agreements. I believe you possess a similar confidence, or we might not be having this discussion."

Tovar regarded the Khalinorhran seated across from him. His quiet, understated, thoughtful manner. The observant eyes and astute mind sharing his thoughts. The mind disciplined, like his. He had not sensed an untoward probing of his thoughts by Governor Nakurinmaral, an intrusion considered rude according to his briefing. But cognizant of the delicate manner in which the Khalinorhran

Governor had referred to Khorabinjolen's removal as "his plan". The Khalinorhran's mental acuity and perception undoubtedly keen, possibly supported by accurate intelligence profiles on Borinorhnus's council members, and the current political situation.

Tovar had not expected his opening gambit to succeed, though he had to attempt it, if only to gauge the extent of Khalinorhnus's information. Nakurinmaral had called his bluff, and had revealed only what Tovar might have already expected.

"The terms of the peace agreement negotiated by our respective delegations are satisfactory Governor," Tovar thought. "If there are no objections from your side I am ready to endorse it. The parameters of the border zones to be established around both our worlds are acceptable. Both of our military fleets have withdrawn inside those borders. And we accept free use of space outside those borders, including the portal. Neither side will interfere in the space facilities or shipping of the other. We enthusiastically endorse the establishment of a council to promote exchanges and joint exercises between our militaries. The remaining item which we both agreed to detach from the accord, is the matter of the incident in the Drixtahl Sector."

"I have been informed our delegations will soon arrive at a resolution Governor Tovarinkara. The lives lost on both sides are regrettable, but by good fortune cooler heads prevailed and prevented even greater loss, or all-out war."

"Indeed. The restraint shown by both commanders during the crisis I consider admirable and worthy of recognition."

"I agree. Discussions are underway on Khalinorhnus to recognize the units involved. I wonder if perhaps a joint ceremony. It would provide an appropriate tribute to both sides, and a commemoration of our new relationship. It may also serve to mend any residual animosity."

"An excellent suggestion Governor Nakurinmaral. I honor and commend you for proposing it."

"As to the other items on the agenda Governor Tovarinkara."

"I am confident our delegations will perform as satisfactorily as they have concerning the peace and other issues. However there is one exception. The matter of the Humans. We agree in principle to their emancipation and freedom. However accomplishing it will place enormous, perhaps destructive stress on our economy and society."

"We recognize and appreciate the enormity of the task. Not only the burden it will place on your society, but also on ours. We will have to absorb the population. And the mental adjustment among Humans whose minds and thoughts have been controlled all their lives requires painstaking psychological remedies. By no means a quick or simple process. We have had experience in such matters. Not all positive. We have had to learn through trial and error. But at the outset Borinorhnus must recognize Humans are sentient beings and declare their immediate emancipation. The hunting and herding of Humans, and their use for labor and food must cease immediately. We can then work together toward eventual repatriation of the population."

"I am uncertain I can deliver acceptance without jeopardizing my position on the council. And in such an event much of what we agree to here will also be in jeopardy."

"The peace we have agreed to is not contingent on the Human issue Governor Tovarinkara. However the character of our relationship moving forward is. Khalinorhnus is prepared to support your efforts on the council, and provide the assistance Borinorhnus requires during the transition. We are prepared to receive all the Human infants and children immediately. And we will provide Khalinorhran personnel, Human and Borinian, and Khalinorhran equipment and technology, to maintain a functioning Borinorhnus economy. You may even discover it will improve efficiency and productivity. You emancipate the Humans governor, and you will gain the full economic and technological support of Khalinorhnus."

"Your offer is most honorable and generous Governor Nakurinmaral."

"It is a measure of the importance this issue holds for us. It is worth any price we have to pay. Some among us even entertained consideration of this war as an acceptable price."

"I believe I understand."

"I believe now you do. A final matter Governor Tovarinkara. The issue of fission."

"A fait accompli Governor Nakurinmaral," Tovar's series of vocal clicks reflecting his impatience and dismissal of an issue he considered important only to a Khorabinjolen type mentality. "The Borinorhnus council will recognize fission. And we anticipate the swift establishment of embassies on our respective worlds, and to receiving your diplomatic representatives."

"And we yours governor."

Answers

Khal's increasing despondency worried Seraphina. Since their return from Borinorhnus, Khal had worked unceasingly in his laboratory. He had slept little, though Borinians required less sleep than Humans. And neither had Seraphina, a constant presence at his side, assisting Khal, and lately, fussing worriedly over him like a mother hen. She had little reason to return to her ship, Ezekiel away on the governor's delegation working to free the Humans on Borinorhnus.

Seraphina entered Khal's office chamber off the main laboratory, bearing a bowl of Vrechi soup. If not for Seraphina, Khal may have also foregone the need to eat. His disappointment drove not only his despondent mood, but an increasing absent mindedness.

"You will eat this," Seraphina commanded. "While you share your thoughts on what is upsetting you. Do you not think you will find the answers you seek?"

Khal opened his eyes, though Seraphina knew he hadn't been asleep. His small, round, onyx eyes gazed upside down at her, and the bowl she held in her hands. He turned to grasp the handrails of the stairway behind him. He clamored down the wall to the floor of the chamber.

"Science is a fickle master Seraphina," he thought, accepting the bowl without complaint, recognizing in her thoughts the steeled will and strength of mind he'd learned not to engage in argument. To do so a futile exercise.

"It does not give up its secrets easily. And when it does, it is usually a surprising and unexpected discovery which has little to do with the problem you initially sought to resolve. I am much more comfortable digging up relics, and discovering their meaning, than I am in a laboratory. I leave the science to the chemists and biologists and botanists. But in this case I would be just as frustrated waiting for their results, as I am receiving disappointing results."

The spoon travelled from bowl to mouth in continuous repetition as Khal's forgotten appetite asserted itself. He slurped each mouthful as his thoughts streamed into Seraphina's mind. Neither wore a headcap. Khal's thoughts lodged themselves in hers, reading her thoughts as her mind summoned them.

"The answers will come Khal. If not now, then at some other time. The search is the important thing. As you have taught me."

"You honor me with how well you have learned Seraphina. You are an eager pupil, possessing a clever, astute mind. I have not expressed often enough how proud I am of you, and how far you have come since we first met. An impressive journey indeed."

"But you have yet to explain my last dream."

"I wish you to discover the lesson in it yourself. But since there is nothing pressing at the moment, let us consider it together. Begin where you left the story on Borinorhnus."

"My human ancestors were explorers. Once they learned to travel among the stars, they explored and established settlements on many worlds, creating a migration lasting many thousands of years."

"And how did they manage to settle these worlds, and establish colonies? These worlds were different from the homeworld."

"They carried their science and technology with them, as they did to build the portals. And they also carried the seeds of life from their homeworld, which they used to transform the worlds they settled on."

"Carry on Seraphina, you are close."

"But I do not understand the visions of the laboratories Khal. And I suspect they hold the key."

"Correct again. The settlers required food Seraphina. And animals which were used for a variety of purposes. It would have required enormous ships to carry the variety of plants and animals required on the new worlds. And many would not have survived the journey. Instead, the colonists transported them as seeds, to be grown when they arrived at their destination. In fact, I have found evidence suggesting prior to widespread establishment of the portal system, the crews were placed in a stasis state, like a long hibernation. And an entire population of colonists may have also been transported as seeds. Frozen embryos. The embryos later developed in maternal laboratories, or artificially inseminated into females. But what if the plants and animals the colonists transported were unable to adapt to the environments on the new worlds?"

"They would not survive. A problem for the settlers."

"A problem they solved by engineering the DNA while still in the seed."

"The laboratories," Seraphina thought in sudden clarity. "Like the ones on Kheral I saw in the dream. And the one you discovered on Davidia."

"The vision in your last dream is of a laboratory on Davidia. Apparently a central support base for settlements in that sector. Just as Kheralincygninus served the sector which included Cygnus Prime and Beta Cygnus."

"The creatures in the glass cages, and the seeds," Seraphina pondered. "It is what you are describing. But how do you know these visions are correct Khal?"

"In all the dreams I have given you, except the final one, the findings have been substantiated by research teams which followed after my initial discoveries. It is not yet the case on Davidia. But the artifacts found there, similar to those on Kheralincygninus, may provide the corroboration we need to complete the story. It is the reason I have been reluctant to offer an interpretation which might be contradicted by subsequent research."

"But if it is proved correct, then what you believe..."

Seraphina's thought interrupted by a researcher entering the office chamber to inform Khal of a call from the Science Colony Administration. Khal retrieved his headcap from his chest coat pocket and fitted it on his head. He stepped to a communication console on the wall beneath his roost, and synched the headcap to the incoming call.

Seraphina's frustration at again being thwarted from a full explanation of her dream uppermost in her thoughts. But she'd received a fleeting glimpse, like a curtain opened by a breeze to reveal the contents behind it before closing again.

An excited string of clicks and chirps drew her attention. Khal's small round mouth stretched wide in imitation of a Human smile. His clicks and chirps a continuous stream.

"What?" Seraphina asked aloud.

Khal's thoughts entering her mind expressed a cheerful delight and satisfaction. The discussion of her dream had been a welcome distraction from his gloomy thoughts, slightly brightening his mood. But his thoughts now giddy following the call.

"Confirmation Seraphina. The Davidia findings have been corroborated. Now we may fully explore your dream. Although I perceive you may have already discerned its meaning. But you may not yet fully recognize its astounding significance to our history."

"I am happy for you Khal. And yes, I believe I understand its meaning."

Another interruption. Seraphina on the edge of screaming aloud her frustration. Another sample analysis completed. Khal's thoughts anticipated another disappointing result. But his mood lifted by the news from Davidia. His enthusiastic optimism revived.

The test results negative as expected. In the process of reviewing the procedures for the next analysis, Khal's thoughts screeched to a halt. He focused his attention on a console of no importance. The Borinian and Human technicians reacted in alarm. All aware of how hard he'd been pushing himself, and the morose cloud surrounding his thoughts. The latest disappointment perhaps too much for him to bear.

"What is on the monitor?" he inquired of the technician at the console.

"A discarded sample Khalinaltani. An accidental contamination from two different samples."

A series of clicks emanated from Khal. Followed by a low humming.

"Which samples? Which contaminated which?"

The technician consulted the data displayed on the console. Reached for the sample jars and scanned the data chips identifying the location and time the samples had been collected.

"From the first and second sites Khalinaltani. The cave beneath the Bahkalornus lake and the Mukhalnus burial ground."

Khal's humming turned to loud melodious screeching. He hopped from foot to foot. Leapt in the air. Flapped his wings. His vocalizations long and rhythmically musical. His wild gyrations attracted the attention of every technician in the laboratory. Their thoughts reached out to him, and to Seraphina, soothing, consoling, attempting to calm him, concerned he might have finally snapped from his mounting frustration and disappointment. And convinced by Seraphina's loud laughter of her own mental breakdown, probably due to the sight of her mentor's affliction.

Their anguished thoughts rushed into her mind. "Do not be alarmed," Seraphina thought and shouted through the din of concerned thoughts. "It is his happy dance. He has found the answer."

Davidia's Seed

Governor Nakurinmaral entered the spacious commander's cabin, his guest quarters while aboard. The cabin comprised two decks. The upper level contained sleeping roosts and sanitary facilities. The lower level an office and conference chamber. The two levels separated by a gangway around the periphery, and a wide circular opening in the center of the deck, providing access to both levels.

The cabin located in a heavily protected central area of the ship, below the command bridge. Across the central hallway another spacious command cabin, designed for Human habitation. Currently occupied by the vessel's Human commander.

Nakur descended a stairway to the lower office level. He'd received a summons for a transmission from Khalinorhnus. He had the call routed to the secure communications console in the private office.

Nakur stood before the bulkhead mounted console, headcap tuned to the secure encrypted frequency. An image of the Khalinorhnus council chamber filled the com screen as it flickered on. The council members gathered around the circular table. And one other, Khalinaltani Ogadeinus.

"A most pleasant surprise," Nakur greeted the council, his thoughts entering the assembled minds linked together through their headcaps. "Seeing you and sharing your thoughts have reminded me of how much I miss home, even after such a short time away."

"Our pleasure as well Nakurinmaral," their thoughts greeted him. And from his brother General Dogarinmaral, "How is the summit progressing?"

"Well indeed. We have encountered no significant obstacles or changes to the proposals we agreed to prior to my departure. There is a suggestion regarding the Drixtahl ceremonies I wished to discuss. But I had planned to brief the council at the conclusion of the summit. Has there been some sort of emergency?"

"Not at all Nakurinmaral. However there is news we decided you needed to hear before conclusion of the summit. Information of stupendous significance to both Borinorhnus and Khalinorhnus. We are undecided as to whether the information should be passed on to the Borinorhrans. At least at this time. They may not yet be ready to accept it. However you are there and they are there, you may have more insight into this decision."

"What is this news Dogar?"

"I will allow Khalinaltani to brief you. It is his discovery. And we are all still too overwhelmed to give justice to the explanation."

"An honor and pleasure Khalinaltani," Nakur greeted the archeologist, though Khal's unauthorized trip to Borinorhnus still rankled. "I assume you have been successful in your experiments. Proceed."

"We have received a report for the research team on Davidia governor, which confirms my initial hypothesis. In essence, the primitive species which we refer to as proto-

Borinian, which gave rise to our own species, did not originate on, and was not indigenous to Borinorhnus."

Nakur unable to mask his astonishment, perceiving a similar reaction in the thoughts of his colleagues, even though they'd already been aware of Khal's news.

"Quite a discovery Khalinaltani. But I sense from the nature of my colleagues' thoughts there is more to it."

"Correct governor. This proto-Borinian species was transported to the planet by the Human colonists from their original homeworld." Khal paused to allow Nakur time to assimilate the information.

"Astounding indeed," Nakur thought, his astonished reaction similar to others upon receiving Khal's information. His thoughts stilled by what amounted to a bombshell. "I can understand your reticence regarding the Borinorhrans. It will destroy the foundations of their beliefs. Even for us Khalinorhrans, who have long been prepared to accept such a discovery, it is a shocking revelation. You are certain of your findings Khalinaltani?"

"Quite certain governor. Analysis of the site and artifacts from Kheralincygninus, and now Davidia, corroborate each other. We are aware the ancient humans transported flora and fauna from their home world to enhance their survival on the worlds they settled. We cannot be certain of the specific purposes for which the flora and fauna were used. A food source may have certainly been among them. Perhaps vegetation was also used to influence environmental changes and create particular ecosystems. And fauna perhaps used to explore inaccessible areas of a new world. Educated conjecture governor. Though there is strong evidence to support such conclusions. We also believe we can now explain the extraordinary effort and resources the Humans dedicated to this problem, as indicated in the translated texts and excavated sites."

"I beg you to explain Khalinaltani."

"From translated texts we are aware the Human settlers as a rule did not introduce their homeworld species on worlds possessing an indigenous biological species. And many of the species they transported were genetically altered to adapt to alien environments. We therefore conclude, and the archeological record supports the conclusion, there was no such life on Borinorhnus when the first Human settlers arrived. We now believe the appearance of this early species on Borinorhnus represented a consequence the Human settlers did not expect or intend. A contamination they sought to reverse, or eliminate. It may explain why they abandoned Borinorhnus altogether, rather than risk further interference in the development of a species. And may further explain a great many events in early Borinorhran history.

"It appears you have completed the story to which you have dedicated your life Khalinaltani. I honor and congratulate you on your achievement."

"There is more Nakur," Dogar gently interrupted his brother's stream of bewildered thoughts. "And this information is even more alarming, though you may think it impossible after what has already been conveyed. It is also of particular significance to Borinorhnus."

"I am already overwhelmed," Nakur conveyed to his colleagues. "Perhaps I should not be standing to receive the remainder of Khalinaltani's news."

"I have discovered the catalyst governor," Khal thought, ignoring Nakur's attempt to lighten the atmosphere surrounding the assembled minds.

Nakur's vocal exhalation the Borinian equivalent of a sigh. He sat, an involuntary manifestation of his light-hearted thought a moment before, and anticipation of another explosive revelation from Khalinaltani.

"The sudden genetic transformation which produced the Borinian species, and has eluded explanation," Khal continued, "was the result of a chemical in the soil of Borinorhnus. A molecule, apparently the unanticipated result of genetic alterations in a species introduced to Borinorhnus by the Humans, which subsequently produced the species we call proto-Borinian. Over many centuries the molecule leeched into the soil from the decomposing tissues of these proto-Borinians. It combined and reacted with the decomposing tissue of deceased Humans, also buried in the same soil. The molecule attached to DNA strands in the human cells and transformed into a chemical compound. This compound is present in the soil throughout Borinorhnus, and in the water, which transports it around the planet. It is incorporated into almost every living organism on Borinorhnus, plants, animals, insects. We have yet to study its function in Borinorhran plants and animals, but it is incorporated into the cells of every Borinian through ingestion of plant and animal food products."

"I ask your pardon Khalinaltani," Nakur interrupted him. "But all this is producing an ache in my head. And I am certain I will receive your complete report upon my return. Please give me the salient point of its significance."

"My apologies governor, I have grown accustomed to teaching." A fleeting image of Seraphina rose in Khal's thoughts.

"The significance being the long term ingestion and incorporation of this chemical compound in proto-Borinians further altered their DNA, and produced a sudden genetic transformation resulting in the emergence of the Borinian species. A further significance governor, is this process is continuing, and appears to have a function in Borinorhran fertility. Having identified the compound, we have reexamined the historical record. During a decline in the Human population, or death rate, we also see a decline in the levels of this compound, and a corresponding decline in Borinorhran birth rates. It is accurate to consider our species would not exist if not for Humans. And our species cannot continue to exist without Humans."

"You refer to Borinorhrans," Nakur thought, the implications for survival of his species a sudden burdensome weight on his mind, after narrowly averting a war. "Does this not apply to the entire species, including the Borinian population of Khalinorhnus?"

"It does not appear to governor. We have searched the historical record thoroughly and have found no corresponding correlations similar to those found on Borinorhnus. Nor is the compound present in Khalinorhnus soil. We currently have no explanation for it. Perhaps a factor in the different planetary environments. The question will require further study, and may provide a solution to the Borinorhran dilemma."

"The acting Governor Supreme is a person of science," Nakur informed them, the analytical part of his mind sorting through the staggering information other areas of his brain still struggled to process. "I believe he will be open minded regarding this information. And as you correctly infer Khalinaltani, the information regarding Borinorhran fertility I am certain he will consider particularly significant. However, you will be aware from my thoughts the political situation on Borinorhnus is still unsettled and volatile. This information, as the council correctly suggests, may provoke unwelcome consequences. I also believe the manner in which this information may be imparted to Borinorhnus's population must be decided by him, and their council. It is too delicate a time for us to interfere. The most we can do is provide him the truth."

Endgame

Immediately following his ouster, Governor Supreme Khorabinjolen commenced engineering his return to power, and exacting revenge on the traitors who had betrayed him. Still uncertain how the governors had managed to disappear and obtain the information used against him. They all possessed the cunning and resources. But only one the courage to defy him.

Khorab did not as yet have a plan. But he had the resources, and powerful political allies who owed their positions to him. And he had Zepharinlenar, who despite being removed from office, still had contacts who operated in the shadows.

The investigation launched by his former colleagues did not concern him. A ploy to remove him no doubt. And buy them time to complete their treacherous negotiations with the rebellious colony. The council would eventually have to close the investigation for lack of witnesses to corroborate and verify their accusations. Zepharinlenar would ensure as much. Following which Khorab intended to level charges of sedition and treason against the usurping governors. And ensure an ignoble demise of Tovarinkara Pharaxnus.

Khorab piloted the transport himself, headed toward a clandestine meeting in a remote isolated mountain, where his and Zephar's association and political rise had commenced. They had constituted a formidable team. Khorab the mentor and Zephar the protégé. Khorab experienced an exhilarating thrill at the prospect of strategizing and plotting their return to power, and the demise of their enemies. Like old times.

Absorbed in his thoughts, Khorab initially missed the transport changing course. He mentally commanded the craft onto its original heading. The transport didn't respond. He also noted the transport's speed increasing. Khorab's attention now fully engaged as his mental inputs failed to command the transport.

The instruments suddenly blanked in his mind. Khorab, concluding a problem in the control headcap, searched for the backup. His busied mind failed to recognize the cockpit instruments on the panel before him also blank. When he did, he broadcast a mayday. Uncertain if either the headcap, or communications, still functioned. He'd set the headcap for total privacy, his every thought shielded, and all other minds blocked from his own.

"Governor Supreme Khorabinjolen Khucharnus requesting immediate assistance," his thoughts shouted, ignoring he no longer carried the title. "I have lost control of my transport. Repeat, transport is not responding to control input." On the verge of panic, he wondered if his thoughts had been transmitted. And if they had been, was he in range of any other minds. The area he'd been transiting remote, unpopulated. And he had no method of determining his present position, heading, or speed.

"I am receiving your distress call," a thought reached into his mind. Khorab's momentary irritation at the other's informality, in not addressing him by name and title, replaced by the relieved euphoria of assistance and rescue.

"I extend to you my assistance into death Khorabinjolen. In honorable memory of General Supreme Zanthinvolar Abydynus."

"What..." Khorab's initial response cut short by the delayed impact of the thoughts reaching him. Their significance struck him like a physical blow. His thoughts screamed in panic, and he emitted a long anguished shriek as the transport impacted a granite peak head on at full velocity.

A bright white plume blossomed around the vehicle as fuel cells ruptured and set off an electro static explosion. The cloud lit by bright lightening flashes as charged ions flew into the surrounding air. The white cloud hung above the shattered transport as it fell, sliding and bouncing along the cliff face, depositing bits and pieces of its disintegrated carcass as it plummeted toward the mist covered gorge below.

Agar flew on toward his next destination. He dismissed the images of the crash echoing in his mind. Khorabinjolen's demise another installment on his debt to General Zanth. Agar's thoughts instead focused on the immediate matter at hand.

One point five echospans, five kilometers, from his destination, Agar engaged the remote pilot on his transport, the same model used by Khorabinjolen. He leapt from the transport's open hatch, wings spread wide. He piloted the vehicle through a control headcap while he banked and soared to approach the location from the west, hidden by the peak, while the transport approached from the east.

Agar timed his arrival to the transport, gliding undetected toward the gaping maw of the cave, while the transport attracted attention. Agar landed the transport smoothly next to another, already waiting. The waiting transport's hatch hissed open. Zepharinlenar stepped out, strode across the distance separating the vehicles, and waited for Khorabinjolen to exit. Agar remotely opened the hatch of his transport.

In the confused moment while Zephar stared at the open hatch, expecting Khorabinjolen and not detecting him, visually or sonically, Agar fired the dart into Zepharinlenar's fur ringed neck. The force and sting of the needle produced an alarmed shriek, followed by a slow collapse to the cave floor.

Agar approached the prone ex-governor. Zepharinlenar's black eyes stared up at him, expressionless. But the bared teeth, snarled curl of his lips, flared nostrils, and vehement thoughts, expressed a murderous intent his eyes could not.

"I will have your hide, whoever you are. I will skin you like a quiri," Agar heard in his mind.

"You may save your thoughts Zepharinlenar. You are already dead. The dart contained a muscle paralytic. I am certain you are aware of it. Used it on many of your victims. An unpleasant way to die. Suffocating as though the life is being squeezed out of your body. And finally your heart, like all other muscles in your body, will cease to function. But before that occurs, you must know I am the one responsible for sequestering the governors. I am the one who isolated you and Khorabinjolen. I am the one who provided the evidence against both of you."

Zepharinlenar's mind a confused, chaotic, incoherent mixture of disassociated thoughts. Agar no longer a concern, except as an unimportant detail. The instinctive struggle for air, unresponsive muscles unable to gasp, the burning in his chest and his brain, the emerging reality of his imminent demise, the foremost thoughts in his mind. Unable to accept it, even as the toxin shut down his body functions one by one.

"I also killed the assassin known to you as Lasiurinceris," Agar continued, pushing the thought into Zephar's fading brain screaming for air. "And I killed Khorabinjolen just before arriving here for you. I wish you to be aware of all this, in the final moments before you pass from this life Zepharinlenar, so you may depart with the knowledge all who had a hand in the death of General Supreme Zanthinvolar Abydynus are now gone from this world and this life."

As the last vestige of Zepharinlenar's consciousness dissolved in Agar's mind, Agar gazed down at the lifeless body.

"In your honor General Zanthinvolar Abydynus. My friend. May you live long in our memories."

Lost World

Space beckoned. Vast and full of wonder. Dauphin caught in the activated portal's grasp. Inexorably drawn toward the dark mysterious energy in its circular maw. The probe they'd sent ahead had returned, confirming a functioning portal at the other end. The ship outfitted for a journey of indeterminate length. Its systems upgraded, its engines overhauled on Khalinorhnus. An aft section refitted to provide Khal comfortable accommodations.

The three companions fell into their usual, cozy, shipboard routine during the four day journey to the portal, despite the long planet bound stay since arriving on Khalinorhnus. Seraphina and Ezekiel spent hours together in the cockpit, both lost in the vast vista of Orh's binary stellar system. Occasionally joined by Khal.

When not in the cockpit Seraphina wandered her ship, her inspections indicated no need for her customary maintenance chores. Dauphin in excellent condition following the loving attention the ship had received on Khalinorhnus.

Though elated to be on the move again, embracing the comfort and delight of the tiny world they inhabited, and the unknown wonders ahead, they had not forsaken the callings discovered during their shared journey. Seraphina continued to absorb Khal's encyclopedic store of knowledge. Ezekiel maintained communication with members of his delegation, refining plans and strategies for the repatriation of

Borinorhnus's Human population. These thoughts set aside as the three companions gathered in Dauphin's cockpit for portal transit, their gazes glued to the forward viewport, as the portal swallowed the ship, and flung it across the galaxy.

A bright yellow star appeared in the port viewport. Brighter and larger than Orh. Dauphin's instruments reawakened. Seraphina's gaze rested first on the stellar wind indicators. She adjusted Dauphin's sails for maximum collection and thrust. She turned to the navigational display. A solitary star, at the center of eight planets circling it in a flat ecliptic plane. Through the viewports the distant worlds appeared as small pinpoints of light, like stars in a night sky.

Dauphin's spectral instruments depicted four small inner worlds, composed primarily of rock and metal. And four outer planets, gas giants, encircled by rings of dust, rocks and ice. The two largest composed of hydrogen and helium. The outermost comprised largely of frozen water, ammonia, and methane. Between the inner and outer planets a wide belt of scattered asteroids, and beyond the orbits of the outer worlds other smaller concentrations of objects, dwarf planets, comets, centaurs and interplanetary dust.

"The system is believed to have been formed approximately four point seven billion celestial years ago," Khal informed Seraphina and Ezekiel. The number unfathomable to either of them, including Khal, who perceived it only intellectually. "Older than the Orh system by seventy five million years. Our destination Seraphina, is the third planet from the star. How long do you estimate?"

Seraphina examined her instruments. "Two and a half ships days."

"Is Dauphin capable of sensor scans at this distance?"

"Some. We already have spectral readings and analysis of the worlds in the system. Mass, density, circumference, volume, surface area. On the third world a dense atmosphere comprised of nitrogen, oxygen, argon, carbon dioxide, a few other minor gases, and water. It has a single moon orbiting it. And it is emitting strong electromagnetic energy across the spectrum, including radio waves. It is within range of Dauphin's visual scanners, but we are still too distant to see details. And we need to be in orbit to obtain readings of the interior. But Khal, the most wonderful thing, the world is covered by water, like Krilan."

"We must by cautious Seraphina, Khal advised. "You say you have detected oxygen and carbon dioxide in the atmosphere. It is one indication of biological life."

"I share your caution Khal, but isn't it what we wish to find?"

"Yes. However life on that world may not be as we expect."

The time in transit passed swiftly, though the three impatient companions perceived it as agonizingly slow. They gathered again in Dauphin's cockpit at a point midway between the planet and its moon. The world grew steadily in the forward viewport, spread before them. A breathtaking blue and white sphere. Its continents a dusty brown, its atmosphere large patches of swirly white.

Seraphina gazed out at the floating globe in awe and wonder. Ezekiel in reverent admiration as his liquid grey eyes, filled by his childlike wonder, absorbed the magnificent blue-white world beyond the viewport. Khal again requested a full sensor scan before correcting course for orbital approach.

"No artificial satellites or other instrumentation in orbit Khal," Seraphina informed him. "But I am able to detect biological readings now." She turned to face Khal, her eyes wide in reverent awe. "Many many species Khal. This world is filled with life. But none similar to Human or Borinian. And I can detect no signs of a civilization. Are you certain this is the correct world Khal?"

"I am certain Seraphina. It is the original homeworld. It was called Earth by your distant ancestors. This is the origin of the seed. But it has been almost two million years since your ancestors departed this world to spread their seed across the galaxy. Much has changed. But even so, welcome home Seraphina."

About the author

A native New Yorker, Michael W. Smart writes mystery and science fiction novels. Michael traces his passion for science fiction to the pioneers of the genre he read at a young age, authors who continue to inspire his love of reading and writing science fiction.

Michael is also the author of the Bequia Mysteries series, set in St. Vincent and the Grenadines, a tropical archipelago in the Eastern Caribbean where Michael lived and sailed for many years. He is an experienced blue water sailor and airplane pilot, two passions the protagonists in his novels also share.

Thank you for reading my book. If you enjoyed it please take a moment to leave a review where you purchased it and spread the word to your friends. Thank you. Fair winds and following seas.

Experience the Bequia Mysteries

http://www.bequiamysteries com

Subscribe to my newsletter and be among the first to receive news and updates on upcoming Bequia Mystery titles and all my other novels

www.ingramcontent.com/pod-product-compliance
Lightning Source LLC
Chambersburg PA
CBHW070613260626
47161CB00007B/2419